"*High stakes on the high seas. A riveting drama of 21st century warfare ripped from tomorrow's headlines. Jeff Edwards proves again that he is the undisputed master of the modern naval thriller.*"

> — **DIRK CUSSLER**, Bestselling author of '*CRESCENT DAWN,*' and '*POSEIDON'S ARROW*'

"*A fantastic and chilling take on how close to the edge of disaster our world actually might be. The adrenaline-fueled writing sends you hurtling forward like a missile.*"

> — **GRAHAM BROWN**, International bestselling author of '*THE STORM,*' and '*THE EDEN PROPHESY*'

"*Impossible to put down! Jeff Edwards has produced another spellbinder that puts you <u>there</u>! ...eerily prescient about where the next world war will begin.*"

> — **GEORGE GALDORISI**, *New York Times* bestselling author of '*ACT OF VALOR,*' and '*THE CORONADO CONSPIRACY*'

"*Jeff Edwards' talent for the techno-thriller should put him in the same ranks as Dale Brown and Tom Clancy. There may be one or two people alive who know more about antisubmarine warfare, but there is <u>no one</u> who writes about it better.*"

> — **ROB BALLISTER,** Award-winning author of '*GOD DOES HAVE A SENSE OF HUMOR*'

"*Edwards pounds a stake into fault lines separating superpowers... A masterwork of epic intrigue.*"

> — **JOHN R. MONTEITH,** Award-winning author of '*ROGUE AVENGER,*' and '*ROGUE CRUSADER*'

SWORD OF SHIVA

SWORD OF SHIVA

Jeff Edwards

STEALTH BOOKS

SWORD OF SHIVA

Copyright © 2012 by Jeff Edwards

Stealth Books

www.stealthbooks.com

The tactics described in this book do not represent actual U.S. Navy or NATO tactics past or present. Also, many of the code words and some of the equipment have been altered to prevent unauthorized disclosure of classified material.

This novel has been reviewed by the Department of Defense and the Office of the Chief of Naval Operations (N09N2), Industrial and Technical Security Branch, and is cleared for publication in accordance with Notice 12-SR-0115.

U.S. Navy images used in cover art and other illustrations appear by permission of the Navy Office of Information (OI-32), and Navy Visual News. No endorsement is expressed or implied.

Cover Artwork & Design by Martin Saavedra.

www.mtnsvd.com

ISBN-13: 978-0-9850443-8-1

Printed in the United States of America

To my mother, Mary Bowers, who infected me with the reading gene almost before I could walk. For years of wonderful stories, for pinching pennies to buy me my first typewriter, and for having the vision to see my future as a writer before I saw it myself.

ACKNOWLEDGMENTS

I would like to thank the following people for their assistance in making this book a reality:

Rear Admiral John J. Waickwicz, USN (Retired), former Commander Naval Mine and Anti-Submarine Warfare Command, for his excellent technical and editorial advice; Lieutenant Commander Loren "Alien" DeShon, USNR (retired), for technical advice about Navy F/A-18s, aircraft carrier landing procedures, and fighter combat tactics; Commander Cliff "Poker" Driskill, USNR (retired)/former Top Gun instructor, for patiently explaining (and then re-explaining) the intricacies of aerial combat maneuvering; Peter Garwood of the Balloon Barrage Reunion Club (www.bbrclub.org), for permission to use his excellent photograph of a Nazi V1 Rocket on its launch rail; Brenda Collins, for her superb research and editorial assistance; FTG2(SS) Bill Blanchard for talking me through anti-submarine warfare and anti-surface warfare engagements from a submariner's point of view; and my crew of advance readers, for catching many (many) of my blunders before they reached the final page.

I'd also like to thank the contributors who are not named here, either by their own choice, or through accident on my part. The information I received from these people was consistently excellent. Any inaccuracies in this book are either the result of deliberate artistic license, or my own mistakes. Such errors are in no way the fault of my contributors.

As always, I would like to thank my editor, Don Gerrard, for more than a decade of guidance, sterling advice, and true friendship.

If the radiance of a thousand suns
Were to burst at once into the sky,
That would be like the splendor of the mighty one.
I am become Death,
The shatterer of worlds.

Lord Shiva, the Hindu God of Destruction
(The Bhagavad Gita)

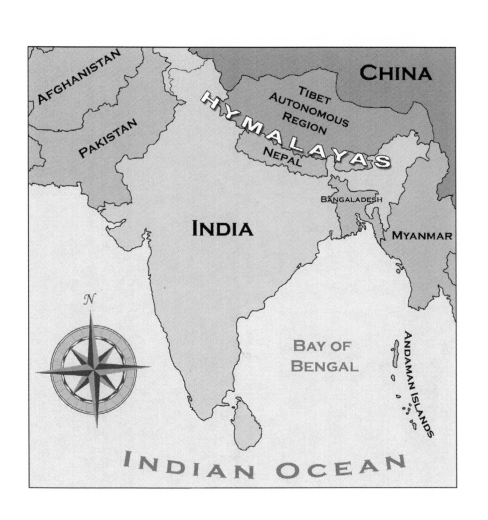

PROLOGUE

QINGHAI-TIBETAN PLATEAU, TIBET AUTONOMOUS REGION
TUESDAY; 18 NOVEMBER
4:49 PM
TIME ZONE +8 'HOTEL'

Jampa flattened his body against the half-frozen earth, and felt the rumble of the oncoming train resonate through his ribcage. His stomach was a knot of nervous tension. The pounding of his heart threatened to drown out the roar of the approaching locomotives.

This was the part he hated—the waiting. Later, after the attack had begun, there would be no time for fear. He would be too busy carrying out the plan. Trying to stay alive, and escape. All doubts would be shoved aside by the need for action and speed. But in these last few moments of inactivity, his mind had time to dwell on all the things that could go wrong—all the ways that he and his men could die—or worse, be captured.

He had chosen this position carefully. The tracks were twenty meters away. The train would pass at a safe distance. Even so, he couldn't shake the notion that the great mechanical beast was racing straight toward them.

The vibration grew stronger, rising through the icy ground to rattle his teeth, and make his ears throb. Jampa imagined the train rearing up off the tracks like a giant steel dragon. He fought the urge to lift his head—to sneak a look at the on-rushing machine—to be certain that it had not somehow left the track, that the heavy steel wheels were not surging forward to grind him and his men into the permafrost.

He kept his cheek flat against a tuft of shriveled winter grass, and reached for the 80mm rocket launcher lying next to his hip. The fiberglass firing tube was smooth and cold under his gloved fingers.

The weapon was a PF89 anti-armor infantry rocket, built as a tank-killer for the Chinese People's Liberation Army. It had been purchased on the black market from a profiteering PLA supply officer. There was something karmic in the knowledge that it would now be used to destroy a train carrying Chinese soldiers.

1

A few meters to Jampa's right lay Nima and Sonam, the other two men assigned to his three-man strike team. If they were following orders, both men would be lying flat, using their rough-woven cloaks to camouflage their profiles against the withered grass of the Tibetan plateau.

Nima wasn't the problem. The old man was a *drokpa*, one of the nomadic herders who roamed the high grasslands and the foothills of the Himalayas, tending yaks and sheep, and wresting a meager existence from this place that foreigners called the roof of the world.

The old shepherd's iron character had been forged by a lifetime of hardship. He had patience, and he could follow instructions. Jampa had no doubt that Nima was lying perfectly still, maintaining concealment until he received the order to attack.

Sonam was not as disciplined, or as predictable. He was a good fighter, but he was young, and too headstrong to follow orders reliably. He might be lying flat right now, as Jampa had commanded. Or he might already be on his feet, eager to get in the first shot at the target.

Sonam had grown up in the refugee city of Dharamsala, on the Indian side of the mountains. He had spent his entire life in exile. For him, Tibet was not home. It was a cause.

He fought fearlessly against the Chinese intruders who occupied the land of his fathers. Perhaps a little *too* fearlessly. Sonam wasn't just *ready* for combat. He *welcomed* it. He wasn't satisfied with being a raider. He wanted to be a warrior, and his eagerness for battle made him reckless.

There were more than two-hundred soldiers aboard that train, and despite Sonam's frequent claims to the contrary, the People's Liberation Army was disciplined, well-trained, and dangerous. More than likely, some of those soldiers would survive the crash. It wouldn't take them long to come hunting for their attackers. The best chance of getting out alive was to hit the train hard, without warning, and disappear before the enemy had a chance to regroup.

If Sonam followed his orders, the chances of escape were about fifty-fifty. If the young fighter did something stupid, the odds might drop to zero.

Jampa had gone to great pains to make Sonam understand how easily this raid could go astray, if everyone didn't stick to the plan. He hoped that some of it had penetrated Sonam's thick skull, but there was no way of knowing.

Jampa had to resist the temptation to lift his head and check. If Sonam broke cover early, they'd just have to deal with the consequences. Jampa could not improve the situation by violating his own order, and breaking cover himself.

The metal thunder of the train grew louder. Jampa waited with a patience he didn't feel. There would only be one chance at this. If he misjudged the timing...

The noise seemed to hit a peak, the rushing sound somehow synchronized with the mad racing of his pulse. The first of the train's three locomotives should be passing him now. Not yet. Not... yet...

He maintained cover for the space of a half dozen more heartbeats. And... Now! He threw the heavy cloak aside and leapt to his feet, swinging the Chinese rocket launcher up, even as he shouted, "*Shi yag!*"— *death*.

He caught brief images of motion as Nima and Sonam tossed back their own cloaks and scrambled into firing position, but he was not watching his men. He had the tube of the rocket launcher over his right shoulder now, his right hand wrapped around the pistol-shaped firing grip, and the flexible cup of the optical sight pressed against his right eye.

The lens magnified the target, making the train seem even closer than it really was. The sides of the cars were suddenly enormous, and they appeared to be passing directly in front of Jampa's face. Although he had practiced looking through the eyepiece, the view was startling and unfamiliar. He swung the weapon a few degrees to the left, and found himself staring through a passenger window into the eyes of a young Chinese soldier.

It couldn't have lasted more than an instant, but Jampa's sense of time had become distorted by adrenaline, and the foreknowledge of imminent destruction. The seconds had become elastic, stretching into minutes, or perhaps even hours.

In that impossibly-frozen moment, he watched the soldier's expression flicker from surprise, to recognition, to fear. Jampa had been a teacher of Science, before the Chinese had burned his school. He understood the workings of the human brain well enough to know that he could not possibly see and register so many details in a mere fraction of a second. It had to be his imagination, his own guilt over what he was about to do, but it seemed real. It *felt* real. It felt like murder.

The train window whipped past and the face of the soldier was snatched out of view, leaving Jampa to stare at the sides of the passenger cars as they careened by. His finger rested on the trigger of the rocket launcher, but he couldn't seem to squeeze it.

His men held their fire as well. They were waiting for him to pull the trigger first—no doubt assuming that their leader had some valid tactical reason for delaying the attack.

The train cars continued to hurtle by, but the face of that soldier was seared into Jampa's memory. He was so young. Not much more than a boy.

And then he remembered his little school in Amchok Bora. He remembered the faces of Chopa, Dukar, and his other students as the villagers had dragged the blackened bodies of the young boys from the smoldering ruin of the school. He remembered the olive green uniforms of the PLA soldiers as they had climbed into their trucks and driven away. The trucks had disappeared into the distance, and not one of the soldiers had looked back. Not one of them had spared a single backward glance for the dead and dying children, or the grief-stricken wails of the villagers.

And now, twenty meters from where Jampa stood, was a train loaded with two-hundred more uniformed thugs from the so-called *People's Liberation Army*. Another load of impassive brutes, shipped down from China to aid in the ongoing oppression of the Tibetan people. More soulless burners of schools and killers of children, come to reinforce the invaders who were strangling the life out of Tibet.

A surge of heated air washed over Jampa's face. His body recoiled slightly as the rocket leapt from its tube. He couldn't remember pulling the trigger, or even *deciding* to pull the trigger, but he had obviously done it. He didn't even know where it was aimed.

The 80mm rocket streaked forward on a thin ribbon of smoke, impacting the underside of a passenger car just above the wheel carriage.

The explosion was instantaneous, and much larger than Jampa had been expecting. The forward end of the railroad car rose above the track, shrouded in black smoke and a mushrooming ball of fire.

To Jampa's right, two more quick ribbons of smoke announced that Nima and Sonam had followed his lead.

The passenger car, already twisting up and away from the first explosion, was blasted sideways in a deluge of sparks and the scream of rending metal. It teetered briefly on its far set of wheels, before leaving the rail completely and crashing onto its side.

The eighteen cars in its wake were still pushing forward at more than 100 kilometers per hour. Several thousand tons of linear force turned the remaining rail cars into an inertial jack-hammer, driving forward with unimaginable relentlessness.

Still burning, the damaged passenger car dug into the ground like the blade of a bulldozer, plowing up truckloads of rock and semi-frozen earth. The inexorable hand of inertia crushed the car into an accordion of fiberglass and steel.

Left with nowhere to go and still driven by the unabated force of the remaining train, the next car rolled sideways off the track, folded in the middle, and began plowing into the earth like the first car, collapsing into a mass of impacted scrap.

Relieved of most of their burden, the trio of locomotives shot ahead, trailing the mangled remains of two passenger cars.

Behind them, the derailment was turning into a chain reaction. As each car was twisted away from the rails and rammed into crushed aluminum foil against the unyielding permafrost, the cars behind drove forward and repeated the sequence. Car after car impacted and collapsed into formless wreckage.

Through it all rushed the fire. The Qinghai–Tibet railway operated at higher elevations than any other train on earth. In some places, the tracks rose more than 5,000 meters above sea level. To prevent altitude sickness for the highest portions of the journey, the train cars were pressurized like the cabins of jet airliners. Every car had its own oxygen concentrators, and its own pressurized oxygen tanks. Under the tremendous heat and force of the crash, the oxygen tanks exploded, sending enormous fireballs coursing down the length of the doomed railroad cars.

Jampa watched in silence, his ears stunned into near deafness by the unending series of impacts and explosions, his mind unable to comprehend the catastrophe unfolding before his eyes. The catastrophe he had caused.

He shook his head absently. He had wanted revenge. But not this…

Someone grabbed his elbow. He turned his head slowly. It was Nima. The old man was tugging at Jampa's sleeve and shouting something. Nima's words sounded like vague mumbles. Jampa couldn't make out what the old shepherd was saying, either because his ears had still not recovered, or because his mind would simply not process human speech.

Sonam appeared at Nima's side, gesturing and shouting as well, but his words were no more understandable.

The fog began to clear from Jampa's brain, and the meaning of the words and gestures began to seep into his consciousness. It was time to run. The old truck was hidden on the other side of a rise a few hundred meters away. If they were going to have any hope at all of getting away, they had to go now.

The crew of the train would already be calling for help. Helicopters would come, and vehicles much faster than the aging truck. The only chance of escape was to get as much of a lead as possible. They needed to be half way to the Indian side of the border before the Chinese could put together an organized response.

Jampa nodded and allowed the expended rocket launcher to fall from his fingers. He took a quick look around to get his bearings, and began to trot in the direction of the hidden truck. After a few unsteady steps, he broke into a run, with Nima and Sonam running a few paces behind.

He was about half-way to the hiding spot when he heard a single muffled crack, like the backfire of a distant car. The sound was barely audible over the ringing in his ears. Maybe it was another explosion from the train, or even his addled mind playing tricks on him.

But when he and Nima topped the small hill that concealed the truck, Sonam was not with them. Jampa looked back over his shoulder and saw the hotheaded young fighter lying face down on the ground.

Jampa was turning to rush back toward his fallen man, when Nima seized his arm and shoved him toward the truck. Nima was shouting again, but Jampa still could not hear clearly enough to make out the words. Even so, he understood the meaning. *"Go. Now. We can't go back."*

Jampa stared at Sonam for several seconds, ignoring Nima's unheard shouts of protest. Sonam was not moving.

Finally, Jampa nodded, and allowed the old shepherd to push him into the truck.

He didn't look back as they drove away.

CHAPTER 1

USS TOWERS (DDG-103)
SOUTHERN SEA OF JAPAN
WEDNESDAY; 19 NOVEMBER
1341 hours (1:41 PM)
TIME ZONE +9 'INDIA'

A half-second after the missile strike, the overhead lighting failed, plunging Combat Information Center into darkness. Electrical relays chattered. The battle lanterns flickered on, replacing the blue-tinged battle lighting scheme with the dim red glow of battery-powered emergency lighting.

The overall noise level in CIC fell by several decibels, as nearly half of the electronic consoles in the compartment dropped off line from loss of electrical power. Cooling fans spun down to a stop, and the whine of high-voltage power supplies trailed off into silence. Even the rustle of the air conditioning faded as the compressors in the nearby fan room shuddered to a halt.

Red and amber tattletales began flashing on many of the remaining consoles, spelling out the details of electronic damage and cascading signal loss. The huge Aegis display screens strobed briefly with a chaotic snarl of tactical symbols, before the video feeds dissolved into static.

In the near darkness, two or three of the wounded Sailors groaned pitifully. Somewhere beyond the steel bulkheads of Combat Information Center, an alarm klaxon was wailing and Damage Control teams were shouting. Their words were muffled into nonsense by distance, the intervening metal barriers, and the unavoidable distortion of emergency breathing masks.

Captain Bowie's voice cut through the blood-colored gloom. "CIC Officer, get me a damage report, now! I need to know where that missile hit us, and how hard!"

Bowie didn't wait for the young lieutenant to acknowledge, but rolled straight into his next set of orders. "TAO, I want an immediate inventory of sensors and weapons. I need to know what we can see, and what we have left to fight with. And as soon as you can get a line on them, we need to know how many of those Bogies are still alive, and where the hell they are!"

The Tactical Action Officer's response was almost instantaneous. "Captain, SPY radar is up on alternate power, but Aegis is off line while the computers reboot. Mount 51 is reporting manned and ready, and it looks like aft CIWS is down. Forward CIWS is operational. Recommend we turn toward the last known position of the Bogies and let the forward CIWS provide some missile cover until we get our eyes back."

Bowie paused for only a split second. "Do it!"

His command was followed almost immediately by a report from the CIC Officer, Lieutenant Westfall. "Captain, I've got comms with CCS. Estimated point of impact was starboard amidships, close to the waterline. Both starboard engines are out, and the engineers are reporting Class Bravo fires in Main Engine Room #1. We're taking on water in several compartments, and #2 Switchboard has been shorted out by flooding water." The young officer paused. "Casualty reports coming in now… CCS is estimating forty-one dead, and about twice that many wounded, sir. The Chief Engineer is dead. The executive officer is unconscious with a head wound and possible skull fracture."

Bowie listened to the growing litany of destruction, and nodded. "Understood."

A voice rumbled through an overhead speaker box. "TAO—Bridge. Forward Lookout reports visual contact on three inbound aircraft off the port bow, bearing three-five-seven, position angle twenty-one. Rate of closure is high."

Bowie looked toward Commander Silva.

The commander stood with her hands thrust deep into the pockets of her dark blue coveralls, her posture erect and alert, her eyes darting quickly from watch station to watch station. She made brief eye contact with Bowie, and then her gaze moved past him. She was taking everything in, like some sort of recording machine—sucking up information— offering nothing in return.

"The Bogies are coming in low and fast," Bowie said. "They're setting us up for another missile strike."

Commander Silva acknowledged with a single nod, but she said nothing in response.

Bowie turned away. "TAO, what's the status of Aegis?"

"Computers coming on line now, Captain," the Tactical Action Officer said. "It'll take SPY a few seconds to sync up and lock onto the targets."

"We don't have a few seconds," Bowie said. "Tell Mount 51 to engage the Bogies using the video feed from the mast-mounted sight. And have the Small Craft Action Team engage all inbounds with the forward fifty-cals, and both of the chain-guns."

Bowie listened as the TAO relayed his orders to the gunnery stations. It was a desperation ploy. The big 5-inch deck gun mounted on the ship's forecastle could probably take out an inbound jet with input from the main radar. Trying to engage three hostile aircraft using only the feed from a black and white video camera? That was a hell of a lot harder. Given the damage the ship had already taken, it wouldn't be much short of impossible.

The .50-caliber machine guns didn't have a prayer, and neither did the 25mm chain-guns. It was probably a waste of ammunition to even try, but—damn it—they couldn't just sit back and do nothing.

USS *Towers* was a state-of-the art naval destroyer. She was a cutting-edge warship, from the bottom of her computer-engineered keel, to the peak of her steeply-raked mast. She'd been designed and built for stealth, speed, and firepower. In her short few years of service, she'd already seen more real-world combat than any other two ships on the current United States Navy Registry.

Bowie smiled a grim little smile. If the *Towers* had to go down, she was damned well going to go down fighting.

He turned away from the static-filled tactical displays, peering around through the red-hued shadows until he spotted the hulking form of an enormous second class petty officer.

Operations Specialist Second Class Kenfield had grown up on a farm in Gordonsburg, Tennessee. The Sailor's first name was Bruce, but the crew called him *Big Country*, partly in reference to his considerable size, and partly because of his molasses-thick southern accent. It was a standing joke among the *Towers* crew that Big Country didn't need a tractor or a mule to plow his family's fields. He just wrapped his oversized hands around the plow, and shoved the blade through the dirt with sheer force of muscle.

Captain Bowie nodded toward the man. "Hey, Big Country... Give us a song."

The air in CIC was as taut as the skin of a snare drum, but the big Sailor's grin shone out in the blood-tinged darkness. "Is that an order, sir?"

"You bet your ass it is," Bowie said.

The Sailor's grin grew wider. "Aye-aye, Captain!" He cleared his throat theatrically, and let out the only sort of song that anyone had ever heard the big man utter—a rebel yell of positively staggering volume.

Commander Silva, still a newcomer to the ways of this ship, nearly jumped out of her skin when the big Sailor's unearthly bellow shattered the air. But the CIC crew had the benefit of long experience. They knew exactly what to expect from one of Big Country's songs. Before the cry could fade into silence, they added their own yells to the mix. Women and men, young and middle-aged, seasoned and inexperienced, their collective yells rising in unison—a defiant refutation of the enemy fighter jets rushing to destroy their ship.

They were a crew. They were one. They would fight together. They would die together. And goddamn it! The *Towers* was *their* ship!

Commander Silva's eyes took in the dimly-seen shapes of the CIC crew. The expression on her face told the tale. She was a seasoned officer, with more than seventeen years in uniform. She'd spent almost her entire adult life at sea, and she'd seen most of what the oceans had to offer. But in all of her years in the Navy, she'd *never* witnessed anything like this. It was crazy. It was utterly futile. But by *God*, it was impressive.

Silva opened her mouth, perhaps to add her own yell to the still-raging caterwaul, but she was preempted by an amplified voice from the overhead speakers.

"TAO—Weapons Control. Aegis is up and tracking. We have five Vipers, short range and closing fast! I say again, we have five inbound missiles, estimated time of impact twenty seconds!"

The ongoing yell was stifled instantly as the watchstanders went frantically about their jobs. Twenty seconds was not enough time to do anything useful, but that didn't stop Bowie's CIC crew from trying.

The Tactical Action Officer's voice broke over the net. "All Stations—TAO, we have in-bound Vipers! I say again, we have multiple missiles in-bound! Weapons Control, shift to Aegis ready-auto. Set CIWS to auto-engage. Break. EW, I need your best course for minimized radar cross-section, and stand by to launch chaff!"

Acknowledgements and follow-on orders began coming over the various tactical nets. Half of the consoles in CIC were still offline. The ship was crippled. A third of her crew were dead or dying, and—worst of all—the clock had run out. But they were still fighting. Still throwing punches.

The Weapons Control Officer's voice came over the net. "All Stations—Weapons Control. Brace for shock! Estimated missile impact in six... five... four..."

Bowie crossed his arms and leaned against the bullnose of a defunct radar console. He whistled softly through his teeth as the amplified countdown continued.

"Three... two... one..." The last word was a near-shout. "Impact!"

The compartment was suddenly flooded with brilliant white illumination as electrical power surged into the lighting circuits.

A different voice came over the speakers. "All Stations, this is the Training Coordinator. FIN-EX this exercise. That is, FIN-EX this exercise. Stop the battle problem; stop the training clock. Restore all power, and return all systems to normal operating condition. This training event is complete at time thirteen twenty-five and nine seconds."

The CIC crew blinked and shielded their eyes against the sudden illumination. Throughout the compartment, "dead" and "injured" watchstanders climbed to their feet, dusted off their uniforms, and went about the business of restoring their equipment to operational status.

A young OS3 lifted a loop of heavy cord from around her neck and examined the yellow cardboard tag clipped to the end. Large block letters on the tag proclaimed: CIC CASUALTY #6 — ELECTRICAL BURNS / BLUNT FORCE TRAUMA / DEATH.

The Sailor handed the casualty tag to a man in orange coveralls, one of the members of the Coordinated Ship's Training Team. "Here," the OS said. "I don't need this. I'm not dead anymore."

The orange-suited observer tucked the tag into the crook of one arm, where he was cradling several similar tags. "Welcome back to the land of the living," he said. "But if I were you, I'd stay dead until time for chow. Then you wouldn't get stuck doing afternoon sweepers."

The Third Class Operations Specialist grinned. "Oh yeah, like *that* would work. Being dead does *not* get you out of pushing a broom." She shrugged. "At least they killed me early. I managed to catch a few Z's down there on the deck while everybody else was busy trying to save the ship."

About ten paces away, Captain Bowie met Commander Silva by the Tactical Action Officer's chair. Bowie raised one eyebrow. "What do you think, Commander?"

Silva nodded. "Impressive, Captain. I've never seen anything like it. You've got one hell of a crew here."

Bowie gave her a wistful little smile. "All modesty aside, they *are* pretty damned impressive. I'm proud to serve with every one of them. Every man and woman on this ship gives a hundred and twenty percent."

He shook his head. "But they won't be my crew for much longer, will they? They'll be yours in just a couple of weeks, Commander."

His eyes traveled around CIC, moving slowly, trying to soak up every detail as though he might never again see such a magnificent sight. And that would be true all too soon. The change of command was only sixteen days away. And then this would not be his ship anymore.

When the final salutes were exchanged, Captain Samuel Harland Bowie would be on his way to becoming Deputy Commander of Destroyer Squadron Fifteen. At that same instant, Commander Katherine Elizabeth Silva would become Captain Silva, the new commanding officer of USS *Towers*.

The most dramatic and important part of Bowie's career would wind to a close. He already knew that nothing would ever fill the hole that was going to leave in his life. And through it all, he'd have to smile and make polite speeches, pretending that he was happy to surrender command of his ship to a near-total stranger.

Damn. *Damn*.

He exhaled slowly. If wishes were fishes…

He turned back to Commander Silva, the prospective commanding officer of USS *Towers*. "Let's head up to the wardroom. We can grab a cup of coffee while we wait for the Training Team to finish prepping their debrief."

Silva started to follow him toward the exit.

Bowie slowed his pace a fraction to allow her to walk alongside. "Your friends call you Kate?"

Commander Silva smiled. "Only my father can get away with that. Everyone else calls me Kat."

"With a K?"

"That's right. With a K." She smiled again. "It's a long story."

Bowie opened the watertight door and motioned for her to step through. When they were on the other side, he dogged the door behind them and they resumed walking.

"How about you?" Silva asked. "Do your friends call you Sam?"

The captain shook his head. "Nope. They call me Jim."

Silva halted in mid-stride. "They call you Jim Bowie? *Really?*"

Captain Bowie grinned. "Really." He started walking toward the wardroom again. "That's a long story too."

CHAPTER 2

BARKHOR SQUARE
LHASA, TIBET
WEDNESDAY; 19 NOVEMBER
3:34 PM
TIME ZONE +8 'HOTEL'

The helicopter came in low and fast, clearing the ornate golden rooftops of the Jokhang temple by only four or five meters. Flying so close to the 1,300 year old building was a blatant violation of a dozen laws and security ordinances. Any other aircraft that dared such a maneuver would be forced to land, or shot down by ground troops or air forces. Today, the laws and regulations did not apply. Not to *this* helicopter.

It was an ordinary looking HC-120 Colibri, the plump dragonfly fuselage noticeably European in design, the paint scheme and markings just as clearly Chinese. But the local police and military commanders knew who was riding in the passenger seat, and no one would be foolish enough to interfere.

The pilot had been ordered to land as quickly as possible, by the absolute shortest flight path. He was following those orders to the letter. He steepened the angle of his approach, practically skimming the top of the tall stone stele at the front gate of the temple wall.

The stele was a rounded obelisk, nearly as ancient as the Jokhang temple itself. The stone had been erected in 822 AD by King Relpachen, to commemorate the Sino-Tibetan peace treaty, which had guaranteed that China and Tibet would forever respect one another's borders. Eroded by centuries of wind, rain, and snow, the words carved in the porous gray stone were still legible. China's public proclamation of Tibet's national sovereignty remained easily visible, for all the world to read. The irony was apparently lost on the occupying Chinese forces. It was not so easily overlooked by the Tibetan locals.

A landing zone had been cleared in the center of Barkhor Square. The usual throng of visitors, pilgrims, and shopkeepers had been pushed back to the edges of the square. The onlookers were now held at a distance by a

13

perimeter of wooden barricades, patrolled by several hundred hard-eyed Chinese soldiers.

Into this temporary enclave, the helicopter dropped the last few meters to the ground, the pilot battling an unexpected crosswind at the last second, before bringing his machine to a brisk landing on the flagstones.

The helicopter's turbine had barely begun to slow when a dark green military vehicle pulled alongside and a young Army major leapt out, ducked under the spinning rotors, and trotted to the passenger door of the aircraft.

The vehicle was a Dongfeng EQ2050, a near carbon-copy of the American-built Humvee. Officially, it was an all-Chinese design, produced completely from parts manufactured in China. In reality, about half of the vehicle's parts were imported from the American company AM General, in South Bend, Indiana—the manufacturer of the original Humvee. This detail was carefully ignored by anyone who did not want to arouse the ire of the Communist Party.

The door of the helicopter swung open, and the major snapped to attention.

The man who stepped out into the downwash of the rotors did not seem to be particularly formidable. He was in his mid sixties, lean, and fit, with crisp black hair and a creaseless face that seemed to subtract several years from his appearance. His dark suit and sharp white shirt were neatly tailored, but not of excessively fine quality. The one stroke of extravagance in his appearance was a red necktie of lush raw silk. He looked like a moderately-successful Chinese businessman in a fairly ordinary business suit.

The mechanical wind from the helicopter rotors whipped at his hair. He paid no attention, crossing the distance to the waiting military vehicle in several quick strides. He did not bow his head as he passed beneath the whirling blades of the helicopter rotors. He walked with his head held erect. Perhaps he carried some internal confidence that no machine of the Chinese military would dare to threaten the head that rode upon his shoulders. Or, perhaps his thoughts were so distant that he was unaware of the danger.

His name was Lu Shi, and he was the First Vice Premier of the People's Republic of China. Technically that made him the second most powerful man in the Chinese government, junior only to the Premier himself, Xiao Qishan. In reality, Lu's role as Xiao's subordinate was no more than a polite fiction.

Premier Xiao was not a young man, and his health had been declining steadily since his most recent heart attack. The old dragon had earned his position, and the honors that went along with it. Lu Shi was quite content to let Xiao wear the formal title for whatever weeks or months he had remaining to him, but no one in the senior ranks of the Communist Party had any serious doubts about who was running the country.

Even if there had been such doubts, Lu was Chairman of the Central Military Commission. That made him the effective commander-in-chief of the entire Chinese military. When the appearances were stripped away, Lu Shi was secondary to no one.

A half-pace behind Vice Premier Lu came a pair of solidly-built men in identical dark blue suits. Their faces were humorless, and their eyes scanned the crowd and the assembled military personnel with the same calculated degree of suspicion. Both men were *Bao Biao*, a Mandarin term most often translated as *bodyguard*, but more properly rendered as *protector*, or *defender*.

Lu Shi disappeared into the open rear door of the vehicle, followed immediately by his two guards, and then the military officer.

The crowd watched from the edges of the perimeter, many of them curious about the identity of the oddly imperious businessman who had dropped out of the sky into their midst. Who was this stranger, and how did he command such sway with the military and the police?

For most of the onlookers, those questions would never be answered. The soldiers shifted several of the wooden barricades, and guarded the procession of the car until it had left the square and disappeared into the streets of Lhasa.

The helicopter's turbine began to pick up speed again. In two or three minutes, the aircraft was lifting away into the sky.

When it was gone, the soldiers began packing up the wooden barricades. In a few minutes more, the soldiers were gone, and people began flooding back into the square. Beyond the aroused curiosity of the crowd, there was no sign at all that anything out of the ordinary had occurred.

⚓ ⚓ ⚓

Lu Shi stared vacantly out the side window as the streets of Lhasa scrolled past. Colors and shapes slid into his field of vision and then slid out again, without making any impression on his conscious mind. His eyes were unfocused, and so were his thoughts.

For a man whose intellect was practically the stuff of legend, such an utter lack of acuity was—quite literally—unheard of. For the first time in his life, Lu Shi could not make himself think. Moreover, he didn't really *want* to think.

One of the heavy-grade military tires hit a pothole. The vehicle's stiff suspension did little to cushion the impact, transmitting the shock directly into the passenger compartment, and sending a jolt up the spine of every passenger. The ride was not smooth; the seats were not at all like the well-padded luxury of the limousines that Lu Shi traditionally rode in. He didn't notice.

His fingers absently fidgeted with his red silk necktie. It had been a gift many years before, from Lu Jianguo. Even the mental recognition of his son's name brought a tremor to his hands.

Unwanted images came surging into his brain. Photographs of the burned and twisted wreckage of the train... Video footage of the wreck site... Smoke still rising from the smoldering remains of the passenger cars. Soldiers and emergency crews carrying stretchers loaded with the bodies of the wounded and the dead.

Lu Shi clenched his eyes shut, and tried to block out the visions of blood and mangled flesh.

None of the photographs or accident footage he had seen contained the face of Lu Jianguo. For that small blessing, he could be grateful. He had not been forced to look upon images of his son's broken body. But Lu Jianguo *had* been there, among the dead and the dying, unrecognized by the first rescue teams to arrive. Known only to the medical personnel and the soldiers as another injured passenger: another victim of the carnage.

Somewhere in Lu Shi's mind—below the threshold of conscious awareness—fear, and anger, and grief were circling like sharks. But for now, his emotions were as paralyzed as his higher thinking processes.

His fingers went through the motions of straightening his necktie, tightening the knot, smoothing the silk, loosening it a fraction, and then beginning the sequence again.

After some unmeasured interval, a hand touched his shoulder. "Comrade Vice Premier, we have arrived."

Lu Shi looked up, willing his eyes to focus. The vehicle had stopped at the entrance to a whitewashed stone building with curved glass doors. He glanced at the raised metal sign long enough to confirm that this was indeed the Tibet People's Hospital, and then allowed his eyes to drift away. His fingers found the red necktie again.

The rear door opened, and Lu Shi followed the Army major out of the vehicle, across a short stretch of sidewalk, and through the double glass doors into the lobby.

A clutch of white-jacketed hospital personnel inclined their heads respectfully, and then shuffled forward to greet him. Some of them were probably doctors, or perhaps the directors of the facility, but Lu Shi's guards weren't interested in credentials. They stepped forward to form a barrier between the Vice Premier and his would-be visitors.

Neither of the guards spoke a word, but their facial expressions and body language announced quite plainly that they would not hesitate to use lethal force on anyone foolish enough to approach the invisible perimeter around their protectee.

The Army major selected one of the white-jacketed men, apparently at random. "You!" He poked a finger in the man's direction. "Take us to the room."

The man nodded vigorously, and said something unintelligible.

Lu Shi, his guards, and the major followed the unnamed man down a hall and into an elevator. Three floors later, the man led them out of the elevator, past the circular desk of a nurse's station, and to the door of a room.

The man opened the door, stepping out of the way so that Vice Premier Lu and his flankers could enter.

Lu Shi stood before the open doorway without moving. He had arrived at a threshold, both figuratively, and literally. This was the place. He had reached the moment that his subconscious had been struggling to postpone, or even to deny entirely.

His senses, which had been dulled into near lassitude, seemed to stir fitfully. The doorframe, the walls, and even the white-coated stranger gradually loomed into sharper focus. His hearing, which had filtered out the majority of the sounds in his environment, began to return. He slowly became aware of the murmur of distant voices, the low hum of electrical equipment, and—he did *not* want to hear this—the cyclical hiss of a mechanical respirator.

This last sound was both repelling, and hypnotic. The high-pitched shush of a forced inhalation, followed by the gurgling rasp of the suction cycle, and then the shush of another forced breath. There was something obscene about the idea of a machine pumping air into a man's lungs, and then sucking it out again.

Lu Shi shuddered involuntarily, realizing as he did so that his sense of smell was recovering as well. Accompanying the surge of returning sights and sounds came a torrent of odors. The sharp alcohol reek of disinfectants. The coppery-tang of blood. The fetid scent of human misery.

The numbness was beginning to recede, but he was not ready to let go of it yet. He wasn't ready to think, or to feel, and he was definitely not ready to walk through the door in front of him.

He became conscious of the fact that his fingers were toying with his necktie. He let his hand drop to his side.

No one spoke.

His guards stood at his elbows like a pair of temple dogs, ready to react instantly, or to wait for a thousand years—hovering one hair breadth away from lethal action.

The Army major waited as well. He was a different breed of warrior. His body and senses were not tuned for instantaneous combat. As a soldier, he was prepared to fight—even to die—if he ever came to a time and place that made such things necessary. But now was not that time, and this was not the place. For the moment, his job was to wait for his superior to make the next move, or to issue the next order.

The stranger in the white lab coat continued to stand without speaking. He did not have the extraordinary discipline of the guards, or even the situational discipline of the soldier. But he was not an idiot. He would stand, holding the door open, for as long as necessary. He would not speak; he would not move; and he most assuredly would not allow the door to close in the face of the First Vice Premier of the People's Republic of China.

The comforting envelope of disorientation was eroding rapidly now, replaced by a growing sense of fearful expectation.

Lu Shi's rise to power had not been uncontested, and it had certainly not been gentle. He was no stranger to conflict or adversity. He was not easily frightened, but he was afraid of what he would find on the other side of that open doorway.

He forced down a fleeting urge to turn and walk away from this place. He exhaled slowly, steeling his nerve. Before he could change his mind, he moved forward, walking briskly through the open doorway.

The room had obviously been intended for at least three patients, but there was only one occupant now. The other beds had probably been bundled off to some storage closet, to make room for the son of Vice Premier Lu. The hospital staff was perceptive enough to understand that this was the most important patient their facility would ever care for.

The lone bed was positioned near the window, surrounded by IV racks, medical sensors, and several pieces of equipment that were less easily identified. The entire array was cross-connected by hoses, ribbon cables, and loops of clear plastic tubing.

On the bed, covered by a green hospital sheet, lay a vaguely human shape. Lu Shi averted his eyes from the shape as he crossed the room toward the bed. He was not ready to look. Not yet. He kept his attention on the baffling collection of medical devices. Nearly every piece of equipment seemed to have a wire or a tube that snaked across the floor to disappear under the green sheet. The patient—Lu Shi could not yet bring himself to think of this inert shape as his son—was wired up like a laboratory rat in some hideous medical experiment.

Finally, Lu Shi forced his gaze to travel up the length of the bed, taking in every detail. He paused when his eyes reached the knee level, or rather where knee level should have been. The sheet lay almost flat against the surface of the bed. There was no tenting of the fabric, no raised contours to indicate the presence of legs.

Lu Shi's throat tightened a fraction. He had been briefed about his son's injuries, but it was one thing to hear the words, and quite another thing to witness the reality for himself.

His eyes continued their journey up the length of the sheet-draped form, gliding over a pair of telltale bulges that must be the bandages covering the stumps of amputated legs. When he reached the upper body, the left arm lay above the sheet, wrapped in bandages, but essentially intact—at least in form. The dressings on the right arm were much heavier, and—like the legs—they ended suddenly, just above the wrist.

Lu Shi raised his eyes still further, to look at the face (if that torn and engorged mass of flesh could be called a face). A thick cervical collar held the neck in place, keeping the head tilted slightly back, to allow for the bundle of plastic tubing that disappeared into the mouth and nostrils.

The right eye and right ear were both swathed in surgical gauze, and the visible portions of the face were swollen, discolored by bruising, and crisscrossed by wandering trails of sutures. The left eye was open, and staring sightlessly toward the ceiling.

As he focused on that unblinking eye, Lu Shi felt an entirely unwelcome stab of recognition. The patient was approximately the correct age: in his middle-to-late thirties, but Lu Shi decided instantly that the similarity in ages didn't prove a thing. He did not want to recognize this face. He wanted it to be the face of a stranger; he *needed* it to be the face of a stranger.

A minute spark of hope still flickered somewhere deep inside of him, just the tiniest glimmer of a chance... This might not be Lu Jianguo. This could be a bizarrely elaborate case of mistaken identity. Somehow, someone had misidentified this poor wretch as his son. And somewhere, somehow—Lu Jianguo was safe, and whole, and alive.

Lu Shi felt the heat of tears on his cheeks. Let it be so. Oh *please*... let it be so... Let this mangled wreck of a man be *anyone* but Lu Jianguo.

And then his final hope was extinguished. He could feel the last tiny flare of the spark as it was swallowed by darkness. The face of the man on the bed was ravaged and distorted, but it was *not* the face of a stranger. The last shreds of denial were ripped from Lu Shi with the force of a hurricane. This thing... this lump of broken humanity... was Lu Jianguo.

Something broke at the very core of Lu Shi's being—something indefinable and incalculably fragile. He could not have named this thing, and he had no idea what it was. But he was instantly aware of its loss, and he knew without question that it could never be restored. Nothing would ever be the same again.

He stared down at the wounded animal that had once been his son. The raw silk of the red necktie flowed smoothly between his groping fingers.

During his early years, Lu Jianguo had brought his father all the usual gifts of childhood... handmade ashtrays... colorful paper ornaments... picture frames decorated with beads and bits of shell. All the worthlessly priceless trinkets made by children for their parents. The necktie had been different, not just because it was expensive, but because of the care that had gone into its selection. It had been Lu Jianguo's first attempt to understand his father's preferences and desires, his first attempt to offer a gift that was utterly appropriate to the tastes and needs of the recipient. It had been a boy's first act of manhood. Lu Jianguo had been nine years old.

At that moment, Lu Shi had known that he had named his son correctly. Jianguo, meant '*building the country.*' Looking into the shining eyes of his nine year old son, Lu Shi had seen his own wisdom in selecting that name. Lu Jianguo *would* build the country. And Lu Shi had not had any doubt that he was standing in the presence of the future leader of China.

Lu Shi blinked, and the memory of that long-past day fell away. He had been so certain that he knew the future of China... the future of his son.

Now, staring at Lu Jianguo's sheet-draped form, Lu Shi was certain of nothing. After a lifetime spent planning and preparing for the future, Lu Shi discovered that there *was* no future. There were only dreams and plans that could be snatched away without a second's warning. The future had been stolen, from Lu Shi, from Lu Jianguo, and from China. For the first time in his life, Lu Shi did not care about tomorrow.

He discovered that his eyes had drifted back down to the flat stretch of bed sheets where his son's legs should have been.

"Where are they?" he asked quietly.

The man in the white coat seemed to follow the direction of Lu Shi's gaze. He cleared his throat nervously. "Your son's legs, Comrade Vice

Premier? I... I'm not really sure. One of them was severed before he arrived, and the other..."

Lu Shi silenced the man with a glare. "Not my son's legs!" he hissed. He turned his head toward the Army major.

The man stiffened visibly. "Yes, Comrade Vice Premier?"

"Where are the men who did this?" Lu Shi asked. "Where are the criminals who..." His voice trailed off in mid-sentence. He paused, and continued at a volume just above a whisper. "The terrorists who... did this thing... Where are they?"

The major swallowed before answering. "We... ah... We believe their plan is to escape through the mountains into India. Given current weather conditions, it is likely that they will travel by way of the Nathu La pass."

"I see," Lu Shi said softly. "Then you do not *know* where they are?"

The major responded with a single shake of his head. "Not yet, Comrade Vice Premier. General Zhou has men and aircraft combing the mountain passes between here and the Indian border. The General has also ordered increased satellite surveillance of the most likely escape routes. We will locate the terrorists, Comrade Vice Premier. They can't hide from us indefinitely."

Lu Shi nodded slowly. "What of the prisoner? The terrorist you have in custody... Has he broken?"

"Not yet, sir," the major said. "But he will."

Lu Shi turned his eyes back to the bed. "Inform General Zhou that the Army is to immediately surrender the prisoner to the Ministry of State Security."

The words were spoken calmly, but the major could not entirely conceal his grimace. "Comrade Vice Premier... That won't be necessary. I assure you that our interrogators will soon have the information we need."

Lu Shi did not look at him. "I'm not offering you a suggestion, major. I'm giving you a direct order. I don't want the information *soon*. I want it *now*. Do you understand?"

The major snapped to attention and saluted. "Yes, Comrade Vice Premier!"

He executed an abrupt about-face, and marched briskly from the room.

Lu Shi stood without moving for several minutes after the major had gone. The only sounds in the room were the sibilant rasp and gurgle of the mechanical respirator.

At last, he looked up and made eye contact with the man in the white lab coat. "Disconnect the machines."

The man's face was suffused by a look of pure horror. "Comrade Vice Premier, we can't do that! These machines provide critical life support functions. If we disconnect them, your son will die!"

Lu Shi turned back toward the bed. "Will he ever be free of these machines? Will he recover enough to leave this bed?"

The man cringed under the hard edge of Lu Shi's voice. "That... That seems unlikely, Comrade Vice Premier. Your son has suffered massive cerebral trauma."

The man swallowed. "I... I don't believe he will ever be entirely free of the need for life support."

Lu Shi's voice was low and cold. "Then my son is already dead," he said. "Disconnect the machines."

CHAPTER 3

QUSHUI PRISON
SOUTHWEST OF LHASA, TIBET
WEDNESDAY; 19 NOVEMBER
7:42 PM
TIME ZONE +8 'HOTEL'

There was a sound somewhere on the other side of the door. Strapped to a steel chair in the dimly-lighted gloom of the interrogation cell, Sonam came awake instantly.

He had been drifting in that strange half-world between consciousness and oblivion. The pain was still too constant and too insistent to let him sleep, but he could find some relief by letting himself slide down into a haze of senselessness.

His face and upper body ached from repeated beatings and frequent jolts from an electric cattle prod. At least two of his ribs were broken, and every breath brought a stab of pain. The bullet hole in his left thigh throbbed in time with his pulse. The vicious bastards had done a good job of patching up his leg; he had to give them that much. The bullet had been removed; the wound had been neatly sutured, and they kept the dressings clean. Of course, their reasons hadn't been humanitarian. The Chinese Army was not concerned with his health. They just wanted him kept alive for questioning.

Sonam's interrogators had been careful to keep well clear of the injury. They had limited their attentions to the parts of his body above the waist. That still left them quite a bit of territory to work with, and they had used it with appalling brutality.

The noise was repeated, and this time Sonam recognized it—the scrape of a boot heel on concrete. It was followed almost immediately by the sound of a heavy key sliding into the door lock, and the dull rasp of the bolt being withdrawn. The soldiers were coming for him again.

Sonam felt a surge of panic, coupled with a sudden urge to urinate, or vomit, or both. He forced himself to slow his breathing.

He could do this. He could withstand another round of the beatings. He could live through another session with the cattle prod. He would clamp his teeth together and summon the will to endure. He told himself again and again that he would not answer their questions. He would not betray his people, no matter what these Chinese animals did to him.

If his interrogators came close enough, he would spit in their faces. With luck, they would become enraged enough to beat him into unconsciousness.

The door swung open, and—after uncounted hours in semi-darkness— even the relatively weak florescent light from the corridor was enough to make Sonam's eyes blink and water. It took him a few seconds to realize that he was not in for another encounter with the soldiers. This was something different.

The man standing in the open doorway was small framed, and very neat in appearance. He was Chinese, like the soldiers, but the resemblance seemed to end with that. He was dressed in civilian clothes, and he had none of the swagger of the military men. There was nothing brutish-looking about him. He looked like a clerk, or a petty bureaucrat. The man's eyes were lifeless, like the eyes of a doll. His features were quite ordinary, and his expression appeared to signal mild indifference.

Squinting toward this unremarkable figure, Sonam wondered if the little man had wandered in by mistake.

He was still puzzling over this new development when another man entered the room, carrying a black nylon zipper bag and a small wooden folding table. Like the clerk, this man was dressed in civilian clothes. He quickly erected the table, laid the nylon bag on the tabletop, and exited the room, closing the door behind him.

The clerk did not look at the black bag, but Sonam felt his own eyes drawn to it. The nylon was scuffed, and the seams were gray with hard use. He knew suddenly that the expressionless little man was not a clerk, and—with equal suddenness—he realized that he did *not* want to see what was inside that bag.

The little man spoke without preamble. "I will ask you questions," he said. His voice was low and inflectionless. He did not mangle the Tibetan language, as so many of the Chinese did. Unlike Sonam, whose speech was shaded by the Indian influence of Dharamsala, the man had almost no accent.

Sonam stared at him without speaking.

"You will answer my questions," the little man said. "Please understand that this is not a boast, and it is not a prediction. It is a simple statement of fact. You *will* answer my questions."

Still, Sonam said nothing.

The man walked to the table and unzipped the nylon bag. He looked up at Sonam, his face as impassive as ever. "You may answer my questions now, in relative comfort, or you can answer them six hours from now, when you have no fingers, no testicles, no eyes, and your throat is raw from screaming."

Sonam knew instinctively that these were not empty threats. There was no hint of malice in the man's voice, but there was not a trace of mercy either.

The man reached into the nylon bag, and pulled out a pair of long-handled pliers with a heavy-looking square head. "I will ask you questions," he said again. He opened and closed the pliers several times, as though testing the movement of the metal jaws. "The first time you refuse to answer, I will clamp these upon the index finger of your right hand, and I will crush it to a bloody pulp."

He stared directly into Sonam's eyes. "Do you understand?"

Sonam's head began to nod almost of its own accord, but he caught himself and held his muscles rigid. He would not answer, even with a gesture.

The little man stepped forward, stopping within easy reach of the chair.

Sonam remembered his plan to spit in the face of his torturer. The man was certainly close enough now, but Sonam's mouth had gone dry. He could not summon a single drop of saliva.

He flinched as the man grasped his right hand. He tried to jerk his hand away, but his forearms were strapped to the arms of the chair at wrist and elbow.

The steel jaws of the pliers were cold as they closed around his finger, midway between the second and third knuckles. There was a brief twinge of discomfort as the serrated teeth of tool pinched his skin, but the little man adjusted the alignment of the pliers, and the sensation vanished.

Sonam saw it when it happened, the minute shift in posture as the little man tensed the muscles of his upper body and rammed the handles of the pliers together.

The pain ripped through Sonam, piercing him as deeply and profoundly as the Chinese rifle bullet had done. The bone in his finger splintered and gave way with an obscenely liquid crack that he heard and felt with equal clarity. His vision narrowed, and then collapsed upon itself until all he could see was a searing pinprick of blood-colored light.

His mouth was flooded with the bitter taste of adrenaline, and still the steel jaws continued to move toward each other—crunching through shards of bone, crushing muscle, tendon, and flesh into a formless mass of pulverized meat.

The heavy square jaws met, the section of finger between them smashed into a ribbon of bloody gel. But the pliers were not finished yet. They twisted and pulled, opening and closing repeatedly, like a crocodile trying to get a better grip on the prey trapped between its teeth. The metal jaws worked their way upward and downward from their starting place, searching for undamaged bits of the mangled finger, finding the broken ends of shattered bones, grinding everything to ragged mush.

Sonam's finger—the thing that had once been his finger—became the very center of the universe. It eclipsed everything. There was nothing else. No life. No world. No thought. Only the ravenous metal jaws, and the pain.

It took him at least a minute to realize that he was screaming. High-pitched keening wails that sounded more animal than human. It took him a minute or two more to force himself to stop. At last, he managed to bring it under control, and he sagged against the straps of the chair, sobbing.

Distantly, through the pounding roar of his pain, he heard the voice of the little man.

"I prefer to begin with a small demonstration," the voice said. "Something effective enough to gain your attention, but small enough for you to recover from if you choose to cooperate."

There was still no malice in the man's speech. No suggestion of threat, and no flavor of sadism. This was not the voice of a man who caused pain for his own pleasure. It was the voice of unconditional confidence, and flawless willpower. And Sonam knew that the little man would not give up the task until his objective had been met. He would not beat his victim into unconsciousness, and he would not make stupid mistakes. He would work methodically and meticulously, and he absolutely would *not* stop until he had the information he had come for. It would happen now, while there was still enough of Sonam's body left intact to call itself human, or it would happen hours from now, when there was very little remaining but pain and shredded flesh.

"We will begin again," the little man said. "I will ask you questions, and you will answer them. Do you understand?"

Sonam nodded.

"Good," the little man said. "The site of my next demonstration will be your left testicle. If you lie to me, or if you refuse to answer my questions again, I crush your testicle just as thoroughly as I have crushed your finger. Do you understand?"

Sonam nodded again. "I..." His voice was a guttural croak. "I will... tell you... what you want to know..."

"Yes," the little man said quietly. "I *know* you will."

CHAPTER 4

USS TOWERS (DDG-103)
UNITED STATES NAVAL STATION; YOKOSUKA, JAPAN
FRIDAY; 21 NOVEMBER
1321 hours (1:21 PM)
TIME ZONE +9 'INDIA'

A heavy layer of clouds hung over Yokosuka harbor. The temperature hovered in the mid-fifties, but the wind blowing in from Tokyo Bay seemed much colder. True winter was still several weeks away, and the bite in the air was just a foreshadowing of things to come.

Silhouetted against the murky Japanese sky, the profile of the American destroyer was unusually angular. The ship's phototropic camouflage had darkened to the color of slate, closely mimicking the gray monochrome of the waves that lapped against the vessel's long steel hull.

Commander Katherine Silva stood on the fantail, and tried to imagine what the ship would look like two weeks from now, when the red carpets had been laid and the patriotic decorations had been hung. The lifelines would be draped with red, white and blue bunting. The American flag that now rustled fitfully at the end of the flag staff would be replaced by the oversized 'holiday colors' that were reserved for Sundays and special occasions.

The decorations and the holiday flag would be visual symbols of a ritual steeped in centuries of nautical tradition. USS *Towers* would undergo a change of command ceremony—the transfer of authority from one commanding officer to another.

That ceremony, just fourteen days in the future, would be the culmination of everything Silva had worked for. After the customary Navy pomp and flourishes, she would step to the podium and assume command of this vessel. With a brief exchange of protocol and hand salutes, her title would change from *Commander* to *Captain*. She would become commanding officer of one of the most advanced warships ever crafted by man.

And at that same moment, Captain Bowie would relinquish command of the ship. When their salutes were lowered, one era would come to an end and another would begin. Bowie would say final goodbyes to the men and women who had served under his command.

Some of the crew were new to the *Towers*, having received orders to the ship recently, like Silva herself. But others had been with Bowie on the last deployment, when the destroyer had gone head-to-head with a rogue nuclear missile sub under the Russian ice pack. A few had been with Bowie on the deployment before that, when the *Towers* had fought a running battle with a wolf pack of attack submarines, from one end of the Persian Gulf to the other.

They had fought for Captain Bowie, and bled for him. Some of the crew had even died for him. In return, Bowie had brought them victory. More importantly, he had given them the opportunity to save the lives of literally millions of their countrymen. He had made every member of the crew, from the most junior seaman to the most senior officer, feel like warriors. And now he was leaving.

Silva had seen it on the faces of the crew members over the last few days, as it gradually became real to them that their captain was leaving. The ship would have a new captain, of course. Silva would be captain. But *their* captain would be gone, and Katherine Silva would be trying to fill the shoes of the man who had made them heroes.

A raindrop struck the side of Silva's face, and ran down her cheek like a tear. It was immediately joined by a hundred other drops, and then a thousand, as the bleak Japanese sky began pelting the harbor with rain.

Silva ran toward the nearest watertight door leading into the skin of the ship. She ducked into the aft passageway and took one last glance at the sky before the door slammed shut behind her. The gray clouds were growing darker and more menacing.

She hoped to God that it wasn't an omen.

CHAPTER 5

MINISTRY OF NATIONAL DEFENSE COMPOUND
AUGUST 1ST BUILDING
BEIJING, CHINA
FRIDAY; 21 NOVEMBER
7:53 PM
TIME ZONE +8 'HOTEL'

There was a quiet tap on the door. Vice Premier Lu Shi didn't look up from the stack of documents on his desk.

He had not been reading the documents. In fact, his eyes hadn't really been focused on them at all. His mind was back in the hospital room in Lhasa, eyes locked on the pitiful wreck that had once been his son … seeing Lu Jianguo's mangled body obscenely violated by the tubes and wires of those damnable machines.

The tap on the door was repeated, slightly louder this time. Lu Shi forced his mind back to the present. He blinked several times, trying to reorient himself to his chair, his desk, his office. "Enter."

The door opened, and his personal assistant, Miao Yin, stepped into the room. She was a beautiful young woman in her mid twenties, her exquisite elfin features framed artfully by the straight-banged pageboy hairstyle that was so popular among female government workers. Her large dark eyes met Lu Shi's gaze, and she nodded, her head tilting with the slightest suggestion of a bow. "Please forgive the intrusion, Comrade Vice Premier. Minister Shen requests a moment of your time. He does not have an appointment, but he assures me that he urgently needs to speak to you."

Lu Shi stared blankly at his secretary. Unlike most senior government officials in China, he was not sleeping with any of his female underlings, but that didn't keep him from appreciating Miao Yin's loveliness. Ordinarily, the mere sight of her would be enough to lighten his mood.

But all such thoughts had been dimmed by the shadows that had descended upon Lu Shi's heart. The presence of Miao Yin barely registered on his consciousness. He had no eye for her beauty, and no real memory of its existence. He had forgotten what beauty was.

His mind was drawn inexorably back to the hospital room. The cloying reek of medical disinfectant. The vaguely human shape under the green sheet. The face of his son, half swathed in bandages—one sightless eye pointed toward the ceiling.

"Comrade Vice Premier?" Miao Yin spoke softly, but her voice startled him.

"Yes?"

His secretary repeated her minimal bow. "Minister Shen... He is waiting in the outer office."

Lu Shi rubbed his hand across his chin, feeling the scrape of stubble against his palm. He had forgotten to shave.

"Minister Shen," he said. He cleared his throat, and sat up straight in his chair. "Yes, of course. Send him in."

Miao Yin backed out of the door, and was replaced a few seconds later by the hulking form of Shen Tao, the Minister of Defense.

Shen paused in the doorway long enough to show proper respect, and then clumped into the room on his sturdy legs. At first glance, the man's barrel-shaped physique could be mistaken for fat, but Shen's round body was solidly muscular. His face was equally misleading. Behind his features and placidly oblivious facial expression, a quick mind was at work.

Lu Shi waved him to a chair.

Nodding his thanks, the Minister of Defense pulled the chair a half-meter forward, and shifted it a few centimeters to the right, before settling himself into the offered seat.

It was an unconscious gesture; Lu Shi was confident of that. It was also typical of the way Shen operated. He accepted everything, from hospitality, to orders, to challenges, on his own terms. *Yes, I will take the chair that you have offered me, but I will move it to a place of my choosing.*

On other days, Lu Shi admired this trait. Today, he had no patience for maneuverings of any sort. He also had no patience for polite apologies, or the niceties of official etiquette, both of which were going to come pouring out when Shen began to talk. Lu Shi preempted the pleasantries by speaking first.

"I understand that the terrorist has broken under questioning. What have you learned?"

'Terrorist' was Lu Shi's label for the murderous young fool who had been captured after the destruction of the Qinghai train.

Shen nodded. "You are correct, Comrade Vice Premier. The subject is now quite responsive to our inquiries..."

Lu Shi felt a flush of cold anger. "He is not a *subject*. He is a terrorist, and a mass murderer. And he is not *responsive to your inquiries*. You have tortured him, and he has broken. Now, may we please stop wasting time with circumlocutions?"

He locked eyes with the Minister of Defense and repeated, "What have you learned?"

To his credit, Shen didn't flinch or break eye contact, but his tone of voice was no longer self-assured. "The subject ... the ... ah ... *terrorist*, is named Sonam Dawa. He is a member of a faction of rebel Tibetan criminals who call themselves *Gingara*, a word that seems to translate as 'the Messenger.' He was part of a three man raiding team, commanded by a man named Jampa Dorjee, also a member of this Gingara. And the third man..."

Lu Shi waved a hand impatiently. "Yes, yes. The third man was an old drokpa shepherd who calls himself Nima. I knew all of this several hours ago. What *else* have you learned? Where have these terrorists gone? What was their escape plan? Where are they now?"

Shen blinked. "Their plan was to ... ah ... escape through the Nathu La Pass, to the Indian side of the Himalayas." He swallowed. "We have not yet located the other two members of the raiding team, but they have had three days since the attack to cross the border. They are probably safe on the Indian side of the mountains by now."

"On the Indian side, perhaps," said Lu Shi. "Whether or not they are *safe*, remains to be seen."

He leaned back in his chair. "Do we know their final destination, Comrade Minister?"

Shen nodded. "Yes, Comrade Vice Premier. This group, this Gingara, has based itself in a small village known as Geku, approximately forty kilometers on the Indian side of the border." He paused. "Were you considering a covert operation? Sending a small team into India, to root out these terrorists?"

His words were nearly lost on Lu Shi, whose thoughts had drifted back to the hospital room in Lhasa. The half-human form of his beautiful son, under the green bed sheet...

He shook his head violently. "No! There will be no covert operation. We will not answer this cowardly raid with a raid of our own."

Minister Shen's eyebrows went up. "I don't understand, Comrade Vice Premier. Are we not going to respond to this attack?"

Lu Shi felt his anger drain away, to be replaced by a clarity of purpose that was almost staggering. "We will respond," he said. "We will destroy them completely."

"The terrorists?"

"No," Lu Shi said. "What was the name of the village? Geku? We will destroy them all. We will show them what it means to harbor the enemies of China."

Shen's face had gone from shock to incredulity. "Comrade Vice Premier... We can't *do* that... The international community..."

"We *can* do it," Lu Shi said. "And we *will.*"

He softened his voice. "Shen Tao, my old friend. Trust me. The international community will do *nothing.*"

"We can't be certain of that," Shen said.

"I am certain," Lu Shi said. "Recent history has given us the perfect example. Think about it. Over the past decade, the United States has conducted so many missile strikes against terrorist bases in Pakistan and Afghanistan that such attacks barely make the international news."

He leaned forward and rested his hands on his desk. "America has laid the pattern. We will simply follow it. We will use our missiles against a terrorist base on the Indian side of the mountains."

He felt his voice harden again. "But we will not stop until that village is completely eradicated. Not a single building left standing. Not a house, or a hut, or anything left alive."

"The Central Committee ..." Shen said. "A military stroke of this magnitude will never be approved."

"I don't need the approval of the Central Committee," Lu Shi said. "The Standing Committee has the power to authorize direct military action."

Minister Shen did not reply. The Politburo Standing Committee was the most powerful decision-making body in China. Of the committee's nine members, one was Vice Premier Lu Shi himself; another was Premier Xiao, whose failing health led him increasingly to defer to the recommendations of the Vice Premier. At least four of the remaining seven members owed their political souls to Lu Shi. It would not have been fair to say that Lu Shi controlled the Standing Committee, but Shen knew that the man wielded great influence over the committee's deliberations.

Lu Shi looked down at his watch. "Tomorrow morning, I will call an emergency meeting of the Standing Committee."

His eyes returned slowly to Shen's face. "And this *will* be approved, Shen. I promise you that."

He nodded toward the door. "Go now, and prepare your missile forces. You will receive your official orders some time tomorrow morning."

The Minister of Defense stood up and walked toward the door in stunned silence. Before he reached it, Lu Shi spoke again.

"Remember, Comrade Minister… Not a hut will be left standing. No one in that village is to be left alive."

CHAPTER 6

FINAL TRAJECTORY:
A DEVELOPMENTAL HISTORY OF THE CRUISE MISSILE

(Excerpted from working notes presented to the National Institute for Strategic Analysis. Reprinted by permission of the author, David M. Hardy, PhD.)

Cruise missile... The term conjures up images of high-tech warfare, and the surgical precision of weapons launched with pinpoint accuracy against targets hundreds (or even thousands) of miles away. For many Americans, the first conscious awareness of cruise missiles occurred in the early 1990s, when the news media began carrying combat video footage from Operation Desert Storm, and the U.S. military's first incursions into Iraq.

Beginning on January 16, 1991, millions of television viewers watched dramatic video of Tomahawk Land Attack Missiles launched from the decks of American battleships, cruisers, and destroyers. Due to the obvious technical challenges in filming a submerged missile launch under actual warfare conditions, there was no accompanying video of submarine launched Tomahawks. Nevertheless, U.S. attack subs in the Persian Gulf and Red Sea were involved in the cruise missile strikes against Iraq from the very first moments of the war.

Americans were captivated by the notion of a 'smart' weapon, intelligent enough to cruise the length of a city street above car level, hang a left turn at the proper intersection, and zigzag its way through a maze of urban businesses and dwellings to locate and destroy the designated target building, and no other.

General Norman Schwarzkopf, Commander-in-Chief, U.S. Central Command, remarked that the Tomahawk missile was so precise that it was possible to pre-select exactly which window of a building that a weapon would fly through.

Post-mission battle damage assessment would ultimately prove that General Schwarzkopf's words were not empty boasts. The BGM-109 Tomahawk Land Attack Missile really *was* that effective.

Desert Storm was the first battlefield demonstration of the extraordinary power of smart weapons. The government and military of Iraq were completely unprepared for the accuracy and power of America's latest tools of war.

As public awareness of these weapons spread, several new pieces of terminology began to filter into the common lexicon. Phrases like Terrain Contour Matching (TERCOM), and Digital Scene-Matching Area Correlation (DSMAC)—while not exactly the stuff of everyday conversation—became generally recognizable components of the technical jargon surrounding next-generation military hardware.

In the years since Operation Desert Storm, the multitude of available media images—reinforced by animated television news diagrams and a sprinkling of explanatory terminology—may have given the average man on the street a false sense of comprehension for cruise missile technology. At the risk of sounding elitist, the core knowledge of many laymen might be summed up in three brief statements:

(1) Cruise missiles can be launched from a variety of vessels, vehicles, and aircraft at targets over 1,000 miles away.

(2) Due to their ground-hugging flight profiles and evasive maneuvering capabilities, cruise missiles are difficult to detect and track by radar, and even more difficult to intercept.

(3) These amazing weapons are the recent result of cutting-edge technological breakthroughs.

The first two of these assumptions are essentially correct. The third statement, as obvious and unassailable as it might seem, is false.

Although the cruise missile has inarguably benefited from refinements made possible by contemporary science, the core technology is not at all a recent development. In fact, the history of the cruise missile dates back at least as far as the First World War.

For all of its exceptional capability, this so-called *next generation weapon* of the modern age was a century in the making. And the tale of its gestation is almost as strangely compelling as the weapon itself.

CHAPTER 7

WESTERN YUNNAN PROVINCE, SOUTHERN CHINA
SATURDAY; 22 NOVEMBER
8:30 PM
TIME ZONE +8 'HOTEL'

A micro switch clicked shut somewhere deep in the electronic belly of the launch computer, channeling power to the firing circuits. Approximately two milliseconds later, the protective membrane at the rear end of the missile launcher was incinerated by a white hot stream of exhaust gasses. With an ear-splitting roar, the missile blasted through the weatherproof cover at the forward end of the launch tube, casting a brief flare of harsh red light against the dark hillside as it hurled itself into the night sky.

For a moment, the big eight-wheeled launch vehicle was wreathed in the smoke left behind by the receding missile. The brisk mountain winds began to shove the smoke cloud aside, but not before the elevated launch tubes spat two more fiery missiles into the cold Chinese night.

The vehicle's mission was complete now. All three of its launch tubes were empty. It had no more threat to offer, no more messengers of death to release into the darkness. But the vehicle was not alone.

There were thirty-five of them in all. Thirty-five Wanshan WS2400 transporter erector launchers, deployed in a staggered formation about a thousand meters west of the road. The matte colors of their camouflage paint schemes blended well with the scrub grasses of the local terrain, but any chance of concealment was stripped away by the roaring streaks of fire unleashed by these strange vehicles.

The launches came in rapid succession, missile after missile climbing away, and vanishing toward the west.

By the time the rising three-quarter moon broke over the foothills of the Himalayas, the area was deserted. The vehicles were gone, their passage marked only by scorched ground, and the tracks of their enormous tires.

Somewhere in the darkness, one hundred and five cruise missiles were hugging the torturous contours of the mountains, following carefully-plotted digital elevation maps toward their mutual target—a small village on the Indian side of the Himalayas.

CHAPTER 8

Jampa stood in the open doorway of the shepherd's house, the soft golden light of the oil lamps at his back, his face turned outward—toward the crisp gloom of the evening. He knew that he should close the door; the heat from the little fireplace was escaping past him, into the night. But he stood for a moment longer, enjoying the sting of the cold air against his cheeks and admiring the soothing near-darkness of the moonlit street.

The village of Geku lay spread out before him, an almost haphazard scattering of small houses and buildings under the emerging stars. It was a beautiful place, this frigid little paradise carved into the mountains on the roof of the world. Harsh. Difficult. Sometimes brutal. But always beautiful.

Most of the inhabitants were already settling down for the evening. The people here led full, but uncomplicated lives. Jampa envied them.

Here, on the Indian side of the Himalayas, there was freedom. Not boundless liberty, but at least the locals could go about their daily lives without fear that their homes would be raided by truckloads of Chinese soldiers. Their schools and their temples would not be burned, or crushed under the boot heels of an occupying nation.

Jampa felt his eyes drawn toward the east, where his own country was hidden behind the rising peaks of the mountains. The Chinese called it the *Tibet Autonomous Region*, which was a typical trick of communist propaganda. There was no autonomy for the people of Jampa's homeland. There was no freedom for them. Not for more than half a century, since the ironically-named People's Liberation Army had surged across the Jinsha River in 1950, to seize control of Tibet.

It had taken the Chinese invaders only thirteen days to conquer the vastly-outnumbered Tibetan defenders. Thirteen days, for one of the most ancient sovereign nations on the earth to become just another oppressed province in the Chinese empire.

Of course, the Chinese were somewhat more subtle about things these days, at least to outward appearances. The brute force of China's military occupation was giving way to something more devious. The Qinghai railway was hauling in trainloads of Han Chinese, to claim and settle the land, forcing the native people into an artificial minority. If no one stopped this unnatural migration, the Tibetan people could be squeezed out of existence in just a few decades.

The ghost of a smile crossed Jampa's lips. He *had* stopped it, for a while at least. He, and Nima, and Sonam had stopped the accursed train. They had blown the mechanical beast right off its tracks.

The smile faded as Jampa remembered staring into the eyes of the young PLA soldier, just before pulling the trigger of the stolen Chinese rocket launcher. The scene flooded into his mind again, the roiling ball of flame, the black smoke, the shriek of rending metal as the wounded train tore itself apart.

Jampa hadn't wanted to kill the young soldier. He hadn't wanted to kill anyone. He had only wanted to destroy the train, to stop the never-ceasing influx of Chinese invaders.

He felt a stab of regret, but it was quickly driven out of his thoughts by the memory of another fire. The smoke rising from the ruins of his little school in Amchok Bora. The faces of Dukar, and Chopa, and his other young students as the villagers had pulled their charred forms from the burning wreck of the school.

Jampa had been a teacher, back then. An educated man. A man of science in a land where academic learning was far too rare.

The villagers in Amchok Bora had treated him with respect. He had been regarded as a man of wisdom and enlightenment.

Jampa did not feel enlightened now. He felt angry, and tired. If there truly *had* been any wisdom within him, it had long since fled, replaced by a single purpose—to free his land from the Chinese oppressors.

He wondered where Sonam was now. He felt guilty about leaving his wounded team member behind after the attack on the train. He hoped—for Sonam's sake—that the young freedom fighter had died from his bullet wounds before the Chinese had gotten their hands on him.

Jampa had a brief image of what the ruthless bastards might do to make Sonam talk. His shudder was amplified by a shiver from the cold evening air.

The shiver was followed by a yawn, and then another one. Jampa tried to push all thoughts of Sonam's capture from his mind. Nothing could be done to help Sonam now. Either the man was already dead, or the Chinese had him in one of their interrogation cells. Either way, coming to Sonam's aid was far beyond the resources of Jampa, or anyone else in the Gingara organization.

Jampa yawned again, and made another attempt to force his thoughts away from the fate of Sonam. There was time for a bit of reading before bed. Tomorrow, perhaps he and Nima could begin planning their next strike against the oppressors.

He started to swing the door closed, and then paused with it still half open. What was that noise?

Jampa tilted his head, and struggled to concentrate on the sound that hovered at the lower edge of his hearing. The noise started softly, but grew louder rapidly. It reminded him of an odd combination of an arrow in flight, and the hissing of a kettle just coming to a boil.

The sound, strange as it was, did not seem completely unfamiliar. He had heard that sound before, or something very much like it.

The memory of the rocket attack on the Qinghai railway flickered through his brain again. He saw himself swing the fiberglass tube of the Chinese rocket launcher up onto his right shoulder. Felt the firing trigger retract under the pressure of his squeezing finger. Heard the whistling hiss of the exhaust gasses as the anti-tank rocket had leapt from the launch tube and streaked toward the side of the nearest railroad car.

The growing hiss in the air… It was almost exactly the *same* sound, but louder. *Much* louder. It was…

Jampa's thought was interrupted by an enormous dark shape that flashed past the half-open doorway, hurtling down the street toward the center of the village. The air current from the big thing's passage washed over Jampa with a warm chemical stench that reminded him somehow of burning kerosene.

The thing, whatever it was, flew about chest-high above the ground. In its wake trailed the strange whistling-hiss, the noise now grown to a painful volume.

Was it some kind of rocket? It *couldn't* be. It was too large. Nearly the size of a telephone pole.

Jampa was thrown sideways as the unknown flying thing reached the center of the village and detonated, splitting the night air with fire and a growing circle of destruction.

Jampa lay on the floor, his half-stunned brain trying to process the idea that the impossibly large thing *was* some kind of rocket after all. His eardrums were ringing from the aftermath of the explosion, but he could still hear the roar of the fireball and the screams of people thrown out of their beds by this deadly and unexpected assault.

He could hear something else, too. More of the whistling-hisses. Not just one of them. *Many.*

That was crazy. Who would fire missiles at a tiny Indian village? Who would *bother*? Who would waste that kind of expensive military hardware on a little town that most people had never even heard of?

And suddenly, Jampa knew the answer. He understood it with a clarity born of his years as a teacher, and a man of science.

He climbed painfully to his feet, and staggered to the doorway. The door hung drunkenly from a single unbroken hinge.

Two more dark telephone pole shapes streaked past the little house, each followed a second or two later by more explosions and more screams.

This was *his* fault. Death was coming to the village of Geku, and it was all Jampa's fault.

The idea had been so simple. So obvious. Strike at Chinese targets on the Tibetan side of the mountains, and then retreat across the border into India. The Chinese government wouldn't *dare* follow a handful of insignificant insurgents into the legal territory of another major nation.

And many of the locals in the northern Indian provinces were sympathetic to the cause of Tibetan liberation. The Indian villagers would gladly give sanctuary to Jampa, and Nima, and their fellow brethren of Gingara.

The plan had always worked, until now. The Chinese counterstrikes had *always* stopped at the Indian border.

What was so different this time? Something had changed. Something major. Jampa had no idea what sort of political shift had occurred, but it was clear that the old rules were suddenly and irrevocably gone.

Whatever the cause of the change in tactics had been, this unfolding catastrophe was almost certainly in retaliation for Jampa's rocket strike on that accursed train.

Another shockwave slammed Jampa against the doorframe. His head bounced off the wooden upright with a bone-jarring whack.

His knees buckled. He was sliding to the floor when the next Chinese cruise missile darted out of the gathering gloom, and crashed through the wall of the shepherd's little house.

Jampa was less than two meters from the warhead when it erupted. He saw no more, heard no more, *was* no more.

And the man who had fired the first shot of the coming war was no longer there to witness the barrage of missiles that continued to fall from the sky.

CHAPTER 9

MINISTRY OF DEFENSE
SOUTH BLOCK SECRETARIAT BUILDING
NEW DELHI, INDIA
SATURDAY; 22 NOVEMBER
7:32 PM
TIME ZONE +5 'ECHO'

Indian Defense Minister Sanjay Nehru was on the phone when the door to his office flew open. The heavy door swung rapidly on its well-oiled hinges, bounced off the burnished oak wainscoting, and nearly swung closed again before the unannounced visitor stopped it with an outstretched hand.

Nehru's eyes jerked toward the door in surprise. He was not accustomed to having people barge into his office without invitation. When Nehru got a look at the intruder, his shock transformed instantly to annoyance. It was that junior captain assigned as an aide to General Singh. What was the young idiot's name? *Kumar*? *Katari*? Something like that.

The young captain was breathing heavily, as though he had been running. He brought his palms together below his chin, and bowed his head quickly. "Namaste, Sri Minister. I apologize for the interruption, but General Singh requests your presence in the Operations Room as soon as possible, and we couldn't reach you by telephone."

Nehru had ignored the plaintive bleating of the phone's call-waiting signal. It was well outside of working hours on Saturday evening, and after half a day of slogging through mind-numbing paperwork, he was trying to enjoy ten minutes of conversation with his favorite nephew.

He covered the mouthpiece of the receiver with one hand. "Well don't just stand there," he snapped. "What is so bloody urgent?"

The young officer had to pause for a half second to catch his breath. "Reports are just coming in," he said. "Missile strikes…"

Nehru hung up the phone, all thoughts of his nephew gone from his mind. "Missile strikes? Where? Are you trying to tell me that we're under attack?"

The captain nodded. "Yes, Sri Minister. So far, the only known target is Geku, a small village in the Himalayas. Based on first-look analysis, approximately a hundred cruise missiles from an unidentified launch point in South Western China."

Nehru was stunned. *China*? That made no sense at all. It was crazy.

"There has to be some kind of mistake," he said. "Some sort of radar error, or a garbled report."

"I don't think so, sir," the officer said. "We've got satellite imagery. It looks like the entire village has been destroyed. There are no signs of survivors."

Defense Minister Nehru glared at the young officer. "Why would the Chinese attack a flyspeck of a village on our side of the mountains? Was there some kind of provocation?"

The captain shook his head. "No provocation that we're aware of, sir. And nothing of strategic value in the area of the village, as far as we've been able to tell."

"Then *why* are the Chinese attacking us?"

"I'm sorry, Minister," the captain said. "We don't know. General Singh requests…"

Nehru nodded quickly and gestured toward the door. "Yes. Fine. Tell General Singh I'm on my way. And inform him that I want a full defense staff briefing in ten minutes."

"Yes, sir," the captain said. He did an abrupt about-face and strode toward the door.

Nehru reached for the phone on his desk. He had to call the Prime Minister immediately. His fingers stopped before they touched the receiver. "Captain!"

The young officer paused in the doorway and looked over his shoulder. "Yes, Minister?"

"Tell General Singh to order a full military alert. Mobilize all air, sea, and ground forces. Maximum readiness."

His voice became quieter, but it took on an edge of steel. "If what you are saying is true, the Chinese have committed an unprovoked act of war against Republic of India," he said. "I don't know what those fools are up to. But if they want a fight, they're going to get one."

CHAPTER 10

FLIGHT LEAD
INAS 303 SQUADRON — BLACK PANTHERS
BAY OF BENGAL (WEST OF ANDAMAN ISLANDS)
SUNDAY; 23 NOVEMBER
0512 hours (5:12 AM)
TIME ZONE +6 'FOXTROT'

In hindsight, no one would ever know what made Lieutenant Ajit Chopra pull the trigger. The pilot's motives, whatever they might have been, died with him when Chopra's Indian Navy MiG-29K was blasted out of the sky over the Bay of Bengal.

In the days and weeks following the First Battle of Bengal, swarms of investigative journalists would try repeatedly to link Chopra's actions with the previous evening's missile strike on the village of Geku. Given the pilot's relative youth and the legendarily all-eclipsing power of young hearts, more than one media pundit would speculate that Chopra had met and perhaps fallen in love with one of the young village women who had been killed in the barrage.

Internet rumors began to spring up, identifying Lieutenant Chopra's lost beloved as a poor but beautiful girl named Mira. The tragic love story of Ajit and Mira would become the modern web's equivalent of Romeo and Juliette, forwarded in thousands—and then hundreds of thousands—of heart-rending emails by uncounted numbers of breathless romantics.

Internet legends tend to grow in the telling, and the compelling tale of doomed young Indian lovers was no exception. Increasingly elaborate email threads offered careful descriptions of Mira's death scene as a murderous Chinese missile shrieked down from the heavens to blow her family's small (but well kept) home into oblivion. Similarly florid descriptions told of Agit's exquisite emotional agony as he turned his Russian-built jet fighter toward a ship of the Chinese Navy, and wreaked teary-eyed revenge upon the godless warmongers who had slaughtered his beloved Mira.

Despite the polished elegance of many repeated tellings, not one shred of evidence would ever be found to support the story. No proof of Mira's existence would ever be documented, and no verifiable link (emotional or otherwise) would ever be established between Lieutenant Ajit Chopra and the bombed-out village of Geku.

From post mission analysis and reconstruction, all that's known for certain is this: on the morning of Sunday, 23 November, Lieutenant Chopra was flight lead for a group of four MiG-29s, operating from the Indian aircraft carrier INS *Vikrant*. At 5:12 AM (local time), apparently acting without orders, Chopra turned his fighter onto an approach vector toward the Chinese guided missile destroyer *Zhuhai*. Approximately ten seconds later, the young Indian pilot armed and launched two Kh-35U '*Switchblade*' anti-ship cruise missiles toward the Chinese warship. Both missiles functioned perfectly, following subsonic flight paths all the way to their target.

The reaction of the Chinese crew was fast, but not fast enough. The *Zhuhai's* Type 360S E/F-band Doppler radar identified the incoming missiles at approximately 17 kilometers, somewhere near the outer edge of the system's threat detection envelope.

Like most of his shipmates, the senior weapons officer aboard the *Zhuhai* had spent much of his career training for combat engagements at sea. But, training and simulations aside, the Chinese officer had never actually participated in live combat actions. He had never fired weapons at a real enemy target, and he had certainly never been on the receiving end of such an attack. When the incoming missile warning appeared on his screen, the weapons officer hesitated for a quick handful of seconds while his brain came to grips with the completely unanticipated idea that this was not a simulation; someone was really trying to kill him.

The man shook his head sharply and then jabbed the button that directed the destroyer's ZJK-4 Thomson-CSF combat management system to engage. The combat management system instantly activated the HQ-7 short-range air defense system, and the eight-cell missile launcher spun to starboard to point toward the inbound threat.

The Chinese weapons officer's hesitation was brief. Given the circumstances, it was also completely understandable. He did not live to regret the error.

Nicknamed *Harpoonskis* for their similarity to the American AGM-84 Boeing *Harpoon*, the Switchblade cruise missiles skimmed above the wave tops at Mach 0.8, or roughly 274.6 meters per second. Each tipped with a 145 kilogram warhead in a shaped-charge configuration, the two missiles were moving at 80% of the speed of sound when they slammed into the starboard side of the *Zhuhai*.

Like the trick of a street conjurer, the Chinese destroyer vanished behind a wall of black smoke and fire. When the smoke had cleared, all that remained of the warship was a spreading oil slick, punctuated by scattered pieces of flaming wreckage.

What happened next might best be described as chaos.

⚓ ⚓ ⚓

The Indian Navy communications net was instantly flooded with radio chatter as every pilot, action officer, and comms officer in the area began talking at once, trying to find out what in the hell was going on. If Lieutenant Chopra's voice was among the babble, it was lost amid the anger and confusion of his shipmates.

⚓ ⚓ ⚓

The *Zhuhai's* escort vessels, the guided missile frigates *Ma'anshan* and *Wenzhou*, did not wait for an explanation. They opened fire on Lieutenant Ajit Chopra's Mig-29K and the other three planes in his flight.

In a matter of seconds, the sky above the Bay of Bengal was a snarl of crisscrossing exhaust trails, as Chinese surface-to-air missiles climbed toward the Indian Navy MiGs, and the Indian pilots unleashed their own Switchblade anti-ship cruise missiles.

By the time the first missiles struck their targets, another flight of MiGs was launching from the deck of INS *Vikrant*.

The entire engagement lasted less than twenty minutes. When it was done, all three warships of the Chinese surface action group were on their way to the bottom of the bay. Seven aircraft of the Indian Navy were destroyed, and three others were able to limp back to their carrier with varying degrees of damage. The sea was littered with the bodies of dead and injured Sailors.

The First Battle of Bengal was over. The true carnage was yet to come.

CHAPTER 11

President Dalton Wainright trailed a Secret Service agent through the door into the Situation Room. As the president walked to his traditional seat at the head of the long mahogany table, the agent stepped deftly aside, taking up a position in the corner to the right of the door, where he could survey the entire length of the room without moving.

In the past, when the primary display screens had depended on ceiling-mounted LCD projectors, the Situation Room had been kept in semi-darkness. But the projector screens were gone now, replaced by six large flat screen televisions along the side walls, and an enormous flat screen master display covering the entire wall opposite the president's chair. With the projectors gone, there was no reason to dim the lights, so the room was well lit.

Although President Wainright would not admit it to anyone—including himself—he would have preferred the semi-darkness of the old days. It wasn't the mystique of the old lighting scheme that he missed; it was the anonymity, the false but reassuring sense of invisibility that sometimes comes from watching a movie in the cozy gloom of a public theater.

Dalton was not at all comfortable in his job. He was certainly not the first holder of the office to experience that particular feeling, but his own brand of discomfort didn't stem from the traditional source. More than one politician had spent an entire career angling for the Oval Office, only to discover that the job was too large, too challenging, and too thankless to reward the effort.

That wasn't the case for Dalton. Like most people who dabble in politics, he had sometimes flirted with dreams of the presidency, but those had been idle fantasies. He had never harbored any thought of trying to make them real, and he was not a bit surprised to find out that the presidency was completely out of his depth.

48

He had been quite happy as the Junior Senator from Maine, content in the belief that his political career had reached its peak. The invitation to join Frank Chandler's dark horse bid for the presidency had come as a surprise. Dalton had accepted the role of vice-presidential running mate, not because he believed that Chandler could win the election, but because it seemed like a logical way to bring his career in politics to a close.

With the possible exception of Frank himself, no one had been more shocked than Dalton when their Republican opponent's campaign had disintegrated in the wake of a well-publicized sex scandal. The resulting backlash in public opinion had propelled Frank Chandler into the Oval Office, with a rather dazed Dalton Wainright clinging to his coattails.

Now Frank was gone too, driven out of office by the public uproar after the fiasco in Kamchatka and the missile attack on Pearl Harbor. His departure had made Dalton Wainwright only the second vice-president in American history to ascend to the Oval Office through the resignation of a sitting president.

During his tenure in the Senate, a *Washington Post* reporter had once described Dalton as 'competent and dedicated, but undistinguished.' Under the undimmed lights of the White House Situation Room, Dalton wondered if even that scrap of left-handed praise might be an overstatement of his abilities. Despite his lack of flamboyance, he'd been qualified for his seat in the Senate. He'd known what he was doing, and he had been equal to the challenge.

The presidency was another matter. He could still lay claim to the words 'dedicated' and 'undistinguished,' but he had serious doubts that he was competent to hold the highest office in the land.

⚓ ⚓ ⚓

According to protocol, the half dozen people gathered around the long table were standing at attention. Dalton waved for them to take their seats, as he settled into his own chair.

The Sit Room Duty Officer, a hard-faced Air Force Colonel with steel-rimmed glasses, remained standing near the far end of the table. He nodded briskly toward his commander-in-chief. "Good evening, Mr. President."

Dalton opened the blue-jacketed briefing folder on the table in front of him, and glanced up to meet the colonel's eyes. He returned the man's nod with an equally abrupt gesture. "Proceed."

The Duty Officer pointed a slender remote toward the enormous screen opposite Dalton's chair. The blue background and presidential seal vanished from the wall-sized display, replaced by a regional map of Asia, overlaid with hundreds of cryptic-looking tactical symbols. The six smaller flat screens along the walls were instantly populated with images of ships, fighter aircraft, submarines, helicopters, and missile systems.

The Sit Room Duty Officer turned toward the master display, and thumbed a button that turned the remote into a laser pointer. The red dot of the laser came to rest in the body of water to the east of India, the Bay of Bengal, where a jumble of colored symbols seemed to indicate a concentration of ships and aircraft.

"Mr. President," the officer said, "the conflict between China and India is escalating rapidly. Both sides are mobilizing military assets across the board, and both countries have clearly demonstrated that they are willing to engage in direct combat action."

Secretary of Defense Mary O'Neil-Broerman spoke up. "The situation over there is going to hell in a hand basket, sir."

"I can *see* that," Dalton said. "I want to know *why*."

He instantly regretted the sharp tone in his voice. He had a tendency to become brusque when he was unsure of himself, and right now he was *very* unsure of himself.

Since the day he'd inherited the presidency, he'd begun every day with a simple prayer, or perhaps it was just a plea to the universe, since it wasn't directed toward any particular deity. *Please do not let anything happen today that I can't handle.*

So far, he'd managed to muddle through without disaster—largely because Frank Chandler had left him with a staff of capable people who were skilled at helping him navigate difficult situations. But he'd also been lucky. Fate had not yet thrown him a problem that was beyond the scope of his abilities.

Dalton's string of good fortune couldn't last forever. He knew that. Sooner or later, it was bound to happen. He would run into some challenge or some catastrophe that was too big for him. Then the people of the United States would find out how horribly things can go wrong when the guy sitting in the big chair is not up to the job.

"Mr. President, we can only partially answer that question," the Sit Room Duty Officer said. "The trigger seems to have been that train wreck in Tibet on Tuesday, the rocket attack on the Qinghai Railroad. The Chinese began calling it an act of terrorism before the smoke had even cleared. They apparently traced the terrorists to the Village of Geku, on the Indian side of the Himalayas. The People's Liberation Army retaliated with a massive cruise missile strike that pretty much wiped the village off the map."

"That can't be right," the president said. "The Chinese are not stupid, and that's too much of an overreaction. You don't retaliate for a localized act of terrorism by launching a large scale missile attack against another country."

The Secretary of Defense leaned forward in her chair. "With all due respect, Mr. President, that's not necessarily true. The U.S. has done it more than once. The first example that comes to mind is August of 1998, when President Clinton ordered the launch of Tomahawk Land Attack Missiles at targets in Afghanistan and the Sudan. It was in retaliation for the embassy bombings in Kenya and Tanzania. We simultaneously launched about 75 cruise missiles against countries on two different continents."

The National Security Advisor, Gregory Brenthoven, shook his head. "Granted that your basic premise is true, but your example is not exactly parallel to the current mess in Asia."

He turned his gaze toward the president. "When former President Clinton gave the order to launch, he knew that both Afghanistan and the Republic of Sudan were a nice comfortable distance from the United States. About six or seven thousand miles. President Clinton also knew that neither country had the firepower or the logistics to bring the fight back to American shores. In other words, the risk of escalating to all-out war was just about zero."

Brenthoven gestured toward the big map of Asia on the master display. "That's not the case with this China-India thing, sir. China didn't launch their missiles against some third-world country on the other side of the planet. They provoked a major military competitor, a nuclear power no less, sitting right on their own southern border. And *that* doesn't make any sense. As you said, Mr. President, the Chinese are *not* stupid. If somebody punches India in the nose, you can bet your last dollar that India is going to come out of the corner swinging with both fists. The Chinese *know* that. But they did it anyway."

The president looked at the map. "Why would they do that? Why would they take such a stupid risk?"

"We don't know yet, sir," the National Security Advisor said. "But right now, we've got a bigger question. What are we going to *do* about it?'

"I've spoken to the Chairman of the Joint Chiefs about this," the Secretary of Defense said. "He's preparing a full tactical briefing now. He can go over the details then, but in broad strokes, he recommends that we get an aircraft carrier on scene up there as quickly as possible. The idea is to establish a presence, and—hopefully—to act as a stabilizing force in the region."

The president nodded slowly. "Who's in the best position?"

The Chief of Naval Operations, Admiral Robert Casey, cleared his throat. "Mr. President, that would be the USS *Midway* strike group, based out of Yokosuka, Japan."

The president turned to look at the CNO. "And the *Midway* is ready to deploy?"

"Yes, sir," the CNO said. "The *Midway* is our ready-carrier at the moment. She's got a full complement of escorts, and they can be underway in a matter of hours."

"Alright," the president said. "Do it. Get those ships moving. We'll figure out the details while they're on the way."

He stared at the wall-sized master display screen with its overwhelming array of strange symbols, and he began to wonder if *this* would be the day that everything came apart.

CHAPTER 12

No matter what the Chinese government or news services might say later, it was not a riot.

Reverend Bill McDonald watched from the window of his second story hotel room, as people began gathering in the square below. At first it was a small group of purple-robed monks, and he wondered if they had come to pray, or meditate, or simply to meet and talk near the gates of the famous Jokhang temple.

But the monks were soon joined by people dressed in street clothes, and more people were streaming into the square, appearing from alleys and side streets. The small group quickly grew to a large group; and the large group blossomed into a burgeoning crowd. Still, the flow of humanity showed no signs of diminishing. As the throng continued to swell, the red, blue, gold, white, and green colors of the Tibetan snow lion flag began to appear—sometimes held overhead as a banner, sometimes draped around someone's shoulders like a cloak.

When the flags were revealed, McDonald knew that he was witnessing something unusual. The snow lion flag was a symbol of Tibetan independence and a rallying point for the separatist movements.

Introduced by the 13th Dalia Lama in 1912, the flag had remained the official banner of Tibet until the 14th Dalia Lama had escaped from the Chinese occupation in 1959, and fled to India. Now, more than a half-century later, the flag was an emblem of Tibetan sovereignty—a reminder of the days before the Chinese invasion, and a token of the freedom that might lie in the future.

The Chinese treated the Tibetan flag as an insignia of terrorism and anarchy. They had outlawed possession of the flag by anyone within the borders of Chinese-controlled territory, including all of Tibet. Public display of the flag was punishable by imprisonment, or worse.

But Bill McDonald could see at least fifty of the forbidden flags from his window. The crowd in Barkhor Square was openly defying the longstanding ban. This was turning into a major act of protest. There must be nearly a thousand people in the square by now, and still more were coming.

His window was closed, but he could hear the crowd now, hundreds of voices chanting in unison. Not ranting or screaming. Not shouting ultimatums. Chanting together in one voice, like an oddly disharmonic choir, all singing from the same sheet of music. It was eerie—mournful and powerful, but utterly peaceful.

McDonald's presence in Tibet had nothing to do with politics or journalism. He had not come to document the conditions of the Tibetan people, or even to question the continuing Chinese occupation of the once-independent nation. Beyond expansion of his own consciousness, he had come with no agenda at all. He was here simply to study with the Buddhist monks, to learn how (and if) their path to enlightenment could shed any illumination on his own spiritual journey.

During the Vietnam War, he had served as a door gunner and Crew Chief in the U.S. Army's 128th Assault Helicopter Company. He'd flown more combat missions than he could count, usually perched in the open door of a Huey gunship with an M-60 machine gun between his knees. He'd been shot down twice, wounded once by enemy fire, and—of greater importance than either—he had been transformed.

Bill McDonald had come out of Vietnam with a Distinguished Flying Cross, a Bronze Star, fourteen Air Medals, and a Purple Heart. But on his flight back to the United States, he had carried something much more important than the medals stowed neatly in his Army duffle bag. He had carried a profound sense of his personal spirituality.

Amid the horror of war, he had discovered his own connections to the mystical forces of the universe. He had become what he liked to call a 'spiritual warrior.' He no longer thought in terms of victory over military enemies. Instead, he concentrated on mastering his own mind, and exploring his place within the spiritual realm.

The events unfolding outside his window were at least partly—if not mostly—political in nature. If he knew anything at all about the mindset of the Chinese government, the reaction of the local authorities would be both rapid and brutal.

He'd spent the last several decades trying to avoid politics and violence, and he now had an unwitting ringside seat to an event that threatened to hold both of these corruptive influences in large measure.

Part of him was tempted to turn away from the window, and not allow himself to be drawn into the coming clash, even as an onlooker. But another part of him knew that the search for enlightenment is also the search for truth. Whatever happened in Barkhor Square this morning, the Chinese government would apply its colossal influence to controlling public opinion after the fact.

Like it or not, Reverend William H. McDonald was about to become the witness of history. If any truth at all was going to emerge from today's events, it would be up to him to draw it forth.

Bill fumbled with the window latch, and then spent several seconds wrestling the balky window open a few inches. As the gap widened, the chanting voices of the crowd became louder and easier to make out.

He found his cell phone, and scrolled through the icons until he located the one that activated the phone's video camera. Even through the window panes, the images on the screen of his phone were sharp and clear. He wasn't sure if the phone's tiny built-in microphone was sensitive enough to record the sounds drifting up from the street below. He didn't know how to check, or how to adjust the audio levels (if such a thing were possible).

He decided to add a bit of personal narration, to provide some context for the video, in case the audio was too low or muffled to be intelligible.

"My name is William H. McDonald," he said. "It's approximately nine-thirty in the morning, on Saturday the twenty-third of November. I'm standing at the window of my second story room, in a guest house overlooking Barkhor Square, in the Tibetan city of Lhasa."

He panned the camera phone right and left, taking in as much of the crowd as he could manage. "As you can see, a large group of people—I'm guessing that it's somewhere between several hundred and a thousand—are gathered in the square. They are chanting, but I only know a handful of Tibetan words, so I'm not sure what exactly they're saying. But I want to make it perfectly clear that this is a peaceful gathering. There have been absolutely no signs of violence or unruly behavior. This is not a mob. If this is a rally or a protest, it's calm and orderly."

He paused for several seconds, trying to decide whether or not to add anything else.

"I don't know if my camera is recording their voices," he said. "I hope it is, because this chant, or song… whatever it might be… is beautiful. I've never heard anything like it."

His voice fell silent again, but he continued to move his little camera around to cover the crowd from every angle he could get from his limited vantage. He thought about going down into the square, to capture some of this from street level, but he decided against it. He probably had a better view of the crowd from up here, and if the police showed up—*when* they showed up—they would take away his phone the instant they recognized it for what it was. If he stayed up here, out of the way, he thought he had a fairly good chance of getting his phone and the video recording out of the country intact.

The reaction forces were not long in coming, and McDonald was careful to record their arrival.

"I see three trucks converging on the square," he said. "Each truck contains thirty—maybe fifty—armed men, dressed in what appears to be riot gear. I can't tell if these are soldiers, or some kind of police tactical squads, but they are definitely loaded for bear."

"They're climbing out of the trucks now, deploying in three positions. Doesn't look like they're trying to form a perimeter, or surround the crowd."

McDonald's narration halted again. He listened for several seconds to the unbroken chanting of the crowd. The people in the square had seen the armed squads arrive and deploy, but there was no move to fight or escape.

The crowd seemed to huddle more tightly together, as if drawing courage and determination from one another. The pitch of the chanting seemed to waver, but it didn't quite falter. The singsong cadence continued, regaining its strength.

McDonald was about to comment on this, when he heard the thumps of the first gas grenades. He saw several smoking canisters arc into the crowd, and watched the protesters recoil from the billowing clouds of white vapor.

Teargas. He had encountered it during chemical warfare defense training in Army boot camp, and he had seen it used several times in Nam. He recognized the retching, face-clutching motions as every person who caught even a whiff of the stuff tried to stagger blindly away from the source of their sudden pain. The orderly crowd disintegrated into a chaos of lurching, frightened individuals.

"They're using gas," McDonald said. "I'm guessing that it's teargas. Whatever it is, it's certainly doing the trick. I think…"

But he never recorded his next thoughts, whatever they were, because his attention was shattered by the sound of gunfire, followed instantly by screams of terror and pain.

He felt a flash of nausea as adrenaline surged into his veins, broadcasting and amplifying the ancient chemical reflex to flee from danger. He could feel his palms begin to sweat, and a strange ringing in his ears that had nothing to do with the after-echo of gunshots.

He looked around quickly, trying to identify the source of the shots. He spotted several members of the riot control squad with their rifles unslung. He jerked his cell phone camera around in time to catch at least a dozen of the uniformed men firing directly into the milling throng of civilians. Sharp staccato muzzle reports, in three-round bursts—assault rifles configured for combat shooting.

All thoughts of narration were gone from Bill McDonald's brain. He saw some of the protestors—a lot of them—jerk and stagger under the impacts of bullets. Blood flew; people fell to the ground, all to the accompaniment of rapid gunshots and screaming voices. This wasn't riot control. It was a massacre. But *why* was it happening?

Not all of the soldiers or policemen were firing. In fact, most of them weren't. Did that mean that they'd been ordered to fire, but many of them had disobeyed the command? Or maybe they *hadn't* been ordered to fire, and some of them had taken the decision into their own hands.

That didn't make sense. Or did it?

McDonald remembered something in the news about an attack on a trainload of Chinese soldiers a few days ago. Was this some kind of retaliation for that? Official retribution? Or maybe spontaneous revenge… Angry Chinese soldiers, who found themselves with Tibetan protesters in their crosshairs.

The more Bill McDonald thought about it, the more likely this last idea seemed. This protest had been going on for less than an hour. That wasn't a lot of time for senior Chinese decision-makers to consider and approve a plan to use deadly force against the crowd. Also, the assault, or intervention, or whatever had begun with teargas. That pretty much guaranteed that the crowd would break up quickly. If the plan had been to mow the protestors down, it would have been smarter to corral them together, to allow for greater concentration of firepower.

McDonald continued to sweep the square with his camera. It was nearly empty now, except for the people who were down, and not going anywhere. After the shooting had started, the riot force had made no attempt to stem the escape of fleeing protestors. That also seemed to support the idea that the shooting had been unplanned, carried out in the heat of anger and the flush of violence.

This was the thing he had turned away from in his own quest for enlightenment. The world's problems could not be solved through the

barrel of a gun, the bodies in the square below—maybe eighty or a
hundred of them—were proof of that.

Even the soldiers looked stunned by what had happened. They milled
around for nearly a minute before they began to shamble toward the
downed protestors, to check for signs of life in the bloody unmoving
bodies.

McDonald shut off his phone camera, and backed away from the
window. In a very short time, maybe only a few seconds from now, the
soldiers were going to shake off their disbelief and start looking around for
any witnesses to the shooting. A foreigner with a digital video camera
would not fare well if they happened to spot him.

He slipped the camera into his pocket, and left the hotel by an exit that
opened on an alley opposite the square. Ten minutes later, he was six
blocks away, poking through the wares of a shop that catered to tourists.
He didn't need or want any souvenirs, but it gave him plenty of separation
from the scene of the incident, and he was determined to stay off the
streets until the cleanup was completed and the riot force was long gone.

His hands were still shaking, so he shoved them into his pockets. The
plastic form of the phone was smooth and warm against the back of his
right hand. No one but him had any idea what was recorded on the phone's
memory card. He planned to be well and safely out of Chinese territory
before he revealed the ugly little chunk of history stored on that flat wafer
of digital circuitry.

His first instinct was to arrange the first possible flight out of this place,
but that might not be a smart move. It was probably wiser to wait three
days, and follow the itinerary he'd already established. If he changed his
travel plans without warning, the Chinese authorities might wonder why
this American tourist was suddenly in such a hurry to depart their sphere
of influence. Better to be patient. Safer that way.

By the time he was back on friendly soil, the People's Republic of
China would have implemented their information-control strategy. Based
on past history, it seemed likely that the Chinese government would try to
cover up the incident completely, deny that this bloodbath had ever taken
place. If they did admit that the shootings had occurred, they would
probably try to minimize the size of the protest, and the number of
casualties. They might claim that all reports of injuries and deaths were
fabricated by untrustworthy dissidents. They might even try to blame
everything on the protestors, falsely accusing them of acts of violence
against police or military forces.

Whether they resorted to outright denial or spin control, it was a near
certainty that the Chinese government would do everything within its

power to hide the ugly truth of what had happened here today. The video recording on Bill's phone was absolute proof. It would shatter their denials and evasions. If they found out about it, he had little doubt that they would go to extreme lengths to silence him.

His plans to distance himself from politics didn't seem to be working out too well at the moment, but perhaps that was part of the greater plan of the universe. Perhaps—at this point in his existence—his purpose was *not* to set himself apart from the affairs of man. Possibly, it was his destiny to become the agent of truth.

He would mediate and pray on the matter. That would usually bring him clarity of thought and unity of purpose.

But even if prayer and meditation didn't yield the answers, he had a strong feeling that the universe was about to let him know what it had in mind.

CHAPTER 13

FINAL TRAJECTORY:
A DEVELOPMENTAL HISTORY OF THE CRUISE MISSILE

(Excerpted from working notes presented to the National Institute for
Strategic Analysis. Reprinted by permission of the author, David M.
Hardy, PhD.)

In 1915, Secretary of the Navy Josephus Daniels established a small
panel of inventors to help the United States military prepare for possible
involvement in the Great War in Europe—what we now refer to as World
War I. Daniels observed that the technologies of combat in the early 1900s
were evolving at an unprecedented rate, and he was concerned that the
U.S. military was not properly armed or trained for mechanized warfare.

The resulting organization, the Naval Consulting Board, was comprised
of 24 inventors whose charter was to provide *'machinery and facilities for
utilizing the natural inventive genius of Americans to meet the new
conditions of warfare.'* Floundering under this lofty but somewhat vague
mission statement, the board had no legal status, no funding, and no staff
for the first year of its existence. In August of 1916, Congress appropriated
an operating budget of $25,000, and the Naval Consulting Board was
finally in business.

Despite the high hopes of Josephus Daniels, the board accomplished
very little of note beyond approving camouflage paint schemes for civilian
ships. One of the more significant exceptions was the development of the
so-called *aerial torpedo.*

The brainchild of Elmer Sperry, one of the pioneers of practical
gyroscope applications, the aerial torpedo was intended as an unmanned
flying bomb, capable of attacking distant targets without human guidance
or intervention. Sperry was fascinated by the remarkable potential of such
a weapon, and he hoped that such awesome destructive power might
actually deter countries from starting wars.

It should be noted that Sperry's attitude toward destructive deterrence,
as naive as it may appear in hindsight, was relatively common among arms

developers of the early twentieth-century. Sperry and his contemporaries believed that—if the frightfulness of warfare could be escalated far enough—human beings would have no choice but to abandon war. Sadly, two World Wars, countless smaller wars, and a global nuclear arms race have disproved that theory.

Elmer Sperry may have been wrong in predicting the end of armed conflict, but his vision for an autonomous flying weapon captured the attention of the Naval Consulting Board. In 1917, the board awarded the Sperry Gyroscope Company a $200,000 contract to develop an aerial torpedo.

Sperry began by developing a gyroscopic autopilot system, and installing it on a Curtiss N-9 biplane. He wanted to start by demonstrating that an aircraft could regulate itself in flight, without a human at the controls. The N-9 carried a pilot to handle take-off and landing procedures, but the intent was to eventually transition to fully automatic flying. In the meantime, the pilot was also tasked to observe the plane in flight, and report on its performance under control of the autopilot.

After a number of successful test flights, Sperry supervised the construction of a purpose-built aerial torpedo airframe, powered by a two-cylinder engine. The actual manufacturing and assembly of the torpedo airframe prototype was carried out by the Curtiss Aeroplane and Motor Company.

The torpedo prototype was modified to carry a pilot, on the assumption that human observation and assistance would be helpful in identifying and ironing out bugs during the early developmental tests. Sperry's son, Lawrence, became the test pilot. Although the exact number of test flights is no longer certain, it's commonly accepted that the Sperry Aerial Torpedo crashed at least four times with Lawrence Sperry at the controls. Available technical data suggests that these incidents were caused by mechanical problems in the prototype, rather than error on the part of the pilot.

In spite of these challenges, Elmer Sperry eventually felt that his torpedo design was sufficiently mature to operate without human assistance. The first unmanned flight of the Sperry Aerial Torpedo took place on March 6, 1918, in what is now regarded as the first successful launch of a guided missile.

Operating completely under automatic control, the torpedo climbed from its launch position to a pre-designated altitude, and continued in smooth, stable flight until the autopilot's distance control ended the test at a preset range of 1,000 yards.

The maiden test of the Sperry Aerial Torpedo was a success. Unfortunately, it was not to be repeated.

Future flights did not go well, as the unmanned aircraft failed to achieve stable flight, deviated from its intended flight path, or simply fell out of the air. Ultimately, Sperry engineers discarded the purpose-built torpedo airframe, and returned to the Curtiss N-9 test bed to re-examine their entire approach to the design.

⚓ ⚓ ⚓

While Sperry and Curtiss were struggling with numerous technical challenges, the United States Army Aircraft Board decided to undertake its own aerial torpedo project. The Army asked inventor-engineer Charles Kettering to design an unmanned flying bomb, capable of striking a target at a range of 40 miles or more.

Kettering, who had observed tests of Sperry's aircraft autopilot in 1917, agreed to take on the challenge of developing an aerial torpedo. While he recognized the potential of Sperry's earlier engineering in unmanned flight control, Kettering wanted a cheaper and less complicated design.

Working in consultation with Orville Wright and the Dayton-Wright Airplane Company, Kettering developed a lightweight airframe with dihedral biplane wings and a tapered cylindrical fuselage constructed of wood laminates and papier-mâché. Powered by an air-cooled 40 horsepower De Palma engine, the unmanned craft was 12.5 feet long, weighed 530 pounds, and was designed to carry a 180 pound explosive warhead.

Its official title was the *Kettering Aerial Torpedo*, but people began referring to it as the Kettering Bug almost from the start, possibly in reference to its dragonfly-like silhouette.

Kettering designated independent engineering teams to handle various parts of the developmental research. One of these teams designed an inexpensive portable launch system, consisting of a four-wheeled cradle which rode on two parallel rails.

Although he had set out to develop an autopilot that was cheaper and simpler than the version used in Sperry's earlier N-9 tests, Kettering was not able to produce a workable model of his own. Ultimately, he asked Elmer Sperry for assistance. Although they were technically competitors, Sperry agreed to help with the autopilot problem.

At last, with the preliminary engineering problems resolved, the Kettering Bug was ready for testing in September of 1918. After several preliminary ground trials, the first full test flight was conducted on 2 October.

The flight began with a smooth takeoff, but it did not go well after that. Instead of turning onto its assigned heading and leveling off, the Bug climbed too steeply until it stalled and then crashed.

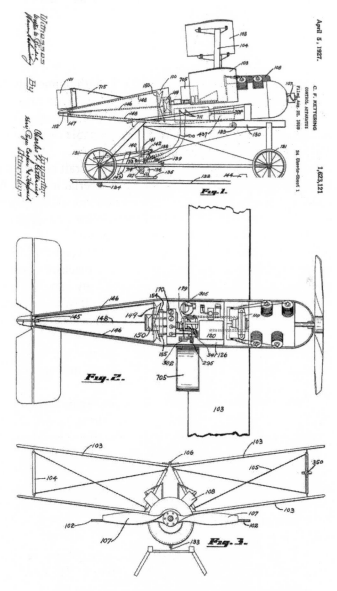

Kettering Aerial Torpedo, Patent Application (1927)

The Kettering Aerial Torpedo was not off to an auspicious start, but a number of subsequent tests were more successful. The Army was encouraged enough to order 100 prototypes, but only about 45 were produced before the Armistice was signed and World War I was over.

Seeing no further immediate need for the technology, and frankly not entirely impressed with the results up to that point, the Federal Government decided to combine the Army and Navy aerial torpedo programs. Competitive test events were more favorable for the Sperry design, and the Kettering Bug was abandoned.

The U.S. military conducted limited experiments over the next two years, before cancelling the project entirely in 1920.

The *War to End All Wars* had come to a close, and so had the aerial torpedo program. Optimists predicted a future of global peace and prosperity, in which there would be no need for the tools of battle. Unfortunately, they were wrong. Mankind was not finished with war, and war was certainly not finished with mankind.

Another global conflict, even larger and more brutal than the first, was looming just over the horizon. And military leaders of that coming war would not forget the idea of an unpiloted aerial bomb that could destroy enemies at a distance.

The first generation of unmanned flying weapons had not carried out a single attack under actual conditions of battle. They had not destroyed a single target, or killed so much as one enemy soldier. But the second generation of such weapons would not be long in coming. And when they *did* arrive, they would change everything.

CHAPTER 14

USS TOWERS (DDG-103)
WESTERN PACIFIC OCEAN; SOUTH OF JAPAN
SUNDAY; 23 NOVEMBER
1348 hours (1:48 PM)
TIME ZONE +9 'INDIA'

Commander Silva opened the door to the wardroom, but before she could step inside, she heard the voices. They were muffled, but she didn't have any trouble making out the words.

"Holy shit!" the first voice said. "We're *really* going into battle? You're not just fucking with me? We're really gonna do it?"

"I don't know if we'll be fighting," the second voice said. "The big dogs don't exactly share their battle plans with junior enlisted types. But we're hauling ass down to the Bay of Bengal, and that's where all the shooting is. I know *that* much."

Silva glanced through the open door. The wardroom was empty of people. The chairs were all pushed neatly up against the long table, and the blue linen table cloth was bare, except for a carefully aligned row of coffee cups, stacked upside down on white saucers.

She stepped through the door, and closed it quietly behind herself. She knew where the voices were coming from now. The small square serving window from the wardroom pantry was not completely closed. A stainless steel shutter could be pulled down to cover the serving window, isolating the pantry from the wardroom to give the ship's officers privacy during meals or meetings. When the shutter was open, the mess attendants could pass food or dishes back and forth between the wardroom and the adjoining pantry as they were serving meals to the officers.

Usually, the shutter was either completely open or completely closed. But whoever had used it last hadn't pulled it all the way down, leaving a gap of four or five inches at the bottom of the serving window. The voices of the two young mess attendants were coming through the opening.

"Yeah," the first mess attendant said. "But the Indians and the Chinese are shooting at each other, right? We're just going down there for like, diplomacy reasons, or something. We're not really going to fight."

"I don't know," said the second mess attendant. "Those crazy bastards are launching missiles all over the place. We could end up in the middle of a shit storm, no matter *what* the big plan is supposed to be."

Silva felt a momentary urge to clear her throat, or make some sudden noise that would let the two young Sailors know that their soon-to-be-captain was in the wardroom. Not that she needed their help to get a cup of coffee. She was quite happy to pour for herself. But it seemed rude to eavesdrop on their conversation.

Still... It was never easy for a commanding officer—or a prospective commanding officer—to find out what the Sailors on the deck plate were truly thinking. Over time, a CO could develop a rapport with the crew that would bridge that communication gap, at least in part. But Silva was new to the *Towers*. She hadn't yet had time to get a good feel for the men and women who would be her officers, much less the enlisted crew.

She would be assuming command soon, but she was a complete stranger to these people. And they were strangers to her. For the moment, any qualms she felt about listening in on a private conversation were outweighed by her desire to know what the junior Sailors were saying amongst themselves.

She picked up the nearest coffee cup, moving carefully to avoid making a noise. The mess attendants were still talking.

"You got *that* right," the first mess attendant said. "This ship has a way of being at the center of the fucking crosshairs when the bombs and the bullets start flying."

The second mess attendant snorted. "Dude, have you seen the pictures? Guys in my division have pics of the damage from that last shoot out, up in the Russian ice pack. The forward gun was totally blown away. Completely fucking gone. Nothing left but a crater in the deck."

"I heard about that," the other sailor said. "But I haven't seen any pics."

Silva *had* seen pictures of the damage from the last deployment, and pictures of the damage from the deployment before that. These kids might be a bit too free with the profanity, but they were right about one thing; the *Towers* did have a way of winding up in the thick of the fighting.

She lifted the coffee pot from its warmer, and poured herself a cup. The liquid was dark, and the odor was acrid. An old Sailor would call this good Navy java, but Silva didn't care for coffee that had been on the burner too long. She could live with it though, and she didn't want to interrupt her impromptu intelligence-gathering session to ask for a fresh pot.

She eyed the dark liquid dubiously, before deciding to double her usual dose of creamer to take the worst of the edge off of the carbon taste.

"I don't know whether to be excited, or scared shitless," the first attendant said.

The second attendant laughed. "I'm going for *both*."

The first mess attendant didn't join in the laugh. "I'm sure glad Captain Bowie is still the skipper. If this crap with the Chinese had happened two weeks from now, we'd be stuck with the new CO."

"What have you got against Commander Silva?" the second attendant asked. "She seems okay to me."

"I don't have *anything* against her," the first attendant said quietly. "I'm sure she's fine, and I'm sure she knows what she's doing. But if we're going into battle, I'd rather have Captain Bowie in command."

"I know what you mean," the other Sailor said. "But we don't get to make that choice. In a couple of weeks, she's going to be the skipper. We've just got to hope she's up to the job."

"Yeah, but what if she *isn't* up to it? Has she ever been in a real combat situation before? What if she doesn't have what it takes when the shooting starts?"

The second mess attendant snorted again. "You need to stop worrying about that shit, and start worrying about these dishes. We've got to start getting ready for evening chow."

Commander Silva set her cup down on the table. She didn't feel like coffee anymore. She walked out of the wardroom, the untasted contents of her cup swirling gently as the door swung shut behind her.

CHAPTER 15

MINISTRY OF NATIONAL DEFENSE COMPOUND
AUGUST 1ST BUILDING
BEIJING, CHINA
MONDAY; 24 NOVEMBER
9:11 PM
TIME ZONE +8 'HOTEL'

Vice Premier Lu Shi sat at his desk, leafing slowly through the stack of photographs for the tenth or eleventh time. The photos varied in size, age, and quality. A few had been composed by professional photographers, and some were recent high-resolution digital images, printed on glossy card stock. Most were ordinary snapshots, taken at various times over a period of nearly three decades. There were even a half dozen Polaroids, alternately fading from exposure to sunlight, or merging into supersaturation by color emulsions that had continued to incrementally intensify with the passage of years.

Lu Shi had scavenged the pictures from every family photo album he'd been able to lay hands on. The collection depicted indoor scenes, outdoor scenes, close-ups, wide shots, group poses, and solo portraits. The images shared a single common element. Every one contained Lu Shi's son, Lu Jianguo.

Here was Lu Jianguo at age six or seven, playing a pickup game of soccer with a gaggle of other boys on the grass in Chaoyang park. And here was plump baby Jianguo, swaddled in orange silk for the traditional red egg and ginger ceremony at which he had received his name. Fourteen year-old Lu Jianguo, wearing the red scarf of the Young Pioneers, marching in ranks with his comrades in Tiananmen Square. A snapshot of the boy at about age eight, sleeping stretched out on the back seat of a limousine, with his head resting on his father's knee. A formal portrait of Lu Jianguo in a severely-tailored gray suit. He must have been about twenty-five in that shot. It had probably been taken shortly after he'd become a junior secretary in the Ministry of Public Security.

The phone on Lu Shi's desk rang, but his brain registered the sound only vaguely. He continued to leaf through the stack of photographs, searching for something that he could neither name, nor fully imagine. Some indefinable sliver of information or fragment of insight that could make sense out of the senselessness that had seized control of his life.

How could Lu Jianguo—this beautiful boy, this bright young intellect, this brilliant communist—be *gone*? How was such a thing even possible? The very idea was wrong. Hideously wrong. *Monstrously* wrong.

At some point Lu Shi's eyes ceased to register the photos as they passed through his fingers. The motions of his hands became mechanical repetition.

In the late nineteen-seventies, when Lu Shi had himself been a rising young star in the Communist Party, he had fought hard to bring China's one-child policy into being. It hadn't been a popular law in those days, and it wasn't much more popular now. But it had been a necessary measure.

By 1976, China's population had multiplied to nearly a billion, and the rate of growth had still been increasing. If the trend had been allowed to continue, the People's Republic would ultimately have devolved into famine, and economic collapse.

The decision to limit each family to a single child had not been made lightly, and it had not been easy to enforce. As with any restrictive regulation, there were exemptions which could be exploited by the privileged elite. Several senior party members had taken full advantage of the loopholes. Lu Shi had not been one of them. The one-child policy was important to China's future. Lu Shi could not very well espouse the benefits of the policy, while violating it himself.

So, he had obeyed the law which he had helped to create. He had fathered only one child. Now, that child was gone, and the future was gone with him.

CHAPTER 16

USS CALIFORNIA (SSN-781)
NORTHERN INDIAN OCEAN
TUESDAY; 25 NOVEMBER
1522 hours (3:22 PM)
TIME ZONE +6 'FOXTROT'

Captain James Patke scanned the tactical display on his command console, carefully studying the wide ring of icons that represented the frigates and destroyers encircling the Chinese aircraft carrier. Like most submarine commanders, Patke had an almost Zen-like level of patience when he was on the hunt, and the current mission was putting that patience to the test.

China was a latecomer to carrier warfare, but their defensive screening tactics were turning out to be surprisingly effective. It had taken Patke and his crew nearly two days of unhurried probing to find a weak spot in the aircraft carrier's defensive perimeter. There had been opportunities to slip in more quickly, but Patke was determined to be even more cautious than usual.

The Chinese and Indian navies were both pretty damned trigger happy right now. If you made the mistake of spooking either one of them, you were likely to get your ass shot off.

Patke looked up from the display and glanced toward his Officer of the Deck. "Take us to periscope depth."

The USS *California* was a *Virginia* class attack submarine, so she didn't technically have a periscope. In place of the traditional Type 18 scopes used by other classes of U.S. attack subs, the *Virginia* class boats were each equipped with a pair of AN/BVS-1 photonics masts. The new fiber optic system was both technically and tactically superior to its predecessors, but no self-respecting submarine officer ever wanted to utter the phrase '*photonic mast depth*.' As a result, much of the old periscope-related terminology remained in use, even though the periscope itself was no longer around.

The OOD nodded. "Sir, periscope depth, aye!" He turned toward the Diving Officer. "Make your depth one hundred twenty feet."

The Diving Officer acknowledged the command and immediately relayed his own order to the Planesman. "Five degree up bubble. Make your new depth one-two-zero feet."

The Planesman pulled back slowly on the control yoke, keeping his eyes glued to the plane angle indicator. "Sir, my bubble is up five degrees, coming to one-two-zero feet."

The submarine began its slow and cautious ascent.

The OOD keyed the mike on his headset. "Sonar—Conn, coming shallow in preparation for going to periscope depth. Report all contacts."

Captain Patke observed the smooth operation of his control room crew at work. This was a good team—confident, but not cocky. If any of them were nervous about penetrating the defensive screen of a foreign carrier strike group, it didn't show.

Patke was actually a tad nervous, himself. This was not a simulation. If something went wrong here, things could turn ugly.

He wasn't particularly concerned about the destroyers and frigates. He took pride in the superb acoustic silencing technology of his boat. The *California* was quiet enough to get fairly close to most surface ship sonars without being detected.

The Chief of the Boat, who held the traditional bubblehead's opinion that all surface ships are targets, liked to claim that the *California* could sneak in close enough to piss on the hull numbers of any surface vessel in the world. Patke wasn't ready to go quite that far, but the COB's boast wasn't completely off base.

But the PLA Navy's antisubmarine warfare helicopters were no joke, and somewhere out there, a Type-93 attack sub was operating in support of the carrier group. Patke's sonar team had maintained an intermittent track on the Chinese submarine for the last two days. At the moment, it was stationed on the far side of the carrier's defensive envelope. If the *California* were detected, the Type-93 would come after her, and the sub would be a hell of a lot harder to shake off than the surface escorts.

⚓ ⚓ ⚓

The *California* reached periscope depth about fifteen minutes later, after a brief pause at 120 feet to check for *shapes and shadows*: the silhouettes caused by ships floating on the surface.

The sensor head of the *California's* photonic mast rose slowly through the surface of the water. The narrow dome-shaped housing contained a color video camera, a high-resolution black and white camera, and a thermal imaging camera for infrared target detection and evaluation. All three cameras scanned continually as the sensor head rotated through a full 360 degree sweep.

The digital video feed from each camera was relayed down to the control room of the *California* in real-time, via high bandwidth fiber optic cables at the core of the photonic mast.

Seated at his command console, Patke jogged the pistol-grip joystick until the cameras spun around to cover the aircraft carrier. He thumbed a button to trigger the video recorders, and zoomed in for a tighter view.

The big Chinese warship had a strange history, and not much was known about her current configuration or capabilities. Built by the Soviet Union during the last years of the Cold War, she had been intended as the newest vessel of the *Admiral Kuznetsov* class. But the ship had been unfinished when the Soviet Bloc collapsed, and she had eventually been sold at auction to a Hong Kong-based travel agency, who supposedly intended to convert the ship into a floating hotel and gambling parlor.

The floating casino plan had never materialized, and the unfinished ex-Soviet carrier had somehow ended up in the hands of the People's Liberation Army Navy. The PLA Navy had re-christened the ship *Liaoning*, in honor of Liaoning Province in northeast China.

Captain Patke nodded to himself as he watched the crisp digital video feed on his command console. This was the closest look that anyone had managed of the *Liaoning* since the ship had gone into operation. The intel weenies were going to have a field day when they got their paws on these video recordings. They would scrutinize every frame of video, from every available angle—examining antenna placements, weapons fixtures, and even the routing of topside cables and pipes—searching for any and all clues to the ship's capabilities or limitations.

The operational parameters of the original Russian design were well known. But the Chinese had made extensive modifications, and no one—with the possible exception of the PLA Navy—had a firm understanding of how those changes would impact the combat potential of the ship.

So Patke was nearly as busy as the video recorders, soaking up and evaluating every detail he could lay eyes on. They were facing the port side of the aircraft carrier, from about twenty degrees aft of the port beam. From this angle, Patke noted the squashed pepperbox silhouette of an FL-3000N missile launcher, and the vaguely robotic form of a Type 730 Close-In Weapon System. Judging from the placement of both systems, it was a fairly safe bet that each of them had a mirror-image counterpart on the opposite side of the ship.

Patke tilted the joystick forward, zooming in tighter, and beginning a slow pan down the length of the Chinese warship. "Alright, you sneaky bastards," he said. "Let's see what kind of surprises you've got up your sleeve."

CHAPTER 17

From: <robert.monkman@navy.mil>

Sent: Tuesday, November 25, 4:31 PM

To: <b.haster@ucsd.edu>

Subject: Missing You

My Dearest Beth,

Just another happy day aboard the mighty USS Midway. At least I think this is the Midway. I've taken so many wrong turns that I might be on a different ship by now. Six weeks, and I still can't find my way around this beast. I have to scatter a trail of breadcrumbs every time I leave my stateroom, or I'll never make it back to my bunk.

Aside from the ever-present danger of getting lost on the way to the briefing room, things are going pretty well. The guys in my squadron are great. I catch the usual ration of bullshit for being a nugget, but I won't always be the new kid on the block. What happens down here doesn't matter all that much anyway. What really counts is what happens in the sky, and nobody can lay a hand on me up there.

Remember Chucky Barnes who reported to the squadron at the same time I did? He's earned himself a new callsign, and he's not real happy about it. He used to be Barnstormer, which isn't too bad, if you ask me. But a couple of days ago, he lost his cookies all over the 0-5 level catwalk. Now everybody in the squadron is calling him 'Upchuck,' and it looks like it's going to stick. (No pun intended.)

My lead, the infamous Poker, has been threatening to change my callsign to 'Monkey Man,' which is apparently the most creative thing that his limited imagination can do with the name Monkman. He's been around so long that his first wingman was Wilbur Wright, so you can't really expect much. But for now, I'm still Rob the 'Monk' Monkman, and I like that just fine. That's me, baby – the Shaolin monk of the skies, kicking butt with my badass aerial Kung Fu.

Okay, enough of that hero-of-the-skies crap. So far, my aerial Kung Fu has been limited to simulators and unarmed practice engagements against other U.S. Navy flyboys. I look pretty damned good in training, but I've never flown against an actual threat. If I ever go up against the real deal, I'll be happy if they don't change my callsign to 'Monkey Butt,' or something equally flattering.

Speaking of the real deal, we'll be entering our Op Area just in time for Thanksgiving. We're only supposed to be doing the observe-protect-stabilize thing, but I'm still kind of nervous. The Chinese and Indian navies have traded shots several times now, and both sides are pretty jumpy. I just hope they remember that we're not the enemy. I'd hate to get my butt shot off while I'm trying to get my turkey dinner on.

Just kidding, baby. I'm sure everything is going to be fine. We've got a full carrier strike group, with all the bells and whistles. We're not here to fight, and nobody is going to be stupid enough to start any trouble with us.

I sure would love to be home tomorrow, helping you get the turkey ready for the oven. We really are going to have to try that one of these days. We can't keep doing Thanksgiving at your Mom's house forever. Or maybe we can... Her sweet potato pie is still the best I've ever tasted, and that bean casserole thing she does is amazing.

Speaking of amazing, I happen to think that your Mother's only daughter is pretty fantastic, now that I mention it. That would be you, Miss Muffin. I wonder if your Mom knows that you do most of your cooking in only panties and my old Chargers jersey. Maybe I should save that piece of information for blackmail at some future date. Hmmm...

Okay, I shouldn't have gone there. Now all I can think about is your cute little butt prancing around the kitchen in panties. Maybe I better go take a cold shower.

I love you, Beth. I miss you more with each second that passes.

Yours always,

Rob

LT(jg) Robert J. Monkman
VFA-228 Marauders
USS Midway (CVN-82)

CHAPTER 18

MINISTRY OF NATIONAL DEFENSE COMPOUND
AUGUST 1ST BUILDING
BEIJING, CHINA
TUESDAY; 25 NOVEMBER
9:48 PM
TIME ZONE +8 'HOTEL'

General Chen Caihou was the first to break the silence. "Comrades, the situation with India is getting out of control. We must act *now*, before it is too late." His words were firm, but the tone of his voice was carefully neutral, pitched to avoid any trace of criticism or accusation. He allowed his gaze to take in each of the other eight men seated at the circular table.

Including himself, all nine statutory members of the Central Military Commission were present. When Chen's eyes came to Lu Shi, they paused for an instant before moving on to the next man.

The table was circular, to symbolize the equality of the commission's members. There was no bourgeois seat of honor here. Just dedicated communists, meeting on equal footing to debate and decide matters of military strategy.

At least that was the theory. In reality, the greatest concentration of authority in the room lay with Lu Shi. His power as Chairman of the Central Military Commission was technically nominal, but the man was also the First Vice Premier of the People's Republic of China.

Although Xiao still carried the formal title of *Premier*, the old leader had long since delegated all serious decisional authority to Lu Shi.

This made Lu a dangerous man to cross. It also put General Chen Caihou and his fellow members of the Central Military Commission in a very delicate position. If the present skirmishes with India continued to escalate, the People's Republic could find itself in a full scale war with a major military adversary. General Chen had little doubt that China would emerge victorious from such a war, but the cost would likely be staggering, in both financial terms, and in terms of human life. The conflict needed to end before things deteriorated that far.

General Chen's eyes circled the table again, his words still lingering unanswered in the air. He had discussed this issue with several other members of the commission in advance, and he had received agreement and promises of endorsement. Chen would flatly (but respectfully) raise the topic, and his covert allies would add their voices in support.

But he had spoken up, and the room was silent.

Lu Shi's eyes also made the circle of the assembled faces. "Someone is letting you down, Comrade General," he said softly. He let his gaze continue to wander until it came to center on General Chen.

"Who is it?" Lu asked. He raised one eyebrow slightly. "Which of our comrades are supposed to be flocking to your banner right now?"

General Chen sat for several seconds, before he turned to meet the Vice Premier's scrutiny. "Comrade Lu, we share your grief over the loss of Lu Jianguo. He was a fine young man, and a true communist. His death was a great tragedy. But is that sufficient provocation for war?"

"This is not about my son," Lu Shi said. His voice was low and hard. "This is about security and national sovereignty. Those who harbor the enemies of China are *themselves* the enemies of China."

General Guo Jinping, Chief of General Staff of the People's Liberation Army, cleared his throat. "With all due respect, Comrade Lu... Is it wise to invite a major military confrontation in order to punish a handful of sewer rats who destroyed a train?"

Lu smiled sadly. *"Xīng xīng zhī huǒ kě yǐ liáo yuán."* It was an ancient Chinese proverb which could be translated literally as '*A single spark can burn the entire prairie.*' Contextually, it was a reminder that leaders must never underestimate the potential destructive power that an apparently minor problem can cause.

"The Qinghai railway is one of the greatest engineering accomplishments in history," Lu said. "In places, the track elevation reaches more than 5,000 meters. Many aircraft don't fly that high. When we brought in the Swiss to develop construction methods for laying rail across the permafrost, the Swiss engineers said it was impossible. The Western press called the entire project a five billion dollar boondoggle. They said it couldn't be done. But we did it. Then, they predicted that the track would fail within a year. But the Qinghai railway carries 3,000 of our people to the Tibet Autonomous Region *every single day.*"

Lu's eyes zeroed in on General Guo Jinping. "Comrade General, we can replace the train cars and the engines. We lost nearly two-hundred of your soldiers in the attack, but the PLA can recruit that many replacements in a single afternoon. Between the dead and wounded, there were more than 1,000 civilian casualties as well, but the People's Republic can also cope with those losses. We can deal with the damaged equipment, and the human victims, and the financial cost. But we cannot permit a direct assault on our national prestige... Our national resolve and our political ideologies have been directly challenged. If we allow such a challenge to go unanswered, China becomes weak in the eyes of our enemies, and the eyes of the world."

Air Force General Xu Zhiyuan, Commander of the PLA Air Force, nodded respectfully. "I believe we will all concede that there are significant political implications," he said. "But is it wise to allow political issues to devolve into outright warfare?"

Lu turned toward the general. "I'm surprised that you would even ask such a question," he said. "Have you forgotten the teachings of Chairman Mao? *'Politics is war without bloodshed, while war is politics with bloodshed.'*"

General Xu nodded again. "Chairman Mao also said that, *'Communism is a hammer which we use to crush the enemy.'* But he was speaking at a time when China was fighting for its very existence. Is that honestly the case now, Comrade Vice Premier? After decades of peaceful relations, have our Indian neighbors suddenly become a threat to our national survival? For that matter, would we be in conflict with them at all if we had not used a hundred cruise missiles to hammer an Indian village into dust?"

Before Lu Shi could respond, General Chen raised a hand. "How we got into this situation is no longer relevant. Regardless of motivation or intention, we did strike their village, and they have retaliated. So far, the skirmishes have been relatively isolated, but that's rapidly changing. We are caught in a cycle of escalating retaliations. The question is; how do we break the cycle before it gets completely out of control?"

"I agree," General Guo said. "If we are not careful, this could become to us what Vietnam was to the Americans. Or what Afghanistan was to the Soviet Union. A bloody quagmire, with no prospect of a graceful conclusion."

"This is already our version of Vietnam!" Lu snapped. "Can none of you see that? Think about it... Vietnam was not a technical failure for the Americans. Nor was it a tactical failure. The American military was well equipped, well trained, well supplied, and well supported. By comparison, their adversaries were a pack of semi-literate monkeys squatting in rice paddies and swinging through the jungles. So, *why* did the Americans lose?"

"The communist ideal," General Guo said tentatively. "The North Vietnamese were sustained by the superior teachings of Marx and Chairman Mao..."

Lu Shi slapped his open palm on the table. "*Bái mù!*" Literally, this could be translated as '*white-eyed*,' or '*blind*.' In this context it meant something like '*you're looking the wrong way, you idiot!*'

Lu's voice was still sharp. "The communist ideal had nothing to do with it," he said. "If it were a matter of ideologies, the Soviets would have used their communist philosophies to triumph over the Afghanis. Instead, the mighty Russian military was vanquished by a few tribes of unwashed goatherds hiding in caves. So I ask you again... *Why* did the Americans lose in Vietnam? *Why* were the Soviets defeated in Afghanistan? How were two military superpowers both routed by inferior enemies? When you know the answer to that question, you'll begin to understand what is at stake in our current conflict."

The room was silent.

Lu Shi looked from one face to the next. "No one? The military brains of our nation are seated around this table, and not one of you can answer such a simple question?"

Still, no one spoke.

"Very well," Lu Shi said. "I'll answer the question for you... The Soviet Union lost in Afghanistan for the same reason that America lost in Vietnam. Because their national will was *weak*."

"With all due respect, Comrade Lu, that may be a bit of an oversimplification," General Chen said.

"It is *not* an oversimplification," Lu said. "It is a basic statement of truth, and any serious examination of the facts will prove it." He jabbed a finger toward General Guo. "Comrade General, how many military deaths did North Vietnam suffer during combat actions against the Americans?"

"Roughly a million or so," the general said.

"Closer to 1.1 million," Lu said. "And how many deaths among North Vietnamese civilians?"

"I'm not sure, Comrade Vice Premier," said General Guo. "I've seen figures as low as 50,000 and as high as 300,000."

"Fair enough," Lu said. "The numbers vary significantly from one source to another. But let's assume a number on the low end, somewhere around 100,000 civilian deaths. Combined, that puts the death toll for North Vietnam at somewhere around 1.2 million."

Lu glanced around the table again. "Can any of you tell me how many American military personnel died in Vietnam?"

"I believe," said General Chen, "that the final count was about 58,000 American dead."

"That's about right," Lu said. He lifted both of his hands, and turned them palm up, shifting each slowly in a reciprocal up-and-down motion, as though they were the arms of a balance scale. "The North Vietnamese lost 1.2 million, and much of their national infrastructure was bombed out of existence. By contrast, the Americans lost fewer than 60,000 soldiers, and the national infrastructure of the United States was completely untouched."

Lu dropped his hands. "America was winning on the battlefield. They were winning economically. Their ability to wage war was not even slightly impaired. So I ask you, comrades... How did the United States *lose* the Vietnam War?"

Again, no one in the room responded.

"Their weapons did not fail them," Lu Shi said. "Their soldiers didn't fail them. Their economy was not in danger of collapse. Only one thing failed them, but it was enough to send the indomitable American military slinking home like a beaten mongrel. Their national *willpower* failed. They lost the desire to win. And because of that, they allowed themselves to be defeated by an inferior enemy."

Lu's eyes blazed. "*That's* what our current conflict is about. It's not about trains. It's not about 200 dead PLA soldiers. It's not about some rat-bitten Indian village. And it's not about my son. It's about the strength of our national will. It's about refusing to bow to a weaker adversary."

"I... ah..." General Guo looked at the other faces gathered around the table, and swallowed. "How far do we go with this?"

"As far as it *has* to go," Lu Shi said. "Until the Indian government backs down."

"But what if they don't back down?" General Guo asked.

"They will," Lu said.

"But what if they *don't?*" Guo repeated.

"They are an inferior adversary," Lu Shi said. "If we raise the stakes far enough, they will have no choice but to back down. And if they don't... Our Indian neighbors will discover that they *do* have a breaking point."

CHAPTER 19

LHASA GONGGAR AIRPORT
SHANNAN REGION, TIBET
WEDNESDAY; 26 NOVEMBER
8:50 AM
TIME ZONE +8 'HOTEL'

The wheels of the China Eastern Airbus A320 left the runway of Lhasa Gonggar Airport exactly on schedule, and Reverend Bill McDonald took his first easy breath in three days. He hadn't slept more than fifteen or twenty minutes at a time since the massacre in Barkhor Square. Now that he was finally in the air and leaving Chinese territory, he could relax.

His cell phone was safe in his pocket, and the memory card with the video recording was still intact. In three and a half hours, he'd be landing in Kathmandu. Then, after a four hour layover, he'd be on a Cathay Pacific flight to San Francisco International by way of Hong Kong.

He'd be home by tomorrow evening, in time for a late Thanksgiving dinner, but he still hadn't decided what to do with the video recording. He needed to get it into the hands of the right people. That much was obvious. Unfortunately, he wasn't sure *who* the right people might be.

He'd considered going straight to CNN or one of the nationally-recognized newspapers, but he didn't have any contacts in the world of journalism. The major news organizations probably got several thousand crackpot calls a day. If he cold-called the offices of any of the big papers or studios, they'd probably lump him in with the xenophobes and the conspiracy nuts. He'd never get a chance to present his video to anyone with the power to make the story public on a national scale. That pretty much ruled out the major media approach, unless he could figure out a way to get someone high up to take his story seriously.

He'd also thought about cutting out the middleman, and going public with the video on the internet. He could post it to the top dozen streaming video sites and wait for it to go viral, like so many of the video clips from the Occupy Wall Street protests in 2011. But there were hundreds of millions of videos on the web, maybe billions. Only a small fraction of them ever captured large scale public attention.

Bill didn't have an established following on any of the popular video websites, and it might take him years to build enough of a reputation to attract a significant audience. He could upload the recording to a hundred websites, or a thousand, but it wouldn't do any good if no one bothered to watch it.

He might get lucky and the video would spread through the internet like wildfire, until everyone was talking about it and politicians were arguing over it on network news. Or it might vanish into the great ocean of the web without creating a ripple.

The irony of the situation was not lost on him. Despite his personal aversion to violence and the machineries of politics, the video clip in his phone was the physical manifestation of both. He had flown to Tibet in search of one sort of truth, but the fates had selected him to become the witness and bearer of an entirely *different* sort of truth. One that could affect the lives of many people, and perhaps even the fates of nations. He quite literally carried the truth in his pocket, but he had no idea of what to do with it.

⚓ ⚓ ⚓

He was still puzzling over the problem when his plane touched down at Tribhuvan International Airport in Kathmandu. And he hadn't solved it four hours later, when his Cathay Pacific flight left the runway en route to Hong Kong.

He was so exhausted now that he was practically a zombie. He reclined his seat, closed his eyes and tried to surrender to sleep, but his brain remained stubbornly awake. His mind refused to let go of the problem, turning it over and over ceaselessly and uselessly.

He tried to meditate, to release the cares of the world, and allow himself to find his spiritual center. He controlled his breathing, and one-by-one, willed every muscle in his body to relax.

He was calm... He was focused... He was at peace...

He was... awake.

His eyes came open. It was no use. Sleep was impossible.

His weary hands fumbled through the seat pouch and came up with an in-flight magazine. He leafed through the pages, only half glancing at the photos, and ignoring the text entirely. His eyes were too tired to make reading seem very interesting. He was just hoping to distract his brain long enough to get some rest.

When he reached the end of the magazine, he started over at the beginning, the glossy pages becoming a repeating collage of random photographs and marketing logos. On the third or fourth trip through the half-seen pages, an image caught his eye. It was a group of paintings by a young Indonesian artist, who was apparently getting his first showing in some upscale New York art gallery.

Near the center of the page was a triptych: three rectangular paintings of the same scene, each from a slightly different angle. At the center of each panel was the portrait of an old man with strongly Asian features, shown alternately from the front, right, and left profiles. In all three paintings a circle of rusty barbed wire hovered in the air in front of the old man's face, like a strangely offset halo or the bevel of an old fashioned cameo.

McDonald stared at the three paintings, focusing not on the old man's face, but on the circles of barbed wire. They reminded him of something— a billboard, or an advertisement, or something that he had once seen on television.

He closed his burning eyes and tried to remember. Three circles of barbed wire, lined up in a row...

And then it came to him, a poster he hadn't seen for years. For several weeks before the 2008 Winter Olympics in China, that poster had been *everywhere*. Five circles of barbed wire atop a chain link fence, silhouetted against an overcast yellow sky. Three of the circles had been on top and two on bottom, clearly mimicking the famous five-ring pattern of the international Olympic symbol. In the upper right-hand ring had been a simple but effective message: *Beijing 2008*. A ragged scrap of signboard hanging from the fence had enumerated the extensive human rights violations occurring in China as dissident citizens and social activists were rounded up and imprisoned to keep them out of public view during the Olympics.

Bill McDonald's exhausted brain could somehow remember the poster perfectly, and he could still see the logo at the bottom of the signboard. Amnesty International.

That was it! As soon as those two words popped into his head, he knew he had found the solution to his problem. He might not be able to capture the attention of the major media, but a global human rights organization could. If *they* brought the video clip to the major media, they would be listened to. CNN and the other news networks wouldn't dare to ignore a story this big, not if it came from Amnesty International. They wouldn't risk being left out of what might turn out to be the biggest human rights story since Tiananmen Square.

Amnesty International. It was the obvious answer. So simple. Why hadn't he thought of it before?

The video clip in his pocket had dwindled from a massively insoluble problem to a series of easily accomplished steps. It shouldn't take more than a few quick phone calls to arrange a meeting with someone who would listen—someone whose entire job was to look for exactly the kind of evidence that Bill McDonald carried, and bring it to the attention of the world.

He could probably get a contact number right off the Amnesty International website. And then he could…

Before he could formulate his next step, the Reverend William H. McDonald—former Soldier, spiritual warrior, and bearer of the truth—fell asleep in Seat #31B, somewhere over the South China Sea.

CHAPTER 20

As usual, Lu Shi's guards were stopped at the front door, and he had to enter alone.

Lu didn't like being forced to leave his guards behind. Not because he didn't feel safe here; the Premier's residence was one of the most secure buildings in China. Lu's objection was of a more attitudinal nature. After a lifetime of careful and methodical maneuvering, he suddenly found that he was impatient with anything which resembled an obstacle.

Having his guards held up at the entrance was an unwelcome reminder that there were certain places and circumstances in which his desires were not the deciding factor.

He had to remind himself that he was still officially the number two man in the Chinese government. The fact that Lu effectively ran the country was an open secret, but the formal power belonged to Xiao Qishan, who was the Premier of China—at least in title.

Lu generally tried not to think of Xiao as a figurehead. Xiao was a good man, and in his day, he had served the party well. Nevertheless, the term *figurehead* was not entirely inaccurate. The old man's political clout had dwindled away to practically nothing. His leverage was gone. He had no more favors to call in.

Xiao held office now, because Lu Shi permitted it. If Lu pulled his support, Xiao Qishan would not be sitting in the Premier's chair a month later.

What's more, the old man *knew* it. Although neither one of them ever spoke about it directly, there was an understanding between Lu Shi and Xiao Qishan. Xiao gave speeches and held press conferences, and Lu made the major policy decisions that kept the nation moving forward.

85

That made this meeting doubly annoying. Xiao Qishan had *sent* for him, as though Lu was a low-grade bureaucrat, or some minor political functionary. Lu Shi was *not* pleased. Not at all.

He'd been tempted to ignore the summons. He could have used the opportunity to remind Xiao of where the power in China really lay. But such a blatant show of strength wasn't necessary, and it wouldn't harm Lu to humor the old dragon.

Lu made a deliberate effort to smile when he was shown into Xiao's office. The old man was seated at his desk, reading from a small book with a tattered red cover. Lu Shi recognized it instantly as *hong baoshu*, Quotations From Chairman Mao Tse-Tung, popularly known in the west as the '*Little Red Book.*'

Xiao looked up, and smiled.

Lu inclined his head—a gesture somewhere between a nod, and a minimal bow. "You sent for me, Comrade Premier?"

Xiao closed the book, using a finger to mark his place within the pages. "Ah, Comrade Lu. Thank you for coming, old friend."

Lu Shi inclined his head again. "I am always at your service, Comrade Premier." Not an accurate statement, but it sounded appropriately polite and respectful.

Xiao waved toward a chair. Lu pretended not to see the gesture. He remained standing.

A slight frown creased the Premiere's brow, but he didn't insist. "I would like to speak to you about this... *situation*... with our Indian neighbors. Some of our esteemed comrades on the Central Military Commission are... *concerned*..."

Lu Shi's laugh contained more bitterness than humor. "Some of our esteemed comrades are timid old women."

Xiao laid the red book on the desk top, his finger still marking the spot where he had been reading. "You are, of course, more familiar with our comrades on the commission than I am," the old man said. "And perhaps some of them are overly cautious. But this seems to be an area in which caution may be prudent."

Lu Shi resisted the temptation to roll his eyes. "I have no problem with caution," he said. "And prudence is a virtue in leaders. But I'm not talking about caution or prudence. I'm talking about timidity. Fear. The lack of courage."

He nodded toward the red book. "Comrade Premier, you are more dedicated to the words and spirit of Chairman Mao than any man I've ever met."

That much was certainly true. As Xiao's once-formidable power bloc continued to erode, the old dragon's thoughts were becoming increasingly buried in the past. He spent his days studying the speeches and writings of Mao, in the forlorn belief that such studies made him a wiser leader. In the process, he somehow managed to ignore the fact that his leadership was now mostly imaginary.

But Lu Shi was not above delving into the words of Mao, in order to bring the conversation around to a more favorable angle.

He reached for the red book, and lifted it gently from the old man's fingers. "Do you remember what Chairman Mao had to say about communists who are too timid to make difficult decisions?"

Xiao nodded. "Of course…"

Lu returned the nod. "And I'm certain, Comrade Premier, that you remember what Chairman Mao wrote about those who protect the enemies of the communist revolution?"

The old man nodded again. "I remember…"

Lu Shi held the unopened book between his palms. "In his wisdom, Chairman Mao cautioned us to unite with our real friends, in order to attack our real enemies. He reminded us that leaders must always follow this principle, in order to avoid leading the masses astray."

"March, nineteen-twenty-six," Xiao said. "The chairman was speaking about the analysis of the classes in Chinese society…"

"Yes," said Lu Shi. "But was Mao speaking metaphorically? Or did he mean for future leaders to put his ideas into action?"

"He meant for us to *act*," Xiao said. "He meant *always* for us to act."

"I agree," said Lu. "If we apply Mao's teachings to our current situation, should we consider our Indian neighbors to be enemies, or friends?"

Xiao hesitated. "I'm not sure we have enough information to make such a stark distinction."

"They are deliberately sheltering known enemies of China," Lu said. "Enemies who have destroyed billions of Yuan in property, massacred our soldiers without provocation, and killed hundreds of our citizens. Yet, our Indian neighbors welcome these terror mongers, and treat them as honored guests. Protect them from extradition, and punishment, even while they're plotting further acts of destruction and murder."

Lu Shi returned the red book to the desk top, laying it next to Xiao Qishan's hand.

"According to our law," Lu said, "if a man gives shelter and assistance to a criminal, that man is *also* a criminal. So, what must we call a man who gives shelter and assistance to our enemies?"

This time, Xiao's hesitation was much longer. When he finally spoke, his voice was not much more than a whisper. "Such a man must also be our enemy…"

Lu stared into the old man's eyes. "And, do we hold nations to a lower standard than we hold men?"

Xiao shook his head, slowly.

"Then, we must ask ourselves a very simple question," Lu Shi said. "What did Chairman Mao tell us we must *do* to the enemies of China?"

CHAPTER 21

CIA HEADQUARTERS
LANGLEY, VIRGINIA
THURSDAY; 27 NOVEMBER
8:26 AM EST

Kurt Gray yawned heavily as he worked through the multi-step process for bringing his computer on line. He slid his electronic key card into the card reader next to his monitor, and waited for the red LED on the fingerprint scanner to light up.

Between digital tokens, biometrics, and seventeen-digit complex pass phrases, his system was encrypted about nine different ways. In recent years, the Agency had taken information security to levels of obsession approaching pathological mania. Kurt and his fellow analysts agreed that the access protocols would eventually be expanded to include DNA samples and rectal examinations.

That was only half-funny, as there was every sign that the CIA's cyber paranoia was continuing to escalate. Kurt yawned again as he typed in the first of his pass phrases. It probably wasn't fair to think of it as paranoia, because there really *were* people trying to get their grubby little cybernetic fingers on the Agency's databases. A *lot* of people. Hostile governments, foreign militaries, criminals, conspiracy theorists, nut cases, garden variety hackers, and even a few friendly governments. For that matter, there were plenty of people in the U.S. government who'd pay good money for an inside look at the CIA's information stash.

When the red light came on, Kurt gave the fingerprint reader the obligatory peek at his right index finger, and then punched in his second-level password. The machine responded with a satisfied bleat, and Kurt sat back in his chair while his computer shuffled its way through whatever technical voodoo it used to decrypt his local hard drive.

He reached for his ever-handy cup of Starbucks, and took a healthy swig of hot rich coffee. Pumpkin spice latte, one of the specialty flavors that only show up around the holidays.

Kurt lowered the warm cardboard cup from his lips, and tilted it toward the flat screen monitor in a mock toast. "Happy Thanksgiving, Mr. Computer. Hope you don't mind working on Turkey Day, 'cause I'm not real fucking happy about it myself."

He took another swallow of coffee as the report queue opened on his monitor and began populating itself with a column of filenames. The process took more than a minute. The list wasn't short. Kurt scrolled down the line of document titles and groaned.

The operating model of the Directorate of Intelligence had been developed in the 1960s and 1970s, before the internet—when email and search engines were unheard of, and rotating-drum fax machines were the cutting-edge of electronic information transfer. There had been no cell phone frequencies to intercept in those days, no web-servers to hack, and no flash drives for stockpiling and transporting gigabytes (or terabytes) of stolen documents. Back then, intelligence analysts had labored to piece together tiny snippets of useful intelligence, in a climate of extreme information scarcity.

Now the Directorate of Intelligence struggled with the opposite problem: information overload. The so-called 'information superhighway' had become a tsunami of ever-growing and ever-mutating data. Add in video feeds from unmanned surveillance drones, signal intercepts, and actual reports from field agents, and the average intelligence analyst was inundated with more incoming files than any human could possibly assimilate. Unfortunately, about 98% of the flood was worthless, from a national security and foreign policy perspective. The trick was to reach into that ocean of crap, and pull out the 2% that actually meant something.

That was Kurt's job, and while it was frequently tedious and frustrating, he was good at it. He paged back to the top of his incoming file list, and began to sort.

He had been hoping for a light load today, but he wasn't going to get it. Still, it might not be all that bad. He could tell from the filenames that many of the documents were regional intelligence summaries. Some of those would be recaps of the previous day's summaries. He could skip those, and he could get by with skimming most of the remaining summaries.

"Okay," he said softly to himself. "Let's see what's shaking in the far off and exotic land of India…"

Kurt had been attached to the CIA's South Asia Desk for three years, the last two of which he had been assigned specifically to *Bhārat Gaṇarājya*, the Republic of India. He could read Hindi like a native, and speak it somewhat less fluently, but his facility with the language was less useful than it might have been in other regions, as more than half of the documents coming out of India were written in English.

Since the days of the British Raj, English had been the default language of politics and major business in India. There had been several moves to shift officially to Hindi after the country had gained its independence in 1947, but the cultural inertia of a century of British rule had left an indelible mark on the Indian government.

As was his custom, Kurt dragged a quarter out of his pocket and flipped it briskly into the air. Heads, he would plow into the Hindi files first. Tails, he would start with the English files.

The quarter landed on his desk top, bounced, wobbled, and came to rest with George Washington's shining profile facing up. "Hindi it is," he said, and he opened the first document.

⚓ ⚓ ⚓

Two hours later, and getting a bit bleary-eyed, Kurt called up one of the last files in the Hindi list. A few more, and he'd be ready to wade through the English pile.

The document was slow in opening. When it finally appeared on the monitor, Kurt could see why. It contained at least a dozen imbedded graphics.

Kurt glanced at the first of these, and then double-clicked it to enlarge the image. The result was a black and white architectural diagram of a large rectilinear structure, like a bridge, or maybe a train trestle. Judging from the associated scale legends, the structure had to be enormous—kilometers long, and about 200 meters high.

Kurt increased the magnification of the image, and began trying to read the associated text boxes. The printed text was rendered in some form of Asian-looking characters that Kurt couldn't decipher. Chinese, or maybe Japanese, or Korean. Something like that. But there were handwritten notations at various spots around the diagram, and these Kurt *could* read, because they were in Hindi. Several of the Hindi notes were accompanied by hand-drawn arrows and arcing lines that converged, diverged, and crossed at what appeared to be strategic points on the architectural structure.

It took Kurt about thirty seconds to realize that the huge rectangular construction was not a bridge or a trestle; it was a dam. A gigantic hydroelectric dam, dotted by more sluice gates than he had ever seen.

Kurt minimized the diagram, and worked quickly through the remaining images in the document with a growing sense of both excitement and dread. An idea was beginning to take shape in his mind, and it was not a pleasant thought at all.

He stared at the monitor for several minutes, hoping for the first time in his professional career that he had *not* found something interesting.

"Not good," he said to himself as he reached for the phone. "This is *definitely* not good."

CHAPTER 22

FINAL TRAJECTORY:
A DEVELOPMENTAL HISTORY OF THE CRUISE MISSILE

(Excerpted from working notes presented to the National Institute for Strategic Analysis. Reprinted by permission of the author, David M. Hardy, PhD.)

The outbreak of World War II brought renewed interest to the search for unmanned aerial weapons.

In 1940, British engineer Frederick George Miles proposed the development of a remotely piloted lightweight aircraft, capable of carrying a 1,000 pound bomb. Designated the *Miles Hoop-la*, this design was not intended as a single use weapon. Instead, it would drop a bomb payload on a designated target, and then return to its home field to be refueled and rearmed for future attacks. The airspeed of the Hoop-la was estimated at over 300 MPH, but this was never verified, as the project was cancelled shortly after it reached the mock-up stage.

In 1941, the German *ReichluftMinisterium* (Air Ministry) began to investigate designs for 'composite' aircraft, i.e. multiple aircraft which are physically connected together and flown as a single unit. Nazi interest in this concept may have derived from Soviet studies in the 1930s, in which fighter planes were attached to the fuselages or wings of large bombers, ready to launch whenever the host-bombers were threatened.

One German scheme involved using an attached fighter plane to guide an explosive-packed unmanned Junkers Ju-88 bomber to a target. Upon reaching the designated site, the fighter pilot would aim the drone bomber toward its final objective, detach his own plane, and depart the area as the Junkers dove into the target and detonated.

The concept met with initial resistance among senior Luftwaffe leadership, but the ReichluftMinisterium ultimately authorized project *Beethoven*, to build a composite flying bomb under the codename *Mistel* (mistletoe).

The first operational test of a Mistel occurred in July of 1943. The control plane was a Messerschmitt Mf-109E fighter, mounted to the top of an unmanned Ju-88A bomber, and wired directly into the larger aircraft's throttles and flight controls. The fighter pilot made a smooth takeoff, and flew the composite aircraft directly toward the target area. At the appropriate range, he detached his Messerschmitt from the bomber, allowing the Ju-88A to make its final approach on autopilot. The accuracy of the attack could not have been better, and the explosives aboard the bomber utterly destroyed the target.

US Soldiers Inspect a Captured Mistel

The Mistel did not much resemble the Sperry Aerial Torpedo, or the Kettering Bug of the previous world war, but this new German design was the direct descendent of those earlier flying weapons. In the space of a single test flight, the Mistel had proven that the concept of an unmanned aerial bomb was both valid, and deadly.

The officers of the Luftwaffe high command forgot their reservations, and became instantly enthusiastic about the Mistel. They quickly began planning ways to improve the Mistel design, and push the weapon into production and use.

The Mistel went into operation in June of 1944, almost exactly a year after the first test flight. The final configuration utilized a Focke-Wulf Fw-190A fighter atop a Junkers Ju-88A-4. The nose and crew cabin of the bomber were removed, and replaced by a 7,720 pound hollow-charge warhead.

Tests demonstrated that the enormous Mistel warhead could penetrate virtually any thickness of reinforced concrete. A trial attack against an old French battleship wrought astonishing damage to the target vessel, revealing the Mistel's potential as an anti-ship weapon. This potential was to be tested quickly, as several Mistels were used to conduct attacks against Allied ships during the weapon's first month of operational service.

The Nazi high command began planning a massive coordinated Mistel campaign against the Allies, codenamed Operation *Eisenhammer* (Iron Hammer). Over 250 Mistels were built, but Operation Eisenhammer never took place. The accumulated Mistels were expended in numerous smaller attacks, mostly directed against bridges in the path of the Allied advance.

The Luftwaffe developed a number of minor variants to the Mistel, incorporating modifications and/or aircraft substitutions to accommodate various mission profiles. A jet-powered model was considered, to be built around the Messerschmitt Me-262 jet fighter, but the concept was never implemented. Still more variants were proposed, some of which were far-fetched, even by the standards of the Mistel program. Most of the more drastic ideas did not ever progress beyond the drawing board.

⚓ ⚓ ⚓

While Germany was developing and deploying its new pilotless killing machine, on the far side of the Atlantic, the United States was once again pursuing the idea of the aerial torpedo.

During a visit to England in 1936, Chief of Naval Operations Admiral William H. Standley witnessed a live firing exercise against a British *Queen Bee* training aircraft (a radio-controlled version of the de Havilland Tiger Moth biplane, configured as an unmanned flying target). Impressed by the Queen Bee's performance, the CNO contacted Rear Admiral Ernest J. King, the head of the Bureau of Aeronautics, and directed him to research options for developing remote-controlled aircraft for the U.S. Navy.

At the CNO's suggestion, Rear Admiral King chose Lieutenant Commander Delmar S. Fahrney to lead the project. A veteran pilot with a masters degree in aeronautical engineering, Fahrney was experienced and technically skilled. He was also a visionary.

Working in cooperation with the Naval Aircraft Factory, Fahrney supervised the modification of two Curtiss biplanes and two Stearman biplanes into "drones." (It's fairly certain that Fahrney was the first person to use the term "drone" in the context of unmanned aircraft. This was

probably intended as a friendly acknowledgement of the British Queen
Bee from which the U.S. Navy program had taken its inspiration.)

By 1937, Fahrney's team was conducting flight tests of these
unmanned drones. A year later, the team's drones were utilized for anti-
aircraft firing tests against gun crews aboard the aircraft carrier USS
Ranger. The drones turned out to be difficult targets, surviving barrage
after barrage during simulated attack runs against the warship.

The success of the drones, and the ship's failure to knock them out of
the sky, forced a sweeping reevaluation of anti-aircraft capabilities
throughout the fleet. The tests with USS *Ranger* also convinced Fahrney
that radio-controlled aircraft could be used as offensive weapons,
conducting direct bomb or torpedo attacks against enemy ships.

Fahrney quickly arranged an operational test, sending an "assault
drone" armed with a dummy warhead against the battleship USS *Utah.*
Unfortunately for Fahrney, the gunners aboard the *Utah* were better shots
than their shipmates on the *Ranger.* As the drone was commencing its dive
bombing run, a burst of flak made a direct hit on the unmanned aircraft.
The drone crashed into the sea, ending the simulated attack.

Fahrney was not discouraged. His demonstration had been cut short by
a lucky shot, but he had no doubt that the underlying concept was both
practical and achievable. A remote-controlled drone *could* attack an enemy
warship, without risking the life of a pilot.

While investigating options for improving his assault drone, Fahrney
encountered Dr. Vladimir Zworykin, a brilliant immigrant from Russia
who had become the chief scientist for the Radio Corporation of America
(better known as RCA). Zworykin, who would eventually hold key patents
for the technology behind both the television and the electron microscope,
had been trying for years to interest the U.S. Navy in the idea of a flying
torpedo guided by an electric eye. Navy leaders had regarded Dr.
Zworykin's concept as unnecessary, expensive, and—in all likelihood—
impossible.

Fahrney took one look at the proposal, and disregarded all previous
evaluations of its potential. He quickly arranged a contract with RCA to
develop a series of experimental television systems for use aboard Navy
aircraft.

Because Zworykin had been tinkering with the idea for years, he had a
functional prototype ready in only a few months. The first model weighed
340 pounds, far too heavy for a relatively small drone, but light enough for
testing aboard a manned aircraft. The initial tests were successful, proving
that video signals from one airplane could be seen and interpreted from
another plane up to 20 miles away.

While the prototype tests were underway, Zworykin's team at RCA was working on a new and smaller model. Dubbed 'Block-1' because of its rectangular shape, the new model weighed only 97 pounds, and fit into an 8x8x24 inch box (i.e. the *block*).

Before the Block-1 prototype could be installed on an airframe for testing, the Japanese Imperial Navy conducted its now infamous bombing raid on Pearl Harbor, Hawaii, inflicting unprecedented damage on the U.S. Pacific fleet. The American aircraft carriers and some light escort ships emerged unscathed, because they were absent from Pearl Harbor during the raid, but the majority of the fleet was devastated.

The U.S. Navy was thrown into chaos. The battleships, the primary might of the fleet at that time, had been mauled. Some of the damaged hulls would be salvaged and returned to service, but—with the Japanese Imperial Navy rampaging through the Pacific—the United States could not sit idle and wait for the battleships to be repaired. The American Navy needed to be combat-ready immediately.

The aircraft carriers were a major part of the solution. They represented a radical departure from the big guns and heavy armor of dreadnought warfare. In the coming months, the carriers would clearly establish themselves as the future of naval power projection, but in the immediate aftermath of Pearl Harbor, their reliability and capability had not yet been proven. In this climate of uncertainty, Fahrney's television-guided assault drone suddenly seemed like a very promising idea.

In February of 1942, the Navy issued a top secret directive known as *Project Option*, making the assault drone a national defense priority. Fahrney and Zworykin didn't even have a functional prototype ready, when they abruptly found themselves with a full-scale development program under the leadership of Commodore Oscar Smith.

Only two months after the program's inception, the Project Option team launched a successful test attack against the USS *Aaron Ward*, a destroyer moving at 15 knots with full evasive maneuvering. The unmanned assault drone, which had been converted from an existing torpedo plane, was guided from remote control by the pilot of a plane circling 8 miles away—completely out of sight of the destroyer under attack.

Watching the remote video feed from a television camera in the nose of the assault drone, the pilot had no trouble guiding the drone into a perfect attack run. The torpedo ran straight under the hull of the wildly evading destroyer. If the weapon had been armed with a live warhead, USS *Aaron Ward* would have been blasted out of the water.

Senior political officials and upper echelon military leaders were stunned by the motion picture films of the test attack. Few people who watched the films had any doubt that they were witnessing a major shift in the nature of warfare.

Admiral King, who had recently been promoted by President Roosevelt to Chief of Naval Operations, ordered Commodore Smith to proceed with the production of 5,000 assault drones. King also directed Commodore Smith to create eighteen drone squadrons, to serve under the command of a new Special Air Task Force.

Although Project Option had support at the highest level, the program was not by any means universally popular. Ironically, the fiercest opposition came from Rear Admiral John H. Towers, who had replaced Admiral King as head of the Bureau of Aeronautics. Admiral Towers insisted that it was unwise to commit valuable resources to an unproven weapon system. (His opposition seems doubly ironic in view of the struggle that Towers himself had endured in the 1920s and 30s, while attempting to gather support for naval aviation over the objections of leaders who openly doubted the effectiveness of aircraft carriers and airplanes in a world dominated by cruisers and battleships.)

While Fahrney clearly believed in the assault drone concept, he recognized the need to give the program's detractors as little justification for criticism as possible. He decided that the full-production model torpedo drones should be manufactured using the smallest feasible quantities of war-critical resources. As a result, the first generation of torpedo drones, designated *TDN-1*, were constructed almost entirely of wood.

TDN-1 Torpedo Assault Drone

With a high wing and small twin engines, the TDN-1 could carry a torpedo or 2,000 pound bomb under its fuselage, at an average airspeed of

175 MPH. The drone was light, inexpensive, and it required a bare minimum of critical materials. Unfortunately, the TDN design was not well-suited for mass production. Only about 114 units were built, nearly all of which were used for evaluation, or expended as unmanned flying targets. None of the TDN-1 drones saw actual combat.

Official enthusiasm for the assault drone concept was beginning to decline, in part due to continuing derision from Admiral Towers and other vocal critics of the program. Commodore Smith and Commander Fahrney were undiscouraged. The Project Option team immediately moved forward with production of the TDR-1 series, a second generation of assault drones that were more suited to rapid manufacturing.

In May of 1944, after intense lobbying on the part of Commodore Smith and Commander Fahrney, Special Task Air Group One (STAG-1) deployed to the South Pacific for combat against the Japanese.

The TDR-1 drones of STAG-1 were controlled by specially-modified Grumman Avenger torpedo bombers, outfitted with radio control systems and television reception antennas. The drone flight controls included a joystick for use by the Avenger pilot, and a telephone dial connected by radio to the TDR-1's autopilot system to manage flight patterns and the arming and dropping of torpedoes or bombs. The control system was only equipped with four radio channels, limiting each Avenger aircrew to controlling a maximum of four drones at a time.

The first live TDR-1 attack occurred on July 30, 1944, against an abandoned Japanese freighter that had run aground near the island of Guadalcanal. Six TDR-1s were committed to the mission: four designated for the attack, and two standing by as backups. All six drones were armed with 2,000 pound bombs.

It was not to be an auspicious beginning. Two of the drones cracked up during takeoff. Two others hit the target, but their bombs turned out to be duds. The remaining two drones conducted successful attacks, and their bombs destroyed the target ship.

The film footage of the exploding Japanese freighter was impressive, but the popularity of the assault drone concept had fallen so low that Commodore Smith had to lobby intensely to prevent immediate cancellation of the program.

Approximately eight weeks later, STAG-1 embarked on an intensive series of drone strikes against Japanese installations on the island of Bougainville. The attacks began on September 27th and ended on October 26th. A total of 46 TDR-1s were expended, 37 of which penetrated Japanese antiaircraft coverage and successfully reached their assigned target areas. At least 21 of these struck their intended targets.

The Japanese were stunned by the fury of the drone strikes, believing that the American Navy had taken up aerial suicide attacks—a tactic that Imperial Japan had embraced only weeks earlier.

While the results of the Bougainville attacks were encouraging, they were not dramatic enough to prevent the cancellation of the assault drone program. The officers and men of Project Option were understandably disappointed, but by late 1944, it was clear that the war in the Pacific was going to be won without the help of STAG-1's strange flying bombs. The TDR-1, which had once seemed like a crucial technological breakthrough, was no longer regarded as a significant factor in the outcome of the war.

The next generation of drones, the TDR-3, was already under development when the program was cancelled. A number of photographs of the TDR-3 still exist, but it's no longer clear if this was a functional prototype, or merely a mockup of the airframe. Either way, the Navy's quest for an unmanned aerial assault drone, was effectively dead.

⚓ ⚓ ⚓

Running roughly parallel to the Navy efforts, the U.S. Army Air Force was engaged in its own attempts to develop an unmanned flying bomb. The *A-1* program centered around a radio-controlled monoplane that could carry a 500 pound warhead to targets over 400 miles away. A handful of A-1s were built before the effort was terminated in 1943.

Under a program codenamed *Project Aphrodite*, the USAAF worked jointly with the Navy in developing a series of aerial torpedo designs with the cryptic designation of '*BQ*'. One of the most ambitious examples was the BQ-7 concept, in which aging B-17 Fortress bombers were modified for radio control, and packed with 20,000 pounds of explosives for use as unmanned assault drones.

Each BQ-7 was manned by a human pilot and copilot during takeoff. The roof of the cockpit was cut away, allowing the crew to bail out and parachute to earth after the plane was airborne. In theory, the BQ-7 would then continue to its target under radio control.

About 25 BQ-7s were built. Most were earmarked for use against hardened military installations in Germany, under a plan known as *Project Perilous*. Regrettably, the codename turned out to be accurate.

There were a number of attempts to use the BQ-7 in combat, none of which were notably successful, and several of which were nearly disastrous. In one reported case, a BQ-7 lost radio lock and circled repeatedly over an English city before the terrified controllers were able to reestablish a radio link and divert the malfunctioning bomber to a safe area. In another case, a BQ-7 failed to respond to radio control signals and crashed in the English countryside, leaving a massive crater to mark the site of the explosion. Project Perilous was abandoned before more serious mishaps could occur.

A follow-on effort, codenamed *Project Anvil*, utilized converted B-24 bombers in a new (and supposedly improved) BQ-8 configuration. But the BQ-8s were not destined to fare any better than the BQ-7 series had done.

The first Anvil mission took place on August 12, 1944. The modified bomber exploded in flight, while the two crewmen were still aboard. The pilot and copilot, Navy Lieutenants Wilford J. Willy and Joseph P. Kennedy Jr., were both killed instantly.

It's of historical note that Lieutenant Kennedy was the eldest son of prominent businessman and political figure Joseph Kennedy Sr. At the time of his death, Joseph Junior was being groomed for the American presidency. His younger brother, John Fitzgerald Kennedy, would later go on to become the 35th President of the United States.

The second Anvil mission was launched on September 3, 1944. This time, the BQ-8 missed its assigned target due to spotty television reception, but managed to inflict some damage on an unrelated German facility.

The BQ series was subsequently cancelled, due to lackluster—and sometimes dangerous—performance.

Like the U.S. Navy, the U.S. Army Air Force was out of the flying bomb business, at least in the short term. Nearly three decades had passed since the first efforts of Elmer Sperry and Charles Kettering, and the United States military had still not managed to produce an operationally reliable unmanned aerial weapon.

Unfortunately for the inhabitants of England, the Germans had finally cracked the problem wide open.

The citizens of London were about to find out the hard way just how deadly such weapons can be.

CHAPTER 23

WHITE HOUSE SITUATION ROOM
WASHINGTON, DC
THURSDAY; 27 NOVEMBER
10:34 AM EST

President Dalton Wainright ignored the blue-jacketed briefing folder on the table, and nodded toward the image on the wall-sized Situation Room display screen. "Okay, gentlemen, what am I looking at here?"

The Sit Room Duty Officer was a Navy Captain with a hawk nose and gray at his temples. "Sorry to interrupt your Thanksgiving morning, Mr. President," he said. "This is an architectural diagram of the Three Gorges Dam, on the Yangtze River, in the People's Republic of China."

He allowed the image to linger on the display for a few seconds, and then pointed a remote at the screen. The architectural drawing was replaced by an aerial photograph of what was presumably the retaining wall of the dam, with the expansive spread of its attendant reservoir lake.

"This is the largest hydroelectric project ever built, sir," the Duty Officer said. "It's also one of the largest manmade structures in the world, second only to the Great Wall of China. The site reached full operational capacity in 2011, and now it produces approximately 85 terawatt-hours of electrical power per year. That's slightly more than twice the annual output of China's entire nuclear power industry."

"Impressive," the president said. "I assume there's a reason that you're bringing this to my attention?"

The Duty Officer nodded. "Yes, sir. A few hours ago, we received preliminary intelligence that the Indian military may be planning to destroy the Three Gorges Dam."

"Destroy it? *How*? That thing is a monster!"

The National Security Advisor, Gregory Brenthoven nodded. "It *is* a monster, Mr. President. But the Indians are apparently planning to bring it down with a coordinated cruise missile strike: seven *Nirbhay* missiles armed with advanced hard target penetrator warheads."

President Wainright raised a hand. "Two questions, Greg... First, what's our source for this information? Second, will it *work*?"

He looked back toward the screen. "That thing really is a beast. Unless they're planning to nuke it, I can't see cruise missiles bringing it down."

The National Security Advisor fished a small leather-bound notebook from his pocket. "The source was HUMINT," he said. "A CIA field operative in New Delhi, with contacts in the Indian Ministry of Defense. He, or *she*—I don't know which—managed to lay hands on a copy of the engineering analysis and targeting plan for the strike. The operative's report was forwarded to the South Asia desk at Langley, and the analyst who received it was smart enough to flag it for immediate high-level attention."

The president nodded. "So we're relatively sure that this information is legit?"

Brenthoven flipped open his notebook and scanned a few lines of text. "The confidence level is listed as 'moderate.' That basically means that the information is plausible and the source is considered credible, but there isn't enough external corroboration to support a higher level of confidence."

"Then I assume that we're going after corroboration," the president said.

"Of course, sir," the National Security Advisor said. "We've got CIA, DIA, and ONI all searching for confirmation. But if the plan is locked down tight enough, we may not find a corroborating source. Our current source may be all we have to go on."

The president paused for a few seconds, and then nodded. "Understood. Let's move on to my second question. What are the odds that a few cruise missiles can knock out a structure as massive as the Three Gorges Dam?"

"Sir, we've got the Office of Naval Research running simulations on that right now," Brenthoven said, "but our quick-look analysis suggests that it might be feasible, if the missiles carried the correct kinds of warheads."

"Do the Indians have the right kind?" the president asked.

Secretary of Defense Mary O'Neil-Broerman leaned forward in her chair. "We think they do," she said. "The Indian military inventory has an indigenously-produced hard target penetrator that might well be powerful enough to crack that dam wide open."

The president turned to stare at his Secretary of Defense. "You're telling me that the Indian military developed a highly-specialized missile warhead, on the *off* chance that they *might* one day have to bomb a giant Chinese hydroelectric site?"

SECDEF shook her head. "No, sir. Ironically enough, they developed the warhead for the Air Force. *Our* Air Force."

President Wainwright rubbed the back of his neck. "Tell me you're kidding, Mary."

"Unfortunately, I'm *not* kidding, Mr. President," the Secretary of Defense said. "The warhead was developed by India's Defense Research and Development Organization to capture a U.S. Air Force contract for a *Next Generation Penetrator*. What the Air Force calls an *NGP*. The Indian defense industry apparently decided that a major Air Force R&D project would be a great way to get their foot in the door for future U.S. defense programs. Their design didn't make it through the down-select, but they decided to move ahead with developing their own Next Generation Penetrator. They call it the *Rudrasya khaḍgah*. From what we understand, it's incredibly effective."

The president frowned. "What was that name again? The *Rud…*"

"Rudrasya khaḍgah," the Secretary of Defense said. "Apparently that's Sanskrit for '*Sword of Shiva.*'"

The president's eyebrows went up. "Shiva? The Hindu god?"

"Yes, sir," SECDEF said. "Shiva is the Hindu god of creation and destruction. But when he manifests in his Rudra aspect, he is specifically the god of storm, wind, destruction, and death."

President Wainwright raised one corner of his mouth in a humorless half-smile. "Well, that sounds promising, doesn't it? What other good news have you got for me?"

"We're still looking at preliminary assessments, sir," the National Security Advisor said. "But if the Rudra—the Sword of Shiva warhead—turns out to be as effective as the initial simulations suggest, then seven missiles may be overkill. It's feasible that four would be enough to bring down the dam, with proper placement and timing, of course."

"Of course," the president said. "Okay, the intelligence on this plan is reasonably credible, and it's possible that this kind of missile strike could punch a hole in the dam. It sounds like one hell of a mess for the People's Republic, but how does that add up to a national security problem for us?"

The Sit Room Duty Officer spoke up. "The Indians aren't just planning to knock holes in the dam, sir. Their apparent goal is to cause a complete failure of the retaining wall. This will trigger catastrophic flooding of the entire Yangtze River basin, all the way from the site of the Three Gorges Dam to the East China Sea."

The Duty Officer keyed his remote, and the Sit Room master display changed to a topographic map of eastern central China. The meandering blue line of the Yangtze river cut across the middle of the map, dividing the northern and southern halves of the visible landmass. The black dots of three cities hugged the wandering curves of the river: *Wuhan, Nanjing,* and *Shanghai.*

"The Yangtze River runs right through the heart of China's largest concentration of human population," said the Situation Room Duty Officer. "Approximately 400 million people live within the boundaries of the Yangtze River basin. That's nearly a third of the total population of China."

He gestured toward the screen. "If the Three Gorges Dam should fail, three of the largest and most heavily-populated cities in China will be directly in the path of destruction."

The National Security Advisor nodded. "The combined populations of Shanghai, Nanjing and Wuhan are closely equivalent to the collective populations of New York, Los Angeles, and Washington, DC. And these three cities form the backbone of China's industrial and financial base. The loss of any *one* of these cities would seriously damage the Chinese economy. The loss of all *three* of them..." Brenthoven allowed his voice to trail off.

"We're talking a nightmare scenario for China," the president said. "Millions of short term casualties, and massive damage to their national infrastructure, followed by a crippling economic aftermath."

"That's correct, Mr. President," Brenthoven said. "Not quite a doomsday scenario for the Chinese, but pretty damned close."

President Wainwright shook his head. "Then *why* in God's name did they even build the thing? The Chinese are many things, but they're not stupid. Why would they put so many of their own people at risk?"

"They probably thought they had factored out the serious risks," the Secretary of Defense said. "From a structural standpoint, the Three Gorges Dam is significantly over-built. They designed in more than enough safety margin to compensate for earthquakes and other natural disasters, and— short of a nuclear attack—there frankly aren't very many bombs or missiles in the world that could put a serious dent in that thing. The Chinese politburo probably felt like they had all the important angles covered."

"But they didn't count on this new Indian warhead," the president said.

"Apparently not, sir," said Brenthoven.

President Wainwright stared at the wall-sized display screen for several seconds. "How will the Chinese government react, if India manages to carry out this plan?"

"That's the big question," the National Security Advisor said. "How would *you* react in that situation, Mr. President? Suppose the U.S. was engaged in hostilities with some hypothetical enemy, and suddenly—without warning—our adversary wiped out New York, Los Angeles and Washington, DC, killing about a third of our national population in the process. How would *you* retaliate, sir?"

"I like to think of myself as a man of peace," the president said. "But if someone hit us with an attack that vicious and that massive, I'd go after them with every weapon at my disposal. I'd do my damnedest to turn their entire country into a parking lot."

The Secretary of Defense sighed heavily. "I hate to say it, sir, but I would too. Any leader with the power and ability to strike back would retaliate just as strongly. When somebody slams you that hard, you don't trade punches. You *crush* them."

"That, I'm afraid, is our answer," Brenthoven said. "If India really does this… If they bring down the Three Gorges Dam, China is going to hit them with *everything…*"

His last word hung in the air, and no one had any doubt at all what 'everything' meant in this context.

President Wainwright sat back in his chair. "We're missing something here," he said.

"We're in the early discovery phase on this, sir," Brenthoven said. "We're still missing a lot of things. It may take the intelligence agencies a while to develop corroborating sources, and assemble the critical details."

"I'm not talking about details," said the president. "And I'm not talking about independent confirmation of the facts."

He looked at the enormous aerial view of the Three Gorges Dam on the display screen. "We're missing a critical piece in the chain of logic."

"I don't think I'm following you, sir," Brenthoven said.

"Mary just summed it up perfectly," the president said. "You don't sit around trading punches when somebody slams you that hard. You *crush* them. *Right?*"

Brenthoven nodded, but didn't speak.

"I don't claim to understand the mindset of the Indian government," the president said. "But they can't possibly be too blind to know what will happen if they cripple China with an assault of this magnitude. This entire plan is practically *begging* for nuclear retaliation. So why in the hell are they even *thinking* about it?"

No one offered an answer.

"We're missing something here," the president said again. "Some vital piece of logical thinking."

The Chief of Naval Operations drummed the fingertips of his left hand lightly on the table top. "What if it's *not* logical?" he asked. "Before that nutcase, Zhukov, bombed Pearl Harbor, I would have said that nobody is fanatical enough to do something that idiotic. But these days, Mr. President, I'm not quite as quick to underestimate the power of stupid and crazy."

President Wainwright grimaced. "You've got a point there, Admiral" he said. "But—crazy or not—our friends in India have got something up their sleeve. And we had damned well better find out what it is…"

CHAPTER 24

Gita Shankar, the Republic of India's Ambassador to the United States, rose from her seat as the American National Security Advisor was ushered into her office. She came around her desk to meet him, and extended her hand to be shaken as he crossed the last few meters of carpet.

The ambassador wore a dark blue sari of raw silk, over a simple gray blouse and a pleated business skirt. The broad strip of rich fabric wound around her waist, and crossed her upper body diagonally, allowing the loose end to drape over her left shoulder in a businesslike approximation of the traditional fashion. Around her neck was a single strand of pearls, and her short black hair was drawn back to reveal matching earrings.

Ambassador Shankar smiled as her visitor accepted her proffered hand and shook it. "Welcome, Mr. Brenthoven," she said. "It appears that we have coordinated our colors today."

Gregory Brenthoven glanced down at the sleeve of his suit. It was almost exactly the same shade of gray as the ambassador's blouse, and his blue Salvatore Ferragamo necktie was a surprisingly close match for the color of her sari.

Brenthoven smiled. "I phoned ahead, Madam Ambassador, to find out what you were wearing. Then I dashed home and dressed myself to match."

The ambassador laughed, and then motioned him to a pair of sofas rendered in the British Colonial style that remained popular among representatives of the Indian government.

"Please," the ambassador said. "Make yourself comfortable, and then tell me what takes you away from your family on such an important American holiday."

Brenthoven seated himself on one sofa, and the ambassador chose a seat across from him, on the other sofa.

Brenthoven's eyes made a quick sweep around the elegantly-appointed office. "I don't want to sound melodramatic, Madam Ambassador, but is this room secure?"

This brought a raised eyebrow from the ambassador. "It should be reasonably secure," she said. "My office is swept daily for electronic eavesdropping devices, and my security staff employs certain technical measures to disrupt remote surveillance by other means. I'm sure you're accustomed to similar precautions in your own government buildings."

"Of course," Brenthoven said.

"And I'm equally sure," the ambassador said, "you realize that such defenses only reduce the threat of hostile surveillance. They do not guarantee privacy."

The American National Security Advisor hesitated. He was not a representative of the State Department, and he had no diplomatic credentials. He was also not a trusted confidant of the Indian government, which meant that the rules of protocol would not allow him to request the use of the embassy's 'bubble.'

Like nearly every other embassy in the world, the Indian chancery building was equipped with an acoustically-isolated Plexiglas security chamber with specialized coatings to repel electromagnetic radiation. In diplo-speak, such a chamber was commonly referred to as a *bubble*. Theoretically, a properly-designed bubble was immune to external surveillance devices, and virtually impossible to bug internally. In reality, the ceaseless evolution of technology meant that any room—no matter how carefully protected—was potentially vulnerable to eavesdropping. Even so, a properly maintained bubble was as close to absolute security as it was possible to come.

Ambassador Shankar had not missed Brenthoven's not-too-casual visual sweep of her office, and she had no doubt that he was fishing for an invitation to use her embassy's bubble. But he had asked for this appointment on very short notice, and had circumvented many of the political niceties in the process. He had also not offered any hints about the topic he intended to discuss, which gave the ambassador and her deputy chief of mission no opportunity to prepare an official position on whatever it was that he wanted to talk about.

In view of these diplomatic lapses—minor as they were—she was not inclined to grant the man any immediate favors. When he revealed the mysterious topic of this meeting, she might change her mind and suggest a recess to the bubble, if she judged that such a precaution was necessary. Until then, it wouldn't kill the man to deal with a bit of discomfort.

"I'm afraid that I don't speak Sanskrit," Brenthoven said, "so I must ask you to forgive my poor pronunciation."

The ambassador smiled and waved a hand dismissively. "Of course."

Brenthoven gave a final glance around the office and paused again before speaking. "Madam Ambassador, have you ever heard of a missile warhead with the codename '*Rudrasya khaḍgaḥ*'?"

Ambassador Shankar frowned slightly. "I don't believe so."

"It's my understanding," Brenthoven said, "that the phrase refers to a sword owned by the Hindu god, Shiva, when he manifests himself as Rudra—the bringer of storms, death, and destruction."

"That sounds like a reasonable translation," the ambassador said. "But I'm not aware of any missile with such a codename."

"It's a Next Generation Penetrator," Brenthoven said. "It was developed by your country's Defense Research and Development Organization, to attack and breach exceptionally-hardened targets, such as massively-reinforced underground bunkers, or armored concrete missile silos."

The ambassador shifted slightly in her seat. She didn't know where this conversation was going, but she was already becoming uncomfortable with the tone. "I will take your word for that," she said. "I believe I have a solid fundamental grasp of my country's military capabilities, but I can't claim to know every detail of every weapon system under development."

Her voice grew a fraction sharper. "Is the United States suddenly concerned that this warhead you speak of is somehow in violation of international laws or treaties?"

"Not at all," Brenthoven said. "It's my understanding that the Rudrasya khaḍgaḥ warhead design is perfectly legal under all existing agreements."

The ambassador relaxed back into the sofa cushions. "Then, may I ask what the problem is? It must be something serious, for you to show such concern regarding the security of this conversation."

"It *is* serious, Madam Ambassador," Brenthoven said. "We have received credible indications that your military is planning to use a number of these advanced penetrator warheads to force a catastrophic failure of the Chinese Three Gorges Dam."

"I have not been briefed on any such plan," the ambassador said. "But my country is engaged in defensive combat operations against an unprovoked aggressor. India was *not* the instigator of the current hostilities, Mr. Brenthoven, as I'm sure you are aware. So—given your own admission that the proposed weapons are not prohibited by treaty or law, and also given the fact that we are reacting to the slaughter of an entire village of unarmed civilians—I'm curious to know why my country's military intentions have suddenly attracted the attention of the United States Government. I don't mean to sound abrupt, but *how* does this qualify as your business?"

"We've done some initial assessments of the potential consequences if the Three Gorges Dam should suffer catastrophic failure," Brenthoven said. "Our analysts estimate that the death toll in China could go as high as 350 million. It's also likely that three of China's most prosperous cities will be completely wiped out, crippling the Chinese economy for several decades."

"I haven't seen any such projections," the ambassador said, "but that sounds like a bit of an exaggeration to me."

"We don't think so," Brenthoven said. "In fact, our early calculations may actually turn out to be optimistic."

Ambassador Shankar said nothing. All of this really was a surprise to her. She had no idea how much of it—if any—might be true.

Brenthoven closed his little notebook and slipped it back into his pocket. "Madam Ambassador, if this attack on the Three Gorges Dam takes place, we believe there's a very strong chance that the People's Republic of China will retaliate with a major nuclear strike."

"That's absurd!" the ambassador said.

"We don't think so," Brenthoven said. "If you hit the PRC that hard, we think they'll strike back even harder."

The ambassador found her own eyes travelling around her office. "We shouldn't talk about this here," she said. "We should move this discussion to the bubble."

"That's an excellent idea," Gregory Brenthoven said. "Why don't we do that?"

CHAPTER 25

The Tactical Action Officer, Lieutenant Ben Lambert, kept an eye on the giant Aegis display screens that dominated the central section of Combat Information Center. On the tactical display, four unknown-aircraft symbols were moving rapidly toward the perimeter of the USS *Midway's* defensive ring of surface ships.

Lambert pressed the electronic soft-key that patched his comm headset into the ship's telephone system, and he punched the three-digit phone number for the captain's stateroom. "Captain, this is the TAO. Sorry to disturb you, sir, but we've got four Bogies inbound from the west. No modes, no codes, and no IFF."

"Thank you," Captain Bowie said. "I'm on my way. Do me a favor, and give Commander Silva a call. I'm sure she'll want to be in on this."

"Will do, sir," the TAO said.

⚓ ⚓ ⚓

Less than three minutes later, Captain Bowie and Commander Silva were standing behind the TAO, looking over his shoulder at the tactical display.

"Whose tracks are we seeing, here?" Bowie asked.

USS *Towers* was running quiet and dark—taking full advantage of her cutting-edge stealth capabilities to hide from the sensors of other ships and aircraft. The odd angles of the destroyer's hull and superstructure had been meticulously calculated to deflect incoming radar, robbing potential enemies of the return signals needed to detect and track the ship. This advanced geometry design was enhanced by the radar absorbent

112

polymerized carbon fiber tiles and phototropic camouflage that covered the majority of the ship's exposed surfaces.

Coupled with acoustic masking and thermal suppression systems, these technologies did an astoundingly effective job of concealing a 9,800 ton warship on the open sea. But no amount of crafty engineering could disguise the transmissions of the ship's own radar systems. If the *Towers* energized her radars, they would light up the electromagnetic spectrum like the proverbial Christmas tree. Any chance of concealment would be instantly gone.

The only way to achieve effective stealth was to shut down all radars and transmitters, and depend on sensor feeds from other U.S. Navy assets in the area.

That's what the *Towers* was doing now, sliding quietly through the night, guided only by tactical data inputs from the ships and aircraft in the USS *Midway* strike group.

"These tracks are coming in from Hawkeye," the TAO said.

'*Hawkeye*,' referred to one of the E-2D Airborne Early Warning planes providing long-range radar surveillance coverage for the aircraft carrier and the air wing.

Commander Silva nodded. "Doesn't look like they're going to overfly us directly," she said.

The TAO checked his console for amplified target motion data on the four unknown aircraft. "Good eye, ma'am. The Bogies won't overfly us. Unless their flight profile changes, they'll CPA us about ten miles to the north, in roughly eight minutes."

"They're going after the *Midway*," Silva said.

"Looks that way to me," the TAO said. "They're flying low and fast, with their radars shut down. I think they're trying to give our carrier a little goose."

"That sounds like a pretty fair assessment," said Captain Bowie.

His eyes stayed fixed on the four aircraft symbols. "If I had to guess, I'd say we're looking at J-15s from the Chinese carrier group. Two flights of two."

"Could be," the TAO said. "Do we let them pass, or do we challenge?"

"We *could* let them go," Bowie said. "That Hawkeye has got them nailed. Our Bogies will have F-18s crawling all over them before they get close to the carrier."

"True," the TAO said. There was a wistful note in his voice, as though he'd been hoping for something a bit more exciting out of his first real-world encounter with a potential air threat.

Bowie smiled. "On the other hand, our current EMCON status is self-imposed. We're running dark and quiet for the practice, not because we have orders to maintain emission control."

The TAO grinned. "Think we should rattle their cage, sir?"

The captain returned his grin. "Why not? No fire control radars. It's okay to spook these guys, but let's not give them an excuse to shoot."

The TAO keyed his mike. "All Stations—TAO, now set Modified EMCON Delta. Unrestricted emissions except for fire control, effective immediately. Maximum safe power levels. I say again, all transmitters on line immediately at maximum safe power levels. Break. Air—TAO, I want a high-power SPY sweep of sector two-niner-zero to three-five-zero."

The AN/SPY-1D(V)2 phased-array radar was the backbone of the ship's Aegis integrated sensor and weapons suite. With a power output of over four million watts, SPY could confuse or even damage the sensitive avionics in most aircraft.

The TAO was still grinning. Those Chinese pilots were about to get the surprise of their lives. One second, they're sneaking along in the dark, hugging the waves and trying to be invisible. Everything is nice and quiet—no sign of anything at all between them and their objective. The next second, bam! A U.S. Navy destroyer right in their faces, pumping out four megawatts of microwave power, making their warning buzzers scream and their instruments go haywire.

The Air Supervisor's voice came over the net. "TAO—Air. SPY is on line and transmitting. Full power sweep of sector two-niner-zero to three-five-zero in progress."

"And here we *go...*" the TAO said.

On the Aegis tactical display, the four unknown aircraft symbols swung hard to the left, sheering away from the *Towers* and the *Midway.*

A half-second later, the Air Supervisor's voice came over the net again. "TAO—Air, Bogies are bugging out. Looks like they're running home to the barn."

The TAO keyed up. "Roger, Air. Keep an eye on them anyway. We don't want them sneaking back around to return the surprise."

"*That* was easy," Commander Silva said.

The Tactical Action Officer nodded. "Just a friendly gesture, to let our Chinese buddies know that the United States Navy is in the neighborhood. Sort of like the Welcome Wagon."

Silva shook her head. "We were early," she said. "We should have waited, and done that *next* month."

The TAO looked at her. "I'm not sure what you mean, Commander..."

"Thanksgiving is over," Silva said. "And we just gave those guys their Christmas goose a whole month ahead of time."

The TAO grinned again. "I think they'll forgive us, ma'am."

"I hope you're right about that," Captain Bowie said. "I hope you're right."

CHAPTER 26

FINAL TRAJECTORY:
A DEVELOPMENTAL HISTORY OF THE CRUISE MISSILE

(Excerpted from working notes presented to the National Institute for Strategic Analysis. Reprinted by permission of the author, David M. Hardy, PhD.)

With the V-1 rocket, the Luftwaffe's flying bomb effort made a complete break from the propeller-driven airframes and remote control systems of previous designs. The new German weapon was a self-controlling robot, utilizing automatic onboard guidance mechanisms in place of a remote human operator. The new design eliminated propeller-driven engines, in favor of a rudimentary (but effective) pulse jet engine that was little more than a tube-shaped fuel combustion chamber.

The weapon was formally designated as the *Fiesler Fi-103*, but the Nazi propaganda corps began referring to it as the *Vergeltungswaffe Einz* (Vengeance Weapon 1), a title that was quickly shortened to *V-1* in common usage.

Unlike prior generations of drones and aerial torpedoes, the V-1 did not resemble conventional aircraft of the day. Its sheet-steel fuselage was streamlined and severely tapered, giving it a profile similar to a throwing dart. The weapon's abrupt cruciform wings were skinned with plywood, to reduce weight and minimize cost, and the narrow stovepipe engine at its tail was like nothing before seen outside of the fictional stories of Buck Rogers and Flash Gordon.

Indeed, the entire look of the V-1 was more like something out of a space opera adventure story than real life. But the V-1 was not a figment of creative fantasy. It was very real, and it was lethal.

Until that point, three decades of effort and expense had yielded only a few hundred unmanned flying weapons. Not one of those programs had met with more than marginal success under actual wartime conditions. By contrast, the Nazis manufactured nearly 30,000 V-1 rockets, thousands of which were used in combat, with brutal effectiveness.

German V-1 Rocket and Launch Rail
(Photo courtesy of Peter Garwood, of the Balloon Barrage Reunion Club)

With an operational range of about 155 miles, the V-1 could not fly directly from Germany to England. The Luftwaffe compensated for this shortcoming by building 96 launch sites in occupied Northern France, well within range of London.

The first V-1 attack was launched on June 13, 1944, one week after the Allied D-Day invasion of Europe. The rocket reached the end of its flight path, and dropped out of the sky near a railway bridge in the East End of London. Eight civilians were killed in the blast.

A handful of additional V-1 attacks were launched over the next day and a half, before the first serious barrage began. Between the afternoon of June 15th and midnight of June 16th, the German Flakregiment 155 launched 244 V-1s toward London. Approximately 90 of these failed to cross into British territory, due to problems during (or shortly after) launch. Roughly 50 impacted in uninhabited areas south of the target city, and another 22 were shot down by British antiaircraft fire. The remaining 73 weapons struck targets in London, causing significant structural damage and killing hundreds of people, most of whom were civilians.

The strange throbbing cadence of the V-1's pulse jet engine reminded many witnesses of the buzzing of an insect. This characteristic droning sound led to diminutive nicknames like *doodlebug*, and *buzz bomb*. But— odd noises and funny nicknames aside—there was nothing comical about the V-1 weapon itself. The people of England would soon come to associate the insectoid buzzing sound with destruction, and death.

Controlled by a gyro-magnetic autopilot, a vane anemometer to calculate elapsed distance, and a weighted pendulum mechanism for attitude adjustment, the V-1 guidance system lacked the precision to strike small targets. Its simple guidance system was accurate enough to strike a city-sized target, and that was good enough to satisfy the tactical employment needs of the Luftwaffe.

According to a report written by American General Clayton Bissell, Germany launched an estimated 8,025 V-1s at targets in England during a single nine-week period in 1944. More than a million houses and other buildings were damaged or destroyed, and tens of thousands of people were killed.

Although England was the primary target of the program, the Belgian city of Antwerp was hammered by nearly 2,500 V-1 attacks.

In March of 1945, the last V-1 launch sites in France were overrun by the advancing Allied armies, just five and a half weeks before the collapse and surrender of the Nazi Third Reich. Hitler's infamous Vengeance Weapon #1 would no longer darken the skies over England or Belgium. The deadly reign of the buzz-bomb was over, but its legacy was only beginning.

Captured German V-1 sites, including hundreds of unfired weapons, fell into the hands of the United States, France, and the Soviet Union. All three countries began reverse-engineering the V-1 design, and producing their own versions of the robotic flying weapon.

Many military historians now consider the German V-1 rocket to be the first true cruise missile. There are points of argument to support this assertion, and (perhaps) an equal number which challenge it. Regardless of the accuracy of the label, it's obvious that the V-1 program became a catalyst for the future development of cruise missile technology.

The concept had been proven with brutal effectiveness. An unmanned aerial weapon could locate and strike a distant city, with no human intervention whatsoever. In the years following the Second World War, research and development teams all over the planet rushed to duplicate— and then exceed—the Nazis' success with the V-1.

The age of the cruise missile had arrived. The future of warfare would be changed forever.

CHAPTER 27

President Wainright shook the Indian Ambassador's hand, and gestured for her to take a seat in one of the nine wingback chairs that formed the meeting area of the Oval Office. "Thank you for coming on such short notice, Madam Ambassador. I apologize for the late hour."

Ambassador Shankar took the offered seat and smiled pleasantly. "Please do not trouble yourself, Mr. President. It is my duty and my pleasure to answer your summons, whenever it may come."

The president took his traditional position at the head of the circle of chairs, his back to the famous presidential desk—crafted from the timbers of the nineteenth-century British sailing barque, HMS *Resolute*.

The ambassador's chair was to his right, and the chair to his left was taken by National Security Advisor Gregory Brenthoven.

"I appreciate your indulgence," the president said. He made a loop in the air with one finger to encompass the nearly empty circle of chairs. "As you can see, we are dispensing with the usual trappings of protocol, in the interests of both speed and privacy."

The customary staff of diplomats and advisors was missing. Ordinarily, a direct meeting between the president and a foreign ambassador would include his chief of staff, the Secretary of State, the Assistant Secretary of State for Southeast Asian Affairs, the National Security Advisor, and a scribe from the National Security Council. Except for the National Security Advisor, everyone on that list was now absent.

"I understand," the ambassador said. If she was uncomfortable with the departure from established White House protocol, she didn't show it. And this *was* a departure. Apart from the lack of the usual participants, it was rare for the president to meet directly with an ambassador, and even more unusual for such a meeting to occur in the Oval Office.

119

Ambassadors almost always dealt with representatives of the State Department, and the meetings would typically take place in the Roosevelt Room, or—if the ambassador happened to be in ill favor—the West Wing Lobby. For Ambassador Shankar, the current meeting was contrary to all expectations: face-to-face with the president, in the Oval Office, with no diplomatic support team.

"I'm glad to hear that," the president said. "I hope you will forgive me if I skip past the polite small talk, and go directly to the matter at hand."

"Of course," said the ambassador.

"Good," the president said. "Because I would like to know whether or not your country intends to carry out an attack on the Three Gorges Dam."

He nodded toward Brenthoven. "It's my understanding that Greg... that is to say my National Security Advisor... has relayed our concerns to you regarding the potential consequences of such an attack. Have you had an opportunity to discuss this issue with your government?"

"I have been fully briefed on my government's intentions in this matter," the ambassador said. "Officially, there is no plan to attack the Three Gorges Dam."

"What about *unofficially*?" the president asked.

"The unofficial answer, I'm afraid," said the ambassador, "is somewhat different. *Unofficially*, I have been authorized to inform you—in strictest confidence—that the destruction of the Three Gorges Dam is considered a valid and necessary military option, if hostilities with the People's Republic of China continue to escalate."

President Wainwright rubbed the back of his neck. "I see. Your government is aware that China will almost certainly regard such an attack as a direct strategic assault against their critical national infrastructure? And is your government also aware that such a devastating blow will likely result in nuclear reprisals?"

"My government has been advised of your concerns," the Indian Ambassador said. "But we do not agree with your assessment of the PRC's response. My government does not believe that the Chinese politburo will resort to nuclear retaliation."

"What if your projections are wrong?" the president asked. "Why would you even risk the possibility?"

The ambassador folded her hands in her lap. "Mr. President, China is not my country's only concern. As your satellites have no doubt revealed to you, our Pakistani neighbors have begun massing troops near our eastern border, in the provinces of *Punjab* and *Sindh*. Even as we speak, *Pak Faza'ya*—Pakistan's Air Force—is carrying out a campaign of intensive air patrols just within the boundaries of Pakistani airspace.

Although these measures technically do not qualify as military action against my country, the armed forces of Pakistan are moving to an aggressive footing. The Pakistani government is clearly preparing to take advantage of India's current discomfort."

She raised her eyebrows. "To use an American idiom, the sharks are circling, Mr. President. Both to our north, and to our east. We cannot allow them to smell blood in the water."

"I understand your concerns," the president said.

Before he could continue, Ambassador Shankar spoke again. "With all due respect, Mr. President, you do *not* understand our concerns. If the United States truly understood the cultural and political tensions in our portion of the world, you would not be so quick to sell weapons to Pakistan, or to back up the regime of terrorists who sit in power in Islamabad. Nor do you understand our concerns about China. I turn your attention to the so-called Sino-Indian War of the early 1960s. My people know what it is like to have the People's Liberation Army come crashing across our borders. Your country, I am pleased to say, has never had such an experience."

"For us, this is not an exercise in foreign policy," she said. "It is not political theory. We are faced on two sides by enemies who have historically demonstrated their will to destroy India, and are currently taking actions which are directly hostile to my country. We will *not* show weakness. And if that means that the Three Gorges Dam must be destroyed, then such is the price China will pay for massacring our villages without warning or provocation."

The president shook his head. "Madam Ambassador, I beg you not to do this."

Ambassador Shankar sat for several seconds before speaking. "Can you offer us an alternative? Will you align your military power directly with ours, and signal to China and Pakistan that to fight India is to fight the United States of America?"

The president said nothing.

The ambassador smiled sadly. "There is your answer, Mr. President. If you will not stand with us, then we will defend ourselves without your help. And we will use whatever means are at our disposal."

"What if your projections are wrong?" the president asked again. "What if China retaliates with nuclear weapons?"

Ambassador Shankar sighed. "Then they will discover that India *also* has such weapons, and—if we must—we are not afraid to take the war to our enemy's doorstep."

CHAPTER 28

CNN CENTER
190 MARIETTA STREET
ATLANTA, GEORGIA
SATURDAY; 29 NOVEMBER
10:19 AM EST

The video came to an end, and Irene Schick immediately hit the play button again. She had watched the clip five times in a row, and she still couldn't believe it. She fast-forwarded to the point where the assault rifles started firing into the crowd, and the bodies began hitting the ground.

The audio was muffled and nearly unintelligible, but the video footage was *amazing*... Chinese troops gunning down peaceful protestors with no visible provocation of any kind. Blood. Raw panic. The terrified crowd stampeding like cattle.

Tibetan activists had been accusing China of similar atrocities since the 2008 riots, but the evidence—what little there was—had nearly always been lacking in quality or persuasiveness.

But the scene unfolding on her computer monitor was the real deal. As tactless as the cliché sounded in this context, this footage looked like the proverbial smoking gun. Not just one or two rioters fired at under questionable conditions, but a hundred people dead or injured. Maybe more. She'd have to assign a crew to analyze the video frame-by-frame, count the bodies, and pull up subtle details that might be overlooked without meticulous study.

According to Byron Maxwell at Amnesty, the recording had been shot from a cell phone. Judging from the quality of the video, it must have been a good one. Even when expanded to full size on Irene's 25 inch LCD monitor, the images were clear and well-defined. Far short of professional quality, but more than good enough for broadcast.

The video would lose some detail and pick up some digital artifacts when it was enlarged for A-roll, but that would only add to the drama, and confirm the authenticity in the minds of the viewers.

They could get the tourist guy who shot it into a local affiliate studio in California, or maybe just do a voice interview while his video ran in the background. They'd also have to let one of the Amnesty International spokespeople sneak in some air time, as payback for the tip and the video. Irene was already starting to plan the first segment in her head. This was going to be the lead story for *days*. She could already feel it.

She picked up her phone, punched a number, and started talking as soon as the call was picked up on the other end. "Roger, this is Irene. How long will it take to get Tom Gwinn or Kelly Spencer into Tibet with a full crew?"

There was a half second pause before Senior Producer Roger Calloway spoke. "Are you serious?"

"Damned *right* I'm serious," Irene said. "We're going to need one of the headliners on the ground in Tibet *fast*."

She looked at the slaughter playing out on her computer screen. "Hang on to your ass, Roger. I'm about to drop a stick of dynamite in your lap."

CHAPTER 29

USS CALIFORNIA (SSN-781)
NORTHERN BAY OF BENGAL
SUNDAY; 30 NOVEMBER
1824 hours (6:24 PM)
TIME ZONE +6 'FOXTROT'

The Sonar Supervisor's voice came over the net, "Conn—Sonar. Sierra One Five bears zero-three-niner. Contact shows slow right bearing drift."

Captain Patke touched his Officer of the Deck on the shoulder. "Let's come a couple of degrees to starboard, and keep as close to the center of his baffles as we can."

The OOD nodded. "Aye-aye, sir." He began issuing quiet orders to the helmsman.

Sierra One Five was the current sonar tracking designator for a Chinese *Shang* class nuclear attack submarine. USS *California* had been trailing the Chinese sub for nearly twenty-hours, and now they were about to follow it past the perimeter ships of the Indian aircraft carrier strike group.

Patke and his crew had performed a similar operation five days earlier, when they had slipped past the defensive ring of ships surrounding the Chinese aircraft carrier, near the southern end of the Bay of Bengal. Then, they had received orders to break off their surveillance, to locate and trail this Chinese attack submarine. And here they were at the northern end of the bay, following the sub as it tried the exact same maneuver against the Indians.

There was a good chance they would succeed, too. The Chinese sub skipper was skillful and cautious, and his boat was reasonably quiet. As quiet as Chinese submarines ever got, at any rate.

Captain Patke glanced at the master dive clock. It was coming up on 1830 hours. Above the surface, the world would be experiencing that strange period of illumination known as *nautical twilight*, when the sun was below the horizon, but its rays continued to light up the sky. The surface of the sea would be too dark to make out visual details, and the still

124

illuminated sky would be too bright to allow the human eye to properly acclimate to the darkness.

This was the time of day when aircrews and shipboard lookouts would have the hardest time spotting the silhouette of a submerged submarine, or the feather of an exposed periscope.

Patke nodded. The Chinese sub commander was doing it right. If the noise of his boat's reactor plant didn't give away his position, he would make it past the defensive ring of Indian destroyers and frigates, and into the heart of the aircraft carrier's screen.

⚓ ⚓ ⚓

A half-hour later, it was clear that the skipper of Sierra One Five had succeeded in his objective. His boat was well inside the screen of the Indian aircraft carrier, INS *Vikrant*. Patke's own boat, the *California* was still trailing silently behind, using the screw noise and reactor plant noise from the Chinese sub as a mask against detection.

Contact Sierra One Five, the *Shang*, was one of China's second-generation subs, and its acoustic signatures were significantly reduced from the older *Han* class boats. But there was a world of difference between *less noisy*, and *silent*. Despite the skill of her commander, Sierra One Five might be just a smidge too noisy to escape detection by the sonar operators in the Indian battle group. And given the close trailing-distance, that would probably mean detection of the *California* as well.

Patke pulled off his wire rimmed glasses, and rubbed the bridge of his nose before returning his glasses to their usual perch. Following close on the ass of a potentially hostile submarine was risky on the best of days. Doodling around inside the defensive perimeter of another navy's aircraft carrier brought an entirely different order of risk. Now, the *California* was suddenly doing both at once. If anything went wrong at all, it would take about three seconds for this entire situation to go straight down the frigging toilet.

Patke took at last look at the tactical plot, and then strolled over to the accordion door that led to Sonar Control. He leaned against the door jam, and stared into the dim interior of the sonar compartment. The boat's leading Sonar Technician, Chief Petty Officer Lanier Philips, was the Sonar Supervisor on duty.

Captain Patke caught the eye of the sonar man. "How's it looking, chief?"

The sonar chief looked up, his African American features intense with concentration. He shifted his headset far enough to the side to expose his right ear, and used his left palm to press the remaining earphone tighter against his other ear. "We've got a solid track on this guy, captain. You know that weird little low frequency flutter that the *Han* class boats make in their second-stage heat exchangers? Looks like the *Shang* class has a similar design. The dB level is a lot lower on these boats, but the tonal is still there."

The chief turned back to the array of sonar screens. "If you keep us in his baffles, sir, we can track this guy until the fat lady sings."

Captain Patke nodded. "How about our Indian friends up above? Are their sonars good enough to sniff this guy out?"

The Sonar Chief frowned at the screen, and answered over his shoulder. "Hard to say for sure, skipper, but I doubt it. The primary tonal we're tracking is not all that loud. We detected it, but we're sticking to this contact's butt like a barnacle. Also the contact is running below the layer, and so are we. We're in the same water with him, which makes it easier for us to track him."

The *layer* (also referred to as the *sonic layer*) was a barrier to sound energy caused by the transition from virtually constant water temperature near the surface of the ocean, to the *thermocline*, a zone of rapidly decreasing water temperature that extended down to about two thousand feet. This abrupt shift in temperature could reflect much of a submarine's acoustic signal away from the hull-mounted sonar sensors of surface warships. This did not make submarines acoustically invisible to ships on the surface, but it created a tactical edge that all good sub commanders knew how to exploit.

Patke nodded again. If Chief Philips was right, contact Sierra One Five's presence might go unnoticed by the Indian Navy ships above.

Patke was about to walk away when the Sonar Chief spoke again. "That's weird..."

Patke turned back. "What have you got, Chief?"

Chief Philips tilted his head to the side, and stared at one of the sonar waterfall displays. "Got a transient... It sounds like..."

The sonar man straightened up suddenly and keyed his headset's microphone. "Conn—Sonar. Sierra One Five is flooding his tubes! I say again, contact is flooding his tubes!"

"Holy shit!" someone in the control room said. "He's gonna shoot!"

Patke sprinted the half dozen steps back to the OOD platform. The unidentified author of that comment was correct. Sierra One Five was getting ready to launch weapons.

Damn! Patke had been sure that the Chinese sub had come on a mission of surveillance. He had not expected the crazy bastards to start shooting.

He raised his voice. "All stations, this is the captain. I have the Conn, belay your reports. Helm, right full rudder, new course one-niner-zero! Diving Officer, take us down! Make your new depth six hundred feet."

He didn't wait for acknowledgements before belting out his next set of orders. "Weapons Control, prep torpedo tubes one, three, and five. Do not flood tubes until I give the order. Countermeasures, stand by to launch decoys."

The deck tilted under his feet as the *California* nosed down and heeled to starboard in response to the boat's changing course and depth.

The Sonar Supervisor's voice came over the net again. "Conn—Sonar. Sierra One Five is opening his outer doors."

"Not yet," Patke said softly. "Don't shoot yet, you stupid son of a bitch. Just hang onto your torpedoes a little while longer…"

The *California* needed distance now, to separate herself as much as possible from the bearing of Sierra One Five before the Chinese sub started pumping out torpedoes. Because about thirty seconds after the launches were detected, the Indians were going to pounce on this stretch of water with every antisubmarine warfare asset they could scare up. The area would be swarming with frigates, helicopters, and those new *Kamorta* class ASW corvettes that the Indian Navy was so proud of. Every one of them would be firing torpedoes at anything bigger than a tuna. And the Chinese sub, Sierra One Five, would probably pump out a few reactionary weapons as it struggled to escape.

"Passing three hundred feet," the Diving Officer said.

"Very well," Patke said. Not deep enough yet, but there wasn't any more time. If the *California* was going to get out of this alive, she needed speed. He would just have to accept the increased risk of detection. "Helm, all ahead full."

The helmsman's response was immediate. "All ahead full, aye!"

There were about ninety seconds of relative calm before the Sonar Supervisor's voice came over the net again. "Conn—Sonar. Torpedoes in the water, bearing zero-four-zero! Looks like a pair of wake homers, headed for the Indian carrier."

Patke glanced at the tactical display screen. The range to contact Sierra One Five was opening quickly, but not quickly enough.

"This is going to be just like when I was a kid," the Officer of the Deck said softly.

"How do you figure?" Patke asked. He couldn't imagine how anyone's childhood could be at all similar to the situation unfolding now.

"My little brother would steal cookies from the cookie jar," the OOD said. "But I was always the one who got in trouble for it. *He* ate the cookies, and *I* got the ass whuppin'."

The OOD nodded toward the tactical display. "I recon that's what's happening right here, sir. Our Chinese pals reached into the Indian cookie jar and grabbed themselves a big handful of snickerdoodles. We didn't *touch* those damned cookies, but we're about to get our asses whupped for it, just the same."

Patke looked at the continually-opening range on the tactical display. "Maybe not," he said. "Maybe we'll get lucky this time."

Four or five minutes later, sonar began reporting torpedoes in the water, but subsequent evaluation located them all at a safe distance to the northeast.

The control room crew began to breathe easier.

"Well, we didn't get any cookies," Captain Patke said. "But at least we didn't get an ass whipping that we don't deserve."

Perhaps it was the tempting of fate. Perhaps it was purest coincidence. Or perhaps it was simple bad luck. But the Sonar Supervisor's next report came over the net less than ten seconds later. "Conn—Sonar. We have just been over-flown by a multi-engine turboprop aircraft. We have multiple active sonobouys in the water!"

"Launch two static noisemakers," Patke said.

The Officer of the Deck turned to the Countermeasures Control Panel. "Aye-aye, sir. Launching static noisemakers now."

A pair of pneumatic hisses and two muffled thumps announced the ejection of the countermeasures.

"That'll give our friends upstairs something to ping on," he said. "Now, let's get a little bearing separation. Left standard rudder, come to new course one-five-zero."

The helmsman acknowledged the command, and turned the control yoke to the left, beginning the *California's* slow turn.

Patke looked up at the overhead of the control room, as though he could see through the intervening steel and seawater to the Indian ASW aircraft circling in the night sky above. "Give us a break here, guys. We didn't shoot at your carrier, and we didn't come to steal your fucking cookies."

CHAPTER 30

21ST SPACE OPERATIONS CENTER
ONIZUKA AIR FORCE STATION
SUNNYVALE, CALIFORNIA
SUNDAY; 30 NOVEMBER
0430 hours (4:30 AM)
TIME ZONE -8 'UNIFORM'

Technical Sergeant Jennifer Thaxton touched a soft-key to silence the alert on her SAWS console. The Satellite Analyst Workstation was monitoring real-time telemetry from GEO-3, a U.S. Air Force infrared detection and tracking satellite currently passing over northern China. The satellite had just triggered an alert, signaling a significant thermal bloom near the Chinese end of the Gobi desert.

Thaxton called up a GPS grid and superimposed it over the site of the bloom. She was ninety-percent sure that she knew the location of the sudden heat source, but she wanted to be absolutely certain. She ordered the software to fix a cursor point at the center of the infrared hot spot, and then read off the accompanying latitude and longitude. Yep. She'd been right.

A flurry of taps on the keyboard summoned up a schedule of known activities for the facility in question. Thaxton scanned it rapidly, and then called up yet another screen—pulling in ballistic tracking data from two Synthetic Aperture Radar satellites belonging to the Air Force, and an Onyx bird from the National Reconnaissance Office.

After a few seconds spent cross-referencing their respective readouts, Sergeant Thaxton swung the microphone boom of her comm-set to a position near her mouth and keyed the circuit. "Watch Officer, this is Operator Fourteen. GEO-3 has detected an unscheduled launch from the Jiuquan Satellite Launch Center in the southern Gobi Desert. Rapid assessment of the trajectory looks like a low orbit insertion."

The Watch Officer, Major Saunders, acknowledged the report. He was standing at Thaxton's elbow almost before she had released the mike button. "What's your analysis, Sergeant?"

"Too early in the launch to know for sure, sir, but it's definitely not a weapons trajectory. If I had to take a wild stab at it, I'd say the Chinese are fielding a low orbit surveillance satellite."

She touched the display screen, and followed an arcing green line with her fingertip. When she reached the end of the arc, she continued moving her finger, extending the curve with her best mental projection of the arc's final shape. "Could be they're getting ready to hang an eye in the sky over their little trouble spot in the Bay of Bengal."

The Watch Officer nodded. "I think you're right," he said. "I'm going to forward your assessment up the chain, along with the tracking data."

"Wait a second, sir," Thaxton said. "That's just a guess on my part. It could be completely out to lunch."

"Understood," the Watch Officer said. "But it's a *good* guess. And personally, I think you're dead on the money."

CHAPTER 31

Admiral Richard Zimmerman sat in his raised command chair, facing the five large-screen tactical displays that covered the forward bulkhead of Flag Plot. Each of the six-foot–square screens was peppered with arcane tactical symbols representing the aircraft, submarines, and ships within the carrier's area of responsibility.

The symbols were color-coded: blue for friendly, and white for neutral or unknown. A third available color-code (red for hostile) was not currently in use, as the USS *Midway* strike group was only in the area to serve as a stabilizing force. Theoretically, the U.S. Navy was a disinterested party, which meant that there were no hostile units in the area. At least not as far as the good old USN was concerned.

The admiral's eyes locked onto the blue half-circle symbol that represented the submarine, USS *California*. Those guys had nearly gotten their asses shot off by the "neutral" Indian ASW assets screening the INS *Vikrant*, only an hour or so earlier. This little act of theoretical non-aggression had occurred after a Chinese attack submarine—also "neutral"—had blown the *Vikrant's* doors off.

Now the *Vikrant* was burning and trying not to sink, somewhere up at the northern end of the bay, while the Indians were pounding the hell out of anything that moved up near that end of the pond. Only God knew how the skipper of the *California* had managed to get his boat out of that mess in one piece.

"Neutral my ass," the admiral said. "If it gets any more '*neutral*' around here, we'll all be going home in body bags."

Not that he could blame the Indian Navy. They hadn't been trying to shoot at the *California*. They'd been going after the Chinese attack sub that had punched holes in their carrier, and they'd gotten a bit too quick on the trigger.

Admiral Zimmerman gripped the arm of his chair. If somebody blasted a couple of flaming craters in *his* aircraft carrier, he might just do what the Indians were doing... Hammer the living shit out of everything within reach.

His eyes swept the dimly lit compartment. Flag Plot was packed with electronic displays and support equipment. The outer bulkheads were festooned with radio comm panels, digital status boards, radar repeaters, and computer workstations—all dedicated to supplying the admiral and his staff with the information needed to command an aircraft carrier and its strike group.

As always when the carrier was deployed, Flag Plot was alive with activity, but quiet. The system operators and radio talkers spoke in hushed voices, through hands-free comm headsets. The collective murmur of their conversations was not much louder than the cooling fans that served the electronic equipment.

"If you have a moment, sir..."

The voice came from the left side of the admiral's chair, about six inches from his elbow. It was that new Flag Lieutenant, the creepy one: Muller, or Moyer... something like that. The one who always seemed to appear out of thin air.

The admiral had watched the man enter and leave rooms, so he knew it wasn't magic or teleportation. You could keep an eye on his movements, if you tried. But if you weren't watching for him, the man had a way of showing up out of nowhere, always with that damned clipboard in his hand.

The lieutenant held out the clipboard. "If you have a moment, sir," he said again.

Admiral Zimmerman accepted the clipboard, resisting the urge to snatch it out of the young officer's hands. The cover sheet was white with a red border and red text, signaling that the document beneath was classified at the Secret level.

The admiral flipped up the cover sheet to reveal a hardcopy of a radio message. He began to read.

//SSSSSSSSSS//
//SECRET//
//FLASH//FLASH//FLASH//
//301332Z NOV//

FM   COMPACFLT//

TO   COMCARSTRKGRU FIVE//
        USS MIDWAY//
        USS TOWERS//
        USS FRANK W FENNO//
        USS DONALD GERRARD//

INFO   COMSEVENTHFLT//
        CTF SEVEN ZERO//

SUBJ/SATELLITE LAUNCH WARNING//

REF/A/RMG/SPACEOPCEN AF/301241Z NOV//

NARR/REF A IS LAUNCH WARNING AND INITIAL TACTICAL SUMMARY FROM
U.S. AIR FORCE 21ST SPACE OPERATIONS CENTER, DETAILING SUSPECTED
PEOPLE'S LIBERATION ARMY (PLA) SATELLITE LAUNCH ON THIS DATE//

1. (SECR) REF A ANNOUNCED THE UNSCHEDULED LAUNCH OF A LOW ORBIT
SPACE VEHICLE FROM THE PLA'S JIUQUAN SATELLITE LAUNCH CENTER IN
THE SOUTHERN GOBI DESERT APPROXIMATELY ONE HOUR AGO.

2. (CONF) TRAJECTORY AND ORBITAL PROFILE ARE NOT CONSISTENT WITH
MANNED SPACE LAUNCH OR ANY KNOWN WEAPON OR WEAPONS PLATFORM.

3. (SECR) INITIAL AIR FORCE EVALUATION IS HAIYANG HY-2F OR HY-3
SERIES SATELLITE, DEDICATED TO OPTICAL, RADAR, AND MULTISPECTRAL
SURVEILLANCE OF BAY OF BENGAL OPERATING AREA.

4. (SECR) SATELLITE TRANSIT SPEED HAS BEEN INTENTIONALLY REDUCED
IN ORDER TO APPROXIMATE GEOSTATIONARY POSITIONING FROM LOW EARTH
ORBIT. 21ST SPACE OPERATIONS CENTER ADVISES THAT ORBITAL PROFILE
IS NOT STABLE, AND WILL DECAY WITHIN TEN DAYS.

5. (SECR) FOR PLANNING AND COMMUNICATIONS PURPOSES, THIS
SATELLITE HAS BEEN DESIGNATED AS REDBIRD ONE.

6. (SECR) DUE TO PREVIOUS OPERATIONAL PATTERNS AND NATIONAL
INTERESTS, THE EXISTING INVENTORY OF DEPLOYED PLA SATELLITES
PROVIDES COVERAGE OF THE BAY OF BENGAL OPERATING AREA ONLY
APPROXIMATELY SIX HOURS OUT OF EVERY TWENTY-FOUR. DURING ITS
PROJECTED LIFECYCLE, REDBIRD ONE WILL PROVIDE THE PLA WITH FULL-
TIME SURVEILLANCE OF THE OPERATING AREA.

7. (SECR) ALL UNITS ARE ADVISED THAT THE FULL CAPABILITIES OF
THE HY-2F AND HY-3 SERIES SATELLITES ARE UNKNOWN AT THIS TIME.
REDBIRD ONE MAY PROVIDE HIGH-RESOLUTION IDENTIFICATION AND
TRACKING OF ALL SURFACE AND AIR ASSETS IN THE AREA. RECOMMEND
THAT YOU ASSUME THAT THE PLA HAS FULL VISIBILITY OF YOUR
OPERATIONS UNTIL ORBITAL DECAY AND SUBSEQUENT FAILURE OF REDBIRD
ONE HAS BEEN CONFIRMED, APPROXIMATELY TEN DAYS FROM THIS DATE.

```
8. (UNCL) GOOD LUCK AND STAY SHARP! ADMIRAL STANFORD SENDS.
//301332Z NOV//
//FLASH//FLASH//FLASH//
//RBT 2034539//
//SECRET//
//SSSSSSSSSS//
```

The admiral read through the message twice before he scribbled his initials at the top and handed the clipboard back to Lieutenant Creepy. "You've got to be fucking kidding me," he said.

The lieutenant tucked the clipboard under one arm. "Excuse me, sir?"

"Nothing," the admiral growled. He waved for the strange little man to go away.

When the admiral looked around a few seconds later, the Flag Lieutenant was nowhere to be seen. The admiral hadn't heard the watertight door open or close, but the lieutenant was no longer in Flag Plot. How in the hell did he *do* that?

The admiral's eyes went back to the tactical display screens. Redbird One would be spying on every move the strike group made, every aircraft sortie, and every course and speed change made by the escorts, or by the *Midway* herself. But there was nothing in Pac Fleet's message which designated the satellite as hostile, which meant that Zimmerman had no authorization to take the damned thing out.

This new Chinese surveillance tool was officially neutral. There was that word again...

The admiral leaned back in his chair. *Neutral.* He was starting to *hate* that fucking word.

CHAPTER 32

Despite Irene Schick's prediction, the video of the killings in Lhasa did not run as the lead story. She was still convinced that the massacre was going to dominate the news cycle for several days, but the news director, Lloyd Neilson didn't agree.

Neilson was damned good at his job, and he and Irene rarely butted heads. But he didn't agree with Irene's evaluation of the story's importance or potential. China and India were escalating toward what could become the first all-out war between nuclear powers. Against a backdrop of that scale, Neilson judged that the shooting of some demonstrators in Tibet would get lost in the shuffle.

He had overruled Irene on both the placement and timing of the piece. Irene had wanted to break the story as a headliner on Saturday evening, with full trumpets, and delivery by one of the big league anchors. Instead, the Tibet piece had been shoved into an also-ran spot on Sunday morning, twenty-two minutes after the lead stories had aired at the top of the hour.

For a lot of news pieces, that would have been the death knell. But not *this* story. As Irene had told Neilson repeatedly, the Tibet thing was *not* going to disappear quietly.

She had no *inkling* of how right her prediction would turn out to be.

135

CHAPTER 33

USS TOWERS (DDG-103)
BAY OF BENGAL
SUNDAY; 30 NOVEMBER
2147 hours (9:47 PM)
TIME ZONE +6 'FOXTROT'

There was a light rap on Commander Silva's door, and then a polite pause before it opened. Captain Bowie stood in the entryway. "Good evening, Kat. Mind if I come in?"

Silva looked up from the stack of paperwork on the tiny fold-down desk of her temporary stateroom. She was still plowing through a mountain of minor administrative details, in preparation for the change of command on Friday.

She had been planning to hit the hay in a few minutes, so she was dressed in her customary shipboard sleeping attire: sweatpants and tee-shirt. Tonight's sweats were standard gray workout pants, and the tee was dark blue with a gold silkscreen image of the surface warfare officer emblem across the shoulders. At home, she preferred to sleep in socks and underwear, but aboard ship she might be called out of bed at any moment of the night. Informal as they were, her tee-shirt and sweats allowed her to respond to drills and emergencies fully clothed.

She leaned back in her chair. "Evening, Jim. Come on in."

Bowie stepped into the stateroom, closing the door behind himself. He held out a routing folder. "I wasn't sure if you'd seen the latest message traffic. I thought you might want to look it over before you hit the rack."

Silva gestured toward the papers on her desk. "The one about the Chinese surveillance satellite? I've seen it. I've got a copy right here."

Captain Bowie shook his head and held out the folder. "Not that one. A new message, from the Bureau of Personnel."

Silva accepted the routing folder, flipped it open, and read the one-page message inside.

136

```
//UUUUUUUUUU//
//UNCLASSIFIED//
//PRIORITY//PRIORITY//PRIORITY//
//301355Z NOV//

FM      BUPERS//

TO      USS TOWERS//

INFO    COMCARSTRKGRU FIVE
        COMDESRON ONE FIVE//

SUBJ/USS TOWERS CHANGE OF COMMAND//

1. (UNCL) BUPERS NOTES THAT USS TOWERS IS CURRENTLY DEPLOYED TO
THE BAY OF BENGAL PURSUANT TO OPERATIONAL ORDERS NOT DISCUSSED
IN THIS TRAFFIC.

2. (UNCL) IN VIEW OF UNANTICIPATED DEPLOYMENT, SUBJ CHANGE OF
COMMAND IS HEREBY POSTPONED UNTIL COMPLETION OF CURRENT
OPERATIONS.

3. (UNCL) CAPTAIN SAMUEL HARLAND BOWIE IS DIRECTED TO REMAIN
ABOARD USS TOWERS AS COMMANDING OFFICER FOR THE DURATION OF
CURRENT OPERATIONS, OR UNTIL USS TOWERS IS ROTATED OUT OF THE
OPERATING AREA.

4. (UNCL) COMMANDER DESTROYER SQUADRON ONE FIVE IS HEREBY
NOTIFIED THAT CAPTAIN BOWIE'S DETACHMENT FROM USS TOWERS WILL BE
DELAYED. NEW DATES TO FOLLOW.

5. (UNCL) COMMANDER KATHERINE ELIZABETH SILVA IS DIRECTED TO
REMAIN ABOARD USS TOWERS AS PROSPECTIVE COMMANDING OFFICER FOR
THE DURATION OF CURRENT OPERATIONS, OR UNTIL USS TOWERS IS
ROTATED OUT OF THE OPERATING AREA. COMMANDER SILVA IS ADVISED TO
UTILIZE THIS ADDITIONAL TIME TO CONTINUE PREPARING FOR
ASSUMPTION OF COMMAND, SUCH PREPARATIONS NOT TO INTERFERE WITH
SHIP'S MISSION REQUIREMENTS.

6. (UNCL) FURTHER DETAILS WILL BE ISSUED VIA SEPCOR.

//301355Z NOV//
//PRIORITY//PRIORITY//PRIORITY//
//UNCLASSIFIED//
//UUUUUUUUUU//
```

Silva closed the folder and laid it on her desk. "I've actually been expecting this for a while," she said.

"So have I," said Bowie. "But I know how frustrating this must be. I was ready to turn over the keys in five days."

He smiled weakly. "Okay, maybe not *ready*. I don't think anyone is ever *ready* to turn over command of a warship, but I was *prepared* to do it."

Silva sighed heavily. "I know you were, Jim, and I appreciate that. And I understand why the Bureau is doing this. You don't change jockeys in the middle of a race. But I can't pretend that I'm not disappointed."

"I understand," Bowie said. "If I were in your shoes right now, I'd be peeling the paint off the bulkheads."

"I'm tempted to do that, myself," said Silva. "But they're not my bulkheads yet, so I guess I'd better leave the paint intact."

Bowie patted the bulkhead next to the door. "They will be yours soon," he said. "Before you know it."

Silva looked back down at the closed routing folder on her desk. "Yeah," she said. The disappointment in her voice was audible. "*Soon.*"

CHAPTER 34

From: <katherine.silva@navy.mil>

Sent: Sunday, November 30, 11:52 PM

To: <harry.silva@nauticalcomposites.com>

Subject: Change In Plans

Dear Dad,

Got a little bad news a couple of hours ago. The Bureau of Personnel has issued orders delaying my change of command until this operational deployment is over. So, Jim Bowie gets to sit in the hot seat a while longer, while your loving daughter cools her heels and waits her turn. (How's that for mixing up the old metaphors?)

I guess I really don't have anything to complain about. Jim is an excellent skipper, and a great guy. He couldn't possibly be any more helpful or thoughtful, and the crew worships him. Needless to say, I'm not happy about the delay, but if I have to warm the bench for a while, it's nice to know that the man playing in my spot is an A-list player.

Before you get started, Jim is not my type, so don't even go there. He has a long-term girlfriend, or a fiancé, or something. I don't know the details, and I'm not going to ask. Whenever I get serious about a relationship, it won't be with a Navy man. Don't get me wrong, I like men in uniform, but I figure one Captain Ahab is enough for any family. Besides, I intend to be married to this ship for a couple of years.

This situation does have an up-side. I'm getting a chance to see my new ship and crew perform under pressure before I take command. We've got an Indian battle group on one side of us, and a Chinese battle group on the other, and that's a little like being between the hammer and the anvil. We're not in combat, and (God willing) we're not going to be, but the situation is tense. The crew is performing beautifully. I'm already proud of every man and woman on this ship, and I'll be proud to lead them when the time comes.

Give Mom a kiss for me, and stop feeding scraps of food to Snickers under the table. Twelve years is getting up there for a pug, and they're prone to heart problems at that age. Scratch him behind the ears instead, and tell him it's from me.

Love,

Kat

CDR Katherine E. Silva
USS Towers (DDG-103)

CHAPTER 35

U STREET CAFE
WASHINGTON, DC
SUNDAY; 30 NOVEMBER
6:30 PM EST

Gregory Brenthoven found an open table near the rear of the café. He chose a seat facing away from the entrance, so he could enjoy the brightly-colored Joel Bergner mural that enlivened the entire back wall.

Brenthoven pulled the lid from his cappuccino, and emptied two packets of raw sugar onto the thick layer of steamed milk at the top. The heavy brown crystals sank quickly through the foam, leaving an irregular tunnel down to the dark liquid below. He gave the mixture a few quick turns with a wooden stir stick and replaced the cover.

The aroma rising from the cup was heavenly. There were plenty of fancier coffee shops in the District, but his long career in Washington had not revealed a single place that served up a finer cup of cappuccino.

He'd bought a sandwich too, grilled chicken and avocado on a brioche roll, but he left that untouched on the table while his eyes feasted on the mural.

Bergner's whimsical rendering of the historic U Street corridor was framed on the left by portraits of jazz legends Billie Holiday and Duke Ellington, and on the right by a throng of revelers, celebrating in the streets on the night of the 2008 election, when the race barrier of the American Presidency had finally been shattered. Between the two ends of the painting lay a curving section of road, with a 1920s era convertible cruising past the façade of the old Roosevelt Theater.

The color pallet of the mural was weighted heavily toward oranges and yellows, giving it a false impression of antiquity, counterbalanced by the strange mingling of resignation and optimism on the faces of the people depicted.

Brenthoven lifted his cup and took a sip of cappuccino. Still a bit too hot, but *damn* it was good.

His eyes danced back and forth across the mural, not focusing on any particular section. He'd seen that painting at least a hundred times since Bergner had created it in 2009, and he still wasn't quite sure why it affected him so profoundly. There was something there, below the surface, some subtly encrypted message of hope and despair. A subliminal acknowledgement that the world could be a much better place... *should* be a much better place... but even in the midst of oppression and injustice, there was still reason to look forward to a brighter tomorrow.

Brenthoven took another swallow of his cappuccino, and started to think about unwrapping the sandwich.

Of course, he could be completely wrong about the intended message of the mural. He had never met with Joel Bergner, and he had never bothered to research the deliberate symbolism (if any) that the artist had attempted to convey. But that was what the painting said to Brenthoven, and—from his perspective—that was the only symbolism that really mattered.

"Good evening, Mr. Brenthoven," said a voice behind him.

Brenthoven glanced over his shoulder. He was surprised to be addressed by name, but even more surprised when he saw who had spoken. It was Gita Shankar, the Ambassador for India.

She held up a paper cup with the café's logo. "May I join you?"

Still a bit put off by the unexpected encounter, Brenthoven took a couple of seconds to respond. "Of course. Yes, please do."

The ambassador took the chair opposite his own, and pulled the lid from her cup.

Brenthoven nodded toward it. "Coffee?"

"Tea, actually," the Ambassador said. "With milk. Apparently it is the closest thing to chai that this establishment can make, unless I want to try something called a *smoothie*."

"If you're not familiar with smoothies, you're probably safer with the tea," Brenthoven said.

He tipped his cup slightly in the ambassador's direction in a toasting gesture, and then took a drink. When he set the cup down, he looked the Indian woman in the eyes. "I have a strong hunch that you are not a frequent customer of this café."

Ambassador Shankar toyed with the lid of her cup. "You are quite correct, of course. I have never been here before."

Brenthoven nodded. "Then, may I ask what brings you here this evening?"

"Surely, you must know the answer to that," the ambassador said. "I am here because *you* are here."

Brenthoven nodded again. "You had me followed?"

The ambassador grimaced. "Only with the best of intentions, I assure you."

Brenthoven met her grimace with a frown of his own. Apparently he was becoming careless. He'd never needed Secret Service protection before, but if his movements were *that* easy to track, it might be time to think about better options for his personal security.

He looked at his unexpected visitor. "You've obviously found me, and I can promise that you have my undivided attention, Madam Ambassador."

"Please," she said. "Call me Gita."

"And you can call me Gregory," he said. "But I'd still like to know why you took the trouble to have me followed here. I assume you want to discuss something outside of the traditional channels. As I said, you have my attention."

The Indian ambassador raised her cup, and then lowered it without drinking. "You're quite correct, of course. I wish to speak to you informally, and outside of normal channels."

Brenthoven took another swallow of cappuccino. "About what?"

"About the hydroelectric site that we have been discussing. And my country's possible intentions regarding the disposition of that site in the near future."

"I see," Brenthoven said. The ambassador obviously didn't want to name the Three Gorges Dam in this public setting, and any discussion about India's plan to destroy it would apparently be couched in indirect terms. That was okay. Brenthoven knew how to talk around a subject as well as any government official.

"Is there something specific you wanted to tell me about your country's intentions regarding the hydroelectric facility in question?"

"Yes," the ambassador said. "Unofficially, I have been authorized to tell you that our planned actions will occur in two days."

She looked at her watch. "Approximately forty-eight hours from now."

Brenthoven sat up. "Forty-eight hours? Are you serious?"

"I am quite serious," said Ambassador Shankar. "That timeline is given to you in strict confidence. We expect you to protect this information as you would defend the military secrets of a close ally. If it should leak to the wrong people, any trust between my government and yours would be irreparably damaged."

"I understand," Brenthoven said. "But I *don't* understand why you are sharing this with us. If this information is so sensitive, and I agree that it *is*, why not restrict the knowledge to your own inner circles?"

"Because there is still time for your government to convince my leaders to divert from the plan," the ambassador said.

Brenthoven stared at her. "How? What do we have to do to convince your government not to go through with this plan?"

Ambassador Shankar smiled. "We have already discussed that. You can enter the conflict on the side of my country, and help us force the People's Republic of China to end their acts of aggression, without resorting to unthinkable strategic options."

"We can't do that," Brenthoven said. "The PRC has done nothing to provoke the United States. We have no justification for entering into direct military confrontation."

The ambassador looked surprised. "Shooting down your military aircraft was not sufficient provocation?"

Brenthoven felt a knot form in his chest. "Madam Ambassador, what are you talking about?"

"Ah," said the ambassador. "I assumed that you *knew*..."

The knot in Brenthoven's chest tightened. "Knew *what*?"

"About the air battle that took place roughly an hour ago," she said. "Two of your carrier-based F-18 aircraft were attacked by two flights of Chinese warplanes. I'm not sure about casualties on the Chinese side, but I know that one of your planes was destroyed. I believe the other was damaged, but I haven't yet been briefed on the details."

Brenthoven shook his head. "That's impossible, Madam Ambassador... *Gita*. I would have been contacted."

He reached for his cell phone, and fished it out of his pocket. It was *off*. The battery had died, or the software had recycled itself, or something else. It didn't matter *why* it had happened. What mattered was that the damned thing had powered itself *down*.

How long had it been off? How long had he been completely out of touch? There was probably a chase team at his townhouse now, and they had no doubt tried his home phone fifty times already. They'd called his cell phone too, of course, but the goddamned thing had been sitting silent in his pocket, like a lump of fucking lead.

He punched the power button, and the phone began its boot-up routine. He didn't have to wait to know what he would find. At least twenty voicemails, and an equal number of waiting text messages.

Damn. Damn. Damn!

He stood up. "I'm sorry, Gita. I have to go."

The ambassador stood up as well. "Of course, Gregory. You have business to attend to."

Her voice hardened. "But don't forget what I said. Forty-eight hours."

CHAPTER 36

COMBAT AIR PATROL
VFA-228 — MARAUDERS
BAY OF BENGAL
MONDAY; 01 DECEMBER
0626 hours (6:26 AM)
TIME ZONE +6 'FOXTROT'

Lieutenant (Junior Grade) Rob "Monk" Monkman eased his crippled Boeing F/A-18E Super Hornet into a slow right turn and tried to ignore the growing vibrations that rattled his fighter. The carrier was only a little more than 60 miles away now. Almost home. *Almost home...*

He didn't feel much like the Monk at the moment. His Shaolin fighter-jock machismo seemed to be on vacation. Right now, he felt like plain old Robby Monkman, and he was just about scared enough to piss his pants.

He ignored the collage of red tattletales blinking on his up-front control display. The touch-sensitive LCD screen was designed to give him fingertip control and status indications for nearly all of the plane's onboard systems, but he had lost track of the ever-shifting jumble of warning readouts. His Hornet was hurt bad, he knew that much. He also knew he didn't have a prayer of sorting out the cascading alert messages to figure out exactly how bad things were.

The Super Hornet's digital flight control system was supposed to detect battle damage and make real-time corrections to compensate. It must be doing its job, because Monk's plane had taken the missile hit more than an hour ago, and he was still in the air.

The starboard engine was fodded out and he'd lost a shitload of fuel, but the quadruplex fly-by-wire controls were still responding to his commands if he didn't push his injured bird too hard. When he'd gone through initial Hornet flight training at NAS Lemoore and the advanced pipeline at NAS Fallon, everybody had talked about how tough the Super Hornet was. Well, the aircraft was definitely living up to its reputation for being able to take a punch.

145

But rugged airframe construction and multiply-redundant systems hadn't been enough to save Poker. Rob had seen the Chinese air-to-air missile punch right through the canopy of Poker's Hornet, blasting the entire cockpit section of the plane into titanium shrapnel. And Rob had reefed his own Hornet back around quickly enough to watch the remains of his flight leader's aircraft cartwheel into the sea.

No ejection. No chute. Not that he'd expected one. He'd known from the instant of the missile impact that Owen 'Poker' Dowell was dead.

But any thoughts of grief had vanished from Rob's consciousness almost as quickly as they had appeared. He had turned his attention—and his fury—on the Chinese bastards who had just blown his mentor and friend out of the sky.

Rob had no idea why the Chinese pilots had opened fire. It had been a routine intercept, two Navy F-18's turning back two pairs of Bogies at the edge of the 300 mile defensive Combat Air Patrol perimeter.

They'd gotten close enough to eyeball the inbound aircraft, and identified them as Chinese J-15's, confirming the classification provided by the E-2D Hawkeye flying Airborne Early Warning support for the *Midway* air wing.

There had been at least a dozen similar intercepts over the past week or so, as the Chinese probed the edges of the USS *Midway's* air defense envelope. But the Chinese Bogies had always turned back, and there had never been any sign of real trouble.

And then they had blasted Owen Dowell without warning. There had been no radar spikes, no fire control acquisition alerts. Just a sudden fireball as Poker took a missile right in the lips. Probably that made the Chinese missile some kind of infrared homer, or something else which didn't require an active seeker that would have alerted the sensors in the Super Hornets.

Rob didn't give a damn about any of the technical details. He had concentrated on going after the treacherous fucks who had just killed Poker.

⚓ ⚓ ⚓

Now, as he made his approach toward the *Midway*, Rob could no longer remember much about the engagement. He knew that he had shot down two of the Bogies, and damaged a third. He knew that he had taken a hit somewhere in the mêlée.

He knew that his wings were bare of weapons, and his 20mm gun was completely out of rounds. Most of the details of the dogfight had faded with his anger, but he had definitely emptied the full magazine on the bastards.

He checked his range to the carrier. It was time to call in, so he keyed his radio circuit. "Strike—Two Zero Nine at fifty-two. Single engine, state four point three."

His report, as short and cryptic as it might have seemed to non-aviators, told Strike Command everything they needed to know. Monk was 52 miles away from the carrier, coming in on one engine, and he was down to only 4,300 pounds of fuel.

Strike responded immediately. "Roger, Two Zero Nine. Flash Ident."

Monk toggled the switch that gave his aircraft's IFF transponder an extra burst of transmit power. This would cause the symbol for his plane to flash briefly on the aircraft carrier's tracking display, verifying his identity, and making it easier to spot him among the cluttered radar signatures of the busy air pattern.

He checked his fuel again. He'd be cutting it close. A healthy Super Hornet burned about 1,100 pounds of gas during a routine landing pass. Monk didn't know what his current burn rate was, but his aircraft was definitely not healthy, and his fuel usage was bound to be higher than normal.

He had survived the dogfight, and limped most of the way home. Was he going to get this close to the carrier, and *then* run out of fuel before he could land? Wouldn't *that* be some fucking irony?

There was no way for him to know how badly his airframe was damaged, or whether or not the canopy would open if he had to punch out. If the canopy was jammed shut, the ejection seat's solid fuel rocket would slam him into the underside of the acrylic bubble at about 12g's. As Poker used to say, *hamburger all over the highway.*

He gave his head a quick jerk to clear his mind. It was time to stop thinking about all the things that could go wrong. He needed to concentrate on keeping his plane in the air. Aviate, navigate, communicate. That was all he needed to do. Aviate, navigate, communicate. Forget about all the shit that could kill him.

⚓ ⚓ ⚓

His Squadron Rep's voice came over the radio. "Two Zero Nine—Barnstormer. Alright buddy, let's work the list."

Back on the carrier, Chuck '*Barnstormer*' Barnes was armed with a copy of the NATOPS systems handbook and checklists for the F/A-18E aircraft. Like all Navy pilots, Monk carried a pocket version of the checklist in his cockpit, but the content of the short list was pared down to a bare minimum, for rapid and easy use. Flying a jet aircraft didn't leave time for reading lengthy technical write-ups, so multiple-failure situations were not covered. Major emergencies called for the full NATOPS manual, and Chuck Barnes was ready to talk Monk through the list of in-flight checks and emergency procedures.

By the time they had done all they could do with the checklist, Monk was coming up on the 25 mile mark. It was time to check in with the carrier's Air Traffic Control Center.

He keyed the radio again. "Marshal—Two Zero Nine at twenty-five. Single engine, three point seven."

"Roger single engine," Marshal replied. "We're going to bring you straight in."

That was a comforting, if obvious decision. Monk was being given clearance to bypass the air traffic control pattern (the stack), and proceed directly in for a landing approach.

He didn't have enough fuel to wait his turn in the stack, even if he hadn't been flying on one engine. As usual, there was a tanker orbiting the carrier at 3,000 feet. The standard procedure would be to rendezvous with the tanker, take on some gas, and make his final approach with a comfortable fuel margin. But one of the many flashing red tattletales on Monk's up-front control display told him that several components of the Super Hornet's fuel system—including the extendible fuel probe—were failing real-time function checks. The decision not to risk an in-flight refueling had been made way above his pay grade.

⚓ ⚓ ⚓

Monk was down to 3,200 pounds of fuel by the time he was five miles out, and it was becoming clear that he would need to trap on the first try. If he missed the wire on the first pass, he *might* have enough gas to make it back around for a second attempt. They'd definitely rig the barricade if he had to make a second approach.

No Navy pilot ever wanted to land that way, his plane caught in a giant nylon net like a fly trapped in a spider web. Not a good way to land, but it was better than ejecting.

The carrier was visible now, a small dark shape in the distance.

Monk spotted the 'ball' about three-quarters of a mile out, the colored lights of the Fresnel lens optical landing system. The orange meatball showed slightly below the green horizontal datum lights. He was a little low, but his lineup looked good.

He added power to his one good engine and keyed the radio. "Marauder Two Zero Nine, Super Hornet ball, two point eight, single engine."

The Landing Signal Officer responded. "Roger ball."

The aircraft carrier that had looked so tiny just a few minutes earlier was growing rapidly, but Monk concentrated on the meatball, his lineup, and angle of attack. Meatball, lineup, angle of attack. Nothing else. Just like in training. Meatball… Lineup… Angle of attack…

The LSO's voice came over the radio. "Little power."

Monk edged the throttle forward on his good engine and his flight path shallowed a fraction. A few seconds later, his wheels slammed into the deck. He instantly shoved the throttle forward, his lone engine shrieking to full power in case he missed the wires and boltered.

His tailhook caught the number two wire. Not a perfect landing, but good enough. His body surged forward against his restraint straps as the arresting cable decelerated his aircraft, and brought it to a stop.

He was down.

A yellow shirt ran toward him, giving the throttle-down signal. Monk brought the port engine back to idle, and the voice of the Air Boss boomed over the radio. "Two Zero Nine—Boss. We're gonna shut you down right there."

Monk acknowledged the order, acknowledged the yellow shirt's 'chocks-in' signal, and powered down his port engine. The silence in the cockpit was almost deafening.

The flight deck crew was already moving toward his plane, bringing the tractor to tow Monk's injured aircraft to its designated landing spot.

And then, with his plane safely on deck, Monk's bladder cut loose and he pissed in his flight suit.

Great… He would hear about that for the rest of his fucking career. No one would ever talk about the two Bogies he had downed, or the third that he'd shot holes in, or how he had kept a severely damaged plane in the sky for 300 miles, and then managed a difficult trap.

All he'd ever hear about was how he had wet his fucking diaper.

But no one ever mentioned the urine soaked flight suit. No one ribbed him about losing control of his bladder. No one even hinted at changing his callsign to *Potty Boy* or *Diaper Man*. If Rob's temporary lapse of continence was discussed by anyone, he never heard a word of it.

And no one ever called him *Nugget* again.

CHAPTER 37

President Wainright strode into the Situation Room, accompanied by a Secret Service Agent. The agent took his usual station in the corner as the president dropped into his chair. "Would someone kindly tell me just what in the hell happened?"

The Sit Room Duty Officer opened his mouth, but Admiral Casey, the Chief of Naval Operations, responded first. "It was an aerial combat engagement in the Bay of Bengal, Mr. President. Two F/A-18 Super Hornets off the USS *Midway* were vectored in to warn off four Chinese J-15 strike fighter aircraft from the aircraft carrier *Liaoning*. Planes off the *Midway* have conducted ten or twelve similar intercepts over the last week or so. Until now, they've always ended peacefully, with the Chinese fighters heading for home after the Hornets show up."

"We're not sure why it went differently this time," he said. "All we know for certain is that the J-15s opened fire on our Hornets, and an air battle ensued. One of our Hornets went down and the other one took some damage, but made it back safely. At least two of the Chinese planes were destroyed. A third Chinese aircraft was damaged, but it was still in the air when it passed out of our radar coverage, so that one probably wasn't a kill."

The president stared at the CNO. "We are *positive* that our pilots didn't shoot first?"

The Secretary of Defense, Mary O'Neil-Broerman, answered. "Absolutely positive," she said. "We have the report from the Hornet pilot who survived, and his account is confirmed by the recovered sensor data from his onboard computers. It's further corroborated by the mission tapes from the E-2D Hawkeye that was providing Airborne Early Warning for the carrier at the time. I haven't seen the data myself yet, sir, but we have it directly from Admiral Zimmerman that the Hawkeye's radar tracks show conclusively that the Chinese aircraft attacked without warning or provocation. One of our Super Hornets was destroyed by the first missile hit. The other Hornet engaged the Chinese fighters and sent them packing."

The president raised an eyebrow. "Our pilot was outnumbered four to one, and he managed to get the upper hand?"

SECDEF nodded. "Yes, sir. I have it on good authority that he pretty much kicked their collective asses, Mr. President."

"Well, it certainly *sounds* like it," the president said. His voice was calmer now.

"Okay, what are we doing about it?" he asked.

This time, it was the CNO who spoke. "For the moment, Mr. President, USS *Midway* is doubling her Combat Air Patrols, and extending her defensive air perimeter by an additional twenty miles. Also, the screening ships in the strike group are on full alert, with Rules of Engagement that allow them to engage any potentially hostile air targets that ignore radio warnings and attempt to penetrate the carrier's screen."

No one at the table remarked on the fact that the word "targets" had just entered the conversation for the first time.

"I see," the president said. "Are these additional measures enough to protect our carrier?"

"Frankly, Mr. President, they're probably *not* adequate," the CNO said. "But that's about as far as we can go without putting our forces on a more aggressive footing."

The president turned to face him. "What do you suggest, Admiral?"

The admiral pursed his lips. "With all due respect, sir, our people are flapping in the breeze right now. If they're going to fight, we should take them off the leash and let them carry the battle to the other guys. If they're *not* going to fight, we should pull them out of the area before any more of them get killed by so-called neutral forces. At the risk of mixing my metaphors, we need to fish or cut bait, Mr. President. You can't win by waiting for the other guy to shoot you in the head, and then deciding whether or not you want to shoot back."

"This is not meant to be a combat operation," the president said. "We put the *Midway* strike group in the Bay of Bengal to act as a stabilizing influence."

"Then I think we can safely say that it's not working, sir," the admiral said. "The *Midway's* presence didn't stop the Chinese from blasting the hell out of the Indian aircraft carrier. It didn't stop them from trying to penetrate our carrier's airspace. And it didn't stop them from shooting at our defensive air patrols. I don't know what we're accomplishing over there, but we're definitely not stabilizing the situation."

The Chairman of the Joint Chiefs of Staff, Army General Horace Gilmore, adjusted his eyeglasses. "I have to agree, Mr. President. The Chinese don't seem to be interested in stability. They've taken shots at our Navy and the Indian Navy. And now they've got a dedicated surveillance satellite sitting right over the operating area, watching every move we make. Every time we launch a helicopter or refuel a ship, they see it. If you ask me, sir, they're tooling up for major combat operations."

"We don't know that for a fact," the president said. "Right now, that's just speculation."

"You're right, sir," SECDEF said. "We *don't* know it for a fact. But we probably won't get ironclad confirmation until it's too late. What the CNO said is true, Mr. President. If you wait for the other guy to shoot you between the eyes, you may not be alive long enough to get off a shot of your own."

The president shook his head. "I'm not letting anybody buffalo me into making a hasty decision on this."

The National Security Advisor spoke up. "Sir, it's not my place to make military policy, and I don't want to buffalo you into anything. But this is one of those cases where we don't get to choose the timetable."

The president looked at him. "What do you mean, Greg?"

Brenthoven looked at his watch. "I remind you, sir, that the Indian government intends to carry out their Shiva attack on the Three Gorges Dam in just about forty-five hours. If the Chinese response is anywhere *close* to what we think it will be, we may be looking at a significant nuclear exchange in southern and eastern Asia."

"I haven't forgotten," the president snapped. "I'm just trying to focus on one crisis at a time."

"Understandable," Brenthoven said. "But I don't think we can really separate one problem from the other. Anything we do *for*, *with*, or *against* China will impact India. Anything we do *for*, *with*, or *against* India will impact China. And if we try to maintain the status quo, India will press forward with their plans to devastate Central China."

Brenthoven lifted a hand with all five fingers extended. "As I see it, we have five possible courses of action here..."

He folded down a finger. "One—we do nothing, and hope that India is bluffing about the Three Gorges attack. Of course, if it turns out that they're *not* bluffing, the USS *Midway* strike group will be fairly close to ground zero when the nukes start flying."

He folded down a second finger. "Two—we actively try to stop India's attack on the Three Gorges site. This essentially means taking direct military action against India. It also means aligning the United States with China, who happens to be the aggressor in this whole bloody mess."

A third finger went down. "Three—we leak the plan for the Three Gorges attack to the Chinese government, and trust to China to protect the dam. This is risky for several reasons, one of which being that the Indian government will pretty much know that we did it. This falls short of actually attacking India, but they will definitely move the United States over to their 'enemies' category."

He folded the fourth finger. "Four—we agree to India's terms, and throw in on the side of the Indian military. This means direct military action against China, but at least we wouldn't be siding with the aggressor. Also, as China has attacked our forces and India has not, it makes more sense from a political and foreign policy standpoint."

The last finger went down. "Five—we pull our forces out of the region immediately, and hope that there aren't mushroom clouds all over Asia by this time next week."

Brenthoven lowered his fist. "I hate to say it Mr. President, but General Gilmore, Admiral Casey, and Madam Secretary are right. It's time to either take decisive action, or get the hell out of there and cross our fingers."

President Wainright massaged his temples. "You're saying that I've backed myself into a corner, and I don't have any viable options?"

The Secretary of Defense shook her head. "Not at all, Mr. President. We're saying that circumstances have backed us *all* into a corner, and we don't have any *attractive* options. We've got choices, sir. *You* have choices. Unfortunately, they just don't happen to be the particular choices we want right now."

"It comes down to the same thing," the president said.

General Gilmore frowned. "We don't always get to choose the battlefield," he said. "But we do get to choose *how* we fight, and *who* we fight against. That doesn't mean we can force someone to become our ally, but it does mean that we can make them regret becoming our enemy."

The president made a dismissive gesture. "Alright. Enough with the saber rattling. I take it your recommendation is that we throw in with India."

"Yes, sir," the general said. "Either that, or pull out of the region, and keep our heads down until the Indians and the Chinese sort it out for themselves."

The president sat without speaking for several minutes. Finally, he leaned forward and rested his elbows on the conference table. "I'm not ready to decide yet. I need to think about this."

"We don't have a lot of time, sir," the CNO said.

"I realize that," the president said. "You've all made that point abundantly clear. But this is an enormous decision, with far-reaching repercussions. I'm not going to make it on the spur of the moment."

"Understood," the Secretary of Defense said. "But I have a recommendation while you're thinking it over."

"What's that?" the president asked.

"I think we should authorize the Navy to take out that Chinese satellite," SECDEF said. "If you decide to pull out of the region, it will make repositioning our forces a lot safer. And if you decide to fight, we sure as hell aren't going to want that thing hanging over the battlespace."

President Wainwright glanced around, taking a silent census of everyone at the table. Every head nodded.

"Fine," he said. "Do it. Shoot the damned thing down."

CHAPTER 38

USS TOWERS (DDG-103)
BAY OF BENGAL
MONDAY; 01 DECEMBER
1127 hours (11:27 AM)
TIME ZONE +6 'FOXTROT'

Lieutenant Lambert, the ship's Combat Systems Officer, walked into CIC and headed straight for the spot where Captain Bowie and Commander Silva were standing.

"Looking good, Skipper," Lambert said. "The patch is loaded, and SPY is back up and tracking."

The 'patch' was a software application that modified the operating parameters of the ship's AN/SPY-1D(V)2 radar system, to allow it to track targets at altitudes above 200,000 feet. With an output power level of over four megawatts, managed by a high–data-rate multi-function computer control system, SPY was quite capable of detecting objects from the surface of the earth all the way up to low orbit. In addition to near-earth satellites, the system could (and would) track any piece of space junk large enough to provide a detectable radar return. As there were an estimated ten-million pieces of manmade debris left in orbit by more than a half-century of manned and unmanned space launches, this could easily flood the radar's display screens with useless false contacts.

To prevent this irrelevant data from overwhelming the system operators, the SPY software had a built-in subroutine that forced the radar to disregard all contacts above 200,000 feet during normal operations. On those rare occasions where it was tactically desirable to track objects in space, there was the *patch*: a small packet of uploadable program code that removed SPY's electronic muzzle, and allowed the radar to see to the very edge of its power radius.

The Combat Systems Officer's report confirmed that this task had just been completed. The patch had been uploaded. SPY had been unmuzzled, and the radar was now capable of tracking targets in space.

Captain Bowie nodded. "Good work. How long will it take us to get a track on Redbird One?"

"Shouldn't be long," the Lieutenant said. "SPY has probably already latched on to it, but it'll take our operators fifteen minutes or so to sort out the sheep from the goats, and get solid identification on the target."

⚓ ⚓ ⚓

It took eight minutes for the Air Search operators to identify the particular radar reflection that corresponded to the Chinese surveillance satellite, and another twelve minutes for them to cross-check the contact's position and motion against the orbital tracking data provided by the Air Force.

Finally, the Air Supervisor's voice came over the tactical net. "TAO—Air. We have a high-confidence track on Redbird One. This contact designated as Track Zero Zero One."

The Tactical Action Officer keyed his mike. "TAO, aye."

The TAO turned to Captain Bowie. "Locked on and tracking, Captain. Request batteries released."

The captain smiled. "You're absolutely totally completely *positive* that we're tracking the right satellite? Because if I give the order and we accidentally take out the Disney Channel, I'm never going to be able to show my face in the O-Club again. Not to mention the NEX or the commissary."

The Tactical Action Officer answered with an exaggerated shrug. "I can't say that I'm absolutely totally completely positive that we're tracking the right satellite. But I'm absolutely totally *mostly* positive. Is that good enough?"

"I guess it'll have to be," Bowie said. "Very well. You have batteries released."

The TAO grinned and spoke into his headset. "Weapons Control—TAO. Engage Zero Zero One with missiles."

"TAO—Weapons Control. Engage Zero Zero One with missiles, aye."

⚓ ⚓ ⚓

An armored hatch flipped open on the destroyer's aft missile deck, exposing the weatherproof fly-through cover that sealed the upper end of a vertical launch missile cell. A half millisecond later, the fly-through cover was blown to shreds as an SM-3 Block II missile roared out of its launch cell and shot into the sky on a ribbon of fire and exhaust gasses.

⚓ ⚓ ⚓

In Combat Information Center, the Weapons Control Officer keyed the microphone of his headset. "TAO—Weapons Control. Bird away, no apparent casualties." The thunder of the departing missile was already fading as he spoke.

⚓ ⚓ ⚓

SM-3 Missile:

The first stage booster fired for six seconds before it burned out and dropped away, to tumble back into the ocean. By the time the Dual Thrust Rocket Motor of the second stage ignited, the missile was above the troposphere and climbing past 70,000 feet, where the blue of the sky began to darken.

The initial high-velocity pulse of the second stage burn lasted seven seconds, and then the missile coasted for nearly a half minute without thrust, passing out of the stratosphere and into the mesosphere. The sky was fully black now and the apparent flatness of the earth had given way to the curvature of its true spherical shape.

Temporarily deprived of thrust, the weapon lost only a fraction of its speed, due to a combination of inertia, the reduction in mass caused by the ejection of the first stage, and the rapid decline in atmospheric drag. Although the tenuous wisps of the ionosphere extended out to an altitude of about 700 miles, the majority of the planet's atmosphere—more than 99% of its molecular gas content—had been left behind.

The second stage reignited for a thirty-five second sustainment burn before its fuel reserve was consumed, and the empty hulk of the expended booster was ejected. Nearly three-quarters of the missile's mass had now been used up and jettisoned.

The guidance section of the missile took a GPS fix, and made minor corrections to the burn vector of the third stage rocket motor. This stage was also designed for two firings, the first at high-thrust, and the second at lower-thrust with lateral corrections to refine the trajectory in the terminal phase.

The third stage did not immediately detach when its final boost was complete. Instead, the onboard computer triggered the third stage attitude thrusters and pitched the nose of the weapon downward, away from the direction of the flight path. A ring of tiny explosive blocks detonated simultaneously, fracturing the locking collar that held the nosecone of the missile in place. In the near-vacuum of space, the protective aerodynamic shell was no longer required. It fell toward the atmosphere, where it would burn up on reentry.

This final task complete, the third stage attitude thrusters fired again, swinging the weapon back up to the proper angle for the intercept. With the nosecone removed, the odd elongated torus shape of the Lightweight Exo-Atmospheric Projectile was exposed.

The LEAP weighed only twenty pounds, and it carried no explosive charge. It didn't need one. The kinetic warhead was moving more than 5,900 miles per hour. Combined with the orbital speed of the target satellite, this yielded a closing velocity of 22,783 miles per hour.

Thirty seconds prior to impact, the LEAP detached itself from the third stage booster. Its onboard sensors acquired the target without difficulty, took a final GPS fix, and utilized a series of rapid pulses from its maneuvering thrusters to refine the angle of approach.

⚓ ⚓ ⚓

The Chinese Haiyang HY-3 satellite was hardened against shock damage. It was designed to withstand micro meteor impacts, and collisions with manmade space debris. It was not designed to survive 96,000,000 foot-pounds of brute mechanical force from a twenty pound projectile with a combined impact velocity of more than 22,000 miles per hour.

Exactly 297.352 seconds after launch, the LEAP warhead obliterated Redbird One with 130 megajoules of thermo-kinetic energy. A human observer, had any been present, would have been instantly and permanently blinded by the fierce intensity of the resulting flash.

But the only human witnesses were 130 miles below, watching the engagement from their radar screens. Their sensors and display systems would recognize and record the fact of the satellite's destruction, but they would carry no sense of the raw power that had just been unleashed on their command.

USS *Towers*:

"TAO—Air. We have confirmed intercept on Track Zero Zero One. We are picking up a growing debris field downrange from the projected impact point."

The Tactical Action Officer turned toward the captain. "I'd call that a kill, Skipper."

Bowie acknowledge the report, and looked around CIC until he spotted OS2 Kenfield. The beefy Operations Specialist was huddled over an electronic plotting table.

Captain Bowie caught the man's eye, and nodded. "Hey, Big Country... Give us a song."

The big Sailor grinned. "Is that an order, sir?"

"You bet your ass it is," Bowie said.

The Sailor nodded. "Aye-aye, Captain!" He cleared his throat and took a very deep breath.

Commander Silva was now familiar enough with OS2 Kenfield's musical repertoire to know what was coming next. She suppressed an urge to cover her ears.

If anything, Big Country's rebel yell was even louder than the last one. It seemed to rattle the very air, and—as before—it was instantly joined by the yells of every man and woman in Combat Information Center.

Bowie smiled in approval and appreciation.

As the collective bellow trailed off into silence, Commander Silva leaned closer to Bowie. "Before we get too carried away with the celebration, somebody better make sure that the Disney Channel is still on the air. If we just whacked the wrong satellite, we're all going to have to change our names and move to Cleveland."

CHAPTER 39

WHITE HOUSE
WASHINGTON, DC
MONDAY; 01 DECEMBER
1:09 AM EST

President Dalton Wainright sat alone in the Oval Office, hunched over his desk. His forehead rested on the polished wooden surface that had once been the hull timbers of HMS *Resolute*. With the exceptions of Johnson, Nixon, and Ford, every U.S. president since 1880 had used the *Resolute* desk, either in the Oval Office, the presidential office that had preceded the oval, or president's study in the White House residence.

Wainright wished that he could somehow use the desk to mentally summon the wisdom of his predecessors. Perhaps if he concentrated deeply enough, their collective knowledge and insight would well up from the russet-colored wood and seep into his brain.

In 1899, William McKinley had signed the treaty with Spain from the *Resolute* desk, bringing a formal end to the Spanish-American War. Nearly a half-century later, the modesty panel had been installed to cover the kneehole, because Franklin D. Roosevelt preferred to keep his leg braces out of public view. Roosevelt had died before the modification was completed, leaving both the desk and the closing chapters of World War II in the hands of Harry Truman.

Truman had sat at the desk while agonizing over whether or not to drop atomic bombs on the cities of Japan. John F. Kennedy had coped with Bay of Pigs and the Cuban Missile Crisis from this spot, managing to drag the world back from the edge of nuclear war, despite Nikita Khrushchev's promise that the Soviet Union would 'bury' the United States of America.

So much history had been made at this desk. So many bills had been signed into law or vetoed here. The futures of nations had been decided from the very place where Dalton Wainright now sat.

But if there was such a thing as genius loci, Wainright could not tap into it. For all its impressive legacy, the desk was not a talisman. It contained no power and conferred no special insight.

He raised his head about two inches and then let it drop back to the wooden surface with a dull thud.

"I've told you before, Dal" a voice said, "you're not going to get anywhere by banging your head on the desk."

Wainwright sat up. No one entered the Oval Office without an invitation, especially not at one in the morning.

Standing in the doorway of the presidential secretary's office was former president Frank Chandler, Wainwright's old boss, and the man who had dumped the presidency in his lap.

Wainwright stood up. "How the hell did you get in here? Did somebody forget to take your key when they booted you out of the building?"

Chandler grinned. "Nah. I left a window open so I can sneak back in whenever I want."

The two men walked toward each other. They met near the middle of the room and shook hands.

"Damn, it's good to see you, Frank," the president said. "But seriously, how did you get in here? Am I going to have to fire the Secret Service or something?"

Frank Chandler shook his head. "Nope. I'm here as the personal guest of your Chief of Staff. He called and told me that you were banging your head on the furniture again, so naturally I came right over."

"Ratted out by my own people," Wainwright said in mock disgust. "Where is my faithful Chief of Staff, anyway? I want to kick his ass for hauling you in here without talking to me first."

"I think he's skulking in his office," Chandler said. "Probably hoping that you won't kick his ass for hauling me in here."

"I'll fire the little traitor tomorrow," Wainwright said. "Or maybe I'll have him shot."

Chandler glanced toward the *Resolute* desk. "That thing is a national treasure, Dal. If you've got to thump your skull on the furnishings, we can get you something from IKEA, so you don't go damaging presidential heirlooms."

Both men laughed. They found seats in the big circle of chairs, and settled in comfortably. And suddenly, the humor was gone from the room.

"I wouldn't have called you," Wainwright said. "But I'm glad you're here."

Chandler loosened his necktie. "Well, you know the old saying... I serve at the pleasure of the president."

Wainwright stared at his former chief executive for a few seconds, but there was no trace of irony in the other man's voice.

"I'm in over my head," he said finally. "I mean, I knew that I was out
of my fighting weight the moment you asked me to be your running mate.
But I didn't really think we could win the election, and a vice-presidential
bid seemed like a nice way to finish out my political career."

Chandler shrugged. "I didn't expect to win either," he said. "I think you
knew that when I invited you on to my ticket. But here we are..."

President Wainwright nodded. "Here we are... Or at least, here *I* am.
Because you left me holding the bag, Frank."

The former president shrugged again. "My political career was dead
after Kamchatka. You know that, Dal. I was the first president to order a
nuclear attack since Harry Truman. And unlike Harry, I hadn't just
accepted the surrender of the Nazi powers."

Chandler sighed. "If I hadn't resigned, I would have been impeached.
Either way, you were going to end up sitting in the big chair. So I decided
to go gracefully, while that was still an option."

"I know you didn't have much of a choice," Wainwright said. "And I
know you played the best hand you could with the cards you were dealt.
But what I don't know, is what I'm supposed to do *now*..."

Frank Chandler leaned back in his chair. "Oh... That's simple. Listen
to your people, but think for yourself. And try to make the best decisions
you can."

He wiped his hands briskly, as though brushing off the dust at the end
of a job well done. "If that's all you need to know, I'm going to get back
on the plane and head home."

"I'm not joking," the president said. "I've got serious problems here."

"I'm not joking either," Chandler said. "And that was a serious answer.
It may seem trite, but I just told you everything you need to know to
handle this job."

Wainwright snorted. "Look, I'm not sure how much you know about
the situation in Asia, but the whole damned continent is getting ready to
implode."

He looked at his watch. "A little over an hour ago, we shot down a
Chinese surveillance satellite over the Bay of Bengal. About forty-one
hours from now, the Republic of India is going to conduct a crippling
attack against the national infrastructure of the People's Republic of
China. Unless my military advisors and the entire intelligence community
are completely out to lunch, China is probably going to respond with a
strategic nuclear strike. And the only way I can get the Indian government
to back down, is to step into the fight and help them take on the Chinese
military."

He closed his eyes and rubbed his temples. "No matter what I do, the shit is going to hit the fan."

"You're probably right," Frank Chandler said. "But you can't let that stop you."

The president opened his eyes. "What do you mean?"

"It sounds to me like you're trying not to screw up."

"Of *course* I'm trying not to screw up," the president snapped. "If I handle this the wrong way, a lot of people are going to get killed over there."

Chandler turned his hands palm-up. "Well, I don't exactly get Sit Room briefings any more, but from what I've seen on CNN, people are getting killed over there already. Tibetan protestors. A whole village full of Indian civilians. Chinese sailors. Indian sailors. Some of our own fighter pilots. And it's only going to get worse as this situation drags on."

The president stared at him. "What's your point?"

"My point is this," Chandler said, "you can't lead by trying to avoid trouble."

He smiled. "Let me share a piece of genuine wisdom with you. Sometimes, we get so wrapped up in trying *not* to do the wrong thing that we forget to do the *right* thing."

"That sounds familiar," the president said.

Chandler nodded. "It *should* sound familiar. You said it to me about six hours after my first inauguration."

Wainwright waved a dismissive hand. "I was babbling. As I recall, we went to nine or ten different inauguration parties that night. The champagne was getting to my head."

Chandler shook his head. "Pardon me for saying so, Mr. President, but that's pure unadulterated horseshit. You were as sober as a judge. And that turned out to be a damned useful piece of advice. It kept me moving forward every time I found myself with a tough choice that I didn't want to make."

He smiled again. "So, now I'm handing your own advice back to you. Stop trying not to screw up. That's a recipe for permanent indecision. Forget about it, and concentrate on doing what you believe is right. There might be consequences. Hell, there almost certainly *will* be consequences. That's the nature of the game."

He stood up. "Listen to your people, but make your own decisions. It's all you can do. That's all anyone has ever managed, including the men who sat in this office before us. And now, Mr. President... It's *your* turn to do it."

Without another word, Frank Chandler walked to the door and was gone.

⚓ ⚓ ⚓

The president sat for several minutes after the former commander-in-chief had left the room.

Finally, he stood up, walked to his desk and picked up the phone. He punched the number for the Situation Room Duty Officer.

"This is the president," he said. "Start waking people up. I want the full battle staff in the Sit Room in an hour."

He hung up the phone. It was time to get to work.

CHAPTER 40

FOX NEWS CHANNEL STUDIOS
1211 AVENUE OF THE AMERICAS
NEW YORK, NEW YORK
MONDAY; 01 DECEMBER
5:30 AM EST

The screen filled with an establishing shot of a computer-generated globe, circled continually by a swarm of CG satellites, each casting a translucent ring of simulated coverage on the rotating earth below. Superimposed over the lower left hand corner of the screen was the red, white, and blue logo of the Fox News Channel.

The voice of early morning news anchor, Ted Norrow, cut in—providing background narration for the animatic.

"This is low earth orbit, where approximately thirty-eight-hundred manmade satellites are circling the world at any given time, providing telephone communications, television broadcasts, GPS navigation signals, weather tracking, internet access, and many other services that are indispensible to modern civilization."

The view cut to a close-up of Ted Norrow's handsome face, staring into the camera with a charmingly somber expression. After two beats, the camera pulled back to a medium shot of the Fox News studio desk, with the satellite animatic reduced to a cameo window over Norrow's left shoulder.

A teaser bar at the bottom of the screen flared with the Fox logo and a wireframe graphic of a satellite bracketed by an artist's conception of targeting crosshairs. The words 'Breaking News' appeared in simulated chrome lettering below the graphics.

"Approximately seventy percent of the satellites in low earth orbit are commercially owned and operated," the news anchor said. "The other thirty percent belong to the militaries and intelligence services of the United States, and other countries."

The animatic changed to a close-up of a satellite hanging in the blackness of space.

"According to unconfirmed reports," Norrow said, "approximately five hours ago, a U.S. Navy warship engaged and destroyed a Chinese military surveillance satellite in orbit over the Bay of Bengal."

"Again," Norrow said, "I have to emphasize that these reports have *not* yet been confirmed. We're expecting a statement from the Department of Defense shortly, but for the moment, we do not have corroboration from a reliable source."

The scene cut to a moving helicopter shot of the Pentagon. Ted Norrow continued in voiceover. "In view of the escalating hostilities between the U.S. and the People's Republic of China, the downing of a Chinese satellite could have serious international repercussions."

Another cut revealed a pair of side-by-side video windows, each containing a head-and-shoulders shot of a man in a suit. The man on the left was middle aged, with an immaculately tailored charcoal jacket and a maroon necktie bearing the Harvard crest. His political opposite in the window on the right was younger and more casually dressed, in a rumpled tweed sport coat and an open necked shirt.

The news caster's voiceover continued. "From our Fox affiliate studios in Arlington, Virginia and Philadelphia, Pennsylvania, we have Dr. Martin Crane from the National Institute for Strategic Analysis, and Jason Walsh from the Center for Global Progress. Gentlemen, thank you both for joining us at this early hour."

The older man nodded. "It's a pleasure to be here, Ted."

The younger man smiled and nodded as well. "Thanks for inviting me."

"Dr. Crane, let's start with you," Norrow said. "If this report is true, and the U.S. Navy has—in fact—downed a Chinese military satellite, what are the most likely implications for the current conflict? And, perhaps more importantly, could this be the beginning of an escalating cycle of satellite warfare?"

The man in the left hand window straightened his necktie. "First, let me say that it's a little early to be jumping to conclusions. We don't have any reliable information about the engagement, if—indeed—it even took place. Second, if we assume—for the sake of discussion—that the U.S. Navy *has* destroyed a Communist spy satellite, then we can't judge the wisdom or the implications of that action until we understand the circumstances in which it was *supposedly* carried out."

The screen cut to a three-shot, with Ted Norrow shown in profile at the anchor desk, facing the video windows containing his interview subjects.

The anchor man nodded. "Can you expound on that?"

Before Dr. Crane could respond, the other interviewee laughed. "That's a silly question, Ted. You should know by now that our learned doctor can expound on *anything*, whether he understands it or not."

Crane ignored the barb. "We have to look at the situation in the Bay of Bengal," he said, "beginning with China's unprovoked attack on two U.S. Navy aircraft, and the death of an American pilot in the hours leading up to the satellite incident. And even *before* that, when the Chinese crippled the Indian aircraft carrier, INS *Vikrant*. What Mr. Walsh doesn't seem to understand—"

The other interviewee cut him off. "I'll *tell* you what I don't understand, Dr. Crane. I don't understand why we're getting involved in yet *another* military confrontation that doesn't concern us. I don't understand why we're still trying to play policeman to the entire world. Didn't we learn anything at all from Iraq and Afghanistan?"

Ted Norrow raised a hand. "Just a second... Are you suggesting that the stability of Asia is not a legitimate concern of the United States?"

Walsh shook his head. "I'm not saying that at all. But why do we keep assuming that military intervention is an effective tool for regional stabilization? When has that *ever* been the case?"

"What about World War Two?" Dr. Crane asked. "Do you honestly believe that Hirohito would have relinquished his stranglehold on the Pacific if we had sent him a letter of complaint? And how about Adolf Hitler? If the Allies hadn't thrown their combined strength at the Third Reich, most of Europe and Africa—if not the entire world—would be living under the iron boot heels of the Nazis at this very moment. Except for the Jews, of course, because they'd be completely exterminated by now."

Walsh rolled his eyes. "Oh, here we go with Hitler again. Whenever you need a boogieman to justify your military expansionist theories, you *always* trot out the Nazis. I hate to break it to you, doctor, but that was nearly three-quarters of a century ago. How is any of that relevant to the current political situation in Asia?"

"We're wandering off the topic here," the news anchor said.

"No," said Dr. Crane. "We're not off topic. Because, apart from Mr. Walsh's inability to learn from history, there's a strong correlation between World War Two and the present conflict with China."

Ted Norrow lifted his right hand in a gesture of invitation. "Can I ask you to explain that?"

"Yes, *please*," Walsh said. "Enlighten us. Dispel our ignorance."

"I can sum it up in a single word," Dr. Crane said. "*Isolationism.*"

He punctuated this one-word proclamation with a sardonic smile. "In the late nineteen-thirties and early nineteen-forties, the isolationist movement in America was powerful enough to keep our troops at home," he said. "We sat on our hands while Germany and Japan were carving up the rest of the earth, and massacring millions of people. Back then, the isolationists were singing the same tune that Mr. Walsh and his buddies are singing today. *Stay out of foreign problems. It's not our business. We're not the policemen of the entire planet.* But where would the world be right now, if the isolationists had gotten the final word?"

Walsh snorted. "Once again, Dr. Crane is oversimplifying my position. I didn't say that U.S. military intervention is *never* necessary. Of *course* it's necessary in some situations. I'll go a step farther, and say that—in certain cases—American military action is not just the *best* answer, it's the *only* answer. But does that make it the solution to *every* foreign conflict that occurs? Are our options always so limited that we have to reach for our guns *every* time there's a crisis somewhere in the world?"

Crane opened his mouth to respond, but Ted Norrow raised a hand to forestall further comment.

"I'm going to have to interrupt," the newscaster said. "My producer informs me that Fox News has just received a statement from the Pentagon, confirming that the USS *Towers* did *indeed* shoot down a Chinese surveillance satellite over the Bay of Bengal. We're expecting additional details in the next few minutes, but for now, we can confirm that the initial reports were accurate."

"So much for our supposed role as impartial peacekeepers," Walsh said in a sarcastic tone. "Just remember, whatever happens next, we brought it on ourselves."

CHAPTER 41

Captain Bowie was alone in the wardroom when Commander Silva arrived. An American Forces Network news broadcast was playing on the television, but Bowie had the sound muted while he jotted down a few changes that he wanted to make to the ship's night orders.

He looked up when Silva walked in. "How's it going, Kat?"

She headed straight for the coffee maker. "Pretty good," she said. "But I'd wrestle a medium-sized alligator for a cup of Starbucks right now."

She peered into the interior of the pot, bent to sniff the aroma, and decided that it was fresh enough to drink. She poured herself a cup, and then looked up at Bowie. "You want one while I'm pouring?"

"Sounds good," Bowie said. "I'll have my usual… a Grande Caramel Macchiato and a blueberry scone."

"Coming right up," Silva said. She poured him a cup of the plain black Navy coffee. "Will that be credit, or debit?"

She handed Bowie his coffee, and dropped into a chair from which she could see the television.

On the screen, a throng of demonstrators was waving handmade signs and banners, across the street from a high-walled enclosure. The protestors were visibly agitated, but they appeared to be respecting the line of police barricades that kept them from approaching the walls. Many of them were clearly shouting, but no sound came from the muted television speakers.

The image cut to another crowd scene. The people were dressed differently and the architecture and color of the walls were not the same, but the anger of the picketers was just as palpable.

The news feed cut to yet another crowd, and this one seemed on the verge of riot. Some of the demonstrators were hurling rocks and bottles over the top of the wall. Occasionally, one of the bottles would smash into a wall and shatter, splattering the stone façade with what must have been red paint. In the background, trucks were disgorging squads of helmeted riot police.

The scene cut again. Another crowd, this one lighting red flags on fire, and dropping them in the street to burn.

Silva looked at Bowie. "What the hell's going on?"

Bowie glanced up at the screen. "I was watching that earlier," he said. "From what I can tell, Chinese troops gunned down about a hundred protestors in Tibet last week. The PRC kept a lid on the story until a video popped up on CNN. Some American tourist—McDowell, or McDonald, or something like that—witnessed the whole thing from his hotel window. He recorded the whole thing on his cell phone, and gave the recording to the media. This is the backlash. Tibetans and Tibetan sympathizers are protesting outside of Chinese embassies and consulates all over the world."

"Some of those demonstrations don't exactly look peaceful," Silva said.

"Yeah," said Bowie. "And the Chinese government is blaming this on the U.S."

Silva stared at him. "What?"

Bowie set down his pen. "A politburo spokesman was on a little while ago, reading a statement. They're saying that this tourist guy, McDonald, was some kind of CIA plant, sent into Tibet to stir up unrest. They're also claiming that the American news networks are operating on instructions from the federal government, and the United States is deliberately trying to turn global opinion against the People's Republic."

Silva raised an eyebrow. "The media taking orders from the U.S. government? They obviously don't understand how that whole freedom-of-the-press thing works."

"They understand," Bowie said. "But they've gotten themselves into one hell of a mess with India, and they're trying not to come off like the bad guys—at least in the minds of their own population."

He rotated his cup on the table, causing the coffee to swirl within its porcelain confines. "If I'm reading the tea leaves correctly, we're going to see some action pretty soon. China is pretty pissed at us about this Tibet thing, and shooting down their satellite probably hasn't done anything to improve their mood."

Silva was about to respond when the wardroom door opened and the executive officer, Lieutenant Commander Matthews, walked in with a routing folder in his hand.

The XO nodded to each of the other officers. "Good evening, Captain. Evening, Commander. I apologize for interrupting."

He strode across the room and held out the folder to the captain.

Bowie accepted the folder and flipped it open. "What's up, Brian?"

"A change in ROE," the XO said. "Our Chinese pals have just been officially designated as hostile."

Bowie gritted his teeth, and scanned the message rapidly.

```
//SSSSSSSSSS//
//SECRET//
//FLASH//FLASH//FLASH//
//011027Z DEC//

FM      COMPACFLT//

TO      COMCARSTRKGRU FIVE//
        COMDESRON ONE FIVE//
        USS MIDWAY//
        USS TOWERS//
        USS FRANK W FENNO//
        USS DONALD GERRARD//

INFO    COMSEVENTHFLT//
        CTF SEVEN ZERO//

SUBJ/RULES OF ENGAGEMENT SUPPLEMENT//

REF/A/DIR/CJCSI 3121.01F/

REF/B/RMG/COMPACFLT/210114Z NOV//

NARR/REF A IS THE CHAIRMAN OF THE JOINT CHIEFS STANDING RULES OF
ENGAGEMENT (ROE) FOR U.S. MILITARY FORCES//

NARR/REF B IS THE PREVIOUS RULES OF ENGAGEMENT SUPPLEMENT,
ISSUED TO U.S. NAVY UNITS IN THE INDIAN OCEAN AND BAY OF BENGAL
OPERATING AREAS//

1. (SECR) REF B IS HEREBY CANCELLED. YOUR ROE ARE AMENDED AS
FOLLOWS:

2. (SECR) PEOPLE'S LIBERATION ARMY (PLA) MILITARY ASSETS WITHIN
YOUR AREA OF RESPONSIBILITY ARE NOW REGARDED AS HOSTILE. YOU ARE
DIRECTED TO ENGAGE AND DESTROY PLA MILITARY FORCES TO THE
MAXIMUM EXTENT POSSIBLE, CONSISTENT WITH LAWS OF ARMED CONFLICT.

3. (SECR) MILITARY ASSETS OF THE REPUBLIC OF INDIA ARE TO BE
CONSIDERED FRIENDLY. ALTHOUGH NO JOINT U.S./INDIAN OPERATIONS
ARE CURRENTLY PLANNED, YOU ARE DIRECTED TO AVOID INTERFERENCE
WITH INDIAN MILITARY ACTIONS TO THE MAXIMUM EXTENT POSSIBLE,
CONSISTENT WITH LAWS OF ARMED CONFLICT.

4. (SECR) THERE ARE TIME-CRITICAL GEOPOLITICAL FACTORS WHICH
NECESSITATE A QUICK AND DECISIVE END TO THIS CONFLICT. THOSE
FACTORS CANNOT BE DISCUSSED AT THIS LEVEL, BUT SECNAV CAUTIONS
ALL RECIPIENTS THAT FAILURE TO ACHIEVE RAPID MILITARY DOMINANCE
IN YOUR REGION MAY HAVE FAR-REACHING CONSEQUENCES TO NATIONAL
SECURITY AND GLOBAL STABILITY.
```

```
5. (UNCL) MOVE FAST. STRIKE FAST. STRIKE WELL. GOOD LUCK AND
GOOD HUNTING! ADMIRAL STANFORD SENDS.
//011027Z DEC//
//FLASH//FLASH//FLASH//
//RBT 2034539//
//SECRET//
//SSSSSSSSSS//
```

Bowie finished reading the message, and passed it to Commander Silva.

She had only read the first few lines when a sharp electronic klaxon came blasting out of the ship's 1-MC speakers.

The alarm was quickly replaced by the amplified voice of the Officer of the Deck. "General Quarters, General Quarters. All hands man your battle stations. Set Material Condition Zebra throughout the ship. Commanding officer, your presence is requested in Combat Information Center."

Captain Bowie was out of his chair and headed for the door before the GQ alarm cut in again. "Coming, Kat? Looks like it's going to hit the fan a little sooner than I thought."

CHAPTER 42

From: <robert.monkman@navy.mil>

Sent: Monday, December 1, 5:34 PM

To: <b.haster@ucsd.edu>

Subject: Poker

My Dearest Beth,

I have to tell you that I'm still pretty screwed up over what happened to Poker. I mean, one second, he was right there on my starboard wing, and the next second his 18 was going down in flames.

I can't even understand how it happened. He was a good pilot. A great pilot. For all my bragging, he was a hell of a lot better than me. But he's dead now, and somehow I'm still alive.

I wish I could take back all the stupid shit I said to him. His first two initials were O. W., and I used to tell everybody that they stood for Orville Wright. All I ever talked about was how ancient he was, and how it was time for him to get his crotchety old ass into a retirement home, and make room for some real pilots.

Poker was a good guy. A good officer, and a good man. He looked out for his people. He looked out for me. He taught me, and guided me, and kept me out of trouble. I would have never gotten my night landing quals if Poker hadn't been covering my six.

How did I thank him? I sat back like an idiot while those Chinese fuckers blew him right out of the sky. Now he's gone, and I'll never be able to tell him how much he meant to me.

I'm sorry. I know I keep droning on and on about this, but it's killing me. Everybody keeps treating me like some kind of badass because I shot down two J-15s, and blasted the shit out of another one. But if I'm such a badass, where the hell was I when Poker needed me?

I'm back in the patrol rotation, but I'm not sure I should be. What kind of a wingman lets his lead go down in flames? What if it happens again? What if I'm some kind of jinx, and anybody who flies with me gets iced?

I don't know, Beth. I don't know anything anymore. I wish I could talk to you right now. I wish I could hear your voice, and talk this through with you until it starts to make some kind of sense.

I wish…

Hang on. The GQ alarm is going off. Got to get to my battle station.

Love you!

More later,

Rob

LT(jg) Robert J. Monkman
VFA-228 Marauders
USS Midway (CVN-82)

CHAPTER 43

The Tactical Action Officer pointed to the Aegis display screens. "Raid warning, Captain. Twenty Bogies coming in high from the southwest. No modes, no codes, no IFF. Threat axis is about two-one-four. Looks like they're lining up for an air strike against the *Midway*."

Bowie nodded. "What does Hawkeye say?"

"Hawkeye concurs that this is a probable strike against the carrier, sir. They're vectoring in three flights of Combat Air Patrol for mop up work, in case any leakers get past us."

Bowie looked at the cluster of hostile air symbols. Twenty red inverted v-shapes were moving toward the *Towers*, and toward the aircraft carrier on the other side of the destroyer's protective missile envelope.

It took him a couple of seconds to realize that something didn't look quite right about the geometry of target motion playing out on the big display screen. The hostile air symbols were approaching steadily, but the rate of closure didn't seem high enough.

"How fast are those Bogies moving?" he asked.

The TAO checked a digital readout on his console. "Airspeed around four hundred knots."

Bowie frowned. "Four hundred knots? That's a little slow for a strike approach, isn't it?"

"It's definitely not typical," the TAO said. "But we've never actually seen the Chinese navy carry out a strike mission against a carrier. Nobody knows exactly what their tactical doctrine looks like for this kind of thing."

"You're right about *that*," Commander Silva said quietly, "but four hundred knots is *still* awfully damned slow for a strike approach."

Before the TAO could respond, a report came over the tactical net from the Electronics Warfare module. "TAO—EW. The Bogies just lit up! I am

175

tracking twenty—that is two-zero—active X-band emitters. Pulse-doppler signature indicates KLJ-10 fire control radars. First cut looks like Chinese J-10 strike fighters."

The TAO keyed his microphone. "EW—TAO. Copy all. Stand by on jamming and chaff."

He released the mike button and turned to his commanding officer. "Captain, request batteries released on inbound Bogies."

Bowie hesitated. Something wasn't quite right about the way the Bogies were acting. The EW emissions and angle of approach added up to a large raid of strike fighters from the Chinese aircraft carrier, but the relatively low airspeed of the raid was puzzling.

Two-thirds the speed of sound wasn't exactly poking along, but the J-10 was capable of better than Mach 2. Why weren't they taking advantage of the aircraft's speed? It didn't make sense.

Or rather, it didn't make sense to *Bowie*. It obviously made sense to whoever had planned the raid. There was definitely a reason for the departure from accepted aerial tactics. Of course, there was little or no chance that Bowie was going to spontaneously guess what that reason might be within the next few seconds. Low airspeed or not, the hostile planes were heading toward the American aircraft carrier. It was up to the *Towers* to ensure that they never got close enough to launch their missiles at the *Midway*.

That made the decision a no-brainer. Bowie made eye contact with his TAO. "Do it," he said. "You have batteries released."

The Tactical Action Officer keyed the net again immediately. "Weapons Control—TAO. Engage air tracks Zero Zero One through Zero Two Zero with missiles."

"TAO—Weapons Control. Engage air tracks Zero Zero One through Zero Two Zero with missiles, aye. Stand by…"

A series of rapid shudders propagated down the length of the warship's hull, accompanied by a sequence of muffled roars as nearly two dozen SM-3 missiles streaked into the sky.

The Weapons Officer's voice came over the net. "TAO—Weapons Control. Twenty birds away. No apparent casualties."

They appeared on the Aegis display within a couple of seconds: the blue shapes of twenty friendly missile symbols, closing rapidly on the hostile air symbols.

Bowie watched the converging symbology for several heartbeats before he reached for a communications headset and punched into the ship's 1-MC system. When he spoke, his voice came from every speaker within the skin of the ship.

"All hands, this is the Captain. We're currently launching missiles against a large raid of hostile aircraft. This is the real thing, people. This is what you've been training for, and I know you're ready. Stay sharp. Stay tough. And be prepared for anything."

He released the mike button and spoke under his breath. "Good luck. To all of us."

⚓ ⚓ ⚓

Xianglong:

With its top-mounted jet engine and v-configured tail wings, the *Xianglong* Unmanned Aerial Vehicle was similar in appearance to the Northrop Grumman RQ-4 Global Hawk that had drawn so much media attention during U.S. military operations in Iraq and Afghanistan. But despite its physical resemblance to the American UAV, the capabilities of the Xianglong were still largely a mystery to the analysts and engineers of the United States.

Its name could be translated loosely into English as '*flying lizard*,' but the UAV's builders preferred the more auspicious translation of '*soaring dragon*.'

Western analysts were correct in believing that the Xianglong's primary purpose was long-range, high-altitude strategic reconnaissance. But the mission modules currently attached to the UAV's wings had a quite different purpose.

The module under the port wing was an electronic blip enhancer, designed to amplify and retransmit incoming radar signals, to make the 7.5 ton UAV seem much larger to enemy sensors. For this mission the drone's apparent radar cross-section had been effectively doubled, giving the slender Xianglong a radar profile that closely mimicked the 16 ton airframe of a Chinese J-10 fighter.

The module under the starboard wing was a microwave transmitter, and it was busily broadcasting X-band signals that were virtually indistinguishable from the pulse-doppler emissions of the Chengdu KLJ-10 fire control radar carried by J-10 aircraft.

The decoy modules and electronic emulators of the deceptive mission package did an extraordinary job of simulating a J-10 fighter jet. The primary flaw in the deception was the drone's lack of speed.

The jet-powered Xianglong was one of the fastest UAVs on the planet, more than 100 knots faster than the American MQ-9 Reaper. But—as impressive as the Xianglong's top speed was for an Unmanned Aerial

Vehicle—it was not fast enough to accurately simulate the airspeed of a real J-10.

The Soaring Dragon was not perfect bait, but it was *very* good bait, and its lack of absolute perfection was offset by numbers. The UAV was not operating alone. It was surrounded by nineteen other drones of the exact same design and capability. Their collective spoofery was intended to make them such attractive targets that minor details like airspeed would be overlooked.

And the deceptive mission packages had not yet exhausted all the tactical cheats at their disposal. They still had a few tricks left to play.

⚓ ⚓ ⚓

USS *Towers*:

"TAO—Air, Bogies are launching chaff and going evasive!"

"TAO, aye!"

The maneuvers were quickly visible on the Aegis display screens, as the enemy aircraft dodged and weaved to avoid the missiles bearing down on them.

Bowie's eyes stayed locked on the dancing blue and red symbols. It still didn't feel right. He couldn't quite put his finger on the problem, but he couldn't shake the idea that there was something wrong with the way the Bogies were maneuvering.

Then, it hit him. He tapped the TAO on the shoulder. "Check their airspeed now. How fast are the Bogies moving?"

The Tactical Action Officer punched a quick series of keys on his console. "Looks like... about four hundred knots. Give or take."

The TAO looked up at his commanding officer. "That's not right..."

"No," Bowie said. "It isn't. Those Bogies are jinking and jiving like crazy, but not a single one of them has kicked in the afterburners to get away from our missiles."

"They're some kind of decoys," the TAO said.

Bowie nodded. "They've got to be."

He reached into the overhead, jerked the red handset of the Navy Red terminal out of its cradle, and shoved it against his right ear. He keyed the mike, and waited a half-second for the crypto burst—a rapid string of warbling tones that the UHF transmitter used to synchronize its encryption signal with the secure communications satellite. "Alpha Whiskey, this is Towers. Hostile strike raid from my bearing two-one-four, is evaluated as a ruse. I say again, Bogies bearing two-one-four are probable decoys! My unit will continue to engage and monitor, but expect additional attacks from other vectors, over!'"

The Air Warfare Coordinator on the aircraft carrier responded within ten seconds. "Towers, this is Alpha Whiskey. Roger all, and concur. We have rapid pop-ups on multiple inbound Vipers, threat axis zero-seven-five. Keep your head down. Alpha Whiskey, out!"

Vipers (mid-flight):

They came in very low, and very fast—forty 3M-54E2 anti-ship missiles, flying three and a half meters above the waves at Mach 0.8.

By official NATO designation, they belonged to the family of SSN-27 cruise missiles lumped together under the code name *Sizzler*. The Chinese variants of this missile class had been alternately over-hyped and under-hyped by the U.S. Department of Defense for more than a decade.

The western press had taken to referring to the 3M-54E2 as China's *Carrier Killer*. That assertion had never been demonstrated under battle conditions. Until now.

Each missile had its radar seeker turned off during this phase of its trajectory, following a pre-programmed flight path, adjusted by periodic updates from the Beidou navigation positioning satellites that comprised China's indigenous version of the Global Positioning System.

The missiles were flying blind, but their nose-on radar cross-sections were relatively low. Coupled with their lack of active emissions and wave-hugging flight profiles, this made them difficult to detect and track.

That would change in a few hundred milliseconds, when the missiles would all energize their target acquisition radars at the same instant. All forty missiles would instantly become visible to the sensors of the American ships and aircraft, but the missiles would compensate for the lack of stealth by accelerating to Mach 2.2 for the terminal phase of the attack.

This supersonic 'sprint' would give potential interceptors only seconds to identify the threat and react. Theoretically, the window of opportunity for defensive engagement would be too narrow for the target ship to exploit.

That theory was about to be tested.

USS *Towers*:

The drama played itself out on the tactical display screens in two acts, separated by both time and distance. To the southwest, the First Act had nearly resolved itself. Evasive maneuvering aside, the ship's SM-3 missiles were shredding the inbound Bogies, which—Bowie was now certain—must be decoys.

The Second Act was playing out to the east. Forty hostile missile symbols had appeared, and were closing on the *Midway* at incredible speed.

Two elements of Combat Air Patrol were vectoring in to intercept the Vipers, but—like everyone else in the strike group—they'd been caught looking the wrong way. Even on afterburner, by the time the F/A-18s arrived on station, the engagement would be over.

The *Midway* had air defenses of her own: a pair of Rolling Airframe Missile launchers, a trio of Sea Sparrow missile launchers, and four Close-In Weapon Systems—the 20mm defensive Gatling guns known to the fleet as *Phalanx*. The carrier could protect herself against a reasonable number of subsonic cruise missiles. But the number of inbound Vipers was not at all reasonable, and they were moving at supersonic speeds.

The only thing between the carrier and destruction was the USS *Frank W. Fenno*, the Arliegh-Burke class guided missile destroyer assigned to the eastern perimeter of the strike group's screen.

As Bowie and his CIC crew watched the tactical displays, the *Fenno* began launching clouds of SM-3 missiles. The friendly missile symbols overlapped and obscured each other for several seconds, and then they began to diverge as the interceptor missiles homed in on individual targets.

They were too many to count visually in the limited time before intercept, but the Aegis tracking software provided the total. Eighty missiles. The *Frank W. Fenno* was following a *shoot-shoot-look-shoot* doctrine. Fire two missiles at each incoming Viper, scan with radar to see how many have been destroyed, and then fire again at any Vipers that survived the first salvo.

Bowie's first instinct was to call that a mistake, but maybe it wasn't. He didn't know the other destroyer's exact weapons load out, but it probably wasn't much different from what the *Towers* was carrying. The *Fenno* had something like ninety SM-3s aboard, give or take a few for minor variations in mission loads. Which meant that the *Fenno's* skipper had just launched about ninety percent of his SAMs in his initial salvo. Ordinarily not the kind of choice that a smart destroyer captain would make. But the Vipers were coming in too fast. The *Fenno* wasn't going to get off a second salvo. Whatever they missed the first time around, was going to hit the carrier.

Bowie slammed the Navy Red handset back into its cradle. "Goddamn it! Is there any way we can help the *Fenno* intercept those Vipers?"

The Tactical Action Officer shook his head. "Not a chance, Captain. Even if we had a clear field of fire, they're too far away. By the time our birds get over there, it'll be too late."

"There's nothing you can do right now," Silva said softly.

Bowie turned, and she was standing at his elbow. He exhaled heavily. "I know. But I don't have to like it."

He turned his eyes back to the Aegis display screens. "Damn it!" he said. "Damn it! Damn it! *Damn* it!"

⚓ ⚓ ⚓

The engagement unfolded on the big displays. Two friendly missile symbols converged on a hostile missile symbol as the first of *Fenno's* interceptors destroyed their assigned Viper. Then the interplay of tactical symbols seemed to shift into overdrive, red and blue icons stuttering, intersecting, vanishing, and rearranging themselves in indecipherable patterns.

When it was over, nine hostile missiles remained on the screen, streaking toward the bright blue circle that represented the American aircraft carrier.

⚓ ⚓ ⚓

USS *Midway*:

Admiral Zimmerman gripped the arms of his chair and watched the onrushing missile symbols on the large-screen tactical displays. He had already double-checked his seat belt. He had no intention of getting tossed around Flag Plot like a rag doll when those damned missiles hit.

He heard the muted growls of outbound RAMs and Sea Sparrows, punctuated several times by the harsh metallic zipper sound of the CIWS guns firing. Friendly missile symbols flickered briefly on the tactical displays, and hostile symbols winked out of existence. They were getting some of the Vipers. How many, he didn't know, but there were two or three left on the screen when the first of the enemy missiles slammed into the starboard side of the superstructure.

The admiral was thrown against his seatbelt so hard that he felt like someone had pounded him in the stomach with a Louisville slugger. The lighting flickered, but the power seemed to be holding, at least in Flag Plot.

His ears rang and his eyes didn't want to focus properly. He could smell smoke, and he could hear someone shouting what sounded like orders, but the words didn't make any sense to him.

He lifted his head and his eyes found the big tactical screens. Four of them were dark, but the screen on the far right still showed the weaving ballet of colorful icons. An odd red emblem bore straight for the heart of a bright blue circle.

The symbols touched, and the admiral felt himself thrown violently against his seatbelt again.

The lights went out.

CHAPTER 44

President Wainright flipped open the blue-jacketed folder and began to scan the top page of the briefing package it contained. After skimming the material for nearly two minutes, he looked up. "Okay, I've seen the charts and figures. Now, I want somebody to translate it into English for me."

He closed the folder and dropped it on the table. "How bad is it?"

Admiral Casey, the Chief of Naval Operations, stood up. "It's not good, Mr. President."

He pointed a remote toward the wall-sized Situation Room display screen. The presidential seal was replaced by a series of still pictures of the aircraft carrier, USS *Midway*. The ship was listing fifteen or twenty degrees to starboard, and several of the images showed smoke billowing from a hole in the superstructure and another (larger) hole in the lower hull. Close-up photos of the two damaged areas had apparently been taken at a later time, after the fires had been extinguished.

"We're looking at the impact points of two anti-ship cruise missiles," the CNO said. "Based on flight profiles, electronic emissions, and battle damage assessment, we believe that both missiles were Chinese air-launched variants of the SSN-27 Sizzler."

The display screen sequenced through a dozen more close-up images, taken from a variety of angles. From this range, the impact points looked like craters. The edges of the blast holes were blackened and irregular, the steel and aluminum structures of the enormous ship broken, charred, and twisted into ragged shapes of chaos.

Admiral Casey halted the march of images with another flick of the remote. The screen showed a medium distance shot of the wounded ship, apparently taken from a helicopter. The angle of the carrier's list seemed to be even more evident than in the earlier shots.

"As you can see," the admiral said, "one of the missiles impacted right at the waterline, causing damage above and below the water, and opening the hull to major flooding. This has resulted in a pronounced list to starboard, which was further increased by firefighting water pumped in to extinguish the fires."

The CNO laid the remote on the conference table. "Given the severity of the damage, personnel casualties have been relatively light. Six dead, and nineteen injured. Three of the wounded are in critical condition, and some or all of them may not make it."

The president sighed heavily. "How much do we know about the attack?"

The Secretary of Defense closed her own briefing folder and stood up. "Well, Mr. President—not to put too fine a point on it—we got suckered."

She reached for the remote, and Admiral Casey handed it to her.

SECDEF thumbed several buttons, and the image of the damaged aircraft carrier was replaced by a map of the Bay of Bengal. The blue iconic silhouettes of three Navy destroyers formed a loose triangle, with the silhouette of an aircraft carrier at the center.

"The raid took place in two waves," the Secretary of Defense said. "The first wave was detected at approximately 1728 hours, that is 5:28 PM local time."

She keyed the remote, and a cluster of red aircraft shapes appeared to the left and slightly below the strike group. "Twenty jet aircraft, inbound from the southwest. We don't know exactly which kind of hardware was used, but it seems likely that the entire wave consisted of Unmanned Aerial Vehicles, equipped with advanced electronic deception systems. We suspect they were launched from the Chinese carrier, but that's only an assumption at this point. They were able to closely simulate a group of Chinese J-10 aircraft. And, due to their angle of approach and radar characteristics, they were misidentified as an actual raid against the *Midway*."

She keyed the remote again, and a group of red missile silhouettes appeared to the right of the strike group. "The second wave appeared from the east, approximately ten minutes later, as the carrier's escorts and aircraft were engaging the decoys of the first wave. The second wave consisted of forty anti-ship cruise missiles, all targeted on the aircraft carrier."

She nodded toward the CNO. "As Admiral Casey pointed out, these missiles were probably a Chinese air-launched variant of the SSN-27 Sizzler. The launching platforms were not detected, leading us to assume that the attacking aircraft stayed extremely low to the water, and fired from close to the maximum range of the SSN-27. Roughly 160 nautical miles. The missiles remained undetected until they switched on their radars for the terminal phase, and accelerated to Mach 2."

SECDEF pressed another key on the remote, and the easternmost of the blue destroyer silhouettes was highlighted on the display. "The only shooter in a position to intercept was USS *Frank W. Fenno*. The targeting window was extremely narrow, but the *Fenno* successfully killed thirty-one of the inbound missiles. The *Midway's* defensive weapons managed to knock out seven of the remaining nine."

The Secretary of Defense sat down. "The last two missiles made it all the way through to the *Midway*. And we've just seen the results of that."

President Wainwright looked at the map on the big screen. "So the second wave, the planes that launched the attack, came from the Chinese aircraft carrier as well?"

The CNO shook his head. "Probably not, Mr. President. To stay outside the radar coverage of our strike group, aircraft from the *Liaoning* would have had to divert east, past the Andaman and Nicobar Islands; turn north and fly up the long axis of the Andaman Sea; and then turn west, back into the Bay of Bengal. Even with several aerial refuelings, that's beyond the capacity of Chinese carrier-based aircraft. And then, they'd have to turn around and do it all in reverse, on the return leg."

"Okay," the president said, "where the hell did they come from?"

"We don't know for certain," the Secretary of Defense said, "but our best guess is Myanmar. They share a border with China, and the PRC is a close ally of the Burmese, as well as one of their top economic trading partners. We don't think the Burmese military actually launched the attack, but they may have permitted their airbases to be used as a staging area for Chinese strike planes."

The president suppressed a grimace. The Republic of Myanmar had no particular love for the United States. The U.S. had been imposing economic sanctions against the country since the late 1990s, to penalize the government for decades of continually worsening human rights violations.

During his days in the Senate, Wainwright himself had led a multinational initiative to convince the European Union to tighten their economic sanctions against Myanmar. The Burmese government didn't have the military or economic muscle to stand directly against the United States, but they might welcome the opportunity to help their Chinese buddies poke America in the eye.

"Alright," the president said. "What are our options?"

No one spoke for several seconds.

Finally, the Chief of Naval Operations leaned forward. The lined skin of his tanned face gave his features the weather beaten gravitas of that famous Gloucester Fisherman painting by Joseph Margulies. "Frankly, Mr. President, I think it's time for us to turn up the heat. Just before the strike on the *Midway*, we issued new Rules of Engagement to our naval forces in the area. Since the attack, we've been on a defensive footing. I say we continue with the plan, and go after the Chinese carrier, and every PRC military unit in the region."

The president shook his head. "How in the name of God did we end up in a shooting match with the Chinese Navy?"

Admiral Casey's eyebrows went up. "Is that a rhetorical question, Mr. President?"

"Hell no, it's not rhetorical," the president said. "When my alarm clock went off this morning, I did not expect to be at war with the People's Republic of China by lunch time."

"Mr. President, we're not at war," the Secretary of Defense said. "Hostilities have escalated farther than we were expecting, but this is still a regionalized conflict, with a limited scope of operations. We are not at war with the PRC."

The president looked in her direction. "But the situation doesn't show any signs of stabilizing, does it? It's escalating, as you just pointed out. Can you guarantee that this conflict won't keep spreading until we *are* at war with China?"

"No, sir," SECDEF said. "I can't give you any guarantees. All I can offer is my best counsel. And I solemnly believe that if we back away now, there *will* be war."

Admiral Casey nodded in agreement. "Mr. President, we got into this dogfight to prevent India from destroying the Three Gorges site. If we walk away now, the Indians are going to carry out their attack, as planned. And you remember what happens after that... Catastrophic flooding of the Yangtze River basin. Three major cities wiped out, and half of China's industrial base washed out to sea. A death toll in the tens of millions— possibly hundreds of millions. When the Chinese retaliate, and they *will* retaliate, they're going to hammer India into the Stone Age."

"I agree," the Secretary of Defense said. "We could be looking at a full-scale nuclear exchange between China and India. But even if the reprisals *don't* go nuclear, the casualty rate could easily dwarf the entire body-count from the Second World War."

"And there's another aspect to this," Admiral Casey said. "If we get a bloody nose, and then back down from the fight, our national deterrence goes down the toilet. We signal to the entire world that China is the dominant military power on this planet. We will be effectively handing them the reins."

The president sat in silence for several seconds. Finally, he nodded slowly. "Okay. We stay in the fight. It looks like every other alternative leads to more bloodshed in the long run."

He turned toward the admiral. "Are we *ready* for this? Our primary means of force projection is damaged. Possibly crippled. It looks to me like we might not have the horsepower to do the job."

"We'll have to shift some additional assets into the operating area," Admiral Casey said. "But our first step should be to get the message out to our forces in the region. Go after the bad guys, and do it *now*."

President Wainwright rubbed the back of his neck. "Can they do it?"

The CNO nodded gravely. "If we give them the word, Mr. President, I *promise* you they'll get the job done."

CHAPTER 45

USS TOWERS (DDG-103)
BAY OF BENGAL
TUESDAY; 02 DECEMBER
0317 hours (3:17 AM)
TIME ZONE +6 'FOXTROT'

Katherine Silva was dreaming of Savannah when the call came. Random snatches of her childhood, strung together in no particular order.

The cobblestones of River Street damp and glistening after an evening rain. Ripples in the dark river tossing back wobbly reflections of the restaurant marquis lights and shop windows. The wind carried the bright salt aroma of the ocean and the hint of cities, countries, and entire continents hiding somewhere below the curve of the horizon.

Kat was eight years old, her father a tall comforting silhouette under the golden aura of the faux colonial street lamps. The world was out there. She knew that. Had known it the first time she had seen the river, and its broad mouth opening to the ocean just a few miles downstream from where she now stood. For her, the world was not here, on the bank of the river—at least not the important parts. It was out *there*, where the sky bent down to touch the sea.

"I'm going to be a pirate," she said in a solemn voice.

Her father didn't laugh. "I thought you wanted to be a shrimp boat captain," he said.

"Or a pirate," Kat said. "Or just build my own boat, and sail around the world."

She threw her arms wide, to encompass the river and the ocean somewhere at the end of it. "I want to be out there," she said.

Her father nodded. "I know." And he *did* know.

⚓ ⚓ ⚓

Kat was twelve years old, standing on the uneven plank deck of her homemade raft, gripping the mast as the unstable vessel bobbed and rolled in the waves. Built from a pair of wooden shipping pallets nailed together with scraps of lumber, the raft was kept afloat by three truck inner tubes and two dozen empty plastic milk jugs, all tied beneath the pallets with carefully-knotted binder twine.

She had christened her raft the *Spray*, after the famous sloop of Joshua Slocum: the first man to sail around the world solo.

This was the maiden voyage of the *Spray*, and Kat had intended it as a brief excursion. Just a quick loop in the Wilmington River, using her bed sheet sail to tack upstream, and then ride the current back to her launch point in an easy glide.

But Kat had not yet equipped her vessel with a centerboard or a keel—a refinement that was apparently more necessary than she had assumed. No matter how she trimmed her sail or which way she turned the plywood rudder, the raft followed the current. She'd been out here several hours now, trying to edge her way back toward the bank as she drifted farther and farther downstream.

She knew that she had a vicious sunburn going, and she had long since guzzled down the bottle of 7-Up that had been her only provisions for the voyage. Out in the channel, a sleek-looking cabin cruiser with a turquoise hull was motoring effortlessly upriver.

Kat thought about trying to wave the boat down, but she was too proud to ask for rescue. She wasn't hurt, and her raft was seaworthy, despite its lack of controlled steerage. She would bring the *Spray* back to port. As captain, that was her job.

She shielded her eyes from the sun, and studied the landmarks along the shore. She'd be sliding past the shrimp boat piers in Thunderbolt pretty soon, and she figured she could get close enough in to snag the end of one of the docks.

⚓ ⚓ ⚓

Kat was five years old, sitting cross-legged under a moss-draped oak tree near the edge of Daffin Park pond. Half a loaf of stale white bread lay on her lap. She was intent on her task, carefully tearing each bread slice into a dozen or so pieces, and flinging the crumbly treats toward a flock of grateful ducks.

The ducks paddled in circles and flapped their wings, darting their heads to scoop up the bread scraps as they landed in the water— occasionally snatching a piece right out of the air. They quacked, loudly and appreciatively. Kat laughed with delight, and reached for another crust of bread.

⚓ ⚓ ⚓

Then the telephone rang, and the dream was gone, like the popping of a soap bubble.

Kat Silva opened one eye, and groped for the phone beside her bed. She pulled the receiver out of its restraining clip, and held it to her ear. "Commander Silva speaking."

The voice on the other end was brisk and alert. "Commander, this is the XO. Captain Bowie is calling a strategy meeting with all senior officers in the wardroom in fifteen minutes. He'd like for you to sit in."

Silva looked at the clock and forced her eyes to focus on the lighted numerals. "Got it," she said. "I'm on my way."

She fumbled for the light switch, flicked it on, and rolled out of bed. She was half-tempted to climb back in and go to sleep. Not that she particularly needed the rest. She was used to getting up at all hours, and she had long ago learned to come instantly awake and respond to the needs of the job.

The problem was that she didn't *have* a job. The Chinese air strike had proven that. Bowie had commanded the ship through the entire engagement sequence, receiving reports, evaluating the situation, and issuing orders. Kat had stood around with her hands in her pockets. She had probably spoken no more than a half dozen words the whole time, none of them particularly helpful or insightful.

She'd come to the *Towers* to assume command. Instead, she was facing real combat for the first time in her life, and she was just along for the ride.

It wasn't Jim Bowie's fault. It was strictly an accident of timing. If the fracas between India and China had started a couple of weeks later, she would have been in command when the *Towers* deployed. It was the luck of the draw—nothing more.

Jim was certainly trying to make the situation bearable for her. He was careful to include her in the inner workings of the ship's upper command structure, and she appreciated that. But the situation was frustrating. This wasn't how things were supposed to work.

She reached for a set of freshly-pressed coveralls. There was enough time to wash her face and run a brush through her hair before she had to head up to the meeting.

⚓ ⚓ ⚓

Silva arrived in the wardroom about five seconds ahead of the executive officer, Lieutenant Commander Brian Matthews. As Silva was taking a seat, the XO did a quick visual inventory of the officers gathered around the table. The ship's department heads were all present. The Operations Officer, Lieutenant Sue Meyer, was in her usual chair across from the door—flanked on the left by the Combat Systems Officer, Lieutenant Ben Lambert, and on the right by the Chief Engineer, Lieutenant Commander Chris Bronson, and the Supply Officer, Lieutenant Pat Connelly.

The XO picked up the phone and punched three digits. "We're ready, sir."

Captain Bowie arrived about four minutes later. He nodded in greeting to the assembled officers, and then poured himself a cup of coffee before taking his seat at the head of the table.

"I apologize for the lateness of the hour and for the short notice," he said. "I know that some of you haven't had much sleep."

Lieutenant Meyer nearly responded by reflex, but she caught herself in time. She was a hard-charger who didn't allow herself a lot of rest. Her favorite comment on the subject of sleep was blunt, politically incorrect, and sexually suggestive. *Sleep is for pussies.* As it was her commanding officer speaking, she decided to keep that particular opinion to herself this time.

Bowie continued without interruption. "Our tactical situation has changed, and we need to make some decisions. In view of the damage sustained during the air attack yesterday evening, Admiral Zimmerman has decided to move the *Midway* out of the Bay of Bengal."

The XO looked surprised. "We're pulling out of the op area?"

Bowie smiled. "That depends on how you define the word 'we.' The carrier is definitely pulling out, but the admiral is thinking about detaching two of the destroyers for independent ops. That's why I called this meeting at oh-my-God-o'clock. The admiral has ordered us to come up with a plan for taking out the Chinese carrier's escorts. He wants to see at least a rough outline by 0600."

Captain Bowie looked at the clock. "That gives us about two and a half hours to hammer out a basic plan of attack."

Lieutenant Meyer pursed her lips. "Why bother with the escort ships? The biggest threat is the Chinese air wing. We should be going after the carrier."

"Admiral Zimmerman has a plan for that," Bowie said. "He's going to use the *Midway's* air power to knock out the *Liaoning*. Our job is to soften up the Chinese battle group in preparation for the main attack."

"I thought the *Midway* was out of action," the XO said. "How is she supposed to launch aircraft?"

"I've been told not to worry about that," Bowie said. "Admiral Zimmerman has a plan. We're supposed to concentrate on wiping out the escorts."

The Combat Systems Officer raised an eyebrow. "Wiping them *out*?"

"Yes," Bowie said. "We're not just supposed to take them out of the fight. Our orders are to sink them. Every escort ship in the Chinese battle group."

Captain Bowie paused to let the assembled officers absorb his words. Not *damage* the Chinese ships. Not *defeat* them. *Sink* them. Destroy them *completely*.

After several seconds of silence, Commander Silva spoke up. "What about the Chinese submarines? Do we go after them? Or do we try to avoid them?"

"USS *California* will be assigned to handle the hostile subs," Bowie said. "If we happen to encounter one, we can engage it. But we're not supposed to seek ASW opportunities."

The Combat Systems Officer raised a finger. "I assume that we'll be operating with the *Donald Gerrard...*"

"That's correct," Bowie said. "The *Fenno* has already expended 80 missiles—the majority of her inventory—so she'll be sticking with the *Midway* to provide cover. That leaves the *Towers* and the *Gerrard* to stick around and do the dirty work."

He took a swallow of coffee and set his cup down. "That pretty much defines our mission parameters. Now all we need is a plan for carrying it out."

No one spoke for several minutes as everyone mulled over the problem and searched for a workable tactical approach.

Again, it was Commander Silva who broke the silence. "I think we should run like hell," she said. "The *Midway* is pulling out, and we should go too. Full retreat. Admit that we got our asses kicked, and run home."

Three or four people started to respond, but Bowie held up a hand. "Go on..."

Silva looked at the shocked and puzzled faces around the table. She didn't speak immediately, enjoying the moment of incredulous silence.

"I was just thinking about Sun Tzu," she said finally. "That famous piece from *The Art of War*, where he talks about all warfare being based on deception... Attacking when you appear to be unable, and making yourself seem far away when you're near. I never bothered to memorize that passage, but the concept applies pretty well to our current situation."

No one responded, so she continued. "The Chinese blasted the hell out of the INS *Vikrant*. The Indian navy responded by pulling their carrier battle group all the way up the northern end of the bay, where it can draw on their coastal defenses and shore-based air cover. That's a reasonable response. When you get your fingers burned, you pull your hand away from the fire. Well... The Chinese have blasted the hell out of our carrier too, and they know that we haven't lost an aircraft carrier in combat since World War II. They also know how important carriers are to our national deterrence. If we circle the wagons and escort our carrier out of the danger zone, I'm betting they'll interpret *that* as a reasonable response too."

Bowie nodded. "Continue..."

"So," Commander Silva said, "we maintain our places in the defensive screen, and cover the *Midway's* retreat from the Bay of Bengal, until..."

The XO slapped his palm on the table. "*Until* we reach the passage through the Nicobar Islands. Then, the *Midway* continues through into the Andaman Sea, while we break off and haul ass down the coast—using the sea traffic and the radar clutter of the island chain to mask our run to the south."

Silva smiled. "You catch on fast, Brian."

The other officers began exchanging interested glances.

Bowie nodded appreciatively. "We could make our final approach after sunset tomorrow evening. Go in dark and quiet—full EMCON, and full stealth mode."

"Exactly," Silva said. "If we do it right, we can get all the way inside their defensive perimeter. Then, we open up and blow their doors off."

Lieutenant Meyer grinned. "I like the way you think, ma'am. You're one sneaky bitch."

The executive officer shot her a look. "*Lieutenant...*"

The Operations Officer raised her hands in a gesture of surrender. "Sorry, XO, but I couldn't think of what else to say. Sneaky bastard didn't seem to fit, and son-of-a-bitch just isn't right..."

The XO pounded the table. "That's enough, Lieutenant!"

The Ops Officer grimaced. "Sorry, XO. It won't happen again, sir." She turned toward Commander Silva. "No disrespect intended, ma'am."

The XO looked like he was going to say something further, but Captain Bowie spoke up again. 'I think it's an excellent plan, Commander Silva. Let's work out the details, and then I'll take it to the admiral."

The tactical discussion began in earnest.

About ten minutes into it, the exchange with Lieutenant Meyer popped into Silva's head again, and she had to suppress a grin. *Sneaky bitch...* She could live with that.

CHAPTER 46

HONG'QI-12 MISSILE DEFENSE BATTERY
ZIGONG, CHINA
TUESDAY; 02 DECEMBER
11:58 AM
TIME ZONE +8 'HOTEL'

The flashing amber light caught Chao Péng's attention immediately. He tapped the button to acknowledge the alert, pre-empting the alarm buzzer that was programmed to sound if the warning went unanswered for more than five seconds.

Chao's rank was *Xia Shi*, the Chinese equivalent to the rank of technical sergeant. He was good at his job, and proud of it. He had been a radar intercept operator for three years, and the alarm had never once sounded while he was on watch. The computer had never caught him napping, and he was determined that it never would.

With a brief flurry of keystrokes, Chao summoned up the system alert queue and scrolled through the flight characteristics of the new target. The data glowed bright red on the screen of his console.

Parked at the center of a circle of six mobile KS-1A missile launchers, the H-200 passively-scanned electronic array was a highly-effective radar sensor. The slab-shaped phased-array antenna was capable of detecting, identifying, and tracking three simultaneous air targets, and it could launch and control up to six interceptor missiles.

The H-200's sensitivity was both a blessing and a curse. It made the radar very difficult to hide from, but it also resulted in a high number of false target alerts. The system latched on to commercial airliners and private aircraft with almost monotonous regularity.

Chao had little doubt that this latest inbound target alert would turn out to be yet another passenger jet. But he was too skilled and too dedicated to deviate from proper procedure. His keen eyes scanned rapidly down the columns of alpha-numeric target data, and then his pulse began to race.

This was not a single airliner straying out of the commercial air corridors; it was ten fast-moving targets, all traveling at altitudes of less

194

than 200 meters. Chao reacted automatically, his right palm shooting up to slam the threat warning alarm.

As the klaxon began its harsh repetitive cry, Chao was swiveling the microphone of his communications headset to a position in front of his lips. He keyed the circuit. "Watch Officer, this is the Radar Intercept Operator. I am tracking ten confirmed inbound targets, converging on this position. Flight profiles are consistent with land-attack cruise missiles. Request permission to arm the missile batteries."

The Watch Officer's voice sounded startled and confused. "Wait! You are certain? This could not be a system malfunction? Or a simulation?"

Chao cursed under his breath and then keyed the circuit again. "Sir, this is not a malfunction. It is not a simulation. This site is under attack, and the inbound missiles are closing at high speed. There is no time to discuss this, Lieutenant. I request permission to arm the missile batteries."

"If you are certain..." the Watch Officer said vaguely. "I mean, *yes*! You have permission to arm the missile batteries! Engage the inbound targets!"

Chao's hands were already moving over his keyboard. "Yes, sir. Arming missile batteries *now*."

The circular formation of twin-armed missile launchers came to life. All six batteries pivoted to different angles as the H-200 radar assigned a target to each launcher. A few seconds later, the first missile leapt off the rail, followed in rapid succession by five others.

The radar array was mounted to the front chassis section of a heavy duty ten-wheeled military vehicle. Chao sat in the H-200's operations cabin, a box-like steel structure which occupied the rear section of the vehicle's chassis, a few meters behind the huge rectangular radar sensor.

Despite the vehicle's heavy shock absorbers, he felt the rumbling vibration of the launching missiles propagate through the soles of his boots and into his feet. On the tracking screen, each of the interceptor missiles arced toward one of the incoming cruise missiles.

Chao Péng's mathematical and spatial orientation skills were much higher than average. He wasn't a genius by any accepted definition of the word, but he had an intuitive gift for solving problems of geometry and mathematics that would challenge or defeat the majority of the common population.

Early in his military training, a PLA captain had recognized Chao's ability to accurately estimate the terminus of a ballistic arc without calculating tools, or even scratch paper. Chao had an instinctive understanding of how objects moved through three-dimensional space, and how influences like gravity and wind resistance could affect their vectors.

His eyes were locked on the tracking screen. He didn't need any of those advanced skills right now to know that he was seconds away from death.

Between them, the twin-armed missile launchers carried twelve missiles: two per launcher. But the H-200 could only control six of those missiles at a time. The other six would have to wait for the second salvo, after the radar's fire control channels had been freed up by the failure or success of the first six missiles. But there wasn't going to be time for a second salvo.

That made the math both simple, and inescapable. There were ten inbound cruise missiles, only six of which had interceptors assigned to them. The other four inbounds were going to get a free ride to the target. As Chao Péng happened to be sitting at the precise center of the target area, that meant he was about to be obliterated.

For a quarter of a second, he considered throwing open the door of the operator cabin and running (literally) for his life. But there was no time to run. There was only time for the briefest possible flare of panic.

The enemy missiles were here.

He didn't hear the impact of the first cruise missile. He had a brief sensation of increasing weight as the heavy chassis of the radar vehicle left the ground on the rising crest of the shockwave. He caught a fleeting glimpse of the thick steel floor plate bending beneath his feet. Suddenly, the world seemed to come apart, with a sound and a fury that Chao Péng had never imagined.

And then there was nothing.

CHAPTER 47

The president took his chair at the head of the table. "Okay, tell me about this missile strike."

The Situation Room Duty Officer pointed a remote at the master display screen, and three high-resolution satellite photos appeared, enlarged to show detail. In each photo, a roughly circular pattern of blast craters was visible. Pieces of mangled machinery lay in and around the craters, blackened and twisted scraps of metal that gave little clue as to their original forms.

The Duty Officer looked at the president. 'Sir, we're looking at the remains of three PLA defensive missile sites, located—respectively—in the Chinese cities of Zigong, Chengdu, and Chongqing."

He thumbed the remote and a map of mainland China appeared, with the named cities circled in red. The three circles formed an almost perfect right triangle, rotated about ten degrees to the west, making the base roughly parallel to the nearby Yangtze river.

"According to NRO's reconstruction, all three sites were hit simultaneously by multiple long range weapons, fired from mobile launch vehicles in the Indian state of *Arunachal Pradesh*. Estimated flight speed of the weapons was Mach 0.7, and the transit range to each target was between 800 and 900 kilometers. Based on performance parameters and the relatively long standoff distance, we believe that the strike weapons may have been Nirbhay series land attack cruise missiles."

President Wainwright nodded. "What do we know about the target sites? Do these three cities have some military or political significance that would lead the Indians to select them as targets?"

The Secretary of Defense spoke up. "Not the cities themselves, sir," she said. "But the geographic locations of the three missile sites may be important."

The president gestured for her to continue.

The secretary took a laser pointer from the conference table, clicked it on, and swung the beam toward the master display screen. The laser dot hovered on the map, near the eastern end of the Indian state of Arunachal Pradesh. "This is the approximate launch site of the cruise missile strike," the secretary said.

She moved her hand, and the laser dot shifted to the east. "This is the location of the Three Gorges Dam, situated on the Yangtze River, near the town of Sandouping."

She began moving the laser pointer back and forth. On the master display, the laser dot traced and retraced a line from eastern India to the location of the Three Gorges Dam. On every pass, the line went right through the middle of the triangle formed by Zigong, Chengdu, and Chongqing.

The president looked at her. "You're saying that the Indians are clearing the flight path for a cruise missile strike against the Three Gorges Dam?"

SECDEF switched off the laser pointer and returned it to the table. "It looks that way, Mr. President. Assuming that they intend to launch from Arunachal Pradesh, they'd need to take out those three Chinese missile sites to get a clear shot at the target."

The president sighed. "So we're still stuck with this damned Shiva thing? I thought the Indians were supposed to call off the dogs when we agreed to help them take on the Chinese carrier group."

The National Security Advisor spoke up. "Sir, I've got an appointment with Ambassador Shankar at ten o'clock. That's obviously going to be the main topic of our conversation."

The president nodded. "But…"

"But I pretty much know what she's going to say," Brenthoven said. "They appreciate our help and our show of solidarity, but our contributions to the fight haven't stopped Chinese aggression."

The president said back in his chair. "So, the clock is still ticking."

"I'm afraid so, Mr. President," the National Security Advisor said. He glanced at his watch. "And we now only have about eleven hours before the Indians move forward with their plan."

CHAPTER 48

GREAT HALL OF THE PEOPLE
TIANANMEN SQUARE
BEIJING, CHINA
TUESDAY; 02 DECEMBER
8:49 PM
TIME ZONE +8 'HOTEL'

Jia Bangguo stood with his hands on the lacquered teak surface of the conference table. His eyes made a rapid circuit of the assembled leaders, taking in the other eight men who formed the Politburo Standing Committee of the Communist Party.

"Comrades," he said, "there is very little time. We must begin an emergency drawdown of the Three Gorges reservoir, and the entire Yangtze River Valley will have to be evacuated."

In nearly any other forum within the People's Republic, Jia's words would have brought a flurry of assents, followed by immediate action. As Second Vice Premier and Party Secretary of the National People's Congress, he was nominally the third most powerful man in China.

If this had been a meeting of the full politburo, he could have leveraged enough votes and proxies to challenge virtually any rival. But among the limited constituency of the Standing Committee, he had no ranks of ministers to flock to his banner. Here, at the heart of China's innermost-circle of leadership, he had only his own persuasiveness to draw on.

"There is very little time," he said again. "If we give the order at once, we can have the water in the Three Gorges catchment down to flood-control levels within two days. Then, if the dam is attacked, the flooding downstream will be a nuisance, not a disaster."

"Completely out of the question!" Ma Yong snapped. "Ludicrous! The hydroelectric turbines from Three Gorges serve almost fifteen percent of our nationwide power needs. If we lower the reservoir to flood-control levels, it will impact our industrial base, food production, transportation, communications… I can't even *begin* to calculate how badly our national economy would suffer."

Ma was Party Secretary of the Leading Group for Financial and Economic Affairs. His first, last, and only concern was the strength of the Chinese economy. This made him an instant opponent of any person or agency which threatened China's financial bottom line.

"Then I suggest a different calculation," Jia said. "Try calculating how badly our transportation and industry will be damaged when half the railroad bridges and road bridges in China are wiped out by catastrophic flooding. And while you are playing with numbers, you should try to estimate how long it will take your precious economy to recover when 400 million of our comrades are killed."

"Where is your proof?" Ma asked in an acid tone. "How do you *know* that the Indians will attack Three Gorges? Have they shared their secret plans with you? Or do you have your own intelligence sources, operating within the Indian government?"

"Of course not," Jia said. "But I can read a map. By eliminating our defensive missile sites at Chengdu, Zigong, and Chongqing, they have cleared a path for a cruise missile strike against the dam. I tell you, comrades—the Indians are planning to attack Three Gorges."

This brought low murmurs around the table.

First Vice Premier Lu Shi raised a hand and all conversation ceased. "Comrade Jia," he said slowly. "I do not doubt your sincerity, and your concerns are worthy of serious consideration. But there is such a thing as too *much* caution. As Comrade Ma has pointed out, we have no real evidence that our neighbors to the south are planning to destroy Three Gorges. Such an attack would constitute a direct and crippling strike against our national infrastructure. The Indian government understands that we would be forced to resort to strategic options."

That last phrase seemed to leave a breath of chill on the air. Among the senior elite of the Communist Party, the word 'strategic' was an accepted euphemism for 'nuclear.'

Wei Jintao, Party Secretary of the State Council, brought his fingertips together. "Perhaps it would be wise to deescalate the situation, before it becomes necessary to consider… ah… *strategic* options."

He looked toward Lu Shi. "If our goal was to punish India for harboring enemies of China, surely we have accomplished that. If our goal was to demonstrate military dominance in the region, we have accomplished that as well. I'm not sure what we can expect to gain by continuing this altercation with India."

Before Lu could respond, Jia spoke again. "Why are we speaking in circumlocutions? We're the top echelon of leadership in this country. If we cannot talk plainly here, how will we make the straightforward decisions that need to be made? If we are talking about nuclear weapons, we should not disguise that fact by referring to them as 'strategic options.' And we should stop pretending that this is some kind of 'altercation.' Everyone in this room knows that we have gone beyond that. When we strip away the ambiguous language, we are discussing the possibility of nuclear war with India."

He tapped a finger sharply on the table top. "Yes. I say the words openly. *Nuclear war.* We all need to think about those words, and we need to think about what they *mean.* Because we're stumbling blindly in that direction, and no one at this table wants to admit it."

Several of the committee members looked as if they wanted to agree, but none of them spoke.

Lu Shi regarded Jia coolly, but his voice remained level. "Again, Comrade Jia, I concede your sincerity, and I don't wish to make light of your concerns. But I think you are overreacting. We have vanquished the Indian aircraft carrier. We have shown the American Navy that they cannot interfere in the affairs of China without consequences. The major engagements are now over. There may be a few skirmishes to deal with, but the remaining tasks will be primarily political, not military."

Wei Jintao raised an eyebrow. "May we ask you to clarify that, Comrade Lu?"

Lu Shi didn't answer. Instead, Premiere Xiao Qishan cleared his throat. Every eye turned instantly in his direction.

Since the Premiere's triple bypass surgery the year before, there had been one overt attempt to force the old dragon out of office, and several behind-the-scenes maneuvers to nudge him into retirement. But Lu Shi had battled tirelessly to keep Xiao in power.

It was widely understood that Lu Shi would succeed Xiao Qishan as Premiere, which made his continued support of the aging leader something of a mystery. No one could understand why Lu Shi would deliberately postpone his own assent to ultimate power. Could it be something as simple as loyalty to the Premiere? Was Lu following a timetable which made the delay necessary, or desirable? Was it something else entirely? Although there was considerable speculation, no one seemed to have an answer.

Lu's motive for continuing to support Xiao Qishan was not clear, but the result was no secret at all. The Premiere repaid that support in-kind, by putting his own power and influence at the disposal of Lu Shi.

Xiao went through the motions of thoughtful deliberation and personal objectivity, but—when the rhetoric was sifted out and his actions were evaluated—the old leader backed Lu Shi's decisions every time.

Premiere Xiao cleared his throat again, more softly this time. Several of the faces turned in his direction had an expectant quality about them, as though some of the committee members were hoping that the gravity of the situation would force Xiao to break with Lu Shi, and reassert the firm hand of leadership. Pull them collectively back from what might be the edge of catastrophe.

If so, they were destined to be disappointed.

"The People's Republic of China is no longer a nation of peasants," Xiao said. "We are a global economic power, and the People's Liberation Army is rapidly becoming the preeminent military force on the planet. The other nations of the world must learn that we can no longer be backed into a corner."

Jia Bangguo and Wei Jintao exchanged glances across the table. The words coming from Xiao's mouth had clearly been scripted by Lu Shi.

The Premiere continued speaking. "I have transmitted instructions to our ambassadors in the United States and India, detailing our demands to the governments of both countries. If India wishes to return to normal relations with China, they must cease harboring our enemies, including the terrorists who continue to incite violence in the Tibetan Autonomous Region. As a gesture of good faith, they must begin by extraditing the criminal agitator, the Dalai Lama. By similar token, the United States is placed on notice... The days of the American military hegemony are ended. If they attempt to intrude in the affairs of the People's Republic, they will discover that their dwindling power is no longer a match for ours."

Lu Shi nodded. "Well said, Comrade Premier."

He pointed his fierce gaze at each of the other committee members. "This is our moment," he said. "The star of the West is falling, even as ours is ascending. If our will remains strong, we will *own* this century."

His voice grew quiet. "This is China's hour. We must not throw it away."

⚓ ⚓ ⚓

Ten minutes after the meeting adjourned, Jia Bangguo caught up with Wei Jintao on his way out of the building. Side by side, the two committee members strolled down the stone steps that led from the Great Hall of the People onto the flat expanse of Tiananmen Square. Both men had limousines idling at the curb, but they signaled for their drivers to wait, and they walked out past the security barriers to stand in the cold night air.

The seven determinative stars of *Bei Fang Xuan Wu*, the Black Warrior of the North, burned bright in the dark curtain of heaven. The ancient Chinese constellation was also known as the Black Tortoise. It was a symbol of winter, and the story of its creation dealt with terror, and death, and the unintended consequences of rash actions by men who were supposedly wise.

"I don't think he cares what happens," Jia said.

Wei Jintao said nothing.

"Lu Shi," Jia said. "I don't think he cares anymore. He is angry, and hurt, and he wants to punish someone for his grief. He destroyed the men who killed his son, along with the entire village where they were hiding. But that wasn't enough."

Wei looked at Jia. "What are you saying, Comrade?"

Jia Bangguo was starting to feel the bite of the winter air now. He flipped up the collar of his coat. "I'm saying that our Vice Premier is looking for an enemy to destroy, and he doesn't really care who it is. But worse than that, I think he has stopped caring about the consequences."

"That's crazy," Wei Jintao said. "I may not agree with many of his decisions, but Comrade Lu would never do anything to endanger the future of China. He loves this country more than he loves his own life."

"That's my point," Jia said. "I don't think he loves his life anymore. I don't think he cares about living at all."

Jia tilted his face up to the stars, his eyes tracing the outlines of the Black Tortoise. "If we don't do something quickly, I'm not sure that China will *have* a future."

CHAPTER 49

Captain Anthony Romano, commanding officer of USS *Midway*, watched the green-shaded areas continue to grow on the integrated damage control display. The screen showed a three-dimensional representation of the ship's interior construction—the decks, bulkheads, and hull fittings sketched out in ghostly shades of translucent gray, to allow the viewer to look through structural features in the foreground to see the compartments and passageways beyond.

The green shading represented sea water. Five of the compartments on the starboard side of the virtual ship image were filled with green from deck to overhead. Those were the parts of the ship that had flooded when the Chinese cruise missiles had punched through the ship's hull.

Thanks to automated damage control systems, good watertight integrity, and fast action by Romano's crew, the flooding had been contained to the smallest possible area. Now, after fighting hard to keep the seawater out, they were intentionally letting it in. On the damage control display, compartments on the port side of the ship were rapidly filling with green shading, as tons of water were pumped into sections of the ship that had previously been dry.

The technique was known as counter-flooding. It was an accepted method for restoring the trim of a warship when she had taken on enough flooding water to endanger her stability.

Romano had known about the concept since his very first course in shipboard damage control at Annapolis. As an intellectual exercise in the comfort of an academy classroom, counter-flooding had sounded like a logical way to cope with shipboard stability problems. But this was not the Naval Academy, and the thousands of gallons of seawater pouring into his ship were not at all theoretical.

204

This bright idea had come from Admiral Zimmerman himself. Just let in a little water on the port side, level the flight deck, and then they could launch aircraft.

Except that it wasn't a *little* water. It was a hell of a whole *lot* of water, and it wasn't going into bare compartments. It was going into two electronics spaces, an auxiliary equipment room, an air conditioning skid, and a fan room. Romano's technicians and engineers had spent several frantic hours trying to unbolt, disconnect, and remove as much equipment as possible from the compartments selected for counter-flooding, but their simply hadn't been time to relocate even a third of the hardware. And now, generators, power supplies, computers, hydraulic pumps, blower motors, and server racks were being immersed in corrosive salt water.

When the mission was over, the additional water could be pumped back out of the ship, but a lot of the equipment wouldn't be worth salvaging by then. The upcoming battle had not even started yet, and the *Midway* had already taken millions of dollars of additional damage. Maybe *tens* of millions.

Romano shook his head and suppressed a curse. The strike group was under Admiral Zimmerman's command, but the ship herself was Romano's responsibility. More than that, he loved the giant metal monstrosity with a fervor that he reserved for few human beings. He cherished every weld, every rivet, and every inch of deck plate from bow to stern. *Midway* was his girl, and he was not disposed to be friendly to anyone or anything that caused her harm.

He understood the reasoning behind the decision to do this, and he even agreed with it. But he damned well didn't have to be happy about it, and he wasn't.

The green shading on the damage control display had reached the overheads of the designated flooding spaces.

Captain Romano turned to his Damage Control Assistant. "What do you think, Steve?"

Lieutenant Steve Cohen checked the readouts on two adjacent computer screens. Then, he glanced up at the bubble inclinometer mounted on a transverse beam in the overhead. He nodded. "Looks like we're back in trim, Captain. The flight deck should be nice and level."

He tapped a few keys and checked a third display. "All that extra water has given us some additional draft, and we're going to lose some speed hauling it around."

"Hopefully, that won't be a problem," Romano said. "The Air Boss assures me that we can offset the loss in wind speed across the deck by cranking up the acceleration and release curve on EMALS. At least that's the idea. We won't know for certain until we try."

EMALS was short for *Electromagnetic Aircraft Launch System*, the next-generation flight deck technology that was replacing steam catapults on the newer classes of U.S. carriers. The new all-electric system was lighter, faster, and significantly more efficient than the mechanical steam systems which had preceded it. More importantly, EMALS provided an entirely new degree of precision control, allowing the system to safely launch everything from lightweight UAVs, to aircraft far beyond the weight limits of previous catapults.

In theory, an aircraft carrier equipped with EMALS could launch planes with less than 10 knots of relative wind across the flight deck. That was a far cry from the 30+ knots of relative wind required by carriers with old-style catapult systems.

They were about to find out if the theory was true.

Romano picked up a phone and punched the number for Flag Plot. "Admiral? This is Captain Romano. I'm on my way up to the bridge. We can set flight quarters any time you're ready, sir."

He listened for a couple of seconds, ended the call with a quick final courtesy, and then hung up the phone and headed for the door.

"This had better work," he said to himself. "This had *better* fucking work."

CHAPTER 50

USS TOWERS (DDG-103)
BAY OF BENGAL
TUESDAY; 02 DECEMBER
2356 hours (11:56 PM)
TIME ZONE +6 'FOXTROT'

The *Towers* moved through the night like a shadow, her phototropic camouflage seeming to wrap the long angular profile of the ship in an even deeper shade of darkness. A little more than 250 miles to the west—on the far side of the Chinese battle group—cruised her sister ship, USS *Donald Gerrard*. Both ships were running dark and quiet—all active sensors and transmitters shut down—their respective headings and speeds calculated to present the smallest possible cross-section to enemy radars.

Even the moonlight had been taken into account. According to the nautical almanacs, official moonset was still five minutes away, but the lower half of the silvery orb was already disappearing below the western horizon. By one minute after midnight, the last of the moon would be hidden behind the curve of the earth. Under simple starlight, the reactive camouflage that coated both ships would make them difficult to detect visually—either by human eye, or by optical sensors.

An adaptive infrared suppression system kept each ship's thermal footprint within half a degree of the ambient air temperature, and the ships' acoustic signatures had been minimized by seventh-generation silencing, active noise-control modules, and acoustically-isolated engineering plants.

Despite the rumors that floated around the internet, this cunning array of technologies did not render the American warships invisible. If there was a way to make 9,800 tons of steel vanish entirely, the engineers of the U.S. defense industry had not yet stumbled across the secret. Even in full stealth mode, USS *Towers* and USS *Donald Gerrard* were not undetectable. They were simply *less* detectable.

The distinction between those two states—undetectable, and less detectable—was very much on the mind of Commander Katherine Silva as she stood next to Captain Bowie in CIC and watched the Aegis tactical display. Under other conditions, the theoretical gap between a *low* detection threshold and a *zero* detection threshold might have been the subject of a stimulating technical debate. But under the current circumstances, that narrow theoretical gap could easily mean the difference between life and death.

On the screen, the blue symbols representing the *Towers* and the *Gerrard* were sliding into the red colored areas which depicted the radar coverage zones of the nearest Chinese warships. The zones were color-coded by estimated probability of detection: lighter shades of red for low probability, darker shades for high probability. Out at the fringes of the enemy's radar coverage, the color was a red so light that it verged on pink. Closer to the Chinese aircraft carrier, the reds deepened to the shade of blood.

The American ships were on nearly reciprocal courses, the *Towers* moving west and the *Gerrard* moving east, both converging slowly on the formation of Chinese warships that lay between them. At some point, the two U.S. Navy destroyers would pass some indefinable boundary, where microwave-deflecting hull geometries and radar-absorbent tiles could no longer hide them from the sensors of their enemies. The goal was to begin the attack *before* crossing that invisible threshold.

If all went according to plan, the Chinese wouldn't suspect the presence of the American ships until they detected incoming missiles. And then it would be too late.

Silva's eyes stayed locked on the display screen. Adjacent to the symbol for the *Towers* was a highlighted data-field containing the current calculated probability of detection, expressed as two sets of numerals separated by a slash: 62.0 / 7.8. The first set of digits—provided for purposes of comparison—was calibrated to the radar cross-section of a standard *Arliegh Burke* class destroyer. The second set of digits was adjusted for the minimized radar signature of a modified Flight III *Arliegh Burke* class ship.

Based on received signal strength at the ship's current position, the Aegis command and decision computer predicted a 62% chance that an unmodified *Arliegh Burke* destroyer would be detected by the Chinese radar, and a 7.8% chance that the same Chinese radar sensors would detect the *Towers*.

While Silva watched, the readout changed to 68.2 / 9.1, as USS *Towers* edged closer to the defensive screen of the Chinese aircraft carrier.

From an intellectual perspective, Silva acknowledged that nine percent didn't seem like bad odds, especially compared to the nearly seventy percent that a less stealthy ship would be facing right now. But for all the cutting-edge technology, there was nearly a one-in-ten chance that a Chinese radar operator would peer into the clutter of random sea returns on his scope, and spot a tiny smudge of pixels that represented USS *Towers*.

Silva tore her gaze away from the probability of detection readout, and took in the overall tactical situation. The enemy aircraft carrier was screened by four surface combatants: a pair of Type 054A (*Jiangkai II* class) multi-role frigates to the northwest and southwest, and a pair of Type 51C (*Luzhou* class) air-defense destroyers to the northeast and southeast. This put both of the Chinese destroyers on the eastern side of the formation—closest to the *Towers*—presumably to provide air coverage against the retreating *Midway* strike group.

The symbols for the Chinese ships were enclosed by ellipsoids of dotted lines, representing calculated areas of uncertainty. The enemy ships were estimated to be somewhere within those areas of uncertainty, but their exact positions were unknown.

With their own radar transmitters shut down, *Towers* and *Gerrard* were relying on tracking information from their AN/SLQ-32(V)3 electronic warfare systems. The SLQ-32 (or *Slick-32*, as the system's operators preferred to call it) was capable of detecting, identifying, and tracking virtually every search, targeting, or navigation radar devised by man. But for all its adaptability and processing power, the Slick-32 was a passive sensor. It could determine the direction of an enemy radar source; but it had no ability to measure how far away the hostile emitter might be. This bearing-only data was sufficient for targeting Harpoon missiles, but lacked the range information critical to most other weapon systems.

If the *Towers* and *Gerrard* had not been operating under strict emission control, they could have exchanged lines-of-bearing through the tactical net, establishing and maintaining cross-fixes for the enemy radars, neatly pinpointing each of the Chinese warships on a continual basis. Instead, they were making due with periodic data feeds from a *NightEagle III* unmanned aerial vehicle flying slow surveillance passes over the enemy formation at 20,000 feet.

Constructed from radar-transparent composites, the UAV was small, lightweight, and relatively stealthy. Every fifteen minutes or so, it pointed an ultraviolet diode laser to the heavens, and squirted a packet of digital information toward one of eleven Fleet SATCOM communications satellites in orbit. The satellite promptly encoded the UAV's targeting data, and transmitted it back toward the earth as an encrypted UHF radio signal, where it was received and decrypted by the two American destroyers.

During these periodic updates, the area of uncertainty for each Chinese ship shrank to a discrete point, and the *Towers* and *Gerrard* knew the exact position of every enemy vessel. But as the minutes ticked away and the Chinese ships maneuvered within their formation, the American Slick-32 systems could only track bearings. The estimations of target range became progressively less reliable, and the ellipsoid areas of uncertainty began to grow again.

The *NightEagle III* was capable of maintaining continuous uplink with the satellites, providing constant position updates for the enemy warships, but the UAV had been programmed to avoid detection. There were at least three flights of J-15 fighter jets circling over the area, providing air cover for the Chinese carrier. The UAV's laser communication link was covert, but it was not completely invisible.

Again, it came down to the difference between *undetectable*, and *less* detectable. The success or failure of this mission—life or death—depended on keeping the UAV and both American warships below the threshold of detection.

Any one of those Chinese planes might bounce a lucky radar echo off the *Towers* or the *Gerrard* at any time. One of the pilots might glance up (or down) at just the right angle, and catch a glimpse of a strange black shape against the waves, or a small winged silhouette against the night sky.

Silva knew she shouldn't be thinking such thoughts, but this was the part she hated. The waiting. The proverbial calm before the proverbial goddamned storm. That frozen eternity of inaction, where every second seemed to draw itself out to an edge as keen as a razor, and there was nothing to do but dwell on the endless list of things that could go wrong.

On the tactical display, the symbols for *Towers* and *Gerrard* were well into the deepening reds of the Chinese radar coverage now. The probability of detection readout said 88.1 / 17.6. There was nearly a one-in-five chance they'd be spotted, and the numbers were still climbing.

Splitting the difference between best-case and worst-case for the areas of uncertainty, the Chinese destroyers were a little over 40 nautical miles away. They were well within Harpoon range, but Silva knew from the pre-mission briefing that Captain Bowie intended to close another three miles before launching the strike.

Like most American surface combatants, the *Towers* carried only eight Harpoon anti-ship missiles. The USS *Donald Gerrard* carried eight as well. That only allowed four Harpoons per target, and the Chinese warships were supposed to have good anti-missile defenses.

Bowie wanted to be close enough to press the attack with naval gunfire, in case the limited inventory of Harpoons was not enough to guarantee a kill.

Even a year earlier, a gun attack from 37 miles would have been impossible. Against surface targets, the effective range of a standard 5-inch naval artillery shell was less than 20 nautical miles—a little better than half what was needed for Bowie's plan. But that had been before *Vulcano*.

Over the past several decades, there had been several attempts to develop rocket-assisted projectiles with enhanced ranges, but none of the U.S. efforts had ever panned out. The two most promising projects—the Ballistic Trajectory Extended Range Munition (BTERM), and the Extended Range Guided Munition (ERGM)—had been cancelled, due to budget overruns and lingering technical challenges.

The U.S. Navy had finally sidestepped the issue by procuring Vulcano rounds from the Italian arms firm, OTO-Melara. The Italian defense industry had succeeded where the American military-industrial complex had failed. OTO-Melara's 127mm Vulcano projectiles were fully compatible with the 5-inch guns aboard U.S. warships, and their maximum range was 40 nautical miles.

The gun crews aboard the *Towers* and *Gerrard* had been trained on the Vulcano rounds, and they'd racked up an impressive number of attack simulations using the new ammunition. But even the most accurate training simulators have practical limitations, and actual hands-on experience with the new projectiles had been limited to a handful of live firing exercises.

In view of this, and in light of the knowledge that the U.S. Navy had never employed Vulcano munitions under real-world combat conditions, Bowie had decided to edge a little nearer to the targets before launching the attack.

Silva agreed completely with the captain's reasoning. It made sense not to push their luck by relying on textbook assessments of a new weapon's capabilities. Better to build in a little safety margin, in case the textbooks turned out to be wrong.

But the probability of detection readout was still climbing. As Silva watched, it changed to 91.6 / 22.9. In another few minutes, the chance of getting caught would reach 30%. Definitely too high for comfort.

Silva looked around and met Bowie's gaze.

He raised one eyebrow slightly. "This must be what it feels like to be a submarine commander," he said.

He turned back to the master tactical display. "Trying to sneak into your enemy's sensor envelope without being detected. Knowing that the only things keeping you alive are silence, and luck."

Commander Silva nodded, but didn't say anything. Her eyes drifted back and forth between the estimated range to target, and the probability of detection. Two sets of numbers—one decreasing, and the other increasing. Silence and luck. Silence… and luck. Silence…

A burst of encrypted UHF came in on the downlink from Fleet SATCOM, carrying the latest targeting fixes from the *NightEagle III*. On the Aegis display screen, the areas of uncertainty for the Chinese ships shrank instantly to distinct points.

Captain Bowie looked over the target geometry, judging angles and distances against whatever image of the battle plan he carried in his head. He nodded, cleared his throat, and spoke loudly. "Let's do it."

And suddenly, it was time.

CHAPTER 51

USS TOWERS (DDG-103)
BAY OF BENGAL
WEDNESDAY; 03 DECEMBER
0013 hours (12:13 AM)
TIME ZONE +6 'FOXTROT'

The Tactical Action Officer keyed the net. "Weapons Control—TAO. You have batteries released. Kill *Surface Contact Zero One* and *Surface Contact Zero Two* with Harpoons."

The acknowledgement came immediately. "Weapons Control, aye."

A handful of seconds later, the steel deck vibrated with the syncopated rumble of anti-ship cruise missiles blasting free of their launch tubes.

"TAO—Weapons Control. Four birds away, no apparent casualties. Targeted two-each on the hostile surface contacts."

Commander Silva watched four friendly weapons symbols blink into existence on the tactical display, and race toward a set of programmed navigational waypoints on the far side of the targets. "How long until the second salvo?"

"About three minutes," Captain Bowie said.

The plan was to launch the attack in two stages. The first salvo of missiles would fly past the enemy warships, remaining below the radar horizon for the Chinese sensors. When the Harpoons had covered half the distance to their respective waypoints, the second salvo of missiles would be launched toward their own waypoints, on the near side of the targets.

The timing of the launches was calculated to bring all of the Harpoons to their final navigational waypoints at the exact same instant. Then, the missiles would simultaneously turn toward the targets and shift into terminal attack phase, their radar seekers going active as they homed in for the kill.

On the western side of the battle group, the USS *Donald Gerrard* would be carrying out a mirror image of the attack against the two frigates on her edge of the enemy formation.

The tactic was called *simultaneous time-on-target*. If it was executed properly, each Chinese escort ship would suddenly find itself with four incoming Harpoon missiles, all converging from different points of the compass.

The *Jiangkai II* multi-role frigates and the *Luzhou* air-defense destroyers were known to carry strong anti-ship cruise missile defenses. Faced with one (or even several) Harpoons coming in from the same general direction, there was an excellent chance that the Chinese ships could intercept most or all of them. But the odds that they could simultaneously engage four hostile missiles from widely-separated bearings were much lower.

If the latest tactical assessments were accurate, a simultaneous time-on-target attack should yield one or two successful hits on each of the enemy destroyers and frigates.

For Silva, time had somehow shifted into overdrive. The three minutes between missile salvos seemed to flash by in a few seconds, and then the deck was vibrating with the launch of the second set of Harpoons. Four new friendly weapons symbols popped up on the Aegis display screen, and instantly began vectoring toward their assigned waypoints.

The missiles had been in flight less than a minute when a report from the Electronic Warfare module broke over the net. "TAO—EW. I have two X-band emitters, bearing two-eight-zero. Signal characteristics and pulse repetition frequencies are consistent with fire control radars for Chengdu J-15 fighter aircraft."

Before anyone had time to react to this message, it was followed by a report from the Air Warfare Supervisor. "TAO—Air. The data stream from *NightEagle III* just chopped off in mid-transmission."

The TAO keyed his mike. "Air—TAO. Clarify your report. Have you lost the satellite downlink?"

"TAO—Air. That's a negative, sir. We've still got a good latch on SATCOM 7, but the satellite has lost comms with the drone."

Silva made eye contact with Bowie. "Captain, unless I miss my guess, a Chinese air patrol just blasted our UAV out of the sky."

Her assessment was confirmed by the Officer of the Deck about two seconds later. "TAO—Bridge. Lookouts are reporting a fireball bearing two-seven-five. Position angle fifty-one."

Bowie turned toward the TAO. "Stand by to go active on SPY. Our Chinese friends have just figured out that we're in the neighborhood. I want to be ready to shift to full Aegis combat mode on a second's notice."

He raised his voice so that the entire CIC crew could hear him. "Listen up, people. It's about to get hot around here. Let's stay sharp, and be ready for anything."

On the Aegis display, the Harpoon missile symbols were reaching their final waypoints and turning toward the enemy warships. The missiles were sea skimmers, hugging the wave tops to remain below the radar coverage of the target vessels until the last possible instant. In another ninety seconds or so, they would become visible to the Chinese radar operators.

Bowie had no intention of giving the enemy ships time to react properly to the incoming missiles. He nodded to the TAO. "Nail 'em with the gun."

The Tactical Action Officer relayed the order to Weapons Control, and the ship jerked as the 5-inch deck gun loosed its first round. The muzzle report reverberated through CIC like a clap of thunder, only partially muffled by the steel bulkheads and insulated lagging that separated the compartment from the gun deck.

The gun cycled into its auto-load sequence, pumping out another projectile every three seconds, with bone-jarring booms. When the first five rounds were in the air, the gun swung its aim toward the second Chinese destroyer, and pumped out another five shells. Then the gun shifted its attention back to the first destroyer, and fired another five-round salvo.

⚓ ⚓ ⚓

Vulcano Round:

Moving at a half mile per second, the first round took just under 74 seconds to close the distance to the target. As the projectile neared the end of its trajectory, the canard control module near the nose took a fix from GPS and compared the result to the position estimate from its own inertial measurement unit. The control module adjusted the angle of the stubby canard fins, and the Vulcano round pitched over into its terminal descent phase.

The infrared sensor locked onto the largest heat source within its field of view. The canard control module made a final angular correction, and the self-guided artillery shell streaked down toward the target like a meteor.

The *Luzhou* class destroyer was powered by two steam turbines of indigenous Chinese design. When the first round of the artillery barrage began falling from the sky, the strongest thermal signature was a plume of superheated gas rising from the forward exhaust stack.

The first Vulcano round punched through the hottest part of the exhaust trail about six feet above the stack, missing the destroyer cleanly, striking the water about fifteen yards off the ship's port quarter. It exploded on impact, sending out a shower of shrapnel that either fell into the sea or pinged harmlessly off the metal flanks of the warship.

Three seconds later, the next Vulcano round missed the Chinese vessel by an even wider margin. Then, the third shell arrived.

⚓ ⚓ ⚓

PLA Navy Ship *Shijiazhuang* (*Luzhou* class destroyer #116):

Junior Lieutenant Dong Jie swung his binoculars to the right, and frantically scanned the sky to the starboard side of the ship. The Watch Officer and Tactical Lookout were gathered at the port side bridge windows, trying to get a look at the points of impact for the two explosions that had occurred so suddenly off the port side of the ship.

But they were looking the wrong way. The rockets, or artillery shells, or whatever they were, had come from the east. Dong had heard them distinctly, a strange whistling noise so high-pitched that his ears could barely detect it. What *was* that sound? What was causing the explosions?

And then he was hearing the whistling noise again, coming from the east, just like the last two times. He turned toward the Watch Officer, and said, "ting!" (Listen!) But the Watch Officer *wasn't* listening.

Dong moved swiftly to the watertight door at the starboard side of the bridge. He yanked up the dogging handle, pulled the door open, and stepped out onto the starboard catwalk under the stars. The cold night air hit him like a blow from a hammer, but he *had* to know where that sound was coming from.

Whatever it was must be too small to see on radar, because the scopes on the bridge were clear of any incoming contacts, and the radar operators were not reporting anything out of the ordinary.

He lifted his binoculars to his eyes and scanned the darkened sky. He saw nothing up there but stars. Who could be doing this? The Indians? The Americans? But they were all gone. Defeated, and chased from the field of battle...

Through the open bridge wing door, Dong could hear the buzz of the telephone. That would be the captain, demanding a report on the source of the unidentified explosions.

The whistling noise was increasing in volume. Dong thought he caught a glimpse of something for a fraction of an instant—a blurred flicker of motion as some small dark shape arced down from the black face of the heavens.

And then he was blinded by an impossibly bright flash of light. His feet left the deck as the shockwave and shrapnel of the detonating shell tore into his body, hurling him back through the open doorway into the bridge.

There were reports coming over the speakers now, the excited voice of the radar Officer jabbering about the sudden appearance of four incoming missiles, all closing from different bearings. Shouted orders to defensive weapons systems.

But Dong Jie's stunned ears were filled with the distant rhythm of his own pulse. Fast at first, but then slowing... Slowing...

He closed his eyes, and then opened them again. The view didn't change. Whether his eyelids were open or shut, he could see nothing but the searing white afterimage of the explosion.

His brain didn't register the chainsaw snarl of the Gatling guns spewing bursts of 30mm slugs into the night. He didn't see the two fireballs erupt in the darkness as the twin streams of high-velocity bullets shredded two of the incoming missiles. He didn't see the Gatling guns swing toward their next targets.

And he didn't see the last of the American Harpoons slip in past the fusillade of defensive fire, and dart in for the kill.

⚓ ⚓ ⚓

USS *Towers*:

"TAO—Weapons Control. Harpoons on top, *now!*"

Bowie didn't hesitate. "Go active on SPY!"

A few seconds later, the giant Aegis display screens began populating with hostile contact information: five hostile surface ship symbols, and four pairs of hostile aircraft symbols.

For a brief instant, sixteen friendly missile symbols were superimposed—in groups of four—on top of the symbols for the Chinese frigates and destroyers. Then the blue missile icons vanished from the display, leaving behind the symbols representing the enemy warships.

Commander Silva watched the Harpoon symbols wink out. How many of the missiles had gotten through, and how many had been destroyed before they could reach their targets? More importantly, how many of the Chinese carrier's escort ships were still in the fight?

With the UAV gone, there was no way to get real-time battle-damage assessment. It might take several minutes to sort out which ships were capable of maneuvering and firing, and which were not. But the out-numbered American destroyers couldn't wait around to find out.

"Keep hitting them with the gun," Bowie said. 'Five rounds, shift targets—five rounds, and shift back."

Every three seconds, the big deck gun barked again, and another Vulcano round began its long flight toward one of the *Luzhou* class destroyers.

Somewhere on the far side of the Chinese aircraft carrier, the USS *Donald Gerrard* was dishing out similar punishment to the frigates on the western perimeter of the enemy formation.

So far, the attack had gone according to plan. The surprise had worked perfectly, but the cat was most definitely out of the bag now. With their SPY radars pumping several million watts of microwave power into the atmosphere, the *Towers* and the *Gerrard* had lost all semblance of stealth.

The enemy fighters knew where they were now. The time for skulking was over.

This was proven about ten seconds later, as the Air Warfare Supervisor's voice came over the net. "TAO—Air. Four Bogies inbound. Two flights of two. Looks like the other four are going after the *Gerrard*!"

"TAO, aye. Stand by."

The Tactical Action Officer looked toward Bowie. "Captain, request batteries released on hostile air contacts."

Bowie nodded. "Granted."

The Tactical Action Officer turned back toward his console and keyed his mike. "Weapons Control—TAO, you have batteries released. Engage and destroy all Bogies within our engagement envelope!"

On the Aegis display screen, two pairs of red hostile aircraft symbols were converging on the *Towers*.

There was another clap of thunder as the 5-inch gun pounded out another Vulcano round toward one of the enemy surface ships. The sound was instantly followed by the roar of launching missiles.

"TAO—Weapons Control. Four birds away, no apparent casualties. Targeted one each on the inbound Bogies."

The TAO was reaching for his mike button when another report broke over the net. "TAO—Air. Bogies are launching. I count eight missiles inbound."

The Tactical Action Officer keyed into the circuit. "All Stations—TAO, we have in-bound Vipers! I say again, we have missiles in-bound! Weapons Control, shift to Aegis ready-auto. Set CIWS to auto-engage. Break. EW, stand by to launch chaff!"

The Electronics Warfare Technician's response came a split-second later. "TAO—EW, standing by on chaff. I'm tracking eight active H-band seekers, consistent with SSN-27 Sizzlers. Request permission to initiate jamming."

"EW—TAO. Permission granted. Jam at-will."

A prolonged series of rumbles announced the launch of multiple SM-3 missiles, followed by the voice of the Air Warfare Supervisor. "TAO—Air. Sixteen birds away, no apparent casualties. Targeted two-each on the inbound Vipers."

The Aegis computers were following a *shoot-shoot-look-shoot-shoot* doctrine: fire two interceptor missiles at each incoming cruise missile, evaluate with radar to see which ones had been destroyed, and then fire two more missiles at any Vipers that survived the first salvo. Unless overridden by human intervention, Aegis would continue to follow this pattern until *Towers* expended fifty percent of her available SM-3 missiles. Then the computers would automatically throttle back to a *shoot-look-shoot-shoot* doctrine.

The Aegis display screen had become a bewildering swarm of cryptic red and blue icons. Silva's eyes darted from symbol to symbol, trying to make sense of the rapidly-evolving tactical situation. The complexity of the battle picture had increased beyond the integration capacity of the human mind. The fight had shifted into the realm of man-machine symbiosis, where the human operators were completely dependent on the processing and correlation capabilities of the computers, and the computers were equally dependent on the humans for intuitive decisions and periodic flashes of tactical brilliance.

The left third of the display screen, corresponding to the western side of the Chinese battle group, was every bit as complex. The *Gerrard* was neck-deep in her own fight, and the missiles—both incoming and outgoing—were flying fast and furious.

Amidst the chaos of iconography, the red symbol for *Surface Contact Zero Two* flashed, and was replaced by a last-known-position marker. The warship had disappeared from radar. Either it had been sunk, or it had been blasted into pieces too small to present a radar return. Either way, it was gone.

Silva tapped Bowie on the shoulder and pointed toward the screen. "Captain, we just got a hard kill on one of our surface targets."

Bowie shifted his attention from the air-battle to the surface symbols, just as the Surface Warfare Coordinator was reporting the destruction of the enemy ship.

The captain gave Silva a nod. "You've got a quick eye." He keyed his mike. "TAO—Captain. Shift all 5-inch gunfire to *Surface Contact Zero One.*"

On the screen, hostile and friendly missile symbols began merging. "TAO—Air. Splash three Vipers. We have five remaining inbounds."

"TAO, aye. Break. EW—TAO. Launch chaff."

The Electronic Warfare operator acknowledged the order. "Launch chaff, aye."

His report was punctuated by a rapid series of muffled thumps. "Six away."

Out in the darkness, a half dozen blunt-nosed projectiles rocketed out of the forward Super-RBOC launchers. The Super Rapid-Blooming Overboard Chaff canisters flew through the air to explode at pre-determined points, scattering metallic confetti and clouds of aluminum dust to attract the radar seekers of incoming weapons.

There was another rumble, as the Aegis computers fired another set of SM-3 interceptor missiles.

"TAO—Air. Ten birds away, no apparent casualties. Targeted two-each on the remaining inbound Vipers."

On the tactical display, the four SM-3 missiles that had been fired toward the Chinese fighter planes were now reaching their targets. One of the enemy aircraft flashed and vanished from the screen, replaced by a last-known-position marker.

"TAO—Air. Splash one Bogie. The remaining Bogies are turning south."

The Tactical Action Officer nodded. "The SSN-27 is a heavy weapon. They might not be carrying more than two."

"Maybe," Bowie said. "But let's not count on that."

The ten outbound interceptor missiles merged with the five incoming Vipers. When the jumble of symbols sorted themselves out, three of the hostile missiles were still closing.

Bowie grimaced. "We're always hearing about how tough it is to intercept the SSN-27, but *Jesus…* What does it take to shoot those damned things down? Kryptonite?"

One of the hostile missile symbols veered abruptly to the side, and then vanished.

"TAO—Air. One taker on chaff. No takers on jamming."

The remaining two Vipers were practically touching the *Towers* symbol on the screen.

"TAO—Weapons Control. Two of the Vipers got through. They've kicked into terminal homing phase, and they're too close to re-engage with missiles. Forward CIWS mount is engaging."

The air throbbed with the staccato growl of the Close-In Weapon System as it sprayed a burst of 20mm tungsten rounds toward one of the incoming cruise missiles. There was a deafening boom as the Viper exploded just a few hundred yards away from the ship.

The CIWS mount spun toward the next target and began firing. It was almost in time.

⚓ ⚓ ⚓

SSN-27:

A half-second before impact, the nose section of the missile was hammered into fragments by a hail of tungsten penetrator rounds, shattering the radar seeker head and the guidance mechanism. If the weapon had been even fifty meters away from its target, the damage might have been enough to send it spiraling into the sea. But the SSN-27 was moving at more than twice the speed of sound, and the resulting inertia carried the blinded missile the last few meters to its destination.

The SSN-27 struck the port side of the American warship, about four meters below the main deck. All of the weapon's sophisticated proximity sensors and influence triggers had been pulverized by CIWS, but the brute simplicity of the contact detonator had survived.

In the microsecond of contact, the mechanical force of the impact propagated down the length of the missile, compressing a simple cylindrical rod of nickel ferrite mounted at the core of a short magnetic coil. Through the physical principle of magnetostriction, the deformation of the nickel rod created a tiny but distinct magnetic pulse, which expanded over the windings of the coil, generating an electrical signal. This signal was calibrated to satisfy the triggering threshold of the primer mechanism buried in the missile's warhead.

Two-hundred kilograms of Cyclotri-methylene Trinitramine flashed into a shaped cone of raw force that punched through the hull of the warship with the power of a runaway locomotive. Steel plating buckled like paper. Reinforced steel beams shrieked and gave way before the unstoppable onslaught of heat and atmospheric overpressure. A flaming torrent of shrapnel and destruction lanced deep into the heart of the ship through the widening hole.

And then there came chaos and death.

CHAPTER 52

There was a strangely-eternal moment when everything seemed to be playing out in slow motion. Silva could hear the Officer of the Deck's voice over the ship's 1-MC speakers, instructing the crew to brace for shock. Someone was requesting an update on the status of the remaining Viper. On the Aegis display screen, the red shape of a hostile missile symbol could be seen merging with the blue circle that represented USS *Towers*.

Silva was standing next to Captain Bowie, a few feet behind the Tactical Action Officer's chair, and there wasn't much within easy reach to grab on to.

Bowie took a grip on a crossbeam above his head, and Silva turned toward a stanchion to her right: a steel support column that ran from the deck to the overhead. She got her hands wrapped around the pole, lowered her head, and bent her knees slightly—trying to mimic the brace-for-shock posture that every Sailor learns, but few expect to ever actually need.

And then the long second ended, and the passage of time jumped from its impossibly languorous stupor, to the speed of sheer pandemonium.

The shockwave tore through Combat Information Center like a hurricane, and the air was suddenly filled with flying debris, body parts, and the screams of the injured and the dying. Every loose article in the compartment, every grease pencil, and clipboard, and coffee mug was instantly airborne, and accelerating away from the point of impact with the speed of the expanding wave front.

The SLQ-32 stations in the EW Module and the radar consoles in tracker alley absorbed and deflected some of the force of the blast. Several of the consoles were ripped from their mounts, display screens exploding

222

into showers of glass, the fragments driving deep into the faces and bodies of the human operators.

Silva's grip was jerked away from the stanchion. She was thrown against a status board hard enough to crack the shatterproof window of Plexiglas. The impact knocked all breath out of her, and the side of her head smacked into the metal frame of the status board. She crumpled to the deck in a senseless heap.

Cooling water sprayed from ruptured pipes, and severed electrical cables arced and shorted, tripping circuit breakers. The overhead lighting went out, and the next half-second of carnage and confusion took place in total darkness.

Then the battle lanterns kicked on, illuminating the devastated compartment in the dim red glow of battery-powered emergency lighting.

The giant Aegis display screens were dark. Red and amber tattletales blinked fitfully on most of the remaining consoles, signaling various degrees of physical and electronic damage.

Silva lay on her back, watching the strange interplay of lights and shadows on the overhead—the glow of the battle lanterns, muted and twisted by tendrils of smoke from the explosion, the pulsing flicker of warning lights, and the dimly-perceived silhouettes of people stumbling around in the semi-darkness. The air was heavy with the acrid odor of burnt chemicals, melted electrical insulation, and scorched flesh.

It seemed likely that fires were burning somewhere nearby, but the possibility didn't seem very important to Silva's addled brain. At some point, she realized that the lower left sleeve of her coveralls was smoldering. The fabric was supposed to be flame-retardant, and apparently it was. Otherwise, her sleeve would probably be blazing merrily right now.

It gradually dawned on her that she was supposed to get up off the deck. There were things she needed to be doing. She just couldn't remember what they were.

Her ears were still ringing from the blast, but she could hear frantic voices coming from the overhead speakers. Reports. Damage inquiries. Requests for orders. No one seemed to be paying attention to any of them.

Her head lolled to the left, and she found herself looking at a man lying on his side, in a spreading pool of blood. His face was familiar. She had seen him somewhere. Maybe she had met him, or something...

No. That wasn't right. She *knew* him. It was Bowie. *Captain* Bowie.

That single coherent thought—that simple and basic act of identification—became the spark that restarted Silva's conscious mind. She began to take in and process information again. The world slid back into focus, and with it came pain, in her head, her ribs, and her left wrist.

More bruises than she could count, and she was bleeding from the area of her left temple, but nothing seemed to be broken.

She tried to lever herself up to a sitting position, and immediately revised her assessment as a wave of stomach-churning pain radiated from her left arm. Okay, maybe the wrist was broken.

Silva rolled to her right, coming up on her knees and her good right arm. There were fires burning near the port side of CIC, and that area of the compartment was hazy with smoke. As Silva watched, three or four Sailors converged on the flames with CO_2 fire extinguishers, smothering the blaze with white clouds of carbon dioxide gas.

Silva was steeling herself to get to her feet when a flicker of motion caught her eye. Bowie was motioning to her, the index finger of his right beckoning feebly.

She got a better look at him. The deck matting around him was slick with dark liquid. His left hand was pulled in tight to his chest, palm pressing flat against a spot near his sternum. The fabric of his coveralls was peppered with small ragged holes, and—judging from the blood that coursed between his fingers—there was a much larger hole under his hand.

His eyes were locked on Silva's. She could tell that, even under the weak red glow of the battle lanterns.

She scuttled over to him as quickly as she could, knees slipping on the slick deck matting. When she was close enough, she reached out with her good hand, and tried to help him maintain pressure on the chest wound.

She tried to call out, but her voice seemed to stick in her throat. She swallowed, and tried again. "Corpsman! I need a corpsman over here!"

She didn't look up from Bowie's chest wound, trying to help him slow the bleeding.

She shouted again, and her voice was startlingly loud. "The captain is *down*! Somebody get a corpsman over here, right fucking *NOW*!"

She began glancing around, trying to spot something she could use as an emergency dressing. Anything to staunch the wound until real medical help arrived.

Something touched her shoulder. She looked down in time to see Bowie's right hand slide off her arm and fall to the deck. His lips were moving.

Silva gave him what she hoped was a reassuring look. "Don't talk now, Jim. Just rest a minute. The corpsman will be here any second."

Bowie grunted, and a rivulet of blood ran from the corner of his mouth. His voice was barely above a whisper. "Closer..."

Silva leaned in until her face was just a few inches from his.

Bowies eyelids slid shut. When they reopened, they moved slowly, as though even the act of opening his eyes took a supreme effort of will.

"She's yours now..." he said. "She's..."

Then someone was kneeling on Bowie's other side. Fast, competent hands searching the captain's body for other injuries.

"Keep the pressure on, ma'am," a voice said. "I'll have a dressing ready in a second."

Silva kept her eyes on Bowie's, so she didn't see the face of the corpsman.

The man yelled, "I need a litter over here, and two bearers! Stat!"

His hands were rummaging through a green canvas zipper bag, fishing out packets of bandages, wrapped in brown sterile paper pouches. "Almost ready," he said. "Just another couple of seconds."

Bowie groaned and then blinked slowly. "She's yours, Kat," he whispered. "You're..."

He coughed wetly, and took a painful breath. "You're the captain, now..."

Silva shook her head. "No, Jim. You're going to be fine. "You're going to..."

"No!" Bowie snapped. His voice was something between a moan and a growl. His eyes blazed with a ferocity that Silva had never seen in him.

The corpsman's fingers were pulling Silva's hand away, working quickly to slide a thick stack of gauze onto the wet hole in the captain's chest.

"This is... my... last... order..." Bowie rasped. "Take command! Take..."

His words trailed off into silence, and he let out a long slow breath. He didn't draw another one.

The corpsman shouted, "Litter bearer! Over here! I need some help!"

And then someone else was kneeling, squeezing in next to Silva on the blood-slick deck.

The corpsman made eye contact with Silva. "Captain? We need a little room here, okay, ma'am?"

Silva nodded, and backed away, shuffling on her knees until she had enough clear deck space to stumble to her feet.

Her head throbbed with the too-rapid motion, and she staggered for a second or two before she found her footing. Her vision was blurry, partly from the rush of pain, and partly from the tears that were suddenly running down her cheeks.

She blinked them away, and took a half dozen unsteady steps to the TAO's station. "Are your comms working?"

The TAO nodded dumbly.

Silva reached for his headset. "Patch me into the 1-MC."

The Tactical Action Officer looked at her, glanced down at the spot where the corpsmen were working feverishly over their downed captain. Then, he looked back to Silva. He punched three keys in succession, and handed over the comm set.

Silva didn't bother with the ear pieces. She raised the microphone to her mouth, and keyed the circuit. When she spoke, her voice came from public address speakers all over the ship.

"All hands, this is Commander Katherine Elizabeth Silva. It is my sad duty to inform you that Captain Bowie is down. He..." She stopped for a second, trying to figure out how to phrase her next words.

She keyed the mike again. "In accordance with my formal written orders from Commander Chief of Naval Personnel, and in accordance with my verbal orders from Captain Bowie, I have now assumed command of this vessel."

She took a breath and continued. "This battle is not over yet, and we are not out of the action. I have every confidence in this ship, and in every man and woman of her crew. Now... Let's get back on our feet and get back into the fight!"

She released the mike button, and scanned the compartment. Every face in CIC was turned in her direction.

She spotted the face she was looking for, and nodded in OS2 Kenfield's direction. "Hey, Big Country... Give us a song."

The big Sailor's face was bruised and bloodied, but his lips parted slowly, in a hesitant grin. "Is that an order, ma'am?"

"You bet your ass it is," Silva said.

The Sailor stood up straighter, and squared his shoulders. "Aye-aye, Captain!" He cleared his throat, sucked a deep lungful of air, and cut loose with his customary rebel yell.

The ship was wounded. Many of the people in CIC were dead or injured. Small sporadic fires were burning in various places around the compartment, and the beloved and heroic Captain Bowie was being carried out the door on a stretcher. But every able person within earshot joined in Big Country's song. The rebel yell seemed to shake the very air, becoming the vocal personification of determination, courage, and defiance.

It was unprofessional. It was silly. It was magnificent.

Captain Silva wiped the last of the tears from her eyes with her uninjured right hand. "Alright people," she said. "Let's go kick some ass!"

CHAPTER 53

USS CALIFORNIA (SSN-781)
BAY OF BENGAL
WEDNESDAY; 03 DECEMBER
0048 hours (12:48 AM)
TIME ZONE +6 'FOXTROT'

The Sonar Supervisor's voice came over the net, "Conn—Sonar. Sierra One Seven is flooding his tubes! Looks like he's going in for the kill, sir!"

Captain Patke scanned the unfolding geometry on the tactical display screen. Contact Sierra One Seven, the *Shang*, was setting up for a torpedo attack against one of the American warships. If the surface plot was accurate, the target would be the destroyer, USS *Towers*. But it didn't really matter which of the ships had fallen into the crosshairs of the *Shang*. What mattered was that a Chinese nuclear attack submarine was about to sink a U.S. Navy vessel. That—in spite of Patke's personal opinions about the shortcomings of the skimmer navy—was not a satisfactory arrangement.

He keyed his headset. "Conn, aye. Any sign that Sierra One Seven is alerted to our presence?"

"Conn—Sonar. Negative, sir. Sierra One Seven has shown no reaction to us at all."

Patke checked the bearing to the Chinese submarine, and thought about coming a few degrees to port, to improve his firing angle on the enemy boat. He decided against the maneuver. No sense in polishing the cannonball.

He glanced over toward the combat control module. "Weapons Control, how's your plot?"

The Fire Control Technician of the Watch looked over his shoulder and gave a thumbs-up gesture. "In the groove, Captain. I have a firm firing solution on contact Sierra One Seven."

Patke nodded. "Very well. Flood tubes one and three. Assign presets, and spin up the weapons."

The Fire Control Tech turned back to his console and began punching soft-keys. "Aye-aye, sir. Flooding tubes one and three. Prepping both weapons for launch."

Patke pulled off his wire rimmed spectacles and polished them with a fold of his dark blue coveralls. His outward demeanor was calm and his voice was even, but he could feel the adrenaline burning at the back of his throat.

This was not a drill. In a few seconds, he was going to give an order that would kill other human beings. Not empty target ships. Not blips on a screen. Not computer simulations. Real living, breathing people, who would neither be living nor breathing after his order had been carried out.

With his eyeglasses off, Patke's vision beyond arm's-length was a blur of indistinct shapes. But he didn't need his eyes to know what was going on. The men and women of his control room crew were moving quickly and proficiently, performing their assigned duties with quiet competence.

They were trained. They were skilled. They were ready. Or, as ready as anyone could ever be for this sort of thing.

He gave the lenses of his glasses a final polish, and returned them to their customary spot on the bridge of his nose. "Open outer doors on tubes one and three. Firing point procedures."

As the orders were being acknowledged and carried out, someone to his left muttered something nearly inaudible.

Patke turned to see the Officer of the Deck. "Say again. I didn't catch that."

The OOD looked surprised. "Oh. Sorry, Captain. I didn't mean to say that out loud."

Patke raised an eyebrow. "If you've got something to say, son... *Now* is the time."

The OOD gave him an expression that was half-grimace, and half-embarrassed grin. "I was just saying '*snickerdoodles*,' sir."

Patke frowned. "Snickerdoodles?"

"Yes, sir," the OOD said. "Like we were talking about last time. Almost getting an ass-whuppin' when somebody else stole the cookies. But *we're* stealing the cookies this time, aren't we, sir?"

"You're right about that," Patke said softly. "We are *definitely* going to steal the cookies this time."

The Sonar Supervisor's voice came over the net again. "Conn—Sonar. Torpedo in the water! Sierra One Seven has a weapon in the water! He's going after the destroyer, sir!"

Patke raised his voice. "Weapons Control, this is the Captain. Match generated bearings, and shoot!"

⚓ ⚓ ⚓

USS *Towers*:

The giant display screens flashed, strobed with random bars of color for several seconds, and then snapped suddenly into focus.

The Tactical Action Officer turned toward Silva. "Aegis is back on line, Captain."

The screens began populating with symbols. First, the *Towers* and the *Gerrard* appeared, followed quickly by the two remaining hostile surface ships: the carrier and one of the Chinese destroyers. Then, the hostile aircraft symbols began appearing, and—for a few seconds—Silva wondered if the Aegis computers were malfunctioning. As new enemy air symbols continued to pop up on the screen, she began to *hope* that it was a malfunction.

She whistled softly through her teeth. "Jesus… How many planes are those guys going to launch?"

The TAO gave her a half-hearted smile. "Looks like *all* of them, ma'am."

The sheer absurdity of the situation hit her then. She had been in command for all of ten minutes. Half of her CIC consoles were out of action. She had no idea how many of her crewmembers were dead or dying. There was a hole in the side of her ship big enough to drive a minivan through. And China's shiny new aircraft carrier was about to shove its entire air wing down her throat.

It was like being twelve years old again. Standing on the uneven planks of her homemade raft, being swept down the river by forces beyond her control. Powerless to fight the current. Her plastic milk jugs and inner tubes bobbing helplessly on the waves.

She felt her jaws tighten. The river had been stronger than she was. Her raft, the *Spray*, had been tiny and frail. But she had gotten her homemade vessel back to shore. She had brought her ship safely home. And she was *damned* well going to do it again.

She made eye contact with the TAO. "We need to go after that destroyer."

"The gun is still off line, ma'am," the Tactical Action Officer said. "And we're all out of Harpoons."

'Understood," Silva said. "Is VLS back on line?"

"Yes, Captain."

"Then hit that contact with SM-3s."

The TAO opened his mouth to speak.

Silva gestured him into silence. "I already know the next half dozen things you're going to say, so you can save your breath. I *know* that the SM-3 missile is not an anti-ship weapon, and I *know* that any effect it has will be marginal, at best. I also know that our orders are to kill that ship. Unless you've got a better plan, we're going to hit that destroyer with the only weapons we have left. Do I make myself clear, Lieutenant?"

The TAO nodded. "Yes, Captain."

He swallowed, and keyed the net. "Weapons Control—TAO. Kill *Surface Contact Zero One* with SM-3 missiles."

There was a pause before the reply came. "TAO—Weapons Control. Say again, sir?"

The TAO keyed the net again. 'Weapons Control—TAO. You have your orders. Kill *Surface Contact Zero One* with SM-3 missiles. *Now!*"

"Ah... Weapons Control, aye."

The deck rattled with the growl of anti-air missiles, tearing into the sky on a mission they had never been designed for. The tumult of the launches was much louder than usual, the sound reverberating freely through the open wound in the side of the ship.

"TAO—Weapons Control. Six birds away, no apparent casualties. Targeted on *Surface Contact Zero One*."

"TAO, aye. Keep hitting that surface track. Don't let up until there's nothing left but a hole in the water."

Silva nodded her approval. She was about to issue amplifying instructions when the Sonar Supervisor's voice blared from the 29-MC speakers.

"All Stations—Sonar has hydrophone effects off the port quarter! Bearing zero-niner-eight. Initial classification: incoming torpedo!"

Silva's eyes darted to the tactical display screen, where a blinking torpedo symbol had appeared. "Come *on*," she said. "You have *got* to be fucking kidding me."

She looked around sharply. The Undersea Warfare Evaluator had surrendered his console to a radar operator, and the Computerized Dead-Reckoning Tracer hadn't been restored after the missile hit.

In the heat of an air and surface fight, anti-submarine warfare assets had been pushed to the bottom of the priority list. Some of the sonar systems were apparently on line, and the sonar team was obviously still doing its job, but CIC was completely unprepared to handle a submarine threat right now.

Where the hell had the sub come from, anyway? There was no time to think about that.

Silva saw the Undersea Warfare Evaluator snatch a comm-set from a dead console, and jack the connector into an overhead panel.

He keyed his mike. "Crack the whip! Bridge—USWE. We have an inbound torpedo. I say again—crack the whip!"

The reply was instant. "Crack the whip! Bridge, aye!"

The Officer of the Deck's voice came over the 1-MC. "All hands stand by for heavy rolls while performing high-speed evasive maneuvers."

In the background came the rising wail of the gas turbine engines as they spun up to maximum rpm. The ship would need flank speed to carry out the *crack-the-whip* anti-torpedo maneuver.

The deck heeled sharply to port as the *Towers* began the first in a series of high-speed hairpin turns. If executed properly, the maneuver would create numerous propeller wakes at narrow intervals. The incoming torpedo would have to sort through a convolution of crisscrossing wakes, as well as a chaotic zone of acoustic interference caused by uncontrolled cavitation from the ship's screws.

According to the tactical manuals, the crack-the-whip maneuver was nearly seventy percent effective, providing it was used in conjunction with the towed acoustic decoy system called *Nixie*. Unfortunately, neither of the ship's two Nixie units were deployed, and there wasn't time to get one of them in the water.

The cant of the deck grew steeper as the ship accelerated into the turn. Silva grabbed the back of the TAO's chair to steady herself against inertia, and the increasing incline of the deck.

She couldn't remember how effective the maneuver was supposed to be without the Nixie decoys, but it was less than seventy percent. A *lot* less.

But this was not the time to get tunnel-vision about problems beyond her control. Given the current situation, the USWE had employed the only available defense against the torpedo. It would either work, or it wouldn't. There was nothing else she could do to cope with the submarine threat, so it was time to focus on issues that she *could* control.

She shifted her attention to the missile symbols tracking toward the remaining Chinese destroyer. The six blue missile icons were packed so tightly together that they overlapped each other on the screen.

The SM-3 missiles were intended for use against other missiles, aircraft, and—occasionally—satellites. Their warheads were not designed to attack hardened warship targets, but they were *fast*. Their top speed was more than ten times as fast as the Harpoon anti-ship cruise missiles they were now pinch-hitting for.

Moving at nearly 5,200 knots, they covered the distance to the target in under half a minute. The six missile symbols converged on the symbol for the Chinese destroyer, and then disappeared. The icon for *Surface Contact Zero One* remained on the screen.

There was no way to evaluate how badly the enemy ship had been damaged by the multiple missile strikes. The Aegis computer system could not apply advanced reasoning, so it substituted simple binary logic. The target was still visible on radar, therefore the target still existed, ergo—it was time to hit the target again.

Another grumbling reverberation went through the ship, followed by an announcement over the tactical net. "TAO—Weapons Control. Six more birds away, no apparent casualties. Targeted on *Surface Contact Zero One*."

The Tactical Action Officer was reaching to key his mike when the next report came in.

"TAO—Air. Four Bogies inbound. Two flights of two."

The next wave of the air assault had begun.

The deck righted itself and then began tilting in the other direction as the ship went hard-to-starboard in its next evasion turn.

Silva spotted the four hostile aircraft closing on the tactical display. And she felt herself start to grin.

This was it. This was her *Kobayashi Maru*. This was her unwinnable scenario. A torpedo in the water, too many hostile aircraft to count, an unfinished shootout with a Chinese destroyer, and an enemy submarine. All happening at once.

Again, there was nothing she could do about it. Nothing, but keep fighting, and try to ride out the storm.

The TAO caught her eye. "Captain, request permission to engage inbound hostile air contacts."

Silva nodded. "Permission granted. Hit 'em! But do *not* let up on that surface contact."

The TAO issued orders to Weapons Control, and eight more SM-3 missiles leapt into the fray.

And then the number of air contacts on the Aegis display began to multiply rapidly.

Silva's grin grew wider. There were at least twenty new air tracks on the screen—more aircraft than she had ever seen, in even the most exaggerated training simulation. But the new symbols were not the warning red color of hostile forces. They were *blue*.

CHAPTER 54

STRIKE FLIGHT
VFA-228 — MARAUDERS
BAY OF BENGAL
WEDNESDAY; 03 DECEMBER
0054 hours (12:54 AM)
TIME ZONE +6 'FOXTROT'

The Air Controller's voice was low, but distinct in the headphones of Rob Monkman's flight helmet. "Hammer, Bandits three-one-zero, for eighty, Angels two-zero."

For all its Spartan brevity, the communication was packed with information. The Air Controller had just informed the leader of Hammer Flight that hostile aircraft had been detected eighty nautical miles from Hammer's position, bearing three-one-zero, flying at an altitude of 20,000 feet.

The lack of the modifiers 'hot' and 'cold' indicated that the enemy planes were not directly approaching, or running away from Hammer. The absence of other modifiers relegated the message to a simple update, for purposes of situational awareness. *No action required, but keep your eyes open for the bad guys.*

The flight lead's response was even shorter. "Hammer." Translation: *This is Hammer Flight Leader. I hear and understand.*

Monk checked his AN/APG-79 radar for any sign of the enemy aircraft. The green-on-green monochromatic display seemed to glow under the image intensification of his night vision goggles, but the screen was clear of hostile contacts. His plane's radar hadn't acquired the targets yet. Not really a surprise, considering the range.

He lifted his head and went back to scanning the sky through the false green brightness of his night vision gear. The APG-79 was excellent for aerial combat, but it didn't have nearly the range of the massive APS-145 radar array carried by the E-2D Hawkeye.

Per standard operating procedure, the E-2D was hanging back outside of the engagement area, supplying Airborne Early Warning coverage for the fighters. With its superior radar sensors and crew of air controllers, the Hawkeye could provide real-time target-cueing and tactical instructions to the American fighter pilots, allowing them to coordinate with a speed and precision that most nations could not even approximate.

Hammer Flight was one of three divisions assigned to the fighter sweep for this mission. Each division was composed of four F/A-18E Super Hornets, which could fight as a single coordinated unit, or split off into two independent sections to engage separate forces.

Monk was wingman to Lieutenant Dan Coffee (callsign *Grinder*), the division lead of Hammer Flight. His job was to keep Grinder in sight, follow the senior pilot's orders, and shut the hell up until his input was asked for.

Monk didn't mind. They'd be getting the order to engage any minute now, and then it would be time to give some Chinese pilots a taste of what they'd given Poker.

Somewhere, about a hundred miles back, was the strike package: a mixed-bag of Hornets and Super Hornets, tooled up for anti-surface action. Their mission was to take out the Chinese carrier with Harpoons and Mavericks.

Monk wasn't thinking about the strike package. He wasn't really thinking about the mission at all. He kept seeing the Chinese air-to-air missile blast through Poker's canopy. No warning. No provocation. Just a shot in the face, and the smoking wreckage of Poker's plane tumbling into the ocean.

The Air Controller's voice came over Monk's headphones again. "Hammer, Bandits three-zero-five, for sixty, Angels two-zero."

Grinder's single word acknowledgement came a second or so later. "Hammer."

Monk glanced at his radar again. Still no enemy contacts, but the screen now showed eight hostile air symbols, being fed to his system from CED, the cooperative engagement data-link transmitter aboard the Hawkeye.

Monk's knuckles tightened on the stick. It wouldn't be long now.

He felt his lips move, and heard the low repetitive murmur of his own voice, but it took him a few seconds to realize that he was actually speaking. It was nearly a chant. "Payback time. Payback time. Payback time. Payback time…"

He chopped it off short, and went back to scanning the night sky for visual contacts. Within a few seconds, the chant started again, apparently of its own accord. "Payback time. Payback time…"

"Hammer, Bandits three-zero-zero, for forty, Angels two-two, hot. Commit!"

Monk grinned. That was the magic word—*commit*. The keys to the kingdom. *Go after your assigned targets, and kill them.*

Grinder's response was as laconic as ever. "Hammer."

A half-second later, Grinder turned left out of the formation, and began closing on the Bandits, trailed by the other three pilots of Hammer Flight: Chuck '*Barnstormer*' Barnes, Sheila '*Redeye*' Lewis, and Monk.

Grinder's voice came over the 'back' radio, the circuit assigned to Hammer Flight for internal comms. "Hammers, sort by desig."

Target designators appeared on Monk's head-up display, bracketing two of the hostile aircraft symbols, identifying the enemy planes he was assigned to kill.

Monk keyed his mike. "Two, sorted."

This was followed immediately by acknowledgements from Barnstormer and Redeye.

"Three, sorted."

"Four, sorted."

Using the old radio-only method, the target sorting process could have taken two or three minutes. With the help of the CED data-link, it was finished in three seconds. Everyone knew who their targets were. Now, it was just a matter of closing to missile engagement range.

Grinder climbed to 35,000 feet and poured on power, gaining speed and altitude for the coming engagement.

Monk adjusted his own speed and altitude to maintain position off Grinder's starboard wing. "Payback time. Payback time…"

At 34 nautical miles, an electronic chime told Monk that his APG-79 had acquired radar contact. He glanced down at the display to confirm that both of his targets were now on the screen. They were.

He selected two AIM-120 AMRAAMs, designated one for each of his assigned Bandits, and allowed the fire control computer to give them their first look at the targets.

The Normalized In-Range Display—better known as the *NIRD circle*—appeared on his head-up display. One of his Bandits was sliding into the engagement envelope, but the second hostile was still slightly out of range. He held fire until the range bar for the second Bandit slipped past the six-o'clock position on the NIRD.

Both targets began to sheer off. Shit! Their threat-receivers had detected his radar lock! The range bars for both Bandits scrolled to the left, rapidly approaching the maximum range caret. He had maybe a second and a half before they slipped out of the envelope.

Shoot now? Or wait for a better opportunity?

It wasn't a conscious decision. He thumbed the weapon selector, shut his eyes, and jammed the trigger twice.

"Fox Three! Fox Three!"

That was the code phrase for launch of an active radar guided missile.

Through his eyelids, Monk could see two green flashes as the missiles tore away into the night. The image processor circuits in his goggles were programmed to keep the output of the light intensification algorithms from harming his eyes, but there was no sense in spoiling his night vision.

The AMRAAMs blew through Mach 2 within seconds, and began gobbling up the distance to the Bandits. The 13,000 foot altitude advantage put the missiles into a dive, gravity and inertia giving them still more speed as they streaked toward the turning Chinese warplanes.

Off Monk's port wing, Grinder pumped out two AMRAAMs of his own, and executed a tight left turn to bring his flight into a lag pursuit behind the J-15s.

Monk nudged his throttle and banked left to maintain his position on the lead plane.

The Bandits dropped chaff, jinked and jived impressively in their attempt to break missile-lock, but the AIM-120 missiles were too close, and moving too fast. A pair of fireballs in the distance told Monk that both of his birds had found their targets.

Grinder's AMRAAMs caught up with their Bandits a couple of seconds later, and two more explosions illuminated the night sky.

Then Monk's own radar warning receiver was shrieking. Somebody had radar lock on him.

A flashing arrow on the HUD told him that the threat was four-o'clock low. He keyed his radio. "Two, spiked, four-o'clock low! Breaking right."

Without waiting for a reply, he broke hard to the right, trading speed and altitude for a violently-sudden change in position. His g-suit clamped down on him like a python as the leg and abdominal modules constricted to keep the blood from pooling in his lower body. He grunted repeatedly through the turn, using voluntary muscle contraction to force blood pressure into his upper torso and brain. His cone of vision narrowed, but he knew where his physical limits were, and he didn't come close to graying out.

The tone was silent when he rolled back into level flight. He had slipped out of the radar lock, for the moment at least.

The adrenaline in his veins screamed for him to go after the threat, find and kill whichever bad guy had locked onto his plane. But that was not his job.

He brought his nose back around to the left, and began to look for Grinder. He keyed his radio. "Two, naked and blind." *This is Hammer-Two. I have broken free from enemy radar lock, but I cannot see my flight lead.*

Grinder's reply came quickly. "One, blind. Furball." *This is Hammer-One. I can't see you either. This fight is turning into a free-for-all.*

Monk acknowledged the transmission. "Two."

Grinder was right, this *was* a furball. The sky had become a seething cluster-fuck of shooting-dodging aircraft.

Monk checked his radar and then did a quick visual sweep. He spotted his next target, and began angling in for the kill.

⚓ ⚓ ⚓

USS *Towers*:

"All Stations—Sonar. Hostile torpedo has broken acquisition."

On the Aegis display, Captain Silva watched the symbol for the enemy torpedo swerve away from the *Towers*. Finally, *something* was going right.

She was about to issue another order when the Sonar Supervisor's voice came over the net again.

"All Stations—Sonar has multiple hydrophone effects off the port beam! Bearings one-zero-three, and one-zero-seven. Initial classification: friendly torpedoes!"

Friendly? That got everyone's attention.

The Undersea Warfare Evaluator punched into the circuit. "Sonar—USWE. Say again the classification of the new torpedoes."

"USWE—Sonar. They're friendly, sir. U.S.-built Mark-48s, and they're locked onto a new broadband contact, bearing zero-niner-zero."

"Sonar—USWE. What's the classification of your new contact?"

"USWE—Sonar. Classification unknown, sir. I've got plenty of blade noise and lots of broadband, but narrowband is too chaotic to get a read. Whoever he is, he just kicked it up to flank speed to get away from those 48s."

Silva keyed her headset. "Sonar, this is the captain. Any sign of the sub that launched the Mark-48s?"

"Ah... Negative, Captain. Whoever our friend is out there, he's running slick and silent. We're not getting a peep out of him."

"He can be as quiet as he wants," the TAO said. "As long as he keeps that bad guy off our back."

Silva nodded. "You've got that right."

On the tactical display, two blue torpedo symbols were racing toward a hostile submarine symbol.

Silva raise an eyebrow. "If I ever find out who's in command of that friendly sub, I'm going to kiss him on the lips."

A junior Operations Specialist spoke up before he could stop himself. "Even if it's a *girl*, Captain?"

Silva gave the young Sailor a mock glare. "Seaman, is that an indirect way of asking about my orientation?"

The Sailor's ears turned bright red. "No, sir! I mean, no, *ma'am!*"

Silva turned back to the Aegis screen. "If our guardian angel turns out to be female, I'll shake her hand and buy her a beer."

"Sounds like a plan to me, Captain," the Operations Specialist said.

Silva scanned the tactical display. "TAO, why did we stop hitting that surface contact?"

The Tactical Action Officer cleared his throat. "It's not *there* anymore, Captain. SPY isn't picking up anything big enough to make a radar return."

"Okay," Silva said. "Then our job is done. We'll wait until the fighter boys have finished mopping up the enemy air cover, and then we move in and pick up survivors."

This pronouncement was met with silence.

Silva examined the faces of the men and women around her. "I know what some of you are probably thinking," she said. "But if we're supposed to be the good guys, we damned well have to *act* like the good guys. When the fight is over, we're not leaving any sailors in the water. I don't care what color uniform they're wearing."

The TAO nodded slowly. "Aye-aye, Captain."

Silva inhaled deeply, and let out a long breath. "Maybe this isn't the kind of order Captain Bowie would have given. But it's *my* order. And it is *not* subject to debate."

The corners of the Tactical Action Officer's mouth curled up in the barest suggestion of a smile. "You misunderstand us, ma'am. This is *exactly* the kind of order Captain Bowie would have given."

There were silent nods of agreement around the compartment.

From somewhere in the semi-darkness, an unidentified voice spoke. "Alright, people. You heard the Skipper. Let's get to it."

⚓ ⚓ ⚓

Hammer-Two:

Monk watched his third kill of the night come apart in midair, scorched fragments of wreckage sifting down toward the dark ocean like flaming confetti. Counting the two J-15s he had nailed during his last mix-up with the Chinese, he now had five confirmed kills. Monk had just officially become an ace, but nothing in the world could have been further from his mind.

He didn't care about honors, or awards, or bragging rights. He was looking for another Bandit to kill.

The mission had gone according to plan. The fighter sweep had cleared away enough of the hostile air cover to allow the strike package to get in and do its job. After ten or twelve air-launched Harpoon strikes, the Chinese aircraft carrier, *Liaoning*, wallowed powerless on the wave tops.

Through his night vision goggles, Monk could see the crippled ship low in the water, listing heavily to starboard, flames rising from her flight deck in several places.

Monk tore his eyes away from the burning ship, and went back to scanning the sky for another enemy aircraft. Three or four seconds later, he found one. Or rather, it found *him*.

The incoming missile must have been a heat seeker, because Monk's threat warning receiver never detected any sign of enemy radar emissions. He was cruising low and fast when the missile struck. The shock was as hard and abrupt as a head-on car crash.

His helmet ricocheted off the inside of the canopy with brain-numbing force, and tattletales began flashing all over his instrument panel. The Super Hornet—lithe and nimble just a few seconds before—was suddenly a shuddering and dying beast.

The cockpit was filling with smoke, and his port engine was on fire. He was losing power and altitude quickly, and the black sea was rushing up to meet him.

He keyed his radio. "This is Hammer-Two. I am hit and going down. This is Hammer-Two. I am hit and going down."

He released the mike and started to reach for the ejection handle between his legs. Then he caught sight of the Chinese aircraft carrier again, the flames billowing green through the lenses of his night goggles.

Maybe there was time to put his dying F-18 through one final maneuver. Nothing fancy: just a simple turn and a change of altitude.

The controls were nearly unresponsive now, and he was almost out of time. He fought the stick to bring his nose around to the left, and then pitched over into a shallow dive with the stricken enemy warship framed squarely within the window of his HUD.

Another nighttime approach on an aircraft carrier, but this time there would be no landing. No surge of deceleration as the arresting gear brought his plane to a straining halt. No coffee and friendly banter in the debriefing room. This was not going to be that kind of landing.

The burning form of the aircraft carrier was growing larger. The moment of impact hurtling closer.

He could do this. He could ride his Hornet all the way down, plunge his sword directly into the heart of the enemy. Bring it all to an end, in a furious cataclysm of fire.

Later, he would never remember reaching for the eject handle. But the yellow and black loop was suddenly in his hand. He wrapped his fingers around it, and pulled.

The canopy blasted clear, and the acceleration hit him in the lower spine as the ejection seat rocketed him out of his plane, and into the night sky. His universe became a maelstrom of darkness and rushing wind.

And then the drogue deployed, pulling his chute open, and he was floating down toward the ocean under an unseen dome of taut nylon.

Monk wanted to see the impact. He *needed* to see it. He prayed that he would be facing the right way when it happened.

Maybe it was luck. Maybe it was fate. Or maybe it was just the wind. But his parachute turned slowly as he descended, and the enemy ship swung into view as the instant of collision occurred.

His wounded Hornet rammed into the superstructure of the Chinese aircraft carrier at several hundred knots. Kinetic energy, the plane's fuel load, and the remaining munitions synergized into an expanding sphere of flame and destruction.

It might not have been the death blow. Perhaps the missile hits had already done that job. But to Monk, it *felt* like the killing shot. The sight had all the brutal majesty of the stone that felled Goliath, or a stake pounded through the heart of some mythical monster.

For the first time since Poker's death, Monk felt himself begin to smile.

"Okay, assholes," he said quietly. "Now we're even."

CHAPTER 55

The telephone on President Wainwright's desk buzzed. He lifted the receiver.

"Mr. President, you have Premiere Xiao on the line. Your translator is patched in and standing by."

"Thank you, Margie," the president said. "Put me through."

There was a brief silence, and then the light on the phone blinked from amber to green.

The president resisted the urge to clear his throat. He'd been mentally rehearsing this call for an hour, and he still hadn't figured out how to say what needed to be said.

Everything was riding on this call. If it went well, maybe he could get China and India to back away from each other before this thing escalated out of control. If it *didn't* go well…

He heard Xiao's ancient voice, speaking in Mandarin. A couple of seconds later, the State Department translator repeated the Chinese leader's words in English. "Good morning, President Wainright. I assume you are calling to apologize for the attack on our aircraft carrier."

The president felt an instant surge of annoyance. They were three seconds into the call, and already the accusations were starting to come out. At least a half dozen responses popped into his head, none of which would help to calm the waters. He needed something firm, but not accusatory.

"The loss of the *Liaoning* was unfortunate," he said. "And so was the attack on the USS *Midway*, which—you may recall—occurred two days before the incident with the *Liaoning*."

Another pause before the State Department translator relayed Xiao's words. "We made no move against your USS *Midway* until after you

241

destroyed a satellite that was the sovereign property of the People's Republic."

The president's annoyance ratcheted up another notch. So much for his hopes of a calm diplomatic dialogue. Fine. If Xiao wanted to play tit-for-tat, he'd discover that Dalton Wainright's years in the Senate had given him certain skills in the shame-and-blame game. And then, maybe after they had bludgeoned each other senseless with blunt rhetoric for a while, they might actually get around to having a productive discussion.

"Premiere Xiao," he said, "your people are apparently not giving you accurate information. I did not authorize the downing of your satellite until two days after your warplanes carried out an unprovoked attack against a pair of American aircraft on defensive patrol. Your planes shot first, killing one of our pilots, and destroying an F/A-18 jet. American naval forces in the region had done *nothing* to justify such an act of aggression."

"You sided with our enemies—"

"We did *not* side with your enemies," the president snapped. "I ordered USS *Midway* into the Bay of Bengal as a stabilizing force. I had hoped that our ships and aircraft could serve as a buffer between Chinese and Indian forces in the region. To give both of your countries a chance to cool off, and seek more peaceful solutions."

The Premier's translated words came a few seconds later. "Mr. President, I find it strange that you speak of peace. You have just destroyed every ship and aircraft in the *Liaoning* battle group. You did not *damage* our ships and planes. You *eradicated* them. You have struck directly at my country's vital strategic assets. You have dealt a serious blow to China's international military deterrence. Now, you wish to cast yourself as a peacemaker?"

Dalton felt his fingers tighten on the telephone receiver. He struggled to keep his voice even. "How this happened is no longer important," he said. "What matters now, is what we do next. Do we continue down the road that we're on? Or do we work together to find a solution to this crisis?"

"You cannot have it both ways," Xiao said through the translator. "Your country's John Adams spoke of holding the sword in one hand, and the olive branch in the other. But we both know, President Wainright, that you are no John Adams. And if we are to speak frankly, you are not even his lesser son, John Quincy Adams."

The words did not just sting. They burned like acid. Because they were true.

If they had come from a different man, they might not have wounded so deeply. Coming from some middleweight bureaucrat, Dalton could have written them off as ill-spirited bluster. But Xiao Qishan was not a middleweight bureaucrat. He was old now, and in the waning days of his political career, but what an extraordinary career it had been.

Xiao had done more to drag China into the twenty-first century than any other man, living or dead. He had earned his place in history. He would be remembered as a great leader. A forward-thinking man of action and results.

Dalton Wainright had no illusions about his own place in history. He was not a great leader. In the future, when he was remembered at all, he would appear as a footnote to the careers of greater men. He knew that, and the knowledge was not pleasant.

Still, he struggled to keep the anger and hurt out of his voice. "I am no John Adams," he said into the phone. "As you have so graciously pointed out, I am not even John Quincy Adams. I am a small man, sitting in a chair that is too large for me. But make no mistake, Premier Xiao, I *am* sitting in this chair. I don't pretend to lead my country with wisdom and greatness, but I *do* lead it."

His fingers were painfully tight around the handset of the phone. "For all of my shortcomings, I intend to discharge my duties. I will *not* accept threats to the security of my country. And I will not accept unprovoked attacks against allies of the United States of America."

The translation of Premiere Xiao's response came a few seconds later. "Are you suggesting that China is *not* an ally of the United States?"

"That is entirely up to you," the president said. "But if you want to be treated as our ally, it's about time that you begin to *act* like our ally."

There was a long delay before Xiao's words came back through the translator. "Is that the sound of your saber rattling, Mr. President? What are you suggesting? Are you hoping to intimidate me with veiled hints?"

Dalton's fist came down on the polished timbers of the Resolute desk. "Goddamn it! I'm not *hinting* at anything. I'm not *suggesting* anything. I am *outright* saying it. The People's Republic of China is dangerously close to being at war with the United States of America. Is that clear enough for you, Premier Xiao? *War.*"

He could hear his voice rising, assuming a strength and assurance that he had not felt since taking the oath of office. He waited for the translator to repeat his words in Mandarin, and then he continued before the Chinese leader could respond.

"There will be no more skirmishes," the president said. "There will be no more diplomatic intimidation. If Chinese forces throw so much as a snowball toward any US person or asset, military or otherwise, we will answer with war. If you continue to press your attacks against the Republic of India, we stand by our allies, and we will bring the fight to your door.

So you need to decide right now... Are you prepared to go to war against the United States?"

There was a long silence, and Dalton could hear his pulse hammering in his ears.

Then, Xiao's aged voice spilled a torrent of Mandarin. "I will not be spoken to this way! You will not—"

President Wainright hung up the phone, slamming the receiver back into its cradle without waiting for the rest of the translation.

He took several deep, slow breaths. When he thought his heart rate was a bit closer to normal, he lifted the receiver and punched the number for the Situation Room Duty Officer.

"This is the president," he said. "Round up the Secretary of Defense, and get the National Military Command Center on line. I want the full battle staff in the Situation Room in half an hour."

He lowered the receiver again, and then glanced at the nineteenth-century John and Thomas Seymour clock near the east door. A little over an hour left before India launched the attack against the Three Gorges Dam, and then this thing was *really* going to get ugly.

CHAPTER 56

GREAT HALL OF THE PEOPLE
TIANANMEN SQUARE
BEIJING, CHINA
WEDNESDAY; 03 DECEMBER
6:31 AM
TIME ZONE +8 'HOTEL'

First Vice Premier Lu Shi pushed his chair back from the conference table and got to his feet. "The loss of the *Liaoning* cannot go unpunished. We will crush them!"

Jia Bangguo raised a hand. "We will crush *who*, Comrade Lu? The *Americans*? Are you saying that we will crush the United States?"

"The Americans have gone too far," Lu Shi said. "They have crippled a major strategic asset, and damaged the credibility of our naval forces. We must show the world that China does not kowtow to any foreign power. We do not back down from India. We do not back down from America. We do not back down from *anyone*. And any nation that challenges the People's Republic does so at its own peril."

Ma Yong, Party Secretary of the Leading Group for Financial and Economic Affairs, nodded toward Lu Shi. "Comrade Vice Premier, I know very little of military affairs, and I know even less about the intricacies of international strategic deterrence. But I do know that the United States and India collectively consume more than thirty-five percent of our manufactured trade goods. America is by-far our best customer, and India is also one of our largest trading partners. Have you considered what will happen to our national economy when a third of our export market suddenly evaporates?"

Lu glared at him. "Comrade Ma, you know that I have always considered you a wise counselor. But you are overestimating the resolve of your adversaries. America is an undisciplined consumer culture, and India is not much better. They cannot live without their toys. If the average American is forced to choose between his political convictions and his iPhone, he will take the iPhone every time."

245

Ma Yong started to speak, but Lu Shi cut him off. "If you examine the true nature of your customers, you will see that there is no real danger of economic reprisals. There will certainly be a few economic sanctions— boycotts of Chinese trade goods, perhaps some short-lived tariffs—to demonstrate America's financial independence and the strength of American character. But any such measures will be short in duration, and they will not significantly impact the flow of our manufactured goods. Because, regardless of their misguided pride, American resolve is weak, and their economy is inextricably tied to ours. If they attempt to cut financial ties with China, they will be cutting their own throats."

"Perhaps you are right about that," said Party Secretary Wei Jintao. "But you are talking about fighting two tigers at the same time."

"Yes," Lu Shi said. "But both tigers have more whiskers than teeth. These are not real tigers. They are make-believe tigers. They will growl and thrash their tails, but India is no match for us, and we will pull America's fangs before they can do much in the way of biting."

Ma Yong raised an eyebrow. "How do you propose to accomplish this? How exactly will we pull the fangs of the United States?"

"Unrestricted cyber warfare," Lu Shi said. "We have been probing strategic elements of their critical infrastructure for years, and their cyber defenses are not capable of withstanding a determined assault. We will take down their national power grids. We will infect their computer networks with military-grade viruses, interrupt their cellular telephone communications, disrupt their air traffic control systems, and paralyze their commercial banking architecture. Within forty-eight hours, the average American won't be able to buy a slice of bread or a liter of water. Bank accounts will be frozen. Planes will be grounded. Telephones will be useless. And the vaunted U.S. military will have its hands full quelling riots, and trying to keep the peace within its own borders."

"An ambitious undertaking," said Jia Bangguo. "But what if your plans for hobbling America are not as successful as you hope? What if you have overestimated the effectiveness of your proposed cyber attacks? Or if you have underestimated the resilience of the Americans?"

"I'm not wrong," Lu Shi said.

"Possibly," Jia said. "But before we commit ourselves to such drastic measures, we must consider all possibilities. So I ask again, what happens if you *are* wrong?"

Lu Shi's voice rose to a shout. "I am *NOT* wrong!"

He turned hard eyes on every face gathered around the table. "Look at yourselves," he sneered. "You are *supposed* to be leaders. You are supposed to be *men*. But you sit around whining like a gaggle of old women. Where is your heart? Where is your spirit?"

His gaze was an open challenge to every man at the long table. "This will happen," he said. "It *will* happen. And when it does, I will remember everyone who opposed me. I have the complete backing of Premiere Xiao on this—"

"No!" said a voice from the far end of the room.

Every head turned toward the newcomer. The wizened form of Xiao Qishan stood in the doorway, flanked by two young and hard-looking PLA officers.

"You do *not* have my backing," Xiao said. He began to hobble toward his chair.

"I don't understand," Lu said. "You were going to speak to the American president. You were going to—"

"I *have* spoken to the president," Xiao said. The old leader was wheezing slightly, as though the act of walking to his chair had used up a significant fraction of his strength reserves. "I am no longer in favor or following your plan."

The expression on Lu Shi's face was one of utter shock. "But Comrade Premiere, you know that President Wainright is weak. We can *do* this. It is our *time* to do this."

Xiao lowered himself carefully into his chair and shook his head. "Wainright is stronger than you think he is. In fact, I suspect that he's stronger than *he* thinks he is."

Xiao was wracked by a series of painful coughs, and when he spoke again, his voice was even feebler than usual. "We will not move against the Americans. I have already called the Indian President. We will cease all hostilities with India, and make immediate efforts to normalize diplomatic relations."

He gave his Vice Premiere a long and patient look. "Comrade Lu, the time for anger is past. Now is the time for healing, and moving forward."

All color drained from Lu Shi's face. "You're too weak for this job, old man. You no longer have the courage to make the hard decisions. It's time for you to retire, and totter off somewhere to die quietly. You're finished here."

The old Premier gave him a thin smile. "I don't think so," he said. "You will be retiring today, my friend. Not me."

He motioned to the pair of PLA officers, and they closed in rapidly on Lu Shi. Before Lu had time to react each man had a firm grip on one of his arms. They began to lead him firmly from the room.

"The Americans are weak!" Lu shouted over his shoulder. "The Indians are weak! We can crush them…"

"Perhaps," Premier Xiao said softly. "But let's see if we can live with them instead."

CHAPTER 57

THREE GORGES DAM
SANDOUPING, CHINA
WEDNESDAY; 03 DECEMBER
7:29 AM
TIME ZONE +8 'HOTEL'

The reservoir extended nearly 700 kilometers upstream from the catchment wall, more than 39 billion cubic meters of water held in check by a concrete edifice that was half as tall as America's landmark Empire State Building.

The wall's internal reinforcements included 463,000 metric tons of steel, enough to fabricate 63 copies of the Eiffel Tower. The entire structure had been designed to withstand accidents, massive seasonal over-flooding, and earthquakes of 7.0 on the Richter scale. But the architects and engineers hadn't known about the Next Generation Penetrator warhead that the Indians called Rudrasya khaḍgaḥ, the Sword of Shiva, and they certainly hadn't known that regional turmoil might push their neighbors to actually utilize such a weapon.

The 370 on-site personnel knew nothing of the Indian plan to destroy the dam. The workers went about their daily routines, maintaining and operating the thirty-two house-sized hydroelectric turbines, and the power distribution plant in its adjacent underground facility.

The inhabitants of the Yangtze River basin were beginning to stir under the first rays of the morning sun. The cities of Wuhan, Nanjing, and Shanghai were gearing up for another busy day of buying, selling, making, and consuming.

Not one person within the footprint of pending destruction knew that India's 48 hour deadline was only a minute away. Not one of the potential victims knew about the seven cruise missiles targeted on the dam, or the meticulous care with which the impact sites had been selected.

The final 60 seconds ticked away, one after another. Forty seconds. Twenty seconds. Ten.

And then, the deadline expired, and the appointed moment arrived.

No missiles fell from the sky. No warheads pierced the hardened concrete of the catchment wall. Downstream from the dam, the brown waters of the Yangtze River continued their slow rolling journey to the sea.

The cataclysm had been averted by a phone call, an act of reason, and the extension of a human hand in the age-old gesture of peace.

The hour of doom had come and gone. And 400 million Chinese citizens went about their morning business, unaware that death had brushed past them in the clear early sunlight.

EPILOGUE

Kat Silva walked down the long row of grave markers until she came to a headstone that was visibly newer than most of the others. The marble was crisply white, and brilliantly clean, having only been exposed to the elements for a few weeks. The inscription read: *SAMUEL HARLAND BOWIE, Capt. USN*, followed by the dates of birth and death.

Silva sighed, and nodded toward the stone. "Sorry it's taken me so long to make it around to see you, Jim. But you know how it goes when your ship is in the yards. The *Towers* is going to be just fine, by the way. When the yard birds are finished sprucing her up, you won't even be able to tell where the missile hit."

Silva felt a yawn coming on, and covered her mouth. "Sorry about that. Fourteen hours in the air, not counting layovers, and I never sleep worth a damn on airplanes."

She glanced up and down the rows of white markers. "I see there are a bunch of old-time Indian fighters buried here. Scouts, cavalry soldiers, maybe even some of the boys from the Alamo. You should look them up. I'll bet some of those guys are relatives of yours. The hero streak in you runs pretty deep, so it's probably in your bloodline."

Silva reached into her pocket and fished out a folded sheet of paper. "I hope you don't mind that I didn't bring flowers. You never struck me as the kind of guy who goes for floral arrangements. But if I'm wrong about that, you let me know, and I'll get you some begonias, or something."

She unfolded the sheet of paper and spent a few seconds smoothing out the creases. "I did bring you something, though. Maybe you'll like it better than a bunch of daffodils. I'll just read it for you, and you can decide for yourself."

She cleared her throat softly. "From: Department of Defense Public Affairs, Washington, DC Naval News Service. Secretary of the Navy

Alexander Fields announced today that the Navy's next *Arleigh Burke* class guided missile destroyer will be named USS *Bowie*, in honor of Navy Captain Samuel Harland Bowie who was killed during last year's naval combat action in the Bay of Bengal. The USS *Bowie* will be the first ship to bear the name…"

Silva folded the paper. "There are four or five more paragraphs, but the rest is mostly about the capabilities of the modified *Arleigh Burke* class, and you probably know more about that than just about anyone. There's also a section about your military career, and the heroic actions of the *Towers* on her last three deployments, but—again—none of that is news to you."

The folded slip of paper went back into her pocket. "The keel laying ceremony is in May at Bath Iron Works. The Navy is inviting everyone who ever served under your command, so it'll be a much bigger dog and pony show than usual. Under the circumstances, I doubt they'll send you a direct invitation. I thought I'd tell you myself, in case you decide to swing by and watch the fun."

Silva's voice took on a more serious tone. "I don't know if you can hear me, Jim. I don't know if you're in heaven, or floating in some ethereal afterlife, or even if there *is* an afterlife. Maybe you're just gone now, and I'm talking to myself. But whether you can hear me or not, there's something I have to say to you.

"The world will probably never understand how much it owes to you, and to the men and women who fought under your command. The average person on the street has no idea that you dragged America—and maybe the entire planet—back from the brink of catastrophe at least three times. Most people will never know how much you did for this country, and how much you sacrificed to give us all a second chance."

She was surprised to find that her eyes were beginning to get misty. "But *some* of us know. We remember what you did, and we know the price you paid. And we're grateful, Jim. I can't even begin to tell you how much."

Silva tried to continue, but her voice had gone husky with unexpected emotion. "I guess that's really all I came to say."

She came to attention, and her right hand performed a slow, deliberate salute. "Thank you."

Her hand came back down to her side. She executed a precise about-face and walked away, leaving the headstone to stand among the ranks of its brothers and sisters under the gray Texas sky.

AUTHOR'S NOTE

Anyone with an understanding of orbital mechanics (or a working knowledge of physics) will spot the fact that I've taken some literary license with the orbit of the Chinese surveillance satellite known as *Redbird One*. The flight path I've described for the satellite is at too low an altitude, and too far from the famous "Clarke belt" to support a geostationary orbit. I haven't attempted to calculate what the duration of such an orbit might be in the real world, but it's a safe bet that it would not remain stable for the ten days predicted in the story.

I could attempt to justify my departure from Keplerian motion by pointing out that Redbird One could be an experimental *statite* (static satellite), a hypothetical satellite which employs a solar sail to modify its orbit. Theoretically, a properly-configured statite could hold itself in a geostationary "orbit" at much lower altitudes and with inclinations far different from the traditional equatorial orbits used for geostationary positioning. I could make such a claim, but I won't. The simple fact is, the story called for a satellite at a lower altitude, and well out of the geostationary belt, and I followed the needs of the plot.

Purists and aficionados of space technology are advised that my criminal misuse of orbital mechanics was premeditated, and carried out with malice-aforethought. In other words, it wasn't an oversight. I done it on purpose.

— Jeff Edwards

HAND THIS TO A HERO

Real heroes don't look like movie stars.

More often than not, military novels and movies portray heroes as larger-than-life characters endowed with stunning good looks, superb physical conditioning, amazing technical capabilities, and combat skills that border on the supernatural. In nearly two and a half decades of active duty, I never met anyone who resembled the kind of lone-wolf superheroes who populate many of the books in the military thriller genre. Real military heroes are ordinary men and women who work together to accomplish extraordinary things. Their only superpowers are training, hard work, dedication, and teamwork.

Those are the kinds of heroes that I write about. Soldiers, Sailors, Marines, and Airmen who know what it's like to accomplish the mission in an imperfect world; to struggle with faulty equipment, often while hampered by rules of engagement that make their jobs many times harder than they need to be. Men and women who step forward to risk their lives for a citizenry that all too rarely recognizes or appreciates their sacrifices.

The novel you're holding in your hand was written with those men and women in mind. I've tried to make it entertaining, but—of equal or greater importance—it's intended as a salute to the real heroes who keep this country strong.

Now that you've turned the last page, I'd like to ask you for a small favor. Please pass this book on to an American service member on active duty, or to someone who once wore the uniform, and remembers his or her service with pride.

In other words, *hand this to a hero*.

Respectfully,

Jeff Edwards

STGC(SW), USN (Ret.)

MORE NAVAL THRILLERS
BY

JEFF EDWARDS

ORIGINALLY PUBLISHED AS "TORPEDO"

JEFF EDWARDS

SEA OF SHADOWS

"A TIMELESS WARRIOR EPIC. JEFF EDWARDS SPINS
A STUNNING AND IRRESISTIBLY-BELIEVABLE TALE
OF SAVAGE MODERN NAVAL COMBAT."
—JOE BUFF, Bestselling author of 'SEAS OF CRISIS'
and 'CRUSH DEPTH'

JEFF EDWARDS

THE SEVENTH ANGEL

"...A SUPERB THRILLER THAT GRIPS THE READER
FROM BEGINNING TO END. A TRULY SPELLBINDING
TALE OF INTRIGUE... BRILLIANTLY EXECUTED."
—CLIVE CUSSLER, International bestselling author
of 'THE SPY' and 'RAISE THE TITANIC'

www.StealthBooks.Com

WHITE-HOT SUBMARINE WARFARE
BY

JOHN R. MONTEITH

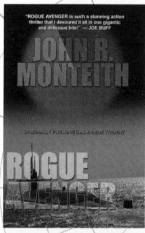

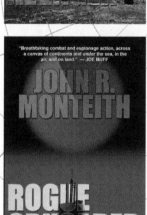

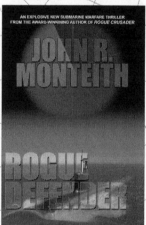

HIGH COMBAT IN HIGH SPACE

THOMAS A. MAYS

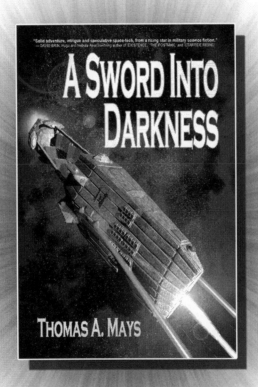

The Human Race is about
to make its stand...

www.StealthBooks.Com

DOME CITY BLUES
(Sample Chapters)

Most readers know me best for my naval warfare thrillers, but I do sometimes wander outside the boundaries of military fiction.

I'm a huge fan of detective novels, and I also happen to be interested in speculative fiction, so it was probably inevitable that I would eventually start dabbling somewhere on the border that separates the two genres.

The result was a sci-fi detective novel called *Dome City Blues*. I like to think of it as a cross between two of my favorite authors, Mickey Spillane and Philip K. Dick. That's almost certainly self-aggrandizing, but I have to find some way to describe the book to people who've never encountered such a thing, and that's my way of thinking about it.

The following pages contain the first three chapters of *Dome City Blues*. If you choose to peruse them, you'll find a book that bears very little resemblance to my naval warfare novels. There's a lot of cutting-edge hardware for my fellow technophiles, and plenty of action (once things start to heat up), but no missiles, no minefields, and definitely no military chain of command.

I invite you to give it a shot. Maybe you'll like it. Maybe you won't.

There's only one way to find out…

CHAPTER 1

||| || | |||||| | || |||| | || | ||| ||| |||| || | |||||| || ||| | ||| |||

The City Planners called it Los Angeles Urban Environmental Enclosure 12-A. Those of us who lived there called it the *Zone*. By either name, it amounted to a geodesic blister of translucent polycarbon fused to the east side of LA Dome #12 like a Siamese twin joined at the hip. It lacked the graceful sweeping arcs of the domes that covered the rest of the city. It was ugly, but then it was never designed to be pretty. It was an afterthought, thrown together after the inhabitants of East LA had made it violently clear that they didn't appreciate being left outside under a sky that pissed acid rain and streamed dangerous levels of solar ultraviolet.

I leaned against a wall and pried a Marlboro out of a squashed pack. The lettering on the box said, "crush proof." It wasn't. The box, like the cigarettes it contained, was a Brazilian knockoff—one of a hundred offshore counterfeit brands that had sprung into existence after the collapse of the American tobacco industry.

I stroked the wrinkled cigarette a few times to straighten it. It was still pretty rumpled, but it didn't look too mangled to be useable. I touched the tip against the black circle of the ignition patch on the bottom of the box. It took two or three seconds for the catalytic reaction to light the tobacco. I took a longish drag, and blew a gout of smoke into the air.

The last rays of the sun were starting to crawl up the tops of the buildings. Night was coming to the Zone. I watched as it crept over the decaying structures, hiding the sandstone texture of crumbling cement and rusting steel under a humid cloak of shadow.

Holographic facades flickered and appeared across the faces of most of the buildings: glamorous mirages that concealed graffiti-covered walls behind idealized projections of fairy tale palaces and pirate ships under sail. Here and there, enough sunlight still filtered through to weaken the holograms, leaving patches of drab reality visible through the bright fabric of illusion. In a few minutes, when the sun dropped a little farther, the holographic facades would become seamless, and the illusion would be perfect.

Above the street, triggered by the failing light, holosigns winked into phantom existence. Neon colored lasers woke up and began painting nightclub logos on the underside of the dome.

1

Two meters above the main entrance to Trixie's, a hologram of a naked woman crackled to life. The woman writhed suggestively through a ninety-second loop of canned video data. A glitch in the software caused the dancer's left leg to vanish in a smear of video static for the last few seconds of the loop. Lately, the glitch seemed to be spreading to the upper slope of her right breast.

Somebody tried to tell me once that the dancer was Trixie herself, the hologram built up from video footage shot when she was young. I've seen Trixie up close. I don't think so.

When half of the cigarette was gone, I ground it into the cracked sidewalk with my shoe and started walking again.

The strip was still mostly deserted, people just beginning to filter in. Four or five early-bird whores staked out their turf. A small knot of sailors cruised the bar fronts, waiting for the action to start. The inevitable sprinkling of tourists wandered around goggle-eyed, too ignorant of street-level protocol to realize that their chances of making it home safely were dropping with the sun.

A nocturnal creature, the Zone hibernated during the day and came to life when the sun went down. After sunset, even LAPD Tactical didn't venture through in less than squad strength.

I passed a pair of muscle-punks leaning against the carcass of a vandalized police car. They were decked out in the severely retro fashion popular in the Zone: black jeans, Gestapo boots, and synthleather jackets with too many zippers.

Both had peroxide white hair shaved close on the sides, left long on the top, and combed into crests like exotic birds. Their well-used leathers reeked of old blood and chemical reflex boosters. They watched me closely as I walked by, predatory eyes sizing up my potential as a target. Some signal passed between them and they decided to leave me alone.

I crossed Santa Fe Avenue, and walked in the front door of Falcon's Nest. I waited a few seconds for my eyes to adjust to the dim illumination, and then scanned the room. I was looking for John Hershell, a friend I was supposed to be meeting for drinks.

John and I were technically cousins on my mother's side, through some geometry that had been explained to me once and then promptly forgotten. We had been buddies right up through our teens. We'd even ended up in the Army together.

John wouldn't be hard to spot. He was strapped into a powered exoskeleton, compliments of a perimeter defense laser that our squad had tangled with in Argentina. The laser had sliced through his spinal cord, leaving his body pretty much null and void from the chest down. Turns out, he was one of those lucky one-in-a-million people who are allergic to the DNA modifying retrovirus that stimulates growth of spinal ganglia.

John wasn't here yet.

Unfortunately, Preacher *was* here, sitting at the bar, and he was in full cry. I slid into the booth farthest from his stool and signaled for my usual: Cutty Sark on the rocks.

Preacher's real name was Robert Treach, and he was an expert on everything. As usual, he was talking loudly to everyone within earshot.

"Natural selection," he was saying. "You can't wipe out disease. You just can't do it. They tried it in the Twentieth Century, right? Antibiotics, vaccines, miracle drugs, all that. Wiped out polio, smallpox, measles, and a bunch of other diseases."

Someone in his general area must have asked the obvious question.

Preacher squeezed a swallow from his tube of beer and shook his head. "Hell no it didn't work. It *can't* work. Not in the long run. Nature always figures out a way to restore the balance. When the population gets too high, natural selection kicks in and a new disease shows up, usually something real ugly. Where do you think AIDS came from? And then AIDS II, and AIDS III? Too many people bumping into each other, that's where. It's not healthy. Nature had to cull the herd. Worked too, didn't it? Culled the hell out of the human race."

I ran his words around in my head for a second: *"Culled the hell out of the human race."* Only Preacher would choose such a banal phrase to describe the disease that had ultimately wiped out a third of humanity.

"It'll happen again too," Preacher said. "Nature will keep on weeding out our weak bloodlines until we wise up enough to do it ourselves."

He downed another squirt of beer and nodded in response to something I couldn't hear. "That's what I'm telling you," he said. "Compassion is not a pro-survival characteristic."

I tuned him out just as he was spouting some nonsense about Darwin.

Falcon's Nest was a dark and cozy little blues bar. As far as I knew, it was the last one left in Los Angeles, maybe even the world. It was an anachronism, with its exposed beam ceilings, dark Portsmouth paneling, and worn leather upholstery. The owner, Rico Martinez, had kept it as true to the traditions of his grandfather as possible. It remained an island of quiet sanity in a sea of designer drinks, psycho-rock, and holo-neon.

When Rico finished pouring my drink, he shooed the waitress away and brought it to me himself. Watching him hobble across the room made me wish I'd sat at the bar.

His round face split into a huge grin as he slid the drink across the mahogany table. "You've finished a piece, haven't you?"

I pushed an ice cube around the top of my scotch. "What makes you say that?"

Rico's grin got wider. "You *bastard*, you *have*, haven't you?"

It was my turn to grin.

He slapped the table. "I knew it! When do I get to see?"

I took a sip of scotch. "I'll probably shoot a couple of holos tomorrow. I'll drop you a copy in a day or two."

"Is this piece as good as the last one?"

I shrugged. "You'll have to be the judge of that."

Demi, the latest in a long line of temporary waitresses, slipped up behind Rico and whispered something in his ear.

He glanced back toward the bar and nodded. "Duty calls, Amigo. I have thirsty customers and the booze must flow."

I lifted my glass and toasted him silently as he limped back to the bar.

Rico doesn't talk about it, but rumor says—when he was a kid—his mother sold the musculature in his left leg to a black market organ clinic. I don't know if that's true, but I've seen the leg. From the knee down, it's not much more than skin stretched over tendon and bone.

I asked him once why he's never gotten a muscle graft to replace the missing tissue. But Rico had given me a sad smile, shaken his head, and told me that you never can be sure whether organ donors are volunteers, or victims.

Lonnie Johnson's *Low Down Saint Louis Blues* found its way out of the speakers. I took another sip of the scotch and settled down into listening mode.

"Getting started without me, Sarge?"

I looked up into John's grinning face.

"You're late," I said. "There is scotch to be drunk, Johnny Boy, and you are not carrying your end of the load."

John eased himself into the booth; the servomotors that drove his exoskeleton bleated softly as they bent his unresponsive lower body into a sitting position.

"A problem that can be quickly remedied," he said. He waved Demi over and ordered a drink.

John wore dark colors as usual, slate gray pants and a pleated black jacket with flyaway shoulders. The dark color scheme was supposed to hide the narrow gray ribbing of the exoskeleton. Under the dim lights of the bar, it almost worked; the exoskeleton was nearly invisible.

"What's the big news?" I asked.

"My R&D team is getting close to a breakthrough on the neural shunt," he said.

The neural shunt was one of a hundred crazy schemes that John had cooked up in his drive to free himself from the exoskeleton. I didn't understand most of the technical details, but the shunt was basically an attempt to wire around the damage to John's spine, sort of like jumpering around a bad circuit.

It consisted of a custom-designed microchip implanted in his frontal lobe. The chip was supposed to interpret synaptic firings from John's brain, and transmit the signals through a fiberoptic strand that ran down his spine to a second chip implanted below the injury. It had been an ugly piece of surgery, and it hadn't really done the trick.

"You're going to try that crap again?"

"Of course I'm going to try it again. That's why I built Neuro-Tech in the first place. Owning a medical R&D team isn't exactly my life-long dream. If anybody else would work on the problem for me, I'd sell the company in a nanosecond. Until that happens, I'm going to have to keep trying myself."

I took a swallow of scotch and tried not to frown. "I thought the neural shunt was a dead-end."

John shook his head. "So did I, but my engineers have worked up a new angle on it."

"John, you told me yourself, every time you power up that chip, you go into a full-blown seizure. You've got to stop screwing around with your brain."

John tapped a fingernail on the carbon laminate ribbing of his exoskeleton. "I've got news for you, Sarge. My brain is about all I've got left to screw around with."

I set my glass down a little too hard. "Damn it, John. You know what I'm talking about."

John nodded. "I know," he said. "And I appreciate your concern. I honestly do. But I'm going to be okay, Sarge. *Really*. This is going to work."

I bit back the obvious comment. When it came to getting his legs back, John's weird projects were always 'going to work.'

It was his quest, his single-minded obsession. In an age where medical technology could cure cancer, transplant organs, and rewrite DNA, John was just about the only crippled person left. He wanted out of that exoskeleton, and he didn't care how many fortunes he had to spend to get there.

"What about the seizures?" I asked.

"We're getting a handle on that," John said.

I gulped down the rest of my scotch and signaled Demi for another.

When it came, she waved away my money and jerked her head toward a woman in the next booth. "Already paid for," she said. "Your secret admirer." Her nasal accent made it sound like *saykrit admoyra*.

I glanced at the woman for a second and then felt my eyes drawn to her again. She definitely had the goods. She was also definitely a hooker.

Her hair was a tousled auburn mane falling well past her shoulders. She had opaline green eyes with improbably long lashes. Her lips were a deep glossy red, with a swollen bee-stung look that suggested she had just climbed out of bed. The soft prominence of her cheekbones tapered to a pointed chin.

A skintight bodysuit of dark green synlon clung to her as if sprayed on. The fabric was photo-active, oval cells of the material cycling to transparency, revealing her white skin in sharp contrast to the dark green synthetic cloth.

Tiny windows of nudity drifted slowly across her body like clouds being chased by the wind. I tried not to stare as one of the transparent patches flowed diagonally across her rib cage and up around the curve of her breast, revealing the cinnamon-toast brown of her nipple.

Cinched tight around her waist was a broad black belt with leaves of ivy embroidered in metallic green thread. Her shoes were those impossibly high stiletto pumps that street kids call *fuck-me shoes*.

She was beautiful; as beautiful as surgical boutiques and DNA-modifying viral cultures could make her.

Beautiful. Perfect. Artificial.

"Wow," John said softly. He tipped his drink slightly in the woman's direction and then took a sip.

A second later, the woman stood beside our table. She looked at John. "Are you David Stalin?"

John hooked a thumb in my direction. "There's your man..."

The woman turned toward me and held out one of my old business cards. "I called your office," she said, "but the number is out of service. I tried the address on your card, but it looks like they've turned that whole building into a pump shop for commercial steroids. If you'll tell me where you've moved your office, I'll be glad to drop by during business hours."

Her perfume was delicate, but overtly sensual. It must have been packed with pheromones, because it was down-loading sexual imperatives to my reproductive system on a frequency that I barely managed to ignore.

"I didn't move my office," I said. "I closed it."

I took another sip of scotch, and paused while it ran down my throat. "I'm out of the business."

John watched me, nodding his head slightly as if encouraging me to somehow take advantage of the situation.

The woman's shoulders slumped a little. She stared down at the table top. "I need your help Mr. Stalin."

"I'm sorry, Ms..."

She glanced up. "Winter," she said. "Sonja Winter."

"I'm sorry Ms. Winter, but I don't do that kind of thing anymore."

Her eyes were glassy, as though a tear might find its way down those long lashes any second. "I need your help," she said again. "I've run out of options. You're the last hope I've got."

As I stared into her eyes, I realized that her eye shadow and lipstick were not makeup. They were tattooed on.

I cleared my throat softly. "I'm not anybody's last hope. There are a thousand private detectives out there that are as good as, or better than I ever was. All you have to do to find one is walk to the nearest public terminal and access the business directory."

The entire situation was right out of an old Mike Hammer vid, but even the bizarrely cliché quality of our conversation didn't stop me from feeling like a totally heartless bastard as the first tear rolled down her cheek.

"If you'll let me tell you..." Her voice trailed off. "If you'll please just... reconsider..."

"Cut her some slack," John said. "It might do both of you some good."

"There's nothing to reconsider," I said. "I'm out of the business, and I'm not going back."

The woman closed her eyes for a long second. The first tear was joined by a second, then a third.

She swallowed heavily. "It's my brother," she said. "He's been... he was murdered."

"Then you've definitely got the wrong guy for the job," I said. "You need to call the police."

She opened her eyes and brushed her fingers across her cheeks, wiping away tears. "The police know all about it," she said. "They're not interested in finding the killer."

Out of reflex, I nearly asked the only logical question. I caught myself just in time, and shut my mouth. She was a smart one. She was dangling the bait right in front of my lips. A murder had been committed, and the cops had decided not to investigate. The very idea suggested either ineptitude the part of the police, or some kind of cover-up. What detective (or even ex-detective) could resist finding out which?

I took a swallow of scotch. If I asked that first question, I'd have to follow it up with another one, and then ten more after that. Before I knew it, I'd be up to my neck in this woman's problems. I wanted no part of that.

John nudged me under the table.

I glanced at him out of the corner of my eye. He was nodding nearly imperceptibly, urging me to go for it.

I turned my eyes back to the woman. "I don't know anything about your brother," I said, "but I'm sure the cops have their reasons. I'm not going to second-guess them."

The white skin of her cheeks took on the slightest hint of pink. She swallowed, and then nodded slowly. "I'm sorry I troubled you, Mr. Stalin. Thank you for your time."

I nodded.

She started to turn away and then turned back. "Your new career, do you mind if I ask what it is?"

Her voice was quiet, her carriage dignified. Somewhere behind eye shadow tattoos and fuck-me shoes was a woman with character.

"I'm a sculptor," I said. "Metals."

A feeble smile tugged at the corners of her lips. She dropped the old business card on the table and walked away.

When the door closed behind her, John reached across the table and pressed his fingertips against the inside of my wrist. His lips moved, as though he was counting under his breath.

I stared at him. "What are you doing?"

"Checking for a pulse," he said. "After you let a gorgeous thing like *that* walk out the door, I was afraid you might be dead."

I tugged my arm away.

John raised his eyebrows. "You sure weren't like this in the old days." He grinned. "How about that gun-ship pilot you hooked up with in Porto Alegre? The Nordic blonde with legs up to her neck?"

"I remember," I said.

I picked up the business card and turned it over. The front was iridescent silver with our old logo in blue 3-D capitals.

```
+-------------------------------------------+
|                                           |
|        CARTER AND STALIN                  |
|                                           |
|      PRIVATE INVESTIGATIONS               |
|                                           |
|      M. CARTER  D. STALIN                 |
|                                           |
+-------------------------------------------+
```

The holographic lettering seemed to float two or three centimeters above the card. Across the back was a data strip containing the office's address and phone number.

I'd never liked those cards. They were too flashy and too expensive. I'd voted for black printing on white cardboard. Maggie had loved them, though. She'd liked the final batch best of all, the ones where her last name had been *Stalin*, instead of *Carter*.

John reached out for the card. I handed it to him.

He whistled softly through his teeth. "I still can't believe you didn't go for that," he said. He read the card and then tapped the edge of it on the top of the table three or four times. "I'll bet you haven't seen one of these in a long time."

"A *long* time," I echoed. I downed the last of the Cutty in a single gulp and called for another.

John put his hand on my forearm. "Take it easy, Sarge. We've got all night, buddy."

When my new drink came, I closed my eyes, leaned back into the red tucked leather upholstery, and let the voice of Billie Holiday carry me away.

CHAPTER 2

‖‖ ‖ ‖ ‖ ‖‖‖‖ ‖ ‖ ‖‖‖ ‖ ‖‖ ‖ ‖‖ ‖‖ ‖‖ ‖ ‖ ‖ ‖‖‖‖ ‖ ‖ ‖‖‖ ‖‖ ‖‖

"David, wake up."

I opened one eye and fought to drag the green digits of the clock into focus. The clock won the first round, its readout remained blurry and danced in dizzying circles.

"David, wake up. There is someone at the door."

I opened the other eye and rubbed them both. "Okay, House," I grunted. "I'm awake. What's up?"

"There is a visitor at the front door, identity unknown."

I sat up and stretched, my lower back making unpleasant popping noises. "House, give me half lighting and a picture of our guest, uh... one-way visual, far wall, life-size, no audio."

The room lights slowly faded up to half brightness and the wall across from my bed sizzled to life.

I was starting to wake up. The image on the wall screen wasn't nearly as hard to focus on as the clock had been. It was the woman from the bar: Sonja something... Sonja... Winter. Yeah, that sounded right.

The insides of my teeth felt fuzzy. "House, let me have two-way audio, please."

A soft chime told me that House had enabled the connection.

I cleared my throat. "Good morning, Ms. Winter. To what do I owe the pleasure?"

She looked directly at the camera pickup. "I need to talk to you. Can I come in?"

I squinted at the clock again; it was a little after noon. I climbed out of bed and stumbled toward the bathroom. "Sure, just a minute. House, audio off."

Again the chime.

"House, run a hot shower and start some coffee. Scan the lady for weapons and then let her in. Oh, and keep an eye on her."

"Of course, David."

The sound of the shower starting told me that House was on top of things.

Fifteen minutes later, I was clean and reasonably awake.

After a stop in the kitchen to grab two cups of coffee, I went in search of my guest. I could have asked House where she was; he knew to within a millimeter. I preferred to find her myself. It gave me a little extra time to think.

I knew what my uninvited visitor wanted, and I wasn't prepared to give it to her. I was going to have to disappoint this woman for the second time in as many days.

I found her in the loft, examining one of my sculptures, a hammered-iron casting of a pair of woman's arms reaching up through a plate of blackened steel. The iron fingers were curled and grasping, as though the unseen woman in the sculpture were trying to claw her way up out of some dark pit. I called the piece *The Quest for Air.*

Ms. Winter was dressed more conservatively than she had been the night before: brown slacks and a cream pullover sweater. Gone were the porn queen shoes and pheromone perfume. Only her eye shadow and lipstick tattoos spoiled the girl-next-door image.

She turned around and caught me staring at her.

I handed her a cup of coffee. "I hope you like cream and sugar."

She took a tiny sip. "This is perfect. Thank you."

Her eyes swept the room, taking in the polished oak decking and vaulted ceilings. "This place is *huge*."

I nodded. "It used to be the local LA-Trans office. We bought it for a song when they pulled the MagLev trains out of the Zone."

Her eyes turned back to the sculpture. "I like this. It's, I don't know... dark. It sort of... broods. Is it one of your pieces?"

"Yeah. An old one. I never have decided if I like it."

She reached out to touch it, glancing at me sideways to see if I objected. She gave a little gasp of surprise when her fingers passed through it. "Oh! It's a hologram. But it looks so real."

"The projector is built into the pedestal," I said. "I keep the lighting soft in here, to make it hard to see the scan lines."

She looked around the room at the other dozen-odd pieces. "Are the rest of them holograms too?"

I pointed. "That one's a holo. So is that one, and those two over there. Most of the rest are real. When I sell one, I shoot a holo of it before I let the original go. Silly I guess, but they almost feel like my children. I hate to let them go entirely."

She nodded. We stood without talking for a few moments. It became a stalemate, each of us waiting for the other to break the silence.

I gave in first. "How did you get Rico to give you my address?"

She raised one eyebrow.

"Come on, Ms. Winter, the business card you handed me is four years old, and there's nothing in the data strip to link me to this address. In my book, anyone good enough to follow a trail that cold doesn't need to hire a detective. You got the card and my address from Rico, didn't you?"

She nodded. "He said you were the best."

"Rico exaggerates," I said. "He's a great guy and a damned good bartender. But that doesn't exactly make him an expert on the private spook business. I'm tired; I'm out of the game, and I'm not going back. Rico knows all of that."

"I've tried other detectives," she said. "They think I'm crazy. Rico said you would at least give me a chance to explain. He also said something about you needing to get back on the horse."

She tilted her head slightly to one side. "What do you suppose he meant by that? I've never even seen a horse. They've been extinct since before I was born."

I rubbed the stubble on my chin, and realized that I had forgotten to shave. "It's an old cliché. It means that Rico thinks it's time for me to come out of retirement."

I shook my head. "Rico is starting to sound like John. Both of them seem to think they know what's good for me."

She watched me without speaking.

A good detective or attorney knows how to use silence as a tool. Most people can't bear more than a few seconds of silence at a time. When conversation lags, they feel obligated to say something, *anything* to fill the void. If you let them babble long enough, they will eventually slip up and say something they don't want you to know. Ms. Winter would have made a good interrogator. She remained silent long enough to put the ball back into my court.

Once again, I found myself breaking the stalemate. "All right, I'll listen to whatever you have to day. But don't get your hopes up. I have no intention of changing my mind."

The woman followed me into the den. I climbed into my favorite chair, an overstuffed brown wingback from another age. She chose the couch. I lit a cigarette and wiggled into a comfortable slouch; it was my house and she was an uninvited guest. I had no reason to be on my best behavior.

A plume of smoke left my lips, blossomed and then darted toward the ceiling as House reconfigured the ventilation system to draw my smoke away from our guest. The bastard. His manners always had been better than mine.

Ms. Winter sat stiffly erect, as if she were afraid that I would read something sexual into casual body language.

I settled back and took a healthy swallow of rapidly cooling coffee. This time it was her turn to break the silence. I wasn't going to coax her. She had come here to tell me something. Now she would either tell it, or she wouldn't.

She inhaled sharply, steeling herself to say something she didn't want to say. The breath held for a second, then two, then three. "My brother was Michael Winter... *the* Michael Winter."

The words came out in a rush, as if they were a bad taste in her mouth and she wanted to spit them out.

"Obviously you expect me to know who *the* Michael Winter is, or was... I believe you told me last night that he'd been murdered. I have to confess ignorance. I don't have a clue who you are talking about."

The look on her face was pure surprise. "Don't you watch the vid? Scan the news sites?"

I shook my head. "I stopped paying attention to that stuff a few years ago. The stories don't really change, just the faces and names. What is, or was, this brother of yours? A vid star?"

Her voice was a tense near-whisper. "A serial killer."

Try as I might, I couldn't come up with a clever response. I was still working on it when she handed me something. It was a data chip, the flat fingernail-sized kind, like they use in holo-cameras.

"Here," she said. "Play this. Then I'll explain."

I stood up and walked across the den to the little Queen Anne table that held my holo-deck. The table was one of Maggie's many 'discoveries.' She'd rescued it from a dusty curio shop in West Hollywood. It was supposedly a genuine antique, but we'd never gotten around to having it authenticated.

The holo-deck was a fat lozenge of matte black plastic; its streamlined profile played sharp counterpoint to the inlaid ivory and dark wood of Maggie's table.

I hadn't used the deck in so long that I wasn't even sure if it would work. I plugged in the data chip, punched the power button, and walked back to my chair. The air above the unit snowed video static until I found the remote and punched the *play* button.

A seedy hotel room coalesced out of the snow. The walls were painted hot pink and the paint was peeling badly. One entire wall and—from the looks of it—most of the ceiling, were covered with cheap plastic mirrors. Bolted to the wall just inside the door was a blood-scanner, the kind that used to be standard fixtures in hotel rooms before over-the-counter AIDS III tests hit the market.

The camera had one of those circuits that superimposed the time and date of the recording over the image. It appeared in the lower right hand corner of the picture in electric blue alphanumerics. The very first time code read **11:42 p.m./14APR2063**.

The scene wobbled, as though something had jarred the camera, and then someone walked directly in front of the lens. The image was blurry for a second as the camera's microprocessor compensated for the change in depth of field. When it focused, a man was sitting on the bed. The image was poorly framed, the man well to the left of center, as though he had miscalculated the camera's field of view.

He was young, perhaps twenty-five. His face was familiar. I knew I'd never seen it before, but I had seen another like it: Sonja Winter. Their features shared that too-perfect quality that people like to describe as 'aristocratic.' I revised my opinion of Sonja; maybe her beauty hadn't come from surgical boutiques after all.

The image made it hard to judge scale, but he seemed to be about medium height, well built. His clothes looked European: khaki slacks, too-white shirt, dark blue yachting jacket, black leather shoes, and a matching shoestring belt with silver buckle.

He turned toward the camera, his eyes a familiar shade of blue-green. "I am Michael Winter," he said. "This video chip is my last will and testament. It is my legacy."

He brushed at a stray lock of hair. It was a coppery shade, lighter than his sister's.

"You probably don't know me. It doesn't matter." He smiled, his teeth white and even. "I'm certain that you know my work."

He leaned forward, the image of his face growing larger in the hologram. His features contorted, leered, as if some malevolent creature hiding behind his eyes had decided to reveal itself.

He pulled something out of the right pocket of his jacket: one of those Japanese kitchen knives like they advertise on the vid, the kind that cut polycarbon and still slice tomatoes.

Tilting the knife back and forth, he watched the light run up and down the blade. Narrow bands of reflected silver strobed across his face.

"I cut Kathy Armstrong's heart out with this," he whispered. "Her soul made the most beautiful sound when I set it free."

I heard a squeak behind me. Ms. Winter's face was pale, sickly. Her eyes glistened as tears welled up. But she never cried. Her brother's ghastly recital was tearing her apart, but she never quite let herself cry.

Obviously, she had seen the recording before, so the contents weren't a surprise, but that couldn't have done much to deaden the pain.

I took a last drag off the cigarette and stubbed the butt out in an ashtray.

Kathy Armstrong wasn't the only name that Michael mentioned. Miko Otosaki... Felicia Stevens... Annette Yvonne Laughlin... Charlene Velis... Amy Lynn Crawford... Linda Joan Brazawski... The list continued. All teenage girls, thirteen to fifteen years old. All dead. All butchered by a maniac who carved open the chests of his adolescent victims and ripped out their hearts.

Virginia Mayland... Carmen Rodrigez... Paula Chapel... Jennifer Beth Whitney... Marlene Bayer... Christine Clark... Tracy Lee...

Fourteen girls. Michael Winter described the death of each in grisly detail, complete with dates and addresses. If half his claims were true, he was a one-man slaughterhouse.

When his recitation wound to a close, he sat in front of the camera. His breathing was ragged, his face flushed. "I am finished now," he whispered. "Not because I fear capture; I do not. You could never catch me. I have *seen* the bridge. I have *crossed* the bridge. I have touched the face of God."

His hand slid into the left pocket of his jacket. "He is calling me now. I can hear him. He is close..."

The left hand reappeared, wrapped around the butt of a large-caliber automatic pistol; it looked like a Glock.

"He is touching me now... I can feel his angels dancing in the spaces between my atoms." The left hand brought the gun up level with his head, the muzzle touching his scalp just forward of his left temple. "My work is done..." His finger tightened visibly on the trigger. "I am finished..."

The slug slammed his head to the side. A large chunk of the right side of his skull blew off in a cloud of pink mist.

I swallowed a rush of bile as I watched his head come apart. His body fell to the bed, a marionette with its strings cut. The gathering pool of blood showed hardly at all on the dark red sheets. A gobbet of flesh clung to the mirrored wall for a second and then began a leisurely slide toward the floor, trailing a red smear.

The scene remained unchanged for about four more minutes before the chip ran out. The last time code read **12:12 a.m./15APR2063**.

I pointed the remote at the holo-deck and pressed the *off* button. The image above the unit vanished as the deck powered down.

I lit another cigarette and drew the smoke deep into my lungs. "Let's cover the obvious first. Are you certain that the man in the recording is... *was* your brother?"

A nod. "The police compared DNA structure, dental work, and retinal patterns. The body in that hotel room was definitely Michael."

"Okay. Do the times, dates and circumstances of his confession agree with the police files?"

Another nod.

I swirled the last of my cold coffee around the bottom of my cup. "Is there any physical evidence, other than the recorded confession, to link your brother to any of the murders?"

"I don't know," she said. "When the police found Michael's body and saw the recording, they closed the case. The files are sealed; I don't know why."

"Did Michael have an alibi for *any* of the crimes?"

"Nothing that would stand up in court."

I sighed. "Okay, Ms. Winter, I'm confused here. Just what is it that you want me to do?"

Her gaze locked with mine. "Find out the truth. Prove that my brother was innocent. Find the real killer."

I suddenly understood why all the PI's thought she was crazy. But, I had promised to hear her out.

"You said you were going to explain," I said. "I assume that you have some reason for thinking that your brother was innocent."

"Michael was with me on the eighth of February."

I searched my memory. "Christine Clark?" Michael Winter had confessed to killing Christine on the afternoon of February eighth.

"Maybe he got the dates mixed up," I said. "Maybe he did Christine Clark on February ninth, or seventh."

"Uh-uh, I checked the news sites. They all quote the police as saying that Christine Clark died on the eighth at about 3 p.m. Michael had breakfast in my apartment at about 9 o'clock in the morning, and we spent the day together. He didn't leave until just before six that evening, when I had an appointment with a client."

The look in her eye dared me to react to her use of the word *client*.

I tried to blow a smoke ring. The modified air currents pulled it apart and snatched it into a vent on the ceiling. "Are you sure about *your* dates? The day you spent with Michael could have been the eighteenth, or the twenty-eighth. Remember, we're talking six months ago."

"It was a Saturday," she said. "I do a lot of business on Saturdays. Mike usually worked Saturdays too. When he called and asked me to spend the day with him, I had to reschedule several appointments. There are notations in my date book. It was most definitely the eighth of February. Harmony remembers it as the eighth too."

"Harmony?"

"The Artificial Intelligence that runs my apartment."

"Is Harmony tapped into DataNet? If she is, there should be a time signature stamped over any footage shot by your apartment's security cameras. Your brother may have an airtight alibi locked up in your AI's data core. For one of the murders, at least."

"No good," she said.

"You're not on the net?"

"I'm on the net all right, but my apartment doesn't have any video cameras. My clients tend to be rather jealous of their privacy. All of Harmony's interior sensors are either infrared or Doppler sonar. Good enough to chase burglars or keep house by, but not good enough for an ID that would stand up in court."

I sucked a lung full of smoke and put out the cigarette. A crumb of tobacco stuck to the tip of my tongue. I bit the crumb in half with my front teeth and blotted the pieces off the end of my tongue with a finger. "Let's say you're right. Let's say that your brother was at your apartment during Christine Clark's murder. He still could have killed one of the others. Or *all* of them."

"You're looking at it from the wrong angle, Mr. Stalin. If my brother confessed, in vivid detail, to *one* murder that he didn't commit—maybe he didn't commit *any* of them."

My stomach rumbled. It was starting to forgive me for exposing it to Michael Winter's suicide. It was starting to think about breakfast.

I stood up and wandered over to one of my favorite pieces, a tall, asymmetrical piece of twisted black grating that I called *Broken Concrete by Moonlight*. "Why is it so important to clear your brother's name? Is there an inheritance, or are you just interested in justice with a capitol *J*?"

She answered from the couch. "I admit that I have an ulterior motive."

I waited. My stomach growled again.

"Michael was a software engineer," she said, "a good one. He specialized in high-speed data compression and retrieval. Several of the big companies tried to seduce him into a contract, but he wanted to stay independent. He wasn't getting rich, but he was living pretty well.

"About four years ago, he started having these fainting spells. I finally convinced him to see a doctor. It turned out to be a brain tumor, and the tests showed that it was malignant. He needed a major operation and he didn't have nearly enough money. I had a few marks stashed away, but nothing like the kind of cash he needed. A big Eurocorp called Gebhardt-Wulkan Informatik ended up fronting Mike the money. He had to indenture himself to them for ten years. He was pretty screwed up physically, and I guess the company execs were afraid that he would die before they got their investment out of him. I had to co-sign his indenture. If Michael died or skipped out, I'd have to work off the remainder of his contract.

That's the bottom line. If I can prove that Michael was murdered, his life insurance will pay off his indenture. If the official cause of death remains suicide, I end up working off the indenture in GWI's Leisure Department. Since their girls get paid bottom-scale, it will probably take me about fifteen years."

I scratched my jaw and thought about trying to crack my neck. "So all I have to do is prove that your brother didn't commit the fourteen murders that he confessed to, find out who *did* commit the murders, and figure out how someone murdered Michael while making it look like a suicide. Sounds simple enough."

I walked toward the kitchen. "You want some breakfast?"

She got up to follow me. "Breakfast? It's after one o'clock."

"I had a late night."

She pulled a small stack of pictures out of her purse and handed it to me.

Most of them were trids, but a few were old two-dimensional photographs. I thumbed through them quickly. "What are these?" I asked.

"Just some pictures of Mike."

"I already know what your brother looked like, Ms. Winter; I saw the vid."

"That video is a fake. I don't know how it was done, or who did it, but my brother did not do those things." She pointed to the stack of pics. "The real Michael Winter is in *there*, Mr. Stalin. I just wanted you to know a little bit about him."

She stood with her arms crossed. The look on her face said she expected me to disagree.

"Okay," I said. "I'll look at your pictures."

She exhaled and uncrossed her arms. "Will you take the case?"

"I'll think about it."

"You will?"

I started rummaging through the kitchen cabinets, looking for my favorite skillet. House knew where it was, but I wasn't about to ask him.

"I'm retired, Ms. Winter. Your story intrigues me, but I really *am* out of the business. I promise to give your request honest consideration, but if I decide against taking the case, you'll have to accept my decision. Agreed?"

She extended her hand. I shook it. Her grip was firm. Her hand was warm, fingers long, nails unpainted. "Agreed."

CHAPTER 3

‖‖‖‖‖‖‖‖‖‖‖‖‖‖‖‖‖‖‖‖‖‖‖‖‖‖‖‖‖‖‖‖‖‖‖‖‖‖‖

The next evening, I left the Zone and rode the westbound Lev to Dome 15, West Hollywood.

Nexus Dreams was a specialty bar on Santa Monica Boulevard, catering to jackers, wannabe's, and techno-groupies.

The club's holo-facade was a live video feed of the street outside the front doors, pumped through a processor and rendered in simple polygon graphics. The result was a cartoonish video-mirror of the street scene in which all people and objects within about fifteen meters of the bar appeared as computer icons.

I watched my own icon grow larger as I approached the front of the club. My head appeared as a truncated pyramid, my body as two rectangular boxes (a short one for my pelvis, and a taller one for my trunk) and my arms and legs were jointed cylinders.

I walked past my polygon doppelganger, and into the club. The decor inside was intended to suggest a jacker's-eye view of the DataNet: matte black floor, walls, and ceiling divided into neat one-meter squares by low intensity florescent blue lasers. The tables and stools were transparent acryliflex, edge-lit in bright primary colors. Slash-rock pounded out of hidden speakers, an abrasive, atonal barrage masquerading as music.

At twenty after nine, the club was packed: a shoulder-to-shoulder swarm of human beings that seemed to writhe and pulsate in time to the arrhythmic beat of the music.

I fought my way to the bar and wedged myself into a narrow opening between a muscle-boy with florescent tattoos on his face and an androgynous albino dressed in black wet-look osmotic-neoprene. The albino's fingernails were black acrylic, long and pointed like tiny obsidian daggers. His/her features and complexion were flawless testimonials to the possibilities of elective surgery.

When I finally got the bartender's attention, I tried to order a Cutty on the rocks, and received a blank stare in return. I looked at the neon-colored drinks everyone else was having and decided that a beer was my safest bet.

The beer came in a purple octagonal squeeze-tube with raised Chinese characters on the label. I squirted some into my mouth; it tasted like cold aftershave.

20

I scanned the room. I was looking for Zeus, a data-jacker who had hung out here once-upon-a-time, back when Stalin and Stalin Investigations had still been a going concern. We'd hired Zeus several times, when our need for computer-skullduggery had overreached Maggie's talents.

Zeus's real name was Orville Beckley, a fact that he went to great lengths to conceal. I'd found that out as a result of a bet that Orville had made (and ultimately lost) with Maggie. He'd boasted of having erased every trace of his real name from the net. True to his prediction, Maggie hadn't been able to catch even a sniff of his birth records in the net. But he hadn't reckoned with Maggie's tenacity. She'd gone on to teach him three simple facts:

#1 Hospitals are bureaucracies.

#2 Bureaucracies are paranoid.

#3 Paranoid bureaucrats keep duplicate records of *everything...* in hardcopy... in file cabinets.

I could still remember the look of stunned disbelief on Zeus's face when Maggie had whispered the *Orville* word in his ear, the certain knowledge that his secret was not dead after all. The memory brought me a smile.

I looked around again. As far as I could tell, Zeus wasn't in the bar, but I did catch sight of a face I recognized. I threaded my way through the crowd until I came to her table. Her handle was Jackal; I didn't know her real name.

She wore a baggy maroon jumpsuit with a couple of hundred pins and badges stuck to it. I remembered her as thin. Now she looked anorexic.

Her hair was a thick black mop that ended suddenly just above the tops of her ears. It looked as though someone had dropped a bowl on her head and shaved off everything that stuck out. Her eyebrows were shaven as well. As she craned her neck, I saw two, no, *three* gold alloy data jacks set flush into the back of her head. One jack held a program chip. A thin fiber-optic cable ran from the second jack to a box clipped to her belt. The box was about two-thirds the size of a pack of cigarettes, molded from charcoal gray plastic, covered with flickering LEDs. The third jack was empty.

She looked up at me, a bare glimmer of recognition in her eyes. She knew she had seen me before; she just couldn't remember where. She reached into the right breast pocket of her jumpsuit and pulled out a small handful of data chips. She selected one and plugged it into the empty jack.

Her eyes closed for a second. When they opened, her expression was totally changed. She gestured toward a stool. "Stalin, right? Long time."

I took the offered seat and faked a sip of the almost-beer. "Yeah, it has been a while. You still calling yourself Jackal?"

"*THE* one, *THE* only," she said.

She took a swallow from her tall green drink. "Are you looking for Zeus?"

"Yeah," I said. "Have you seen him?"

Jackal shook her head. "Not in a couple of months. The last I heard, he snooped Ishikawa Audio for some pretty fancy technical specs. If he fenced them through the Cayman Islands, like he usually does, he's probably off spending his bankroll in the skin-bars in Bangkok. We probably won't see him for at least another six or eight weeks."

I nodded, and studied Jackal's face. As near as I could figure, she must have been about twenty-eight. She looked forty.

Jackal returned my stare. "Are you looking for Zeus for social purposes, or are you here on business?"

We had to lean close to hear each other over the crowd and the music.

"Business, actually," I half-shouted.

"What have you got? Maybe I can hook you up."

I thought about it for a second. I didn't really know her. I'd seen her hanging around with Zeus from time to time, but I had no idea whether or not she was any good.

She obviously had the skull modifications, and she knew how to talk-the-talk. But, when it came time to ride the data grid through somebody else's security software, could she slip in and out without a trace? Or would she leave a trail of bread crumbs through the net that some AI could follow? Or, worse yet, tangle with a neuro-guard subroutine that would reach through the interface and fry her brain?

My gut instinct told me that she could cut it.

I leaned close to her ear. "I've got two jobs, if you're interested. The first is a protected database. Are you up to that?"

"Depends. Whose?"

"LAPD. Homicide Division. I need a complete data pull on a closed murder investigation. The files are sealed."

Jackal rummaged through her pocket full of chips and selected one. She popped a chip out of one of her jacks, and plugged the new chip into the empty slot.

"The Boys in Blue have good security," she said. They just upgraded their AI about four months ago. Not cutting-edge, but real good stuff."

Her eyes went vacant for a second as the chip continued to download arcane technical data into her brain. "I can crack that base," she said. "Not easy, but I can do it." She looked back at me and smiled. "Also not cheap."

I nodded. "I didn't think it would be."

She pushed her drink around the table top leaving a smear of condensation on the clear surface. "You mentioned a second job."

"A personal database," I said. "It probably has fairly standard consumer-grade protection. Shouldn't be too difficult to penetrate."

She smiled again. "If it's as easy as all that, I might just throw it in as a bonus. But if it turns up any surprises, it's going to cost you."

We talked for another half-hour: price, time schedule, data format.

I elbowed my way out of the bar and caught a hovercab to the eastern perimeter of Dome 12. The cab was a beat-up old Chevy with a patched apron and a wobble in the left rear blower that threatened to loosen my teeth.

The driver was an attractive African woman, her proud cheekbones decorated with the inverted chevrons of ritual tribal scars. Over her shoulder, I could see the tattletales on the taxi's liquid crystal instrument panel. Every few seconds, one of the status bars would blink from blue to red. When it did, she would tap the display with her right index finger until it blinked back to blue.

She dropped me off at the corner of 55th and Fortuna, a couple of blocks short of the barricade. Nobody's been dumb enough to drive a cab into the Zone in years.

The MagLev doesn't run through the Zone anymore either. People kept stealing the superconductor modules out of the track, maybe for the resale value, maybe for the hell of it.

A few years ago, somebody stole five modules in a row. Ordinarily that wouldn't have been a big problem; the computers at LA Transit Authority are smart enough to spot damaged track and stop the train. Unfortunately, the thief managed to bypass the track sensors and trick the LA-Trans computers into thinking the track was safe. A Lev derailed, killing twenty-nine people and wiping out a half dozen buildings.

Now, unless you actually have your own car, the only way in or out of the Zone is on foot.

The cops at the barricade let me through with a quick wave of their scanner and a token pat down. It was a formality. They don't much care who or what goes into the Zone. They're worried about what gets out.

The Fearless Leaders of our fair city like to keep most of their bad eggs in one basket. Don't get me wrong, they have crime in the other domes too, but not like we've got it in good old Urban Environmental Enclosure 12-A.

I should have moved ages ago. Just stubborn I guess.

When I got home, I laid down on the couch with my eyes closed and told House to play some blues. House responded with Blind Willie Johnson's *Lord, I Just Can't Keep From Cryin'*. I tried to lose myself in the music, but even Blind Willie's gently gruff voice and sensuous slide guitar couldn't distract my racing brain.

After a few minutes, I stood up and lit a cigarette. I couldn't even pretend to relax.

I kept telling myself that there was nothing to get keyed-up about. I didn't have to take the case. I hadn't promised Sonja anything.

No, that wasn't true. I had promised to give her case serious consideration. But I was doing that, wasn't I? Hadn't I hired Jackal to scope the police files on the case? When I got access to those files, I would go over them in detail and prove to myself what I already knew: that Michael Winter was guilty.

I would be off the hook. I could stay snuggled up in my little cocoon, listen to ancient blues, drink scotch, smoke bootleg cigarettes, and weld pieces of metal together in patterns that amused my simple mind. I could tell Ms. Sonja Winter that her late unlamented brother was a murderous psycho-pervert, who deserved to have his brains blown out.

Except...

I didn't want to do that. I didn't want to tell Sonja that her brother was a killer. I didn't want to tell her that she was going to spend the next fifteen years as a corporate sex-toy.

Maybe a lot of people wouldn't appreciate the difference that would make in her life. She was a whore, right? So what if she had to punch a time clock for somebody else instead of set her own hours? She still made her living flat on her back, right?

The difference was in *control*. As an independent call girl, Sonja could select her clientele. She could take a day off if she wanted. She could say *no*.

It was the difference between freedom and slavery.

Still, none of that was my problem. I had troubles of my own. I didn't need to shoulder someone else's burden.

I jump-started a second cigarette off the butt of the first and then ground out the butt in an ashtray.

I wanted a drink. There was a bottle of Cutty hidden somewhere in one of the kitchen cabinets. I went looking for it.

On the counter next to the refrigerator was Ms. Winter's little stack of pictures.

I picked them up. The picture on top was a dog-eared photograph of Michael Winter as a boy, twelve, maybe thirteen. He was skinny, his hair a much brighter red than it had been in the video. On his left hand, he wore a baseball glove; a bat was draped across his right shoulder.

I paged through the stack slowly. A trid of a high school graduation, Michael and two other grinning teens in caps and gowns. Michael in his early twenties, sprawled on a couch with a huge tabby cat sleeping on his chest. The shot had probably been taken a year or two before North America had been hit by the genetic plague that made cats an endangered species.

I flipped to the next picture, another flat photo, Michael at four or five, in a bathtub full of bubbles. An obviously staged trid of an adult Michael surrounded by electronic equipment and wrapped in a tangle of test sensors and wires.

The last trid in the stack caught my attention. Michael as an adult, his arm around the shoulders of a pretty young woman dressed in orange surgical scrubs. The woman carried a data pad and had a stethoscope strung around her neck; she was obviously a doctor or nurse. It took me a couple of seconds to recognize the woman as Sonja Winter; the holo had been shot before she'd gotten the eye shadow and lipstick tattoos.

I wondered if the surgical getup was a Halloween costume. If so, why wasn't Michael in costume as well?

I dropped the pictures on the counter and opened the door to a cabinet. The Cutty was around somewhere. I closed the cabinet and opened another.

As I reached up to rummage through the shelves, I realized that my hand was trembling.

Maybe a drink wasn't such a good idea. I closed the cabinet and went to bed.

I had the dream again...

I am in a dark labyrinth of rusty steel walls and worn cement floors. The tops of the walls and ceiling are lost in shadow. Somewhere, I can hear water drip slowly into a stagnant pool. The air is damp and has a weird echoing quality that makes me think of indoor swimming pools. The darkness is interrupted by irregular patches of light.

I hear a series of muffled thumps. Someone is pounding on a wall. I don't know how I know it, but I'm certain that it's Maggie. She's in some sort of danger. I have to find her! I listen carefully to the pounding, trying to figure out where it's coming from. I can't tell. I touch first one wall, then another. It's no good; I can feel the vibration through all the walls.

The pounding becomes faster, more urgent.

I start to run through the maze, taking turns at random. I've got to find her! I will goddamn it, I will!

I run faster, my feet skidding through puddles of water, stumbling over unseen debris. Sometimes I lose my balance and bounce a shoulder painfully off one of the walls or sprawl headlong on the floor. When that happens, I scramble to my feet and take off again, rushing blindly on through the labyrinth.

The pounding grows weaker, less frequent.

Every time I turn a corner, I promise myself that Maggie is just around the next one. At each new corner, the promise turns into a lie.

The pounding is very weak now. I have to stop running to hear it over my own footsteps. She hasn't got much time left. Oh God, don't do this to me... PLEASE God... I'll do anything...

I found myself sitting up in bed whispering "Please God..." over and over as the tears streamed down my face.

I knew better than to try to stop it. I just let it out in great wracking sobs that left me gasping like a fish on dry land.

When it was over, I felt wrung out. I laid down and listened to the sound of my own breathing until I drifted off again. If I dreamed, it wasn't anything worth remembering.

The next morning, I was in the shower when House played that pleasant little chime he uses to get my attention. I paused in mid-scrub. "Yeah House, what have you got?"

"As you requested, David, I have downloaded the morning news feed."

I resumed scrubbing. "Great, check the Personals for any messages addressed to Igor."

The *Igor* thing was Jackal's idea. I guess jackers have an obsession for code names.

"There is one message addressed to Igor," House said. "Shall I read it to you?"

"Please."

House made a quiet throat clearing sound. It was an obviously superfluous gesture, since he didn't actually have a throat. I guess something in his programming told him that it was an appropriate sound to make, prior to reading aloud. "To Igor, From J — The job is done. Come see me."

"That's all?"

"Yes."

"Thanks, House."

"Don't mention it, David."

Nine hours later, I walked to Dome 12 and caught the Lev to West Hollywood.

Nexus Dreams was every bit as crowded as it had been the night before. One end of the room had been cordoned off into a makeshift stage. The attraction was a computer performance artist who billed himself as "Insanity." The performer's long black hair was slicked back and pulled into a point, giving his head a sort of teardrop shape.

He wore a white synthleather trench coat that hung to his knees. His entire act appeared to consist of a table top full of computer equipment jacked into a hologram projector. The rig generated an animated hologram of the artist's own face. The holo was enlarged to about five times its normal size, so it could be easily seen from all over the room. It floated over the heads of the crowd, its features contorting themselves through a range of weird expressions as it alternately screamed and whispered bizarre epithets.

"Night is the contrivance of solidified truth!" it shouted. "I am the crystal blood-mist of hyperbolic fuel that mummifies the secret organs of the gods..."

The holographic face ranted ceaselessly, never making an iota of sense.

I watched the thing whimper and rave. At first, I thought it was just a simulation, a vid recording of the artist's face that had been doctored by video morphing software to create bizarre facial expressions. But I began to realize that it was more than that. There was something hypnotic about it, as though the hologram were a living thing instead of a weirdly distorted digital recording.

Somehow, from across the crowded bar, the hologram's gaze met mine. I found myself staring into its eyes, and I saw an agony reflected there that nearly staggered me.

"I can't stop them," the hologram said. "Leaves of corruption are falling on my face, burrowing their way like insects down into the empty chasm of my heart, and I CAN... *NOT*... STOP... THEM..."

It suddenly seemed possible that I might stand there forever, crucified by the power of the holo's gaze. Then the tortured eyes flicked away from me, and began wandering the room again. The spell of pain was broken.

I tore my eyes away and stared at the floor. It took me a couple of seconds to remember why I'd come here. Finally, I lifted my head and started scanning the crowd for Jackal.

I found her sitting at a table at the end of the room opposite *Insanity*. Seated next to her was a kid I'd never seen before. He was augmented cybernetically, *heavily* augmented. Enough of him was hidden behind hardware implants to make it difficult to read his age, but my best guess was about seventeen. He was definitely too young for the bar scene, but no one seemed to be interested in scanning his ID-chip.

Where the kid's eyes should have been, cylindrical electroptic lenses protruded from his eye sockets like the barrels of twin video cameras. His camera eyes whirred softly as the lenses spun to bring me into focus. His right hand looked normal, but his left was cybernetic, an articulated alloy skeleton that made me think of robotic bones. His head was shaved, his scalp tattooed with intricate patterns of circuit runs. The servomotors in his cybernetic hand emitted sporadic electro-mechanical whimpers whenever he moved his fingers. He stared at me for a second and then shifted his electroptic eyes back to Insanity's performance art.

I turned to Jackal. If anything, she looked thinner than she had the night before. In place of the jump suit, she wore blue stretch-pants and a white sweatshirt with the sleeves ripped off. The front of the shirt was a photo-active trid depicting a famous cartoon mouse sodomizing his cutesy mouse girlfriend in lurid 3-D. The mouse appeared to move in and out when Jackal turned her body.

Jackal motioned me to a seat.

I sat down without ordering. I didn't intend to be there very long.

Jackal started to say something, but Cyber-kid interrupted her. "They think that shit is funny," he said.

His voice was gravelly, obviously generated by a speech synthesis chip. I was struck by the certainty that he'd had his own larynx removed, just so he could speak with the voice of a machine.

"They're too stupid to know what they're doing," he said. "Either that, or they're too stupid to care."

Jackal took a swallow of her bright green drink. "It's no big deal," she said.

"That asshole is torturing it," the kid said in his metallic voice. His camera-eyes were locked on the performance artist's floating hologram. "And everybody thinks it's funny."

I forced myself to look down the length of the bar room at the hologram, ready to jerk my eyes away the instant I felt the touch of its electric gaze. From this distance, the face's jabbering voice was hard to hear over the murmurings of the customers.

"It's like it's alive," I said. "At first, I thought it was just a vid recording, but it's more than that, isn't it?"

"It's a Scion," Jackal said.

"A Turing Scion?" I asked.

"Yeah," the kid said. "A digital image of a human mind. And Asshole over there is driving it crazy, on *purpose*."

I knew a little something about Turing Scions. The concept had been around since the nineteen forties, the brainchild of Alan Turing, the British mathematician who'd invented digital computer logic, Artificial Intelligence, and the so-called *Machine Mind*.

Turing had predicted that technology would eventually permit a human mind to be recorded in digital form. Thought, personality, idiosyncrasies, prejudices, the whole ball of wax. Turing had been right; technology had caught up with his ideas in less than a hundred years.

"How can you drive a Turing Scion crazy?" I asked.

The kid turned his electroptic eyes toward me. "Leave it plugged in," he said.

"That doesn't make any sense," I said. "Turing Scions are *supposed* to be plugged in. That's what they're designed for."

"True," Jackal said, "but they're only intended to be active for short periods of time. If you leave one plugged in too long, it goes crazy."

"I still don't understand," I said.

"Look," the kid said. "The entire point behind the Turing Scion is to preserve the knowledge base of our so-called civilization. In the past, if a brilliant engineer died, his knowledge and his creativity died with him. His thought patterns, his ideas, his personal methods of problem solving ... *everything*. All gone forever. That's the way things worked for most of human history. Then, along comes the Turing Scion and changes all the rules. Now, if our hypothetical engineer has a Turing Scion, his knowledge doesn't disappear when he dies. If we have a problem that only Mr. Hypothetical Engineer can solve, we just plug his Scion into a computer node and start asking questions."

"But you can't *leave* it plugged in," Jackal said.

"Why not?"

The kid stared at me like I was an idiot. "Scions are sort of like software," he said. "They're only active when you plug them into a computer node. Unplug one, and it's just an anodized box full of dense-pack memory chips. It can't talk. It can't think. It can't do *anything*. It's inert. Asleep, if you prefer."

"But when they *are* plugged in," Jackal said, "they have dynamic memory, just like AI's. They continue to think, and learn, and grow."

"How does that make them go crazy?" I asked.

"Think about it," the kid said. "Even a low-end computer can process information three or four hundred times faster than a human brain can. For every hour of real-time that passes, an active Scion would experience four hundred hours. That's about sixteen days. Not sixteen days for some piece of artificially intelligent machine code that only *thinks* it's alive. Sixteen days for a human mind who has memories, wants, aspirations."

I nodded.

The kid looked back toward the performance artist's Turing Scion. "Asshole over there has kept his Scion plugged in for over a year. Try to imagine that. Four hundred years trapped inside a machine."

"It's not like it's a real person," Jackal said.

"It *thinks* it's a real person," the kid said.

I looked across the bar at the anguished face of the Scion, and suddenly I couldn't bear the thought of being in the same room with it. I cleared my throat. "This is all very interesting," I said, "but I have business to attend to." I looked at Jackal.

"Sorry," she said. "I got a little sidetracked." She pulled a data chip out of her pocket and slid it across the transparent table top.

I reached into my pocket and pulled out an envelope. "Cash," I said. "As agreed."

We traded.

I wouldn't be able to verify the contents of the chip until I got home. Jackal knew this; out of courtesy, she didn't open the envelope until I was gone.

Outside the bar, I waited for a cab on Santa Monica Boulevard, and tried not to think about Turing Scions. I'd seen one years before, and I hadn't liked it anymore than I'd liked the one inside Nexus Dreams.

John had talked Maggie into letting him make the recording. She'd been excited by the idea: her mind, her *personality* stored in a digital module. All you had to do was plug the Scion into a computer and presto, Maggie in a can. Sort of the electronic version of immortality.

She was in there, all right, or at least an incredibly accurate computer approximation of her personality was. Her memories were in there too, current up to the instant when John had slipped the sensor network over her head.

Maggie had tried to talk me into making one. She and John both had. I'd refused, a decision I had never regretted for a second. Man is not meant to be factored into logic algorithms.

The Scion had just been a novelty to John and Maggie, an interesting trinket. Every once in a while, they would drag the module out and plug it into John's computer. They'd talk to it for hours, giggling over it, like children playing with an amusing gadget. Then they'd unplug it, and it would go back on the shelf.

It might still be there somewhere, gathering dust at the back of one of John's closets. I made a mental note to ask him about it. If the damned thing was still around, I wanted it erased.

The past was dead, and nothing that was recorded on a stack of memory chips could change that.

Dome City Blues is available in hardcover, paperback, and eBook formats.

Made in the USA
Middletown, DE
27 October 2020